LOVE AND DUTY

Visit us at www.boldstrokesbooks.com

LOVE AND DUTY

by
Catherine Young

2022

LOVE AND DUTY

ISBN 13: 978-1-63679-256-9

This Trade Paperback Original Is Published By
Bold Strokes Books, Inc.
P.O. Box 249
Valley Falls, NY 12185

First Edition: September 2022

CREDITS
Editor: Barbara Ann Wright
Production Design: Stacia Seaman
Cover Design by Tammy Seidick

Acknowledgments

Thank you to everyone who provided me with feedback and encouragement. I owe an especially heartfelt thanks to Mary Griggs for reaching out to encourage me to seek publication, to AevumAce and Z for beta reading the first draft, and to Órla for beta reading part of the second draft. I am also grateful to my editor, Barbara Ann Wright, whose edits vastly improved this book, and to Bold Strokes Books for accepting my manuscript.

For Savannah

CHAPTER ONE

Princess Roseli entered the armistice ball with her personal assistant at her side and two guards at her back. From the top of the staircase, she could see the entire imperial ballroom, from the three huge crystal chandeliers on the vaulted ceiling to the great glass windows looking out into the palace gardens.

The air smelled of floor polish, perfume, and too many people pressed together on a warm evening. The crowd fell silent at her appearance, and the orchestra struck up something suitably majestic for her descent of the curving staircase. Roseli did not feel majestic. She felt like several hundred Delphian nobles and a good number of foreign dignitaries were staring at her impatiently. None of them could dance until she opened the ball with the first waltz.

Her thoughts were awhirl, and it took every ounce of her self-control to keep her smile in place. Why the hell had her mother thought it was a good idea to tell her about the engagement right before she had to make a public appearance?

As the heir apparent to the Delphian Empire, Roseli had always known it was her duty to marry as many times as needed to build alliances for the crown, but why did her first marriage have to be to some Calliopean princess she'd never even met? Surely, there were other ways to secure a treaty between two planets.

She wanted to find her lovers and get their counsel, but there was no time. She needed to focus on the task at hand, and at the moment, that meant getting down the grand staircase without tripping over her ballgown.

Her assistant, Meredith Cooper, leaned over to whisper, "Remember, during the dance, tell Ambassador Hansen exactly what your mother told you to pass on. Watch how she reacts. Try flirting and batting your eyelash to keep her off guard."

"Batting my eyelashes?" Roseli paused briefly in her descent. Meredith was wearing a green dress with red poppies drawn on it around her skinny frame, which clashed with her red hair and was garish even for her unconventional approach to fashion.

Meredith shrugged. "It's what people do in books."

"Do you even understand how flirting works?"

"No idea, but better you than me."

Roseli would have liked to glare at her, but they had reached the ballroom floor, and she had to continue alone. By custom, the first dance of the armistice ball must be between representatives of Delphi and Terra Nueva.

Ambassador Hansen crossed the empty dance floor to her and bowed deeply. Her suit was black in the Terra Nuevan style and stood out in strong contrast to the brighter colors and elaborate embroidery favored by the Delphians. The simplicity suited her, as did the short cut of her dark curls. Her face was forgettable, ordinary, but Roseli knew from experience she could be unsettlingly charming.

The ambassador bowed. "May I have this dance, Your Highness?"

Roseli offered her hand. "I would be honored."

The orchestra started the first waltz, and Ambassador Hansen drew her into the first steps. While Roseli had no innate talent for dancing, countless girlhood lessons had left her competent enough to dance and converse at the same time.

"You look lovely tonight, Your Highness," said Ambassador Hansen.

"Thank you."

"I trust you are well."

"Yes."

"And your lovers? You've not added any new ones recently, have you?" There was a hint of suggestion in her tone that Roseli didn't like. Ambassador Hansen always made it sound like there was something lurid in the tradition of Delphian royalty publicly acknowledging lovers and having more than one.

"I am still with the same three paramours as last year and the year before. I've been told I've become a great disappointment to the gossip magazines. What about you?"

"Now, now, you know I am a married woman."

"And I'm sure you dutifully keep faith with your wife back on Terra Nueva." While marriages on Terra Nueva were traditionally monogamous, rumor had it that Ambassador Hansen had seduced several nobles and at least one actress during her time on Delphi.

"In my own way." The ambassador pulled Roseli uncomfortably close as they turned.

It wasn't the opening Roseli had been hoping for, but she took advantage of the proximity. She smiled sweetly and whispered in the ambassador's ear, trying to channel at least a fraction of her mother's talent for intimidation. "Enough of silly banter. We need to discuss why your navy is setting up a base on the smallest moon of Jove in the neutral zone."

The ambassador missed a step, and only Roseli's hand on her arm kept them both upright. Had Roseli had any doubt of the veracity of the information her mother's spies had passed on, she didn't anymore. She also now knew for a fact that the ambassador was being kept abreast of Terra Nuevan naval movements.

It took only a moment for the practiced stateswoman's face to return to a carefully neutral expression. She kept her voice to a whisper. Since they had the dance floor to themselves and with the music and ambient noise of the ballroom, there was little danger of being overheard or recorded. "Your Highness, I do not know where you heard this unsubstantiated rumor, but there is no truth in it."

"We have photos." They didn't.

Ambassador Hansen raised her right hand, guiding Roseli into a turn. When they were facing again, she was grinning in a chilling way. "You realize, sending any kind of scouting ship or drone into the neutral zone is a treaty violation."

Roseli felt a sharp flicker of panic, but it was too late to back down. She pushed her gambit. "Funny, we have pictures of your scouting ships, too. Perhaps we are both unclear on that point of the treaty."

"Tell me, Your Highness, exactly how good are these photos you claim to have? It would be a shame if you're making all this fuss over what could easily turn out to be a space pirate hideout."

"I have never taken you for a fool, Madame Ambassador. I will thank you to extend me the same courtesy. Covering a ship's serial number does not change its shape, and Terra Nuevan naval vessels are distinctive, unless you are suggesting you've lost five dozen to pirates." The spies had been specific about those details.

That earned her a slight inclination of Ambassador Hansen's head. "No, I do not take you for that, even if you aren't half as canny as your mother. May I assume she has sent you as her proxy in this case?"

"In an unofficial nature." Which, she hoped, gave her the advantage. "Within a month's time, she expects to be seeing photos of nothing more than a moon's rocky surface, and we can forget all about this unfortunate incident."

"You do realize, I am only an ambassador."

"And I am a princess, but we both speak for others. See it done, or the matter becomes public. As you have said, my mother is cannier than me. Do you want to face her across the table in an official negotiation? With a treaty violation to hold against Terra Nueva, she may finally get back the disputed Hubble mining colony."

Ambassador Hansen laughed. "I much prefer your far more pleasing disposition. The last time I discussed the treaty with your mother, she called me a pompous proletariat idiot and somehow got me to agree to lift a tariff."

"She only used two adjectives' worth of insults? From her, that is practically a compliment." The song ended, the final chords fading. "Do we have an understanding?"

"Yes, Your Highness." She looked as if she might have wanted to say something else, but she saw someone behind Roseli and merely bowed and walked away.

Roseli turned to find her oldest lover, General Alexis Tate, waiting for her. Alexis made a tall and dashing figure in her dark blue dress uniform with all its shiny buttons. Even after five years of peace, she still possessed a soldier's sinewy build. Although her handsome face, defined by sharp angles and a firm chin, was unmarred by battle, the rest of her was not. Her neck was badly scarred, and she wore her light brown hair longer than military regulation to hide her missing left ear. Although young to hold the rank of general, she was already graying at the temples.

"Your Highness." Alexis bowed deeply. Roseli returned the gesture more shallowly as their respective social statuses dictated.

It was strange to hear such a formal address from such familiar lips, but Alexis was always that way in public, respectful and reserved. Only when they were alone did she use Roseli's first name or dare to call her, "my love." They were anything but alone now. Couples had drifted onto the floor after the opening dance had finished.

The music began again, and they eased into a waltz.

"Did it go well?" asked Alexis.

Roseli had previously told her of the planned confrontation with the Terra Nuevan ambassador. A condition of becoming a royal paramour was the ability to pass the highest level of security clearance.

"Yes, I think so," said Roseli. "We came to terms. I'll tell you more later."

As they danced, Roseli felt the ache of nervousness in her stomach ease. Alexis was not as graceful a dancer as either of her other two lovers, Beatrice or Julia, but there was a confidence in the way she moved that Roseli had always loved. Looking up into Alexis's slate gray eyes, Roseli could almost pretend that all was well.

Sometimes, she dreamed of marrying Alexis, although her mother would never permit it. Despite her success in the military, Alexis was still a lesser noble and of illegitimate birth. A future empress couldn't marry a woman who had neither wealth nor influence to bring to the crown, at least, not as a first or second wife.

When the song ended, Roseli took Alexis's arm, and they left the dance floor before anyone else could ask Roseli to dance again. She needed to greet guests and circulate through the crowd before she could leave the ball.

On Alexis's arm, she greeted senior members of the Delphian navy and military. Unaware of the significance of what had transpired during the first dance, most of the members of the armed forces were in good spirits. General Hollens, who was retired and possibly well on her way to becoming senile, unfortunately, decided to recount the entire Battle of Broken Saber in excruciating detail.

Even Alexis, who had been present at that battle, was yawning when Roseli's second lover, Senator Julia Veritas, swooped in to save them.

"Roseli, dearest, there is someone you simply must meet." Julia bowed to Roseli, giving her a conspiratorial wink as she took her arm before bowing more shallowly to the gathered generals. "My apologies, I need to steal her."

Julia was an undeniably striking woman, and not just for the fiery red hair she had tied back in a ribbon. She had intelligent green eyes set within a narrow, foxlike face and a sly smile she knew how to deploy to best effect. She was slender without being willowy and slightly shorter than Alexis. For the ball, she was wearing a well-cut blue suit embroidered at the cuffs in the current fashion.

Roseli noticed that Julia's makeup was painted more brightly than usual, her lips red and cheeks heavily rouged. It was the way she wore it when expecting to give an important speech on the Senate floor, where the bright lights washed out her already pale completion.

Julia hooked her arm through Roseli's to lead her away from the gathered generals, and Roseli could have kissed her in gratitude. Alexis, no doubt seeing her chance to escape, attempted to follow but was cut off by another military colleague eager to tell her something. Roseli waved at her sadly, and Alexis motioned for her to go while she could.

"Did you come straight from the Senate?" Roseli asked.

"Afraid so. I had to change in the car. Senator Baker tried to push through his fertilizer tariff. We'd have all been there until midnight if the Speaker of the Senate hadn't said she wasn't missing the ball for this and declared a recess until tomorrow morning."

"Smart woman. Was there actually someone you wanted me to meet?"

"Senator Palmer. She promised she'd back my party's agricultural bill, the one the empress wants to pass, if I introduced you."

"What is she after?" Although Roseli's mother had been giving her increasing degrees of royal responsibility since she had come of age, most of that had comprised of attending social events, making public appearances, and sitting in on council meetings. She had a limited ability to dispense royal favors.

"To give you her opinion on the current rate of agricultural taxes. Also, she's hoping you'll autograph a photo for her daughter. Apparently, the little girl is going through a princess phase and is obsessed with tiaras and pretending to wage war."

"I don't wage war."

"The child is five. She probably doesn't have a good understanding of the difference between the authority of a princess and an empress."

Julia guided her adeptly through a series of brief conversations with senators and other representatives, carefully whispering relevant details into her ear, as well as the occasional bit of funny gossip to get her to laugh. Before Julia had come into her life, Roseli had always found interacting with politicians terrifying. Now she had an advantage over most of them. While Julia was still a junior senator, she came from a powerful old patrician family with an extensive information network. She knew what everyone wanted and why.

Julia was the only one of Roseli's lovers of high enough birth for marriage to even be a possibility, but Roseli could never ask her, at least not without forcing her to choose between Roseli and her career.

Members of the royal family were forbidden from holding elected office. Julia's current position as a royal paramour was informal enough for her to skirt past the law, but if they married, she would have to leave the Senate.

After an hour, Roseli was flagging. She felt a soft touch on her arm and turned to find her third lover, Lady Beatrice Swann, smiling at her, dimples and all. Roseli's heart lightened at the sight of her.

Beatrice was a small woman with a delicate, heart-shaped face. She wore golden curls twisted up in a silver clip, and her green ball gown hugged every pleasing curve of her lovely body. Emeralds set in silver shone at her neck, ears, and wrists.

"Hello, darling, I got you champagne and a snack."

"I love you."

"I know." Beatrice handed her a champagne flute and a little cake in a napkin.

Roseli had never let herself dream of marrying Beatrice. A princess might name a retired courtesan as a paramour, but no member of the royal family had ever taken one as a consort, even as a later wife or husband. If Roseli ever tried, even after her mother died, the Senate would never approve the marriage.

When another politician made a beeline for Roseli, Julia dutifully moved to intercept, giving Roseli a much-needed moment of respite.

"Please tell me you don't need me to talk to anyone," Roseli pleaded.

"Nope, Meredith asked me to extract you. Your mother wants to know how it went with the ambassador. Intelligence Director Barker will debrief you."

"She can't wait until the end of the ball?"

"Since when have you not wanted to sneak out of a ball early?"

"Wasn't complaining." Roseli tipped back the champagne flute. "Lead the way."

They slipped out into the hallway, two of Roseli's bodyguards in tow, and made like they were heading toward the women's bathroom and then ducked through a hidden door that led to a secret hallway used primarily by palace staff. A series of hallways took them away from the public southern end of the sprawling palace complex to the military and intelligence offices of the east wing.

Roseli hesitated at the entrance to the mostly dark imperial intelligence office. Giving in to temptation, she drew Beatrice into her arms and kissed her soundly. Beatrice melted against her.

She wanted to never let her go, to stay like this always. That thought brought back all her fears in a rush. She needed to tell her lovers about the engagement.

"Beatrice, can you ask Alexis and Julia to meet me back in my rooms in about a half hour?"

"Of course, darling." Beatrice's expression had grown serious, eyebrows drawing together. "Is this about the ambassador?"

"Not exactly. I promise, I will explain."

"All right, we will be there."

Roseli entered the office with a heavy heart.

CHAPTER TWO

Although Roseli's dance with the ambassador had taken only a few minutes, her debriefing took nearly an hour because Director Barker had her recount the entire encounter, word for word, twice. When at last Director Barker let her go, it took nearly fifteen minutes to walk through the darkened hallways to the residential western wing of the palace. Roseli's mother, her mother's husbands, and her little sister lived in the highly secure Inner Chambers.

Upon coming of age, Roseli had taken a nearby set of rooms, traditionally occupied by the heir apparent. It had been a relief to escape the ornately beautiful rooms and courtyards of the Inner Chambers, still hushed with grief despite the passage of time. When she entered her sitting room, she was glad to find her lovers still waiting for her despite the late hour. Alexis had taken a seat in an ornately carved, straight-back chair and was drinking a cup of coffee. Julia reclined on one of the two low blue-silk-covered couches on either side of the coffee table, reading a tablet. Beatrice was standing by the bookshelf, flipping through one of Roseli's valuable paper books of poetry.

She set the book on the shelf and came to kiss Roseli on the cheek. "Come sit down, darling. I had the kitchen send up some sandwiches from the ball."

Everything was too much at once. She had meant to ease into the conversation, but she couldn't pretend everything was all right, even for a moment longer. Tears welled in her eyes.

Beatrice took her arm and led her to the couch. "What's happened? Did things go badly with the ambassador?"

Roseli shook her head. "No, that went fine. It's…" She forced herself to take a steadying breath. "Right before I went into the ball, my mother told me she finally got the Calliopeans to agree to a mutual defense treaty."

Alexis leaned forward, alert with interest. "How? The Calliopeans have always refused before. They didn't ally with us during the last war until after the Terra Nuevans attacked their colonies."

Roseli looked at the red carpet. "My mother offered the Calliopean emperor a marriage alliance. I'm now engaged to his daughter, Princess Lucia Caron."

The silence was deafening. Alexis had gone completely still, and Julia wasn't doing much better. Beatrice said nothing. Despite the inevitability of her eventually marrying, Roseli and her lovers had never talked about it directly. Alexis would never leave her, regardless of the cost, of that she was certain. Julia would not go willingly, but she would bow to necessity if Roseli asked it of her. As for Beatrice, she would go without a word if it came to it, but Roseli would never forgive herself if she let it happen.

"Have..." Julia had wrapped her arms around herself in a way that made Roseli's heart ache. "Have you been asked to set us aside?"

Roseli stood and stepped around the table to sit beside her, hugging her tightly. "No, and all seven hells will freeze over before I do."

Julia remained tense in her arms. "Princess Lucia is Calliopean. They only marry one spouse and don't publicly acknowledge lovers. What if she insists?" Julia was a fourth Calliopean on her grandfather's side and familiar with their customs.

"I've not seen the marriage contract yet, but my mother would have never agreed to one that excluded me from taking additional wives to build alliances on Delphi. If Princess Lucia has to accept that, I doubt she'll fight me on having paramours." At least, she hoped so.

"What do we know about this woman?" asked Beatrice.

"I know nothing of her character, but she is a competent admiral in her father's navy." Alexis's tone was dispassionate, but Roseli knew that meant she was trying not to show how upset she was. "Her fleet provided orbital support for my troops several times during the battle for the second moon of Brahe."

"Princess Lucia is the second youngest of three siblings. With an older and younger brother, she's third in line for the Calliopean throne since she's a woman," said Julia. She had finally relaxed against Roseli's embrace, and Roseli kept one arm about her.

"Shouldn't she be first in line, then?" asked Beatrice.

"No, on Calliope, men inherit before women. It's the opposite of Delphi," said Julia.

Which was just one more reminder that Roseli was expected to marry a stranger from a completely different culture. Beatrice must have seen the look on her face because she dropped that line of questioning and sat on Roseli's other side. "We don't have to figure out all this tonight. You look exhausted." She took Roseli's free hand and squeezed it. "Whatever comes, we are here for you."

"Always," said Alexis.

"What do you need right now, darling?" asked Beatrice. "Do you want us to stay, or do you need time alone?"

"Stay, please. All of you." The thought of being alone with her thoughts was unbearable.

Beatrice gently touched the side of her face, turning her head so she looked into her piercing blue eyes. "Do you want to be held, or do you need more?"

Roseli felt her face heat. "More, but only if you want to."

Beatrice kissed her. It was a light kiss, more tender than passionate, but it was enough to calm the frantic flutter of Roseli's heart.

"I do," said Beatrice. She briefly traded a look with the others before she asked, "Do you want Alexis and Julia in the same way right now, or will that overwhelm you?"

"I think that's exactly what I need."

"Then come to bed, darling."

Beatrice led Roseli to the bedroom down the hall. The decoration was an odd, magpie-like collection of precious and common elements. While Roseli yielded all decorating decisions to Beatrice's impeccable taste when it came to decorating public parts of her rooms, she did what she wanted with her most private space. Within these familiar walls, with those she loved, she didn't need to be anyone but herself.

The carpet was a woven pattern of bright geometric designs. Roseli had covered the white walls with paintings that she liked, mostly reproductions of works from old Earth. A woman lay in the water clutching flowers, three naked women danced in a circle, a black cat yowled, and a woman in a yellow dress sat reading a small book in a chair.

The bed was large, nearly indestructible, and most importantly, could hold the weight of several people without creaking. It was made of heavy dark wood, carved in a swirling style common to Varcia.

It had been a formal gift from some long-forgotten Varcian empress generations ago and had spent untold years forgotten in the dark until Roseli had discovered it while exploring the palace vaults.

Beatrice drew her to the bed, and as Roseli embraced her, she felt another set of hands on her hips and lips against her neck, kissing and nipping lightly. She knew Julia's touch, confident and sure.

Alexis had followed but hadn't touched her yet, as she might have if they were alone. She tended to be more reserved when the others were present. Roseli knew that Alexis would have preferred for it to have remained just the two of them. If it had been in Roseli's nature to give her that, she would have, but it wasn't. She was still deeply grateful that Alexis had set aside a jealous streak to remain with her.

Beatrice broke the kiss to ask seductively, "What do you need tonight? Gentle or hard, to make love or to fuck?"

Roseli struggled for clarity. "I…" Why was it so hard to say what she wanted? She was the future empress of an empire, yet when she was only with her lovers, her words sometimes failed her.

Beatrice kissed her. "It's all right, love, you're with us. You can say anything. You know we love you." How easily she spoke for the hearts of others. Julia and Alexis would never dream of speaking for Beatrice, and yet they both trusted their voices to her without protest.

The touch of a hand on her arm, sure and kind, caused her to turn her head. Alexis was by her side, gray eyes kind. "What do you wish for, my love?"

She trembled. "Make me forget everything but the three of you." With a sudden burst of courage, she said, "Can we do again what we did at midwinter?"

Beatrice tilted her head slightly. "Are you sure?"

She nodded. "Yes."

Beatrice looked at Julia and Alexis and waited for a nod from both before she continued. "How about I get you ready, and Julia and Alexis can get the toys?"

"Yes," Roseli managed breathlessly.

Beatrice kissed her again and helped her undress. She was tenderly methodical about it. She wasn't the clothes-tearing sort, especially since she'd picked out everything Roseli was wearing. Roseli ached to pull Beatrice back into her arms and tumble onto the bed, but experience had taught her that it was well worth letting Beatrice take her time.

Beatrice unzipped Roseli's ball gown before carefully hanging it up. She tugged Roseli's white silk shift over her head and set it aside on a chair before helping her with her bra and panties. "Unzip me?" she asked, looking coyly over her shoulder.

Roseli pulled down the zipper, running her hands over the warm skin of her back. Beatrice stepped out of her dress and set it aside, turning to give a good view of her red silk bra and panties. She took her time unclasping her bra and then easing her underwear down her legs, letting Roseli appreciate the sight.

When she was gloriously naked, she climbed onto the bed, beckoning Roseli to her with a come-hither motion. Roseli followed, stretched over her, kissing her and running her hands over her body.

Beatrice caught her hand and turned it to kiss the palm. "Lie back, darling, let me pleasure you."

"Bossy," teased Roseli. Still, she did, rolling onto her back, happy to let Beatrice take charge.

Beatrice kissed a trail down her body, sucking on a nipple and then continuing across her ribs and stomach to her thighs. She nudged Roseli's legs open with an elbow and ducked her head.

Roseli gasped when Beatrice breathed on her labia before using her fingers to part them and find her clit with her tongue. Roseli had always been in awe of Beatrice's talents; she seemed to know instinctively when to lick and when to press with the flat of her tongue, when to circle and when to suck.

Roseli ached to pull at her golden curls, but she knew Beatrice didn't like that, so instead, she clutched at the sheets and moaned. She looked up to find Alexis on one side of her and Julia on the other.

Alexis's body was a collection of lean muscles kept toned through hours of fencing. Roseli knew every scar that marked her olive skin. Faded red lines and splotches marred her left arm, side, and leg, the results of the same mortar explosion that had scarred her neck and cost an ear. There was another shallower gash across her right breast, a reminder of an ill-advised duel she'd fought in her youth.

In contrast, Julia's pale skin was unmarked by anything but a dusting of freckles. She'd fought no duels, nor likely ever would. There was a pleasing curve to her breasts and hips, although her body still had the definition of a woman who worked out regularly.

Roseli's pulse sped up when she noticed both wore strap-ons from the box beside the bed. She knew exactly what they were going to do, and her body burned with anticipation. Alexis kissed her as Julia brought her mouth to a breast.

Beatrice worked two fingers into her, fucked her steadily, curling her fingers and pressing a thumb against her clit in hard circles. Roseli tumbled into her first orgasm of the night, her body clenching on Beatrice's fingers.

Beatrice eased her down from her release, slowing her fingers but not stilling them. "Lube," she said.

When Beatrice withdrew her fingers. Roseli was left aching and empty. She felt the bed shift and heard the soft click of a bottle opening, and then Beatrice was pressing a single finger against a lower part of her, circling slowly, letting her get used to the feeling. When Roseli relaxed, Beatrice slowly pressed in up to the knuckle, drew back, then repeated the motion.

Roseli gasped when Beatrice worked the finger deeper and then added a second. It had been a while since they had done this. Beatrice paused. "Darling?"

"I'm good," she managed.

Julia leaned past Beatrice to begin rubbing Roseli's clit.

She couldn't stop her breath from growing desperate and haggard as Beatrice fucked her with two fingers and then three. She wanted to sink into the pleasure, lose herself in it. Infuriatingly, Beatrice stopped instead of bringing her to the second orgasm she craved.

Roseli moaned in protest, but Beatrice kissed her cheek and drew back, "Don't fret darling, you know how much you love what comes next." Roseli heard her telling Alexis and Julia, "I think this will work best with you on your back and her riding you, just like last time."

Roseli collected herself enough to sit up and roll out of the way so Alexis could lie in the center of the bed, bracing her back against a pile of pillows set against the headboard. Roseli climbed onto her lap, the dildo pressed between them. So close together, Roseli could see the warmth in Alexis's gray eyes.

Alexis kissed her. "My love."

"My Alexis."

Beatrice crawled over to them. "Make sure she's still wet enough."

Alexis leaned forward to accept the bottle from Beatrice. Roseli moaned as Alexis pressed lubed fingers into her, curling them a few times inside at just the right angle before withdrawing them and slicking the dildo with the excess.

Roseli rose on her knees, used her hand to line up the toy, and sank down on it. She gave herself a moment to adjust to the feeling and then rolled her hips, braced a hand on Alexis's shoulders for leverage, and moved with purpose. She closed her eyes, focusing on the pleasure that flooded her body.

"You're so lovely like this," Alexis murmured. After all the time they had been together, she still said things like that, as if she was seeing Roseli for the first time. Roseli loved her for it.

Her body burned with need. She was so close to getting off again. She reached to touch her clit as she fucked herself on the toy.

Beatrice kissed her just beneath her ear. "Not yet, darling, you'll tire yourself out."

Roseli's eyes drifted open. She looked toward Beatrice and pleaded, "I need it."

"I know, love, but you must be patient."

A sure hand turned her face to kiss soft lips. "Forget about me, beautiful?" teased Julia.

"Never."

Julia stroked her cheek. "Are you ready for the next part?"

"Yes, so very ready." She didn't think she could wait another moment.

Julia moved behind her. Roseli leaned forward, half lying over Alexis as Julia pressed lubed fingers into her ass. The feeling of being penetrated in two places at once was intense, even with just fingers. She gasped when Julia withdrew her fingers and replaced them with the second dildo, easing the toy into her.

She clutched at Alexis's shoulders, struggling for breath. Her body clenched on the toys, overwhelmed by the intense feeling of fullness. She fought to relax, to accept the penetration. She knew if she could get through the initial feeling of stretching, it would all feel wonderful.

When it had just been Julia and Alexis, she could have never dreamed of a night like this one. She'd lacked the courage to ask them both into her bed at the same time. It had taken Beatrice to draw her true desires and needs out of her.

She barely realized when the toy was fully inside. For an instant, it was all too much, and discomfort warred with pleasure. Beatrice reached between her and Alexis and found her clit. Julia rubbed her back, speaking softly.

Roseli felt completely and utterly cared for. Within that deep feeling of security, she found a wild and intoxicating sense of freedom. In the arms of her lovers, she had no fear of falling. She began to move of her own volition. Alexis and Julia took the cue and did the same.

Julia had more room to maneuver and could thrust into her. Alexis couldn't do much, but she rested a hand on Roseli's hip and guided her as she rose and fell.

Somehow, between all of them, they found a rhythm. Amidst it all, Beatrice kept rubbing Roseli's clit, bringing her closer and closer to the brink. "Go on, darling, let go, we have you."

Roseli came with a flash of euphoria, her entire body tensing and releasing. "Don't stop, please don't stop," she begged, even as her orgasm faded. More than even the pleasure, she didn't want the feeling of intense connection to end.

Julia and Alexis obeyed, taking her to another release. Even as her orgasm crested, she knew she'd gone past the point of overstimulation. She slumped against Alexis, feeling boneless and vulnerable.

Julia eased the second toy from her, and Beatrice helped her rise up enough to free herself from the first. Alexis drew her into her arms, and Julia hugged her from behind.

Beatrice stroked her hair, murmuring, "We've got you, love, we're here."

She knew she was trembling, but she was too content to care. She could have happily drifted off to sleep, but after a time, Beatrice nudged her. "Go pee."

"Can't move."

"Go pee, then you can sleep." She was a stickler about that kind of thing. Beatrice wasn't wrong about the importance of peeing after penetrative sex to avoid getting a UTI, but it was still a pain to get out of bed when her bones felt like jelly.

She slipped from the bed to pad across the carpeted floor to the ensuite bathroom. She returned to find an interesting sight. Beatrice was going down on a reclining Julia as Alexis knelt beside her, pleasuring her with sure fingers. Roseli leaned against the door, enjoying the tableau.

It was rare to see them touching each other without her but not unheard of. Their earlier activities had left them all aching, and with Roseli exhausted, there was little hope of relief from her. It amazed her that they had all grown comfortable enough with each other for what she was witnessing. Julia gasped with orgasm, and then Beatrice did shortly after. Alexis sat back, likely consoling herself to the continuance of her longing. Beatrice roused herself from her brief stupor and drew Alexis into a quick kiss and then urged her down and began doing for her what she had for Julia.

Had the air in the room not felt cold against her naked skin, Roseli would have been content to continue to observe, but she shivered. She returned to the warmth of the bed and settled into Julia's arms as Alexis and Beatrice finished.

She promised herself that she would spend some time alone with each of them over the next few days. For what they had just done to be possible, her individual relationships with each had to remain strong.

After Alexis and Beatrice were done, Alexis went to turn out the lights, and Beatrice lay down beside Roseli. Roseli pulled her into her arms, nuzzling her soft curls that smelled faintly of rose perfume.

The bed shifted as Alexis returned, settling behind Beatrice, throwing an arm over her and Roseli. Roseli searched for her hand in the darkness and clasped it.

At the middle of the complex tangle of limbs, Roseli felt safe and calm for the first time that day. Whatever lay ahead, so long as she had Alexis, Julia, and Beatrice at her side, they could face it together.

CHAPTER THREE

Roseli slept fitfully. She dreamed of the Inner Chambers of the palace and her childhood there, of listening to stories about the stars and the terrible night she lost her sisters.

She had never slept easily, even as a child. Her sisters had been sweet, obedient girls who went to bed when told. Roseli had always begged her nurse to let her play just a little longer, for one more bedtime story or a late-night snack. Eventually, her exhausted nurse would tell her to close her eyes and lie still. Sleep would come soon enough.

It seldom did. Roseli had learned it was easier to pretend that she had been successfully put to bed and then wait until she heard snoring from her nurse's small room beside the nursery. She would slip from her blankets and play with her toys quietly on the floor, listening to her sisters' soft, sleeping breaths. When she was feeling bold, she would slip from the nursery into the nighttime halls of the Inner Chambers. At first, the guards brought her back and told her nurse. After a time, they tired of such an impossible task and simply kept an eye on her. What harm could a child come to within the most secure part of the palace?

It was during her nocturnal wanderings that she stumbled upon her mother's third husband, Prince Ambrose. Her mother had married the Mycenae prince the year before, but he and Roseli had seldom interacted.

Prince Ambrose was sitting beside the reflecting pool and looking up at the stars. He was a tall, lanky young man with his hair cut shorter than most Delphian noblemen wore it. "Can't sleep either?"

She'd shaken her head "No. I'm not tired."

"Sit then."

The invitation had surprised her. Her mother's first husband,

Prince Leon, had never talked to her when he'd come to the nursery to see his daughters. When Roseli had asked her nurse why she had no father of her own to bring her toys or take her on outings, the kindly woman had told her that father had been a great general who'd fallen in battle before she was born.

Roseli had sat beside Prince Ambrose, putting her bare feet in the cool water of the pool.

After a time, he'd pointed out a constellation in the shape of a bear and had told her its story. He spoke in a slow, almost lyrical manner, his Moûsaian heavily accented by his native Mycenaean dialect. She'd liked listening to him.

When Roseli had grown drowsy, he'd carried her back to the nursery. In this way, their strange friendship had begun. On nights Roseli couldn't sleep, which was most of them, she'd sought Prince Ambrose in the garden, and they'd sit and talk.

He'd never told Roseli about his sorrows, but she'd learned his story from other sources when she was older. Roseli's mother had married Prince Ambrose for the sake of a trade agreement with the previously neutral planet Mycenae, an agreement that had quickly proved ill-fated when the Varcians had invaded and had conquered Mycenae a year after the marriage.

The Mycenaean royal palace had burned during the invasion, leaving Prince Ambrose his father's sole surviving male heir. He was a loose end the Varcian empress did not want. A living heir had left the possibility of a future Mycenaean rebellion. To her credit, her mother was not so coldhearted as to hand her husband over to the Varcian empress to be killed when she'd demanded it.

In order to keep the two empires' shaky military alliance against the Terra Nuevans, Roseli's mother had to make it clear she had no intention of defending her husband's potential claim to the Mycenaean throne and that his bloodline would end with him.

She did not divorce Prince Ambrose but set him aside as a husband in all other ways. There could not be even a whisper of the possibility that he'd fathered any of her children. Prince Ambrose had lost his home, his family, and his status as an imperial consort all at once. What few friends he'd been able to make in the Delphian court had abandoned him. Witnessing how the court had shunned Prince Ambrose had been Roseli's first lesson in the harsh ways of politics.

Lonely and grieving, Prince Ambrose had accepted Roseli's

friendship. He'd told her stories from his childhood, as if he could somehow recapture all that he had lost. He'd talked often of his father's court where he'd grown up.

It had seemed like a strange world to Roseli, a place where a man was emperor and women were not allowed to be soldiers or senators. Roseli hadn't liked the idea of a place where her mother couldn't be empress, but she'd loved to listen when Prince Ambrose had told her about his father's hunting lodges and fine horses and hunting dogs.

When Roseli had closed her eyes, she could imagine riding through a dark green forest with dogs running at her horse's feet. She had never ridden a horse or been allowed to have a dog. Horses were rare on Delphi, and dogs were not popular pets. When Roseli had asked Prince Ambrose to take her to Mycenae to see the horses and dogs, he had gone silent and had told her it was too far away.

The night that an assassin had stolen into the nursery and had slit Princess Isabella's and Princess Sarah's sleeping throats, along with their poor old nurse, Roseli had been sitting beneath the Laponian Maple tree in the garden with Prince Ambrose, listening to a story about a winged horse in the stars. He had gone silent, staring toward the rooftop. He'd hit a button on a device on his wrist and had pulled Roseli into the tree's shadow, whispering for her to stay quiet.

She had been terrified. She hadn't known what he had seen or was hiding from, but his fear was infectious. She'd hidden her face against his shoulder and tried not to cry.

He had waited until everything exploded into a chaos of voices and thundering feet before he'd picked her up and ran. They'd passed a dead guard on the floor in the hallway beyond the courtyard. He'd ignored the body, slamming his palm against the keypad for one of the Inner Chambers' safe rooms, and had run inside.

Although no one ever spoke to Roseli about what happened that night, she would later come to understand from official accounts and rumors that the assassins had meant to kill her entire family. Prince Ambrose's insomnia had saved not only Roseli's life but his own. Had he been in his bed, the assassins would have murdered him there.

Her mother and Prince Leon had been equally lucky. Years of paranoia had led her mother to always sleep with a loaded gun beside her bed. On that night, when her mother had awoken to find a stranger in her bedroom, she'd shot him, saving both herself and Prince Leon, who was sleeping beside her.

Prince Ambrose had brought Roseli to her mother after the guards had told him he could come out of the safe room. When they'd come in, her mother was standing in her sitting room in her dressing gown, hair wild and uncombed. Guards were swarming all around as Prince Leon stood at her side.

When her mother's eyes fell upon Roseli, she gave a cry and rushed over.

"Oh, thank the gods." She'd embraced them both, kissing Roseli's head. "Where are the others?"

"I don't know," said Prince Ambrose.

Her mother had drawn back, her eyes wide in panic. "How can you not know? Why did you bring me only one? Where are my heir and baby?"

It was then that a guard had come in to tell the terrible news of what had occurred in the nursery. Her mother had gone utterly still, and then she'd turned her back on Roseli and Prince Ambrose. She'd sunk onto the couch, waving off Prince Leon when he'd tried to lay a hand on her shoulder.

"Get out, all of you, get out."

Prince Ambrose had carried Roseli from the room. They were halfway down the hall before she'd heard her mother sobbing. That night was the last time Roseli's mother had ever hugged her or looked at her without a shadow of grief in her eyes.

Beatrice woke in Roseli's arms in a sea of rumpled sheets. The others had already departed, Alexis no doubt to early morning fencing practice and Julia to a Senate hearing. It was peaceful feeling the warmth of Roseli's breath against the back of her neck. She was tempted to go back to sleep, but the palace's Spring Ball was in two weeks. In the capital city of Delphi, Thetis, early spring was the height of the social season. It was an exhausting time of year but still her favorite.

While Roseli would have happily worn a sack if allowed, Beatrice did her best to make sure she dressed in a manner befitting a princess. She had found her a proper royal wardrobe mistress. That woman had gotten one of Delphi's top designers to provide Roseli a new dress for this ball, and Beatrice wanted to make sure the dress was ready after the alterations from the first fitting.

She slipped from Roseli's embrace and took a silk dressing gown from the closet, drawing it around herself. She padded into the sitting room and used her wrist strap to send for tea. As she waited, she sat on one of the low couches and took up the tablet she had set aside the night before and began to check her correspondence.

She heard the door open. "Thank you. Set the tray on the table, please," she said without looking up.

"You've gotten rather impertinent, haven't you, tart?"

The flat voice of the Empress of Delphi sent a spike of fear through her. She dropped her tablet and fell into a deep bow on the floor beside the couch. "Your Majesty, please forgive me."

"Get up. I've certainly not paid you to get on your knees." The empress was at first glance a rather ordinary-looking woman, gray-haired and thin, well past her middle years. Her face carried the lines of a life of loss and disappointment, but the rigidity of her back spoke of absolute authority. She wore a modestly cut dress of blue silk, with flowers embroidered sparingly on the sleeves and hem. The silk alone, much less the tailoring, had probably cost more than Beatrice had ever made in all her years as a practicing courtesan.

Beatrice rose as gracefully as she could, her eyes still downcast. She knew she looked less than presentable in her current state of tangled curls and last night's makeup. "Thank you, Your Majesty."

"If you are about, I trust my daughter is as well?"

"Princess Roseli is sleeping." As was most of the palace. Beatrice felt deeply unsettled by her presence. What was the empress even doing in Roseli's rooms? She never came there.

"Alone?" The implication was rather clear.

Beatrice bowed again. "Yes, please allow me to wake her for you."

"Go on, then," she said with a distracted wave.

Beatrice hurried into the bedroom. With the bed to herself, Roseli had sprawled across the entire thing and managed to kick off the covers in her sleep. Beatrice gently nudged her. "Wake up, darling."

"A few more minutes," she mumbled without opening her eyes.

"You must get up, darling, your mother is in the next room."

Roseli sat straight up. "What? Why?"

"I don't know, but she is here."

Roseli scrambled from the bed and pulled on the pants and shirt that Beatrice handed her before roughly tugging her tangled hair into a ponytail. The empress was not a woman to be kept waiting.

Beatrice caught her arm as she headed into the next room. "Do you want me with you, or is it better if I stay here?"

"Come with me. She knows I'll tell you anything she tells me."

When they stepped into the sitting room, the empress was sipping the tea Beatrice had sent for, frowning at a delicate porcelain cup as if it had personally offended her. "I don't know how you stomach this weak Calliopean rubbish. It tastes like a flower."

So much for the finest green jasmine tea that could be imported. "I'll send for something else, Your Majesty," said Beatrice as she and Roseli bowed, Beatrice far deeper. She tapped at her wrist strap, sending off an order for coffee.

"Don't just stand there like idiots, sit," said the empress with a generous wave to the divan across from her.

They obeyed.

The empress studied Roseli. As usual, she seemed to find her lacking. "You shouldn't be sleeping so late, not when there is so much to do."

Roseli frowned. "What needs to be done?"

"Preparations for your impending marriage. I've come to tell you that your fiancée is arriving much sooner than expected, at the end of next week."

Roseli started. "How? It's a two-month journey from Calliope to Delphi."

"Her ship and two others were patrolling close to Delphi when the negotiations were finalized."

"Surely, we still need time to prepare for the wedding, even if she is to arrive sooner," said Roseli.

"That…" The empress went silent when the door opened, and a servant brought in a tray of coffee and pastries. She waited until the gray-liveried man was gone to ask, "When was this place last swept for bugs?"

Roseli sighed in annoyance. "Yesterday afternoon. You know I take every precaution my head of security advises."

The empress still looked less than convinced and glanced at Beatrice pointedly.

Beatrice knew when she had been dismissed. She began to stand, but Roseli said, "Lady Swann is to be trusted with anything that I am."

The empress considered this briefly, her gaze not softening. "I suppose you have a point. Courtesans, even retired ones, tend to be good at knowing when to keep their mouths shut, an art you would do well to learn. She may stay."

Beatrice wasn't sure if that had been an insult or a compliment.

The empress sipped black coffee and set it down, seemingly as displeased with it as the earlier tea. "You are to be married by the end of the month, as much of a bother as it will be. That stubborn old bastard of a Calliopean emperor won't send ships until the alliance is sealed."

"Why the rush? I got Ambassador Hansen to agree to remove the base. The armistice is safe. You read my report, didn't you?" asked Roseli.

The empress looked at her over her cup. "You didn't seriously believe there was only one base, did you?"

"What?"

"There are five other hidden bases in the neutral zone on small asteroids and moons."

"And you sent me to the ambassador without telling me that?"

"I had no intention of the Terra Nuevans finding out we know about the other bases. The purpose of your little conversation was never the removal of the base but to see how the Terra Nuevans would react to our knowledge of one."

There was a soft ceramic click as Roseli set her teacup in its saucer. Beatrice saw her hand shaking. She wished she could take Roseli's hand to calm her, as she would have if they were alone.

"Does this mean the truce is over?" said Roseli.

"Hell if I know. It still isn't clear if this incursion into the neutral zone is a genuine act of aggression or a preemptive step on their part because they fear we are doing the same. We must prepare for the worst but make no move to escalate things."

"Except for marrying me off with all haste."

The empress ignored her tone, remaining deathly serious. "Yes, because gods willing, it may help us keep the peace. Adding additional Calliopean ships to the forces patrolling our edge of the neutral zone should make the Terra Nuevans rethink their incursions. We need to remind the Terra Nuevans that Delphi does not stand alone."

"Is it even possible to prepare a royal wedding in a single month?" asked Roseli.

Beatrice knew it was not. While subsequent marriages would require little more ceremony than a ball, the first wedding of a future empress was supposed to be the social event of a generation. With less than a month to prepare, there would not even be time for foreign dignitaries to arrive.

"No, but the alliance matters more. I will see that all palace resources are put to the wedding and that no expense is spared. I will not have my heir's first wedding be a shabby mess."

Considering how much Empress Eleanor disliked extravagant spending, this was rather impressive on her part. While she still held all the traditional royal balls, they were the simplest ones in generations. Beatrice had often listened to the older retired courtesans in the guild reminisce, longing for the lavish events that Empress Ariadne had once thrown, where Calliopean wine flowed like water.

The empress looked at Beatrice again, this time with an almost calculating expression. "Lady Swann, I know you are behind the improvements in my daughter's wardrobe and general presentableness. See that she looks the part of a future empress for the wedding." Almost like an afterthought, she added. "While you're at it, assist the palace steward with the preparations, as well. That old prig is going to have a heart attack when I tell him how soon the wedding is."

Beatrice bowed her head, stunned. Had the empress just put her in charge of Roseli's wedding? What did that mean? "Yes, Your Majesty."

The empress seemed to catch the look of surprise on Roseli's face. "You didn't think I was going to tell you to dismiss her or the other two before you wed, did you?"

"I wasn't sure," admitted Roseli.

Beatrice wanted to hug Roseli and cry with relief, but she could hardly do that in front of the empress.

"You have your share of flaws, but you have been wise in your collection of lovers. They strengthen your ties and influence with the military, the Senate, and the Courtesan's Guild. You'll need those alliances now more than ever. I made sure that the marriage contract has a clause that allows you to keep your current, officially named paramours, although in the future, you'll need your first wife's agreement to add any more." She stood. Roseli and Beatrice did as well, as tradition dictated. "Now, I have other matters to attend to. I trust this matter is settled?"

Roseli bowed to her mother. "Yes."

The empress nodded and swept from the room.

Roseli and Beatrice sat in stunned silence for a moment and then slowly sank back onto the divan.

"A month," said Roseli quietly.

"A month," Beatrice echoed. She could face the impossible, even plan a royal wedding in a month, if it meant she wouldn't lose Roseli.

CHAPTER FOUR

A fter her mother left, Roseli took a short walk through the palace hallways to the Inner Chambers. She needed to speak with Prince Ambrose. He had been the closest thing she'd had to a parent for most of her childhood.

He had raised her in the years after the Massacre of the Inner Chambers, when her mother had sunk into grief. He had sat with her through the night terrors that followed her sisters' deaths, overseen her education, and had always been ready to listen and give advice. Upon reaching her majority, she had officially named him her adopted father. Gaining the title of Father of the Heir had considerably raised his social status in the court, not that he ever seemed to take much notice.

She found him, as she often did, painting beside the main reflecting pool in the central courtyard of the Inner Chambers. He was standing before his easel, brush and pallet in hand. On the canvas was a half-finished image of the great Laponian Maple from Old Terra that dominated about half the courtyard. He had painted it countless times, and yet every painting was unique.

As a child, Roseli had always loved to watch him paint; there was something deeply soothing about watching him methodically mix colors and bring life to a canvas. She had a spring and fall version of Laponian Maple on opposite walls in her sitting room.

He had never had much success as a painter on Delphi, but his work was highly regarded on several other planets, especially Calliope, where prints of his paintings sold well. He never seemed to have much use for the money, but the recognition made him happy.

Unlike most Delphian nobles, he preferred to dress simply, in muted colors. As he stood in the late afternoon light, Roseli noticed that although he had yet to reach the end of his forties, his dark blond hair, so common to Mycenae, was now streaked with gray. The fall of his planet, the murder of most of his family, and his years as a near pariah in a foreign court had aged him before his time.

He must have heard her steps because he set down his pallet and brush on a stool and turned, smiling when he saw her. "Come, let's have breakfast."

Roseli returned the smile, and they went to sit at the base of the maple where a low table and cushions had been set out in Mycenaean style. Servants brought tea and a tray of honey-almond sweets, along with simple flatbread and a honey dip. Even after two decades on Delphi, Prince Ambrose still preferred Mycenaean food when he had a choice.

His forehead wrinkled with worry as Roseli told him about the engagement. "I take it you are not happy with this?"

"Yes." Roseli lifted her heavy rounded cup of spiced black tea. "I knew this day would come, I just…I feel a bit overwhelmed now that it has."

"I understand."

She took a slow breath. "I don't even know why I'm feeling so out of sorts. I should be relieved. At least I'm engaged to a woman and a passable-looking one at that." She had looked up a picture and found her fiancée to be about five years older than herself, with dark brown hair and a rather self-assured smirk. "I worried for years that my mother would try to force me to marry some prince or other, despite the obvious compatibility issues."

"She gave up on that idea a long time ago," he said, sipping his tea. "Especially after you punched Prince Adam of Septia when he visited as a young teenager."

"He pulled my hair." She had no regrets.

"You bloodied the boy's nose," he said with a shrug. "Not that he didn't deserve it. Still, it made things awkward with Septia for a time."

"The royal family there is mostly symbolic, anyway. I don't think we'd have ever gotten a trade treaty with them, even if I had gotten along with that brat." She wasn't sure if she was any happier being married off for ships instead of trade, but at least she wouldn't be stuck with Prince Adam.

"True enough."

They sat, enjoying the warm spring morning. Roseli did not want to break the peace of their meal, but she needed to talk. At last, she said. "I'm to be married in barely a month. It feels like my entire life is laid out before me, and I have no choice in it."

"We always have a choice, even if it is merely how to live the life we are given."

"You love quoting that philosopher." She recognized the sentence from the dialogs of Diotima Aspasia, a famous Galian poet. Galia, like Mycenae, had fallen to Varcia during the last war. The philosopher had written many of her greatest works from captivity within the Varcian royal court after being carried there along with her planet's fabled library.

"Philosophy has no shortage of insights. Although, in this case, I have advice of my own to offer," he said. "It is important that you treat your new consort well regardless of your feelings."

"I'll try. It is an arranged marriage, though. It's not as if I'm going to love her."

He set down his cup, studying her with thoughtful brown eyes. "No one expects you to. Just be kind. She will be alone and far from everything she has ever known. Prove yourself an ally from the beginning, and she will be one to you in the years to come."

Essentially, the opposite of how her mother had treated Prince Ambrose. Roseli knew he would never say that, though. In all the years she had known him, he had never spoken ill of her mother, likely out of a sense of self-preservation.

Instead, she said, "Now you sound like a political strategist."

He smiled. "No, I'm just a painter, but I try. Has what I said made sense?"

"Yes."

He reached for her hand, covering it with his own. "Keep coming to talk to me. I'll try to offer what counsel I can." His hand seemed thinner and more lined than she remembered. The feeling of reassurance was the same. He couldn't solve all her problems, but he would listen, and that was enough.

"I will," she promised. Even if all she ever had with her future wife was trust, she would make sure they had that.

❖

Alexis pushed aside her tablet after reading the same paragraph for the third time without retaining anything. She leaned back in her chair, a fancy leather recliner that was as much a part of the office as the heavy wooden desk and oil paintings on the wall.

When she was assigned the office after being put in charge of the home guard after the war, she had never seen any need to change or replace anything the last general had left. The office was merely one more thing in her life that was only temporarily hers.

She was struck by the intense urge to snatch up her tablet and fling it against the wall. She wanted to scream at the unfairness of it all. She had fought for her planet, she had loyally stood beside Roseli as a paramour for years, and yet she could never ask for her hand in marriage.

She forced herself to lay her hands flat on the table. If she broke the tablet, that would just mean more work for her secretary, who would have to requisition a new one. Even worse, she would ask what had happened, and the last thing Alexis wanted to do was talk.

She was no fool. She knew that Roseli's duty was to the crown before all else. Marrying for the good of Delphi had always been expected of her, and right now, Delphi needed ships. If Princess Lucia insisted Roseli set aside her lovers, despite all her promises, Roseli would have to do so.

It had been hard enough to make peace with Roseli taking other lovers, but at least both times, it had been a matter of love. For all her jealous nature, Alexis could accept sharing Roseli with Julia and Beatrice so long as they made Roseli happy. Julia could draw laughter out of Roseli in a way she'd never been able to, and Beatrice could adeptly see Roseli safely through the treacherous waters of any social situation.

This was different. The thought of Roseli going unwillingly to another woman's bed filled Alexis with something halfway between rage and panic. The only thing that stopped her from planning to challenge Princess Lucia to a duel the moment she set foot on Delphi was that Princess Lucia had no more choice in the matter than Roseli did. Alexis needed to know more about Princess Lucia to be sure she wouldn't mistreat Roseli or come between them.

She would need to be discreet in her inquiries but not overly so. The marriage contract had been sent to the Senate that morning, and the official announcement was scheduled for later in the afternoon. She tugged her tablet back across the desk and looked through several personnel lists. She sent for a lieutenant who had recently returned from a term as an exchange officer with the Calliopean navy. A half hour later, Lieutenant Cartwright arrived from the naval offices several blocks away.

She was an unremarkable-looking woman in her mid-thirties. She had a painfully thin build that was not improved by her long nose, but there was no mistaking the intelligence in her sharp face. "General Tate." She saluted as she entered the office and stood at attention, showing no sign of being intimidated.

Alexis was well versed in the tension between their respective armed services. As a naval officer, Lieutenant Cartwright was not under the chain of command of an army general. She was showing Alexis a professional courtesy by speaking to her outside of an official request. Alexis had to approach this carefully and be respectful, especially as the information she wanted was not of a military or naval nature.

Alexis returned the salute. "Welcome. Please sit. You served under Admiral Lucia Caron, did you not?"

"Yes, on her flagship *Intrepid* during the war."

"What did you make of her?"

"She is a fine admiral and a decent tactician. She had the respect of her crew and every captain who served under her."

"What did you make of her character?"

Lieutenant Cartwright eyed her uncertainly. "As I said, she is a fine admiral."

Alexis folded her hands on the desk. "Lieutenant, you may speak freely. I give you my word that this is off the record. You served with the woman for two years. Even on a large ship, there are few secrets. Did she conduct her personal life honorably?"

The lieutenant glanced toward the door and then back before lowering her voice. "She went to bed with any attractive woman who'd smile back at her, but it's not unheard of for officers of different ranks within the Calliopean navy to be involved. She didn't abuse her power or anything like that. That said, she never stuck with any woman long and broke a few hearts."

"Enough to affect the running of the ship?"

"Nothing serious. I know that a few women she ended things with transferred to other ships. Transfers are common, so it was not the sort of thing to impact a career."

"I see." Alexis considered the woman across from her. "You weren't involved with her, were you?" That could make things considerably more awkward. Alexis could ask an officer her opinion of a former superior officer, but she had no right to ask a woman about a former lover.

The lieutenant's back stiffened, and she said nothing.

"You are under no obligation to answer that. Forgive me for prying," said Alexis.

Lieutenant Cartwright let out a breath. "I'm not exactly her type, but I suppose she got bored because she cast me a glance once. I scowled at her, and that was the end of it." She provided an example of just such a scowl. "She knew perfectly well that I was seeing one of her crew. I don't know what she was playing at."

"How is your wife, by the way? There was an article about your wedding in the paper. It is not often a Delphian sailor marries a Calliopean one."

The lieutenant brightened. "Abigail is still adjusting to Delphi but doing well. She retired from the navy to open a branch of her mother's shipping company here."

"I wish you both the best."

Julia returned to her office in one of the Senate buildings after an early morning vote. Once alone, she fished a pack of gummy candy from a drawer, tore it open, and dumped the contents onto her desk, picking out the red ones and eating those first. Her mind was awhirl with thoughts, possibilities, and worries. She was so afraid of losing Roseli.

She had never meant to fall in love when she had first set out to seduce Roseli for the political influence such a relationship would bring. She'd been lost from their first kiss. It was those big brown eyes, the smile, and the listening. Roseli was good at listening, and Julia loved her for it.

Roseli had been the first lover she had ever truly trusted, who she knew wouldn't turn around and backstab her for a political advantage. The last three years had been the happiest in her life. She should have known nothing good could ever last. Except, maybe it still could. For all her fears, the one thing she was certain of was that Roseli loved her, and she couldn't walk away from that.

Julia finished the red candies and started on the purple. From the start, she had accepted sharing Roseli. Roseli had already been with

Alexis when they met. Even when Roseli had brought Beatrice into their lives, she had still treated all her lovers with equal care and respect. A wife would be different. Even if Princess Lucia had no objections to Roseli having paramours, she would surely expect to be prioritized.

With the purple candy gone, Julia started on the orange. If there was one thing she hated, it was not knowing where she fit into a situation. She needed to learn more about this Calliopean princess who would have a claim to at least the public attentions of the woman she loved.

She swept the remaining green gummies, her least favorite, back into the bag. She used a private line to make an interplanetary call to her second cousin, Sydney Loraine, in the Calliopean Senate. This wasn't the first time she had reached out to Senator Loraine. One reason Julia had risen so quickly within her political party was her source of inside information regarding the political climate of the Calliopean Senate. She and her second cousin had a standing agreement to inform each other how likely their respective senates were to approve trade agreements. This knowledge had helped Julia's party know which agreements to expend political capital on passing and which to abandon.

Senator Loraine appeared on the screen, a plump and friendly woman. Julia had always liked her. She hoped to someday take her up on her offer to visit the family vineyards on Calliope, although if war was brewing with Terra Nueva, that might not be for some time.

"Julia, dear cousin, it is good to see you."

Her Calliopean dialect of Moûsaian sounded stilted and formal, but Julia had grown up listening to her grandfather's dialect and had no trouble understanding her cousin, although she had to slow her speech for Senator Loraine to understand her.

Senator Loraine was already aware of the engagement; the marriage contract had been sent to the Calliopean Senate that morning, so Julia asked what she knew of Princess Lucia.

"She is a war hero and popular among the Calliopean people. She's not boring like her older brother or flighty like her younger one. She doesn't make a lot of public appearances, but when she does, she's well-spoken. When she's on the planet, the tabloids are always trying to get a photo of her with a potential love interest, but they have nothing substantial on her. Rumor is, she mostly sleeps around with other women in the navy while on ship."

Julia could have gotten most of that from a gossip magazine

and wished for something more substantial. Their closely secured interplanetary line wasn't cheap. "What else can you tell me?"

"It's not publicly known, but she's had a failed engagement."

"Oh?"

"It was about two years ago when Calliope and Calypso were in the middle of negotiating a mutual defense treaty."

"I remember being surprised by that treaty, especially after how Calypso kept out of the last war."

Senator Loraine leaned forward and lowered her voice as if they were in the same room. "Well, as everyone knows, Calypso was only able to stay neutral during the war because they had an under-the-table agreement with Varcia. Calypso sold Varcia weapons and other supplies, and in exchange, Varcia promised to protect Calypso if the Terra Nuevans ever attacked. After the war ended, so did the agreement. I think the Calypsonian Queen became worried that the Varcians might eye her planet as a target for future expansion. Calliope was a natural ally to reach out to and offer the same agreement of weapons for protection. Unlike Varcia, we honor our defense agreements."

"I see." Julia already knew this; she was losing patience. Few things happened between planets that could be kept secret. "But how does it relate to Princess Lucia?"

"During negotiations, the Queen of Calypso suggested sealing the treaty with a marriage contract and offered her younger sister, Princess Helena. Princess Lucia traveled to Calypso in secret to marry her."

"Wait, didn't Princess Helena elope with a common-born woman?" She vaguely remembered a scandal, but she mostly followed Calliopean politics, not Calypsonian social pages.

"She did, right before Princess Lucia arrived. The Queen of Calypso was so embarrassed, she had to agree to the treaty without a marriage contract. She sent her youngest son to be fostered by the Calliopean royal family, and the Emperor of Calliope sent a niece to be fostered on Calypso. The matter of the non-engagement was kept quiet."

"Then, the failure of the engagement had nothing to do with Princess Lucia?" Hopefully, that was a good sign.

"No, although when the Queen of Calypso offered to annul her sister's marriage with the commoner and force her to still marry Princess Lucia, she declined. Princess Lucia said she would wed no woman who loved another. She was the one who suggested the fostering exchange instead."

"She's honorable." Would Princess Lucia have the same moral compunctions when she learned that Roseli already loved three women? Would she even understand? Calliope had no concept of paramours, and affairs outside of marriage were taboo, albeit common. Senator Loraine shrugged. "More likely, she didn't want to end up in a miserable marriage with a wife who didn't want her."

"Is there anything else?"

"Not that I can think of. I'll send you everything publicly available I have on her." While they exchanged a great deal of information on their secured and unrecorded calls, they were both careful when it came to files. Nothing classified ever changed hands. The line between back-channel communications and treason was a thin one and, at least on Delphi, they still executed traitors.

"Thank you."

"You'll keep me updated on the status of the marriage contract in the Delphian Senate?"

"Yes." Julia's thoughts were less settled than when she had begun.

Beatrice returned to her rooms across the hall from Roseli's. Despite everything that needed to be done, she let herself take a moment to sit at her makeup table in her dressing room. She was half-sick from relief; she'd been so afraid she was going to lose Roseli. A soft meow informed her that Roseli's cat, Dahlia, was hiding somewhere among her clothes. The small black feline poked her head out from beneath a shoe rack. Beatrice mentally cursed herself for leaving the door to her dressing room open earlier. The fuzzy beast had probably gotten black fur everywhere. She still adored her.

Dahlia meowed again, more pointedly, and came to headbutt her ankles.

"Don't even try begging. I know you've been fed, you little glutton."

The cat jumped into her lap. Normally, Beatrice wouldn't have permitted that, not when those sharp little claws could easily ruin a silk dressing gown. She scratched the cat's soft ears and felt the comforting vibration of her purrs. Before she knew what she was doing, she was hugging the cat and sobbing.

She cried half from the sheer weight of emotions she'd had to keep in check since Roseli's announcement the night before and half from relief. Although Julia had been the one to voice her fears, Beatrice had shared them. She trusted that Roseli would never willingly set her aside, but Roseli's life was not truly her own. The last thing she had ever expected was for the empress to protect her, Julia, and Alexis's place beside Roseli.

Beatrice would never say it to Alexis or Julia, but the stakes had never been the same for all of them. Without Roseli, Julia was still heir to the most powerful southern patrician family on Delphi and a senator in her own right. Alexis was one of the highest-ranking generals on Delphi and had built her military career long before she met Roseli.

For Beatrice, though, Roseli had become her life, and there was no going back. In order to become Roseli's official paramour, the crown had required Beatrice to sign an agreement that if Roseli set her aside or died, Beatrice would not return to her former profession. In exchange, she would receive a modest stipend for the rest of her life.

If Beatrice was dismissed as a royal paramour, she would not starve, but the glittering world of high-society garden parties and balls would be lost to her. She had known the risk she was taking when she'd chosen to be with Roseli.

Love, in her experience, was too rare a thing to let slip through her fingers. She's spent so much of her life playing a part to please others, always looked upon but never seen, listening but not speaking. The first time she'd met Roseli at a poetry reading, Roseli had asked her opinion and had seemed genuinely interested in what she had to say. For that alone, Beatrice had started to fall for her.

With Roseli, Beatrice could let slip the carefully crafted manners and illusions she had relied upon to make her way in the world. Roseli was the only person who knew the name Beatrice had left behind when she'd become a courtesan. Roseli could see past the glamor of Beatrice Swann to the slum girl, Maude Brown, and for that, she would always love her.

The cat wriggled in her arms, and she let her go before she could yowl or deploy her claws. She reached for a tissue, blowing her nose and wiping her face. With the coming marriage, Roseli would need her now more than ever, and she intended to be there for her. The first step was learning more about Roseli's fiancée so she would know how to deal with her.

An hour later, she emerged from her room with just enough light makeup to hide the puffiness of her eyes. She called for a car to take her to the Courtesans' Guild. While officially retired, she still paid a small annual fee to maintain access to the guild's resources and databases. It felt strange going back, but the guild was her best source of information and the only one she could possibly use to learn about a foreign princess. She needed to be sure that Princess Lucia wasn't a violent or cruel person.

The guild kept careful records and not just of clients. While the guild openly blacklisted clients if they hurt courtesans, they also had a gray list of any noble known to be a domestic abuser or rapist whom the guild would not accept as clients. It wasn't unheard of for nobles, especially mothers, to discreetly pay to learn if their daughter's or son's intended had any marks against him or her. What few people knew was that those records went beyond planetary limits. The Calliopean, Calypsonian, Varcian, and Delphian guilds had been sharing records for as long as nobles and courtesans had been traveling between the planets.

When she arrived at the Central Guild Hall, an apprentice courtesan showed her to an inner records room. The head librarian, Madame Adler, was a lean, sharp-faced woman, known more for her intellect than her charm. She was most often engaged to give lectures or improve the conversation of intellectual salons rather than merely grace a noble's arm.

Madame Adler bowed deeply. "Welcome, Lady Swann."

The title still sounded strange in Beatrice's ears. Roseli had officially bestowed it upon her when she became her paramour, as it would not be fitting for the lover of a princess to use a courtesan's title, even a retired one. Being treated with respect and diffidence by a senior guild member was unsettling, especially as she'd always been under the impression that Madame Adler didn't think much of her.

Beatrice had only been moderately successful as a courtesan. She had never held a Guild Council rank or office and had earned only two blue earrings before retirement. Between only accepting women as clients and refusing to take a contract with anyone she genuinely disliked, she'd had a small, if loyal, client base. It had taken her longer to pay back her apprentice fees than most of her colleagues, but she'd been happy and had enjoyed her work.

She returned the librarian's bow and explained the reason for her visit. The lack of surprise on Madame Adler's face confirmed Beatrice's suspicion that rumors of the princess's engagement had already escaped the palace.

"I will have to consult the head librarian of the Central Guild Library of Calliope."

"If possible, I would like to be part of that consultation," said Beatrice.

"It is early morning on Calliope, but I suspect their guild librarian keeps diligent hours. I will make the call, but it may take some time for my colleague to prepare an answer. May I suggest you take tea in the gardens? I'll call you when my colleague is ready to speak with you."

Beatrice knew when she was being dismissed and took it with grace. It still stung. Madame Adler was treating her like a client, not a former guild member. An apprentice led her to a gazebo at the heart of the ornamental gardens, where she served a delicate floral tea. The apprentice poured the tea with meticulous care and then stepped back, eyes demurely downcast.

Beatrice caught her stealing a shy glance. She remembered how in awe of older courtesans she had been as a girl. "It's all right, dear, I don't bite."

The apprentice bowed.

She deployed her best smile. "I was an apprentice once, too, you know. Tell me, does Madame Mabel still wax on endlessly in her classes about the importance of using the right fork at dinner parties?"

The apprentice giggled. "She does."

Beatrice took up her porcelain teacup and motioned the girl to sit across from her at the low table. "Listen to her, she's not wrong."

"I doubt any client will care what fork I use."

"Believe me, they will. If a client just wanted an attractive warm body, they would hire a member of the Prostitutes' Guild. As courtesans, the greatest thing we offer is the illusion of grace and refinement."

"Illusion?" The girl sounded lost.

"No one is born knowing which fancy fork to use. High-class manners are something nobles learn in the cradle, and women like us learn later, but we're all still playing a part." Albeit many had a much harder part to play than others. Beatrice let her high-class accent fall away to reveal the rougher drawl of the Western Slums. "Which part of the city are you from?"

"The Eastern Tenement, Mulberry Street." She could still hear the faint traces of her original accent.

"The guild had you go to a voice coach, I see."

"Yes."

"I had one before my entrance interview." Those voice lessons had cost everything she'd been able to save, but they had been worth it. She'd passed her entrance interview speaking with the even, middle-class vowels of most of the other applicants.

She would have been happy to offer more advice, but the apprentice's intercom buzzed, and the girl told her that the librarian was ready to speak with her again.

When Beatrice reentered the communications room, there was a woman on the main screen. She was older than the Delphian librarian and equally somber.

Beatrice was glad for their help but wished she'd been included in the initial call. It was just one more reminder that she was on the outside now. She could only hope she wasn't about to learn anything troubling.

"Lady Swann," Madame Adler said, "this is Madame Monnier, the head librarian of the Calliopean Courtesan's Guild. Madame Monnier, this is Lady Swann, retired courtesan second rank and paramour of Princess Roseli."

Mistress Monnier nodded curtly. "I have little information to offer you on Princess Lucia, but I can say with certainty that she has no marks against her."

Beatrice let out a breath of relief. "That is good news."

"She does, however, appear in our records."

"As a client?"

"No. I only found several passing mentions. She paid a girl's apprenticeship fees about a decade and a half ago."

"She would have still been a girl herself."

"Rumor is they were childhood friends. The girl was the daughter of palace servants."

"The princess's generosity is to her credit." Beatrice had spent enough of her life among nobles to know how rare it was for most to even notice servants, much less care about their lives.

The librarian tapped at a tablet just out of view. "That was not the end of the matter. She fought a duel for the honor of that same courtesan several years later."

"A duel?" She did not know what duels were like on Calliope, but they were common on Delphi. While it was not unheard of to duel with pistols, traditionally, they were fought with swords to first blood, and the goal was not to kill one's opponent. In her opinion, most duels were more a way for young nobles to show off than genuine matters of honor.

"Yes. Early in her career, a young noble client assaulted and scarred the courtesan. The guild blacklisted him but could take no other action, and the authorities would not pursue a case. When Princess Lucia learned of the matter after returning on leave from the navy, she challenged the nobleman to a sword duel. She scarred him the same as he did the courtesan. This caused something of a scandal."

As far as Beatrice was concerned, this also spoke well of the princess. "Is that all?"

"Yes. If she has any deep dark secrets, the guild does not know of them."

"Thank you for your time."

Beatrice signed off the call and headed back to the palace. Her mood had improved considerably. Princess Lucia sounded like someone she could get along with.

CHAPTER FIVE

In all the chaos, Roseli would have completely forgotten about the Spring Ball if Beatrice had not reminded her a few hours before. She normally attended balls and parties with Beatrice, as she had the greatest talent for it. Roseli would never cease to be in awe of Beatrice's ability to almost painlessly maneuver her through what had once been miserable and overwhelming social obligations.

She went to anything involving the Senate with Julia and all military-related events with Alexis, although Julia could step up and escort her to other events when Beatrice couldn't go. While Alexis was unfailingly polite, she had no skill for social interactions outside of the military. She would loyally remain on Roseli's arm at events, but she could offer little help in remembering names and knew little about the complex court intrigues, petty jealousies, and feuds that Beatrice would normally warn Roseli of. Even worse, she had never mastered the art of small talk. Roseli loved her for trying but knew when she was out of her element.

Once, when asked by a society matron what she thought of a somewhat abstract metal sculpture of a naked woman's torso at an art gallery opening, Alexis had said that it looked like the charred remains of a body after a mortar explosion. Roseli had never taken her to another one.

While it was rare for Roseli to attend any event with all her lovers, the Spring Ball was the second most important social event of the year, and she needed as much support as she could get. Julia and Alexis arrived at Roseli's quarters while she was still getting ready in her dressing room. She sat in a white slip amidst a swarm of women. One was styling her hair with some manner of hot curler, one was doing her makeup, and another was painting her nails.

She had always disliked the impersonal touch of attendants. Being painted and brushed made her feel like a doll. However, as she had no talent for hair and makeup, she had accepted the necessity of stylists long ago.

She never minded when Beatrice did her hair or makeup for her, but at the moment, she was busy directing the entire endeavor. Beatrice was dressed for the ball in a blue taffeta gown that flowed down her body like water. Her golden hair was piled on her head, and sapphires shone on her throat.

Julia entered the room and blew Roseli a kiss before pushing aside a pile of makeup to take a seat on one counter. She wore impeccably tailored black slacks and a beautifully embroidered green silk shirt. She had her hair caught back in a ribbon rather than the neat braid she wore most of the time. Her lips were painted an appealing red, and her long eyelashes had been darkened. Roseli felt a familiar flicker of lust and wondered if they might have time to slip off for a few moments before the ball.

Alexis came in and leaned against the wall. She was wearing her formal dress uniform and had brushed her light brown hair to a shine. Her face was unpainted, as it was not normally the practice of women in the military to wear makeup.

Neither escaped Beatrice's scrutiny. "Alexis, your nose is shiny."

Alexis arched an eyebrow. She was the only one of them who could successfully raise a single eyebrow and use it to full effect. When Julia tried, she always raised both. "My nose is not shiny."

"It is," said Beatrice in a tone that brooked no argument.

Alexis grudgingly allowed Beatrice to pat at her face with a powder puff. Julia observed the whole interaction with amusement until Beatrice turned her attention to her, considering her with slightly narrowed blue eyes. "That bra won't do."

"How can you even see my bra?"

"I can see the outline against your shirt. You are wearing an underwire bra, but you can't do that with a silk top."

"Too late now."

"Hardly, you've got other bras here, off with it."

Julia suffered the indignity of unbuttoning her shirt and shedding her bra after Beatrice returned with several more from the wardrobe in the next room. The servants fussing over Roseli took no note. They were used to seeing nobles in a state of undress, but Roseli couldn't help casting a few appreciative glances.

Julia was just tugging her shirt back down when Roseli's little sister, Roxane, burst into the dressing room in a flurry of taffeta. "Roseli, aren't you ready yet?" She had been born after the Massacre of the Inner Chambers and was nearly eight years Roseli's junior. Aside from possessing Prince Leon's aquiline nose, she had little in common with her father. She had her mother's dark brown hair and short stature but none of her grimness. Where she got her friendly and rambunctious personality was anyone's guess, but it was one of Roseli's favorite things about her.

Her ballgown reflected a deep fondness for pink things and ruffles. Her skirt had as many layers as the current fashion would permit, and she had so many seed pearls sown onto the dress that it rattled. Roseli loved her more than she had words for, but she would be the first to admit that they were highly different people. Roxane was taking to her first season in society like a duck to water. Roseli, at the same age, had responded to her first season like a cat to the same substance. She tolerated balls but only as an official duty. One of Rosalie's sincerest and deepest held hopes was that someday, Roxane could take over attending most of her social engagements for her.

"She's almost ready, dear," said Beatrice.

"She's not even dressed," said Roxane.

"Because her makeup isn't done. When I let her put on the dress before her makeup, she always manages to get it on the dress."

"Save me, please, save me, little sister," said Roseli. "Let's run away and go eat sweets in the garden in our shifts." She was only half joking.

"No way," said Roxane. "Mother would be so mad."

"You're the one who keeps saying you're not scared of her," Roseli teased.

"I'm not. I'm more afraid of Beatrice. She's scary when she's angry."

"You've never seen me angry, child," said Beatrice with half a smile. "Sit down in that chair, your eyeshadow is already smeared."

Roxane sat on the proffered stool carefully, as if trying not to wrinkle her dress. Beatrice set about wiping away and redrawing the ornate eyeshadow, complete with pink swirling spirals, at the edges of her eyes.

"What do you think of Lord John Harper?" asked Roxane.

"The youngest son of the house of Harper?" Beatrice said. "I don't know him personally, but from what I've heard, he's scandalized everyone by playing in a rock group made up of other young nobles from the university."

"I think he's dreamy."

Roseli choked on the water she'd just sipped; through a straw so as not to smear her lipstick. "Him? He looks like a skinny ferret." Then again, in her opinion, that was what most of the boys looked like in the band posters Roxane loved to collect.

"What would you know?" Roxane said with a huff. "You have no interest in men at all."

"Fair enough," admitted Roseli. "But I do know that I'm no fan of his older brother, Jacob. He once tried to chase me with a garter snake when we were children."

"You like snakes," said Alexis from against the wall.

"I didn't say it worked. I ended up running after him and yelling at him to let the poor snake go."

Roxane giggled. "John's nothing like that. He's nice to animals and a total rebel."

"Is that so?" asked Roseli carefully. She still didn't like the idea of her little sister mooning after some teenage musician.

"Yes, he thinks that our entire class system is stupid and needs to change."

"He's not advocating any sort of actual rebellion, is he?" asked Julia.

Roseli felt uneasy. There had been a recent student uprising on the planet Thalia that hadn't ended well for the students. She'd met one of the survivors who had escaped by being smuggled on a cargo vessel and claiming political refugee status on Delphi. She'd never seen a young woman with more haunted eyes.

She didn't think anything like that could ever happen on Delphi; at least, she hoped not. Delphi's universities had always been a hotbed of thought and change but not violent rebellion. Students, like all Delphians, had a constitutional right to protest. Roseli's mother's usual response to any student manifestos sent to the palace was to put the most pedantic staff member she could find in charge of replying with an even more boring rebuttal.

Roxane shook her head. "No, he just thinks that everyone should have equal opportunities and that admission to the universities should be based on merit, not social standing. He says the same about government jobs."

"Sounds like he's got a lot of ideas," said Roseli.

"He does. I really like him." Then, in a rush, she added, "And now that you're finally getting married, that means I'll be allowed to as well."

"You want to marry Lord John Harper?" she asked in disbelief.

Roxane made a face. "No, I don't know. I just want to court publicly. I may have had my debutante ball, but I'm still not allowed to have a formal escort to one."

This had long been the tradition. Until the heir apparent married, all younger siblings could not marry, become engaged, or take part in anything that might be considered a serious courtship. Roxane could attend balls, but she couldn't arrive with anyone or dance too many times with the same person. Roseli hadn't thought about how her upcoming marriage would change things for Roxane. She'd not realized Roxane wanted to take anyone to a ball.

"You do realize you still may not be permitted to choose your first husband," Julia reminded her.

Roseli felt a wave of sadness. While Roxane might be allowed some freedom in choosing her later husbands, she would need to use her first few marriages to form alliances with the major noble houses that Roseli did not end up taking wives from. She wished she could give her more choices and control of her life.

"That's hardly fair."

"Life seldom is, dear," said Beatrice, finishing the final swirl of the makeup. "You can still take this young lord as a lover if you wish."

"I already have. I just want to take him to a ball, too."

"What?" Roseli turned so quickly that she jostled the hairdresser behind her.

Roxane rolled her eyes dramatically. "I am of age."

She hadn't realized her little sister was dating, much less sexually active. Was there some kind of talk she should have had with her? She was sure their mother hadn't. What should she even say?

"You had a lover even before your first ball," Roxane pointed out.

"Don't remind me." She'd have rubbed at her eyes if a warning sound from Beatrice hadn't stopped her from smearing her makeup. Despite all the time that had passed, she still couldn't think of Lady Heather without a deep sense of embarrassment. "I was young and stupid, and I'm still living it down."

"At least you never fought a duel over a woman," offered Alexis.

Beatrice frowned at her watch. "As fascinating as this discussion is, we had all best be going." She nudged Roseli. "On your feet, my darling, we need to get you into your dress."

Even as Roseli finished dressing, she kept worrying. When had she gotten so out of touch with what was going on in Roxane's life? She felt like a terrible sister. She needed to make more time for her.

❖

The ball began as it did every year. Roseli opened the floor, dancing a waltz with Alexis. She danced the second song with Julia and the third with Beatrice. She was careful to lock arms with Beatrice and move from the dance floor quickly at the end of the third song before anyone else could ask her to dance.

She and Beatrice began the slow process of greeting guests. With Beatrice on her arm, she had someone to whisper in her ear and remind her of names and what she should know about each noble. Sometimes, Roseli felt guilty for how much Beatrice did for her. There was no way to repay her for all the countless hours she spent memorizing names and studying court politics, much less return the level of care and attention Beatrice gave her.

She had years of experience with the guilt that came with having lovers who prioritized her more than she could prioritize them. They would drop whatever they were doing when she needed them, but as a princess, she couldn't do the same. None of them had ever complained. They knew what they were getting into when they became involved with her.

She pushed aside her thoughts as she and Beatrice worked their way through the crowd. Little caught her attention until she met the new Thalian embassy director and her wife. She was struck by how attractive the small brunette woman and her willowy blond wife were. Like most Thalian couples, the two were impressively in sync. The blond whispered in the brunette's ear before they came to introduce themselves.

She also noticed how the embassy director looked at her. Her eyes didn't exactly hold an invitation, but there was interest there. Roseli wondered about that. As far as she knew, Thalians were monogamous and had no tradition of taking lovers outside of marriage. Infidelity was a serious enough offense to cause divorce on Thalia.

Roseli was flattered, although she had never had any interest in casual affairs. Her existing relationships were complicated enough. They spoke briefly about a trade agreement, and then the couple went on their way. Once they were out of earshot, Beatrice told her. "Rumor has it that they both had an affair with a Calliopean general at their last post."

"Really?"

"Maybe it didn't count as cheating if they did it together."

That caused them both to giggle. She was glad to have Beatrice with her.

As the night wore on, Beatrice tired. She handed Roseli off to Alexis, who guided her through greeting several high-ranking military members. At least none attempted to tell any long-winded war stories. After that, she did the same with Julia, who handled most members of the Senate.

When Roseli flagged, Julia led her to an out-of-the-way table while Beatrice retrieved food. She ate while Beatrice played buffer. After the brief respite, the thought of standing and returning to her duties was almost unbearable.

Julia got a mischievous look in her eyes. "Look at that. Your makeup is smeared. We should go fix it."

She knew exactly what she was offering. This wouldn't be the first time they had snuck away from a ball; the memory of the last time made her face heat and her body ache with desire.

"Yes, we should," she managed to say.

Beatrice coughed pointedly and said quietly to Julia, "I'll cover for you, but don't you dare actually mess up her makeup. You know how long that takes to fix."

"You're no fun," replied Julia.

"Oh, you know that's not true."

They slipped from the ballroom and down the hall to the bathroom. As was traditional on Delphi, the first room of most formal public bathrooms consisted of a large lounge, complete with couches and an entire wall of mirrors with seats. Two halls branched off; one led to a room that contained the more essential sorts of amenities, such as toilet stalls and sinks. The other led to a series of small rooms, all with mirrors and chairs meant to be a place for women who needed a break to brush their hair in peace.

It would never do for a princess to wait in line, so Roseli had a chip on her wrist device that opened a small, locked bathroom on the first hall and a dressing room on the other. She went ahead of Julia, slipping into the small dressing room. Soon, there was a tap on the door, and she ushered Julia in.

She had always loved this kind of clandestine meeting. She had to be so careful and dignified most of the time, and it was a wonderful thrill to steal a few moments back merely for the sake of impulse and passion.

She reached for Julia, who shook her head and tapped at her wrist strap, quickly scanning the room. Roseli felt her ardor briefly cool at the reminder of how little freedom and privacy she truly had. Palace security had been vastly improved since the "video incident" she and Alexis had suffered several years before, but it didn't pay to be careless.

Julia drew Roseli into her arms, kissing her lightly to save both of their lipstick. With surprising ease, she lifted her onto the makeup counter that ran across one side of the small room.

"I want to touch you first," Roseli told her. Julia was so irresistible with her slightly freckled cheeks flushed and eyes bright.

"But I can't wait to have you. Oblige me, won't you, beautiful?" She grinned impishly, no doubt already knowing she would get what she wanted.

"Impatient woman," said Roseli. "I ought to leave you wanting for your impertinence."

Julia knelt on the carpeted floor, tugging up Roseli's skirts. They both knew better than to try to get her dress off. There were too many internal zippers, buttons, and layers. At least tights had gone out of fashion, one fewer garment in the way.

"You keep threatening that, but you never carry through. We both know you want me far too much." Julia tugged off Roseli's underwear, and Roseli gasped when Julia parted her labia and brought her tongue to her center.

Roseli clutched the counter so she wouldn't mess up Julia's hair. "Fingers, please, fingers."

Julia obeyed, pressing two fingers into her, curling them as she sucked on her clit. Roseli bit the inside of her lip to stay silent as she came. The room was not soundproof.

When Julia slowed her movements, Roseli pleaded, "No, don't stop, harder, please."

Julia shifted, standing to brace a hand on the counter and deepen the thrusts of her fingers.

Roseli was so close again.

"Look at me, beautiful," Julia murmured.

Roseli forced her eyes open as waves of pleasure washed over her. She was met by the intense heat of Julia's gaze.

"You're so beautiful like this, lost to pleasure and yet still so desperate."

Roseli clenched against Julia's fingers as she orgasmed. She was just reaching to unbutton Julia's pants when there was a sudden knock on the door. They both froze.

Roseli was caught between embarrassment, guilt, and anger. Before she could yell at whoever was on the other side of the door to go away, Beatrice's voice called, "Roseli?"

"Let her in," said Roseli, pushing down her skirts. Julia opened the door just enough for Beatrice to dart into the small room. "What's happened?"

"It's Princess Lucia. We just received news that her ship has entered orbit."

"What? She's not due until the end of the week."

"I don't know, but her shuttle is on the way down. We have to leave now to meet her at the spaceport."

CHAPTER SIX

R oseli's assistant, Meredith Cooper, led them to a waiting car. Her current choice of ballgown appeared to have cartoon cats on the bodice, which was restrained for her. Roseli had never understood her taste in clothes but had always been amused by it. As odd as she could be sometimes, Meredith was the only person who genuinely didn't care what anyone else thought.

As soon as the car was in motion, Meredith removed a tablet from her clutch purse, unrolled it like a scroll, shook it out to make it a solid surface, and set to work. Roseli made a mental note to ask Meredith to get one for her. She'd never seen one that small or flexible before.

Beatrice set about adjusting Roseli's hair and makeup while Roseli watched the city flash past her window until they had just passed the city's central square. She had never been carsick in her life, but she was so nervous, she thought she might be now. "Wait, we've missed the turn for the spaceport."

"We are heading for the oversized industrial port outside of the city limits," said Meredith. "Calliopean naval shuttles are too big to land in either the city's regular commercial or the naval spaceport. I don't know why she's coming down in the middle of the night, but you know how dramatic Calliopeans can be."

Alexis's phone tablet rang, and she answered. "What do you mean they were attacked...Wait, they were hit...How many casualties... Well, don't just talk about it, I want emergency teams standing by."

"What's happened?" Roseli knew it wasn't anything good.

Alexis lowered the phone. "Several Terra Nuevan warships attacked Princess Lucia's ship five days ago. Her two escort ships were destroyed, and her ship took damage. Half the crew was killed.

They escaped and went radio silent until they reached Delphi. The ship lost life support just as they reached orbit, and they evacuated in the shuttles."

"Is Princess Lucia all right?" She'd been ambivalent about the engagement, but the last thing she'd wanted was for Princess Lucia to be attacked on the way to her.

"She sent the last message we received, so she's alive, at least," said Alexis.

Meredith started talking into a smaller tablet as she kept typing on the one in her hand. "Block the media. I'm serious. Block all of them, now. We don't know what we're heading into...No, are you even listening? I don't want anything broadcast live."

Julia's tablet rang, and she answered, her tone short and clipped, "No, I don't know what's going on...You can tell the Speaker of the Senate to shove it. I don't work for her. I'm not even in her party... No, don't actually tell her to shove it...Tell her the palace will release an official statement shortly...Yes, moving up the official motion to welcome Princess Lucia would be a good idea...How soon? I don't know, like, right this damn minute."

Beatrice finished fussing over Roseli and took her hands, pulling her back out of the overwhelmed daze she had begun to sink into. "Are you ready for this, darling?"

"Is anyone ever ready to meet a fiancée for the first time?" She wasn't.

"Probably not, but you're going to do wonderfully."

"Do you think she'll like me?" she asked, mostly joking. She was sure she would be pretty low on Princess Lucia's list of concerns at the moment.

"She'd be a fool not to. You're beautiful and smart and even dressed impeccably."

"In a ballgown at a spaceport?"

"At least you won't be underdressed."

Their car and the vehicles escorting it came to a stop and pulled off the road when the lights of the spaceport were just a glimmer in the distance. Roseli hit the intercom beside her and spoke to her head of security, who sat in the passenger seat on the other side of the vehicle's divider. "Why did we stop?"

The driver's voice crackled back over the intercom. "I'm sorry, Your Highness, but we must follow security protocols. Please remain inside."

Beatrice gave a cry of surprise. "Look!"

The sky filled with the lights of descending shuttles. Roseli pushed open the door and stood in the warm spring air despite Alexis's protests that the car was safer. The others followed her out. Beatrice took her hand and Julia her arm. She was glad of the support; her legs felt weak.

As she watched, the lights descended and took form. They looked like silver birds with wings of flashing blue and red, slowly circling downward to the spaceport. One ship broke away from the others, moving in a straight line. Why was it orange? With a growing sense of horror, she realized she wasn't seeing landing lights but flames, and the ship was hurtling toward them.

"Roseli, get down!" Alexis grabbed her and shoved her to the ground, covering her. Beatrice and Julia took cover, too. A second later, the earth shook as the fireball slammed into a nearby field. Dirt rained down on them, as fine as dust. The wind smelled of smoke.

Alexis rolled off and helped her up as the others shakily stood.

"May the gods help them," murmured Beatrice.

"Too late for that," said Julia.

"I hope Princess Lucia wasn't on that one," said Meredith, dusting herself off. "I just ordered the cake."

Roseli made a choking sound and covered her mouth. She wished for once that Meredith had kept her thoughts to herself. To her relief, she neither cried nor threw up. She had just witnessed an unknown number of deaths. With the flames reaching against the dark sky, there was no chance of survivors.

"Never change, Ms. Cooper," Julia said dryly, glancing at Meredith.

"We should turn back," said Alexis. "We don't know what state the other shuttles are in. I won't endanger you, Your Highness."

Roseli brushed the dirt from her dress. "No, my fiancée may be injured. I must see her and her people safely to the palace." Princess Lucia might also be dead, but Roseli felt no need to give that possibility a voice as Meredith had.

"I'll go in your place," said Alexis. "I'll have one of our escort vehicles take me the rest of the way."

"No. I am going."

"Your Highness—"

Roseli cut her off. "Don't you dare try to 'Your Highness' me and then tell me what to do in the same breath."

Alexis flinched. "As you will."

Roseli climbed back into the car. "Whoever is coming, get in now." It wasn't until she sat down that she realized just how badly she was trembling.

❖

It was a brief ride. When they reached the spaceport, which wasn't much more than a paved field with a radio tower, everything appeared to be in a state of controlled chaos. Their car and escorts parked at the edge of the facility, out of the way.

Alexis stepped from the car and surveyed the scene. Roseli and the others followed, ignoring her protests. The smell of burning plastic and metal threw her back to another time in her life when listening for the hissing whistle of falling mortars meant the difference between life and death.

Her chest felt tight, and she couldn't breathe. Every instinct she had told her to grab Roseli and run.

"Alexis?" Roseli's voice grounded her.

"Stay close."

Ten large silver Calliopean shuttles sat upon the concrete landing strip. All but one had flipped its small silver wings back into a vertical position. The tenth ship had one wing out to the side, and the other had broken clean off. It was smoldering, and its emergency hatch was thrown open. If nothing else, someone had lived to trigger the door's release.

A ground crew in a red truck was spraying white foam at the burning wing as others helped people from the ship. A woman in a white Calliopean naval uniform emerged, dragging a smaller figure.

"That's Princess Lucia, unless someone else is wearing an admiral's stripes," said Meredith. "I guess we do still need the cake."

Alexis was surprised the secretary knew anything about Calliopean naval insignia, much less had eyes sharp enough to make out such a thing in all the chaos and smoke. Ms. Cooper was holding up her tablet and using one hand to zoom in on the scene. That was military tech. How did a civilian have it?

She shook away the thought when Princess Roseli tried to start walking across the tarmac. "Please, my love, it's not safe. I will tell her to come to you." Alexis was more than prepared to forcibly restrain

Roseli if she had to. She wasn't letting her anywhere near the smoking ship.

"Do so," Roseli said sharply.

Alexis hurried across the landing pad. She quickly reached the admiral, who was now kneeling beside a limp body, and recognized Lucia Caron from the few times she'd seen her on a video screen. Her face was smeared with ash, and her uniform was stained with blood.

Alexis hadn't been shocked by the sight of blood since she was a young soldier, but she had known five years of peace. How could violence and danger have come back into her life so quickly?

She bowed. "Admiral Lucia Caron, I offer you formal greetings from Princess Roseli Almeda of Delphi."

Admiral Caron looked at her like she was insane. "All that can wait. Help my cousin." She spoke a Calliopean dialect of Moûsaian but was still understandable. Before Alexis could reply, Admiral Caron shoved the limp woman at her and ran back into the smoking ship. Alexis looked at the small woman in her arms and realized she was a girl in her late teens. Alexis had forgotten just how early Calliopean officers entered their armed forces.

The girl's face was deathly pale beneath a layer of grime. She coughed violently, her skinny body shaking, but never opened her eyes. Her hands were tightly bandaged, the white cloth darkly stained. Alexis caught the familiar smell of infection she'd come to know so well in the trenches. Some of the girl's injuries had had time to fester. Her stomach turned with the memory of horror and death. "Medic! Get me a medic." Soon enough, someone was taking the girl from her. She returned her attention to the shuttle in time to see Admiral Caron struggling to drag someone much heavier from the ship.

Alexis ran to help, pushing into the smoke. Admiral Caron had one arm of an unconscious man draped over her shoulder. Alexis grabbed the limp other, and they carried him to safety. As they eased their burden to the ground, Admiral Caron called to one of her crew who'd been right behind her leading a stumbling man. "Was he the last?"

"Yes, Admiral."

She coughed, doubling over with the force of it. Alexis moved to support her, but she pushed her away even as she kept coughing. "I'm fine, help him."

There was no need. Two more medics had reached them. One

checked the prone man and signaled for a stretcher. Admiral Caron knelt beside him as one medic hustled away. "Jonas, don't you dare die. I'm not training another first mate, it's too much damn work."

The man tried to say something but was coughing too hard. The medics got him onto the stretcher and carried him away.

Admiral Caron took a breath that only caused her to cough again. When she could take a full breath, she looked around. "Where's the eleventh ship?"

"It crashed in a field," said Alexis.

"Survivors?"

"I'm sorry."

Admiral Caron slumped as if her injuries had finally caught up with her. Then she caught sight of something that made her shake her head slightly, as if trying to clear a hallucination.

Alexis turned to see Roseli crossing the tarmac. Walking through the smoke in a full ballgown with, Julia, Beatrice, and several guards in tow, Roseli looked like some kind of fairy queen out of legend. Quickly, Alexis said, "As I was saying, Princess Roseli has come to welcome you."

"She what?" Admiral Caron squinted as if doubting what she was seeing.

Roseli reached them. She bowed formally. "I, Princess Roseli Abram Almeda of Delphi, welcome you, Princess Lucia Valdez Caron of Calliope, to Delphi. I have come to offer any assistance you and your crew may require."

Despite the absurdity of the situation, Alexis felt intensely proud. There was nothing that Roseli could not meet with the dignity and compassion of a Delphian Princess.

Admiral Caron bowed in return. "As a princess and admiral of Calliope, I gladly accept. The injured need to be taken to a medical facility. The rest of my crew needs food and beds. I also require a way to send secure communications to the Calliopean naval command."

"We are transporting your injured people to a military hospital as we speak. The others will be housed in the palace barracks. If you come with me, I will take you to a secure line in the military offices on the palace grounds."

Something approaching respect entered Admiral Caron's eyes. "Thank you, Your Highness."

"I have a car waiting."

"I need to see to the safety of all of my people first."

"Please, take all the time you need."

It didn't take long. Admiral Caron called over the officer who had helped the last injured person from the smoking shuttle. "Lieutenant Laurent, status report."

The lieutenant was a slender woman in her early thirties. She had unusually dark skin for a Calliopean and a braid of sleek black hair, now half-loose from her efforts during the rescue. If the sharpness of her nose was any sign, she was likely of Septian heritage, possibly a descendant of a Septian colony Calliope had absorbed a few generations past. Alexis had fought side by side with several Septian Calliopeans in the trenches of Tyco. She still remembered some of the more creative Septian curse words. She saluted. "I have no status on shuttle Lambda." She took a shaky breath. "But the Delphians say they saw it go down and are checking for survivors." She sounded like she doubted there would be any.

Alexis was sure of it. No one could survive the tower of flames she had seen leaping up into the sky.

Lieutenant Laurent fell briefly into a coughing fit before continuing. "All other shuttle leaders report all personnel present and accounted for. The five injured from our shuttle have received medical transport. The twenty previously injured members of the crew are being loaded onto a medical vehicle. The uninjured are awaiting several transport vehicles that should arrive shortly."

"Very good, Lieutenant. Remain until all crew are transported and then go in the last vehicle. Report to me as soon as the crew is settled in the palace barracks."

"Yes, Admiral."

Admiral Caron turned back to Roseli, who had observed the interaction patiently. "We can depart now."

Julia gasped and pointed upward. The sky was alight with thousands of falling stars, brilliant dots of light tumbling across the planet's atmosphere. Admiral Caron looked up, too. She froze, then she raised her arm in a salute.

Lieutenant Laurent called, "All stand and observe." The Calliopeans saluted and stood at attention.

Out of respect, Alexis did the same. How many times had she stood exactly like this before bidding farewell to lost comrades, men and women who would never grow old?

Admiral Caron spoke slowly, her voice ragged from smoke but still commanding. "From the dust, we are born, and to the dust, we return. May the goddess of travelers see our comrades' souls safely home. As it was, as it is, as it will be."

Her crew echoed her last line and dropped their salutes before returning to helping their injured comrades.

"That was my flagship, the good ship *Intrepid*. We scuttled her before we abandoned ship. She couldn't be salvaged, and her orbit would have gradually decayed, so we made sure that happened safely. We're seeing the fragments breaking apart in the upper atmosphere."

What she didn't need to say, but Alexis could guess, was that the remains of the dead were among the debris. She had seen no bodies removed from the shuttles.

They all watched for a minute longer in stunned silence and then made their way to the waiting car. Alexis had not wanted to like Admiral Caron, but after seeing how she cared for her crew, Alexis couldn't help but respect her.

❖

They piled into the back of the car, settling into two rows of facing seats. Roseli found herself between Alexis and Julia and across from Princess Lucia, Beatrice, and Meredith. The entire situation felt unreal to her.

Alexis was silent, her shoulders tense, looking forward at nothing, and Julia had her arms drawn around herself. Beatrice sat still and poised, the way she always did in a crisis. Meredith, being Meredith, was already tapping at her tablet. Princess Lucia's attention was entirely focused on the window and the still-smoldering shuttle, her expression grave.

Now that she had a proper chance to look, Roseli saw that, despite the blood, Lucia was as attractive as her picture. She had a face made of strong lines but softened by large hazel eyes. The ash had made her dark brown hair nearly gray.

They had just left the spaceport when Beatrice gasped. "You're bleeding."

"It's mostly not my blood," said Princess Lucia in a matter-of-fact tone.

Roseli couldn't tell if she was dazed from what had just happened or was normally that calm.

Beatrice was still staring. "Your neck, that red ribbon you've got around it, it's not supposed to be red, is it?"

Lucia reached to touch her neck, drawing the white glove back with a new red blossom across it. "I must have cut it during the crash."

"Let me have a look. I have basic emergency training." As a courtesan, Beatrice had been required to renew her first-aid and CPR certification each year, and she had kept it up after retiring, something for which Roseli was currently glad. "Meredith, get me the first-aid kit."

"I'm fine," insisted Lucia, but Beatrice was already opening the kit that Meredith had handed her. She quickly fished out a pair of medical gloves, tugged them on, and then turned back to Lucia, reaching to untie the carefully knotted ribbon.

Lucia jerked back. "What are you doing?"

"Trying to see where you're hurt."

She covered her neck with a hand, expression deeply scandalized. "You can't."

Beatrice looked at her blankly.

"You can't just expose my neck in public."

Beatrice pursed her lips. "Your Highness, we're in a car with tinted windows. You are bleeding, please let me help you."

Despite her injury and obvious state of exhaustion, Lucia proved stubborn. "It would not be proper, not in front of my fiancée."

"She'll see more than that soon enough," said Meredith, with her usual lack of tact.

"I'll look away. We all will," said Roseli quickly, giving Meredith a warning glare.

"Fine," said Lucia, looking down. Her face reddened beneath the smudges of ash.

It seemed incongruous for a career sailor with a reputation for philandering to be modest about her neck, but she was Calliopean, and women there kept their hands and necks covered. It occurred to Roseli how vulnerable Lucia must be feeling, injured, far from home, and now dependent on strangers who did not share her customs.

"I think you need stitches, but I'm not qualified to do that. I'll bandage you, and a doctor can see to you properly at the palace," said Beatrice. After a few minutes, she added, "All done."

When Roseli looked back, Lucia's neck was wrapped in a clean white bandage. "Thank you..." Lucia hesitated, seemingly unsure how to address Beatrice.

"Lady Beatrice Swann," she said as she stripped the gloves from her hands.

Roseli added, "Forgive me. I failed to introduce the members of my escort. As well as Lady Swann, this is General Alexis Tate, Senator Julia Veritas, and my personal secretary, Meredith Cooper." It did not seem to be the time to explain that three of them were her lovers. Roseli did not know if Lucia had been briefed or what she would think. It was unclear if she had received the marriage contract in full, much less if she had read it.

Soon enough, they were pulling into the palace grounds. Alexis took Lucia directly to the military offices to ensure that she could contact her forces and inform them of what had transpired.

Roseli wanted to help with the arrangements for Lucia's crew, but Julia and Meredith assured her it had already been seen to. Beatrice led Roseli back to her quarters. She didn't realize how exhausted she was until Beatrice helped her from her stained ballgown and urged her toward the bed. Beatrice kissed her once on the cheek before going to shower in the next room.

Roseli lay down but she could not sleep. When she closed her eyes, she could still see the burning shuttle falling from the sky. How many had died on it? How many on the *Intrepid*? How many more would die? She'd been a fool to ever dream that the peace would last.

Of all the ways she had imagined first meeting her fiancée, this was not one of them. She'd expected some arrogant foreign princess, not this competent and somber admiral. She could not deny she was drawn to Lucia. Beyond just her looks, there was something about her calm courage that was captivating. She'd seen Lucia in what had to be one of the hardest moments of her life, and she'd handled it bravely and with compassion for the sailors under her command.

She did not know what Lucia had made of her, if she had formed any opinion at all. Lucia had still managed to be formally polite amid all the chaos, which was rather impressive. Regardless of either of their personal feelings, if a war was coming, they were going to need to learn to work together and support each other quickly.

CHAPTER SEVEN

R oseli woke to someone nudging her. "Lemme sleep, Beatrice, you meanie," she mumbled.

"I'm not Beatrice, but she told me to get you up," said Meredith.

Roseli sat up groggily, noticing only belatedly that she'd kicked off the covers in her sleep, and she was naked.

Meredith was untroubled, as usual. She'd once accidentally walked in on Roseli and all of her lovers in the midst of an ill-timed midmorning tryst in the sitting room and not even blinked. The weird bit was how, instead of apologizing and retreating, she had thought it entirely reasonable to stand there and read Roseli her list of appointments for the afternoon before leaving the room.

Meredith had seemed more annoyed than embarrassed when Roseli had taken her aside later and emphasized the importance of knocking before entering rooms in her quarters, even rooms that weren't the bedroom. Meredith had agreed but still made it sound like Roseli was the unreasonable one.

"Five more minutes," grumbled Roseli, thumping back down onto her pillow.

"Lady Swann said to keep poking you until you got up."

"Who's the princess here, exactly?"

"You, but I'd rather deal with you being cranky than her wrath."

Roseli grumpily sat up again. "Beatrice doesn't have wrath."

"You didn't see her last month when I forgot to pick up a dress order. Her lips got so thin, they lost their color, and her eyes were like narrow blue daggers. She used that scary tone where she speaks so softly, you can barely hear her, but it still feels like she's yelling. She reminds me of my mother when she does that, and it's scary." Meredith shivered.

Roseli had once made the mistake of asking Meredith about her family. She had never made that mistake again. She got up, tugging a blanket about herself, and headed for the bathroom.

"Beatrice said you should shower and then dress appropriately for a royal audience. She laid out the clothes."

"Thank you, Meredith," called Roseli, hoping she took it as a dismissal from the bedroom.

"By the way, Beatrice said your mother called and said the wedding has been moved up to the end of the week, something about military hostilities. I had to expedite the cake. The baker is pissed and charging three times as much."

"What?" She thought she'd have at least a month to get know Lucia.

"I'm just the messenger."

One shower, hasty breakfast, and briefing later, she was on her way across the palace grounds with Meredith and two ever-present bodyguards in tow. Lucia was to be formally introduced to her mother in court that afternoon, and Roseli was sure as hell not going to let her face that unprepared.

When she turned down the hall that led toward the guest quarters, Meredith called after her, "She's not there."

"Where is she, then?" It was still early, but the entire palace was already up.

"She stayed the night in the barracks with her crew," said Meredith. From everything Roseli had seen of her so far, that made sense.

They adjusted their course and soon reached their destination. The palace barracks were not anyone's definition of luxurious. The palace steward had placed the large number of guests in an older barracks building that was normally used for overflow when there were more soldiers garrisoned in the palace than usual. It was behind the recently renovated main barracks, and Roseli couldn't help but notice how badly the paint was peeling when she entered the building.

No one greeted her at the door when she knocked, so she opened it. The cavernous room was mostly deserted, although the bunks looked as if they had been slept in. Likely, they were all in the mess hall used by the castle garrison.

She caught sight of Lucia with Lieutenant Laurent at her side, talking with an imperial guard. Neither was wearing the ruined clothes from the day before. As replacement Calliopean naval uniforms would have been impossible to find on Delphi, so they were wearing blue pants and white shirts that had clearly come from Delphian military uniforms. Lieutenant Laurent still had on her original, if smudged, gloves and ribbon.

No one seemed to have been able to find Lucia a replacement for her bloodstained ribbon and gloves. She was wearing a white bandanna around her bandaged neck. She'd fared little better with the gloves. Instead of the thin white ones that allowed Calliopean women full dexterity, she had a pair of white leather winter gloves. Roseli supposed the palace quartermaster had done the best he could.

Roseli felt shy to approach her. None of her childhood etiquette lessons covered how to greet a crash-landed fiancée in a barracks.

When the imperial guard saw her, he bowed deeply. "Your Highness."

Lucia turned and offered a shallow bow in greeting.

Roseli returned a half bow, as was appropriate for greeting an equal. "Good morning, Princess Lucia. I trust you slept well?"

"Yes," she said. "However, I am having difficulty acquiring transport to the hospital where my injured crew are being treated. It seems that I am not allowed to leave the palace grounds." Her polite words only emphasized her anger.

Roseli looked at the imperial guard. "Did my mother order this?"

The man bowed again. "No, but as I have been attempting to explain, it would be inadvisable to leave the grounds at this time, as she has an audience with the empress at noon."

"I don't care if I have an audience with an entire pantheon of gods. I will see my injured crew."

Lucia did not sound like a woman who was accustomed to being told no. Roseli was again impressed by her dedication to her crew. She glanced at her watch. Wristwatches had fallen out of fashion, but she'd worn one since she was a child and had never broken the habit. Prince Ambrose had given her one for her sixth birthday and taught her how to read the little arrows within the circle.

"We have three hours. I will take you," she promised.

Lucia visibly relaxed. "Thank you."

As they walked to a courtyard where a car had been summoned, Roseli held back a few steps to quietly speak with Meredith. "Go find her some better clothes. Consult my wardrobe mistress if you don't know what that means. I won't have her go before my mother wearing garrison castoffs. Also, get her a Calliopean style ribbon and gloves if you can." She didn't understand the custom, but she would respect it.

"I'll see it done," promised Meredith. She had the fashion sense of a toddler playing dress-up, but she had a talent for finding things if she knew what she was looking for.

The car arrived, and they climbed in. Once they were under way, Roseli felt the awkwardness of being alone with her fiancée for the first time. What exactly was she supposed to say to a woman she was about to marry at the end of the week?

Lucia silently watched the unfamiliar city slide past the car windows. Her broad shoulders were hunched, and there were dark circles beneath her eyes. Her hair was damp from a recent shower, but the scent of smoke and burning plastic still clung to her.

Roseli gave her the silence she clearly needed. It was a brief ride, and soon, they were pulling into the hospital garage. She did not know who had sent the injured Calliopean sailors to an armed-forces hospital instead of a civilian one. She suspected it had more to do with controlling information than anything else.

A staff member quickly led them through a series of elevators and halls to a big airy ward where the injured crew members of the *Intrepid* rested in a roomful of beds. A murmur went up as soon as they appeared. Lucia walked through the room, pausing briefly to speak with each sailor as Roseli followed quietly.

She recognized the hospital and the ward. She had been there several times during the final years of the last war. After her mother had named her heir apparent, one of her first duties had been to visit injured soldiers and sailors. As her mother had put it, "Go be pretty and nice, you're good at that."

She'd never been sure if her mother had sent her because she thought meeting a teenage princess would be any sort of comfort to injured troops or wanted her to see the human cost of war. As far as she had been able to tell, most soldiers had seemed heartened to see her, although she could do little beyond listen to their stories.

At least most of the sailors Lucia was visiting were only there for minor burns and smoke inhalation and appeared to be recovering well. When they finished a circuit of the room, a staff member led them to several private rooms. In the first was a man hooked up to a lot of equipment. He was the first mate Lucia had dragged from the shuttle the day before. The nurse explained that his lungs were badly damaged, and he couldn't breathe on his own for the time being. His eyes were closed, and he made no sign of awareness, even when Lucia spoke to him. Roseli wished there was something she could do to help.

In the next room was a girl with wavy black hair and freckles across her nose and cheeks. She was awake and tried to salute when they entered. By the tight expression on her face, the movement pained her. Both her hands were heavily bandaged.

"This is no time for ceremony. Be at ease," said Lucia. "I'm just checking on you, Penelope. Your mother would have words with me if I didn't." Lucia took a chair beside her bed and motioned Roseli to do the same.

"Who is she? She's pretty," asked Penelope, nodding in Roseli's general direction. "Her dress is all blue and shiny." Her voice was still rough from the smoke.

"She is Princess Roseli of Delphi, my fiancée," said Lucia.

"She looks like a princess in a storybook. Except she doesn't have a tiara or a puffy gown. She must be a real princess, just like you are. Is she an admiral too?" Her voice was slurred, and her eyes drifted shut as she spoke.

"Oh, little cousin, they've given you a lot of painkillers, haven't they?" said Lucia, brushing hair from her face.

"Yes, I woke up screaming from the burns, and then they gave me stuff to make it not so bad."

Lucia's face fell. "How badly are you hurt?"

"They said my hands and arms are badly burned, almost too much to fix. I need skin grafts."

"I'll make sure you get the best care."

"I know, but..." Tears leaked from the girl's eyes. "They already took two fingers from my left hand, and if I don't heal, I could lose more. Even if the grafts take, my hands are going to be so ugly now."

"You can never be ugly, little cousin."

Roseli felt as if her heart was breaking. Penelope looked as young as Roxane.

Penelope cried harder, her dignity lost to pain and fear. "I'll..." She was hiccupping from crying so hard. "I'll end up with a medical discharge, and I'll have to go home. There will be nothing for me there. I can't even have a debutante season now. There's no point. My hands are ruined, and no one will ever marry me."

She broke into helpless sobs. Lucia tilted her face up. "Penelope, look at me. You will not be discharged from the navy unless you want to be. I will see to that."

"What can I even do now?"

"Even if you have limited use of your hands, you're an officer. Your mind and voice are the most valuable things you have."

Penelope smiled lopsidedly. "You always said I was a flighty, forgetful creature."

"Only during the first few weeks after you came aboard my ship. You improved a great deal."

Her tears eased. "You think so?"

"Yes, you have the makings of a fine officer. This injury is not the end of anything," said Lucia.

"I'm still going to die an old maid."

"What of the ensign on the *Bravado* you keep sending messages to? What was his name?"

"Marcus Giovani, but he'll think I'm hideous now."

"Isn't he the ensign who was injured last year when a power coupling blew? Half his face is scarred."

"He's still handsome," said Penelope defensively. "And he's funny. He writes such wonderful letters."

"If you can still see the beauty in him, then you must realize that others will still see the beauty in you."

"What if he doesn't?"

"Then you'll find someone who does." Lucia's tone shifted to something lighter, almost teasing. "Besides, you know I don't approve of ensigns courting. At your age, you should focus on your career, not waste time flirting."

"That's not what the stories say about you when you were my age, cousin."

Roseli wondered how much truth there was to that.

Lucia laughed and then shrugged. "Well, maybe some flirting is okay, but you're too young for serious courtship. You're an officer of the royal navy. You don't need to worry about getting married in your first season like a poorly dowered debutant. You can have as many flings as you wish and never marry unless you want to."

Penelope giggled. "I never had a fling, at least not...you know." Her eyes were drifting shut again.

"You have all the time in the world." Lucia kissed her forehead before she stood.

Once outside the room, Roseli pulled aside a nurse to see what could be done for Penelope. The nurse seemed slightly confused. "We are doing everything we can, Your Highness. Dr. Cunningham is the best skin-graft surgeon there is in the capital. He'll operate on the patient this afternoon, as soon as the vat-grown skin for the grafts are ready. Nothing can be done before then."

"You'll keep me updated on her condition?"

"Yes, Your Highness."

Roseli and Lucia fell silent for the first part of the ride back. At last, Roseli said, "The ensign is your cousin?"

"Technically, Penelope is a first cousin once removed. Her mother, Lady Hannah, is my oldest cousin on my father's side. Hanna will never forgive me for letting her daughter get injured on my watch."

"I'm sorry."

"This is what happens in war. Penelope gave her oath the same as any officer." She sounded like she was trying to convince herself of that.

"She's so young."

"So was I when I began my service."

Roseli almost said that it didn't make things any less terrible. "This happened because of me, didn't it? You were attacked because you were coming here to marry me."

"Yes. The Terra Nuevans don't want this marriage to happen. They know how deadly our fleets will be when combined."

Guilt tore at Roseli. Despite her attempt to keep from frowning, Lucia must have read it on the rest of her face because she added, "Don't blame yourself. I doubt you chose this marriage any more than I did. If you want to blame anyone, blame my traditional old coot of a father who insisted a marriage alliance was necessary for a damn naval agreement."

Roseli didn't know what to say to that. The mention of Lucia's father jolted her. "Speaking of parents, that's why I came to find you this morning. I wanted to prepare you for your audience with the empress."

Lucia seemed unimpressed. "I thank you for your concern, but I have met foreign rulers before."

"You've never met my mother."

❖

At midday, they walked together into the palace's largest audience chamber, arms linked as expected. Lucia was wearing a suit cut in the

Delphian style, with embroidered sleeves. Meredith, with the assistance of Roseli's wardrobe mistress, had acquired a white ribbon for her throat and proper Calliopean gloves.

Even in civilian clothes, Lucia was every inch an officer, from the rigidity of her spine to the watchfulness of her eyes. They were announced at the door of the audience chamber and entered the crowded room.

Every noble that could snag an invitation had come to get a glimpse of the future royal consort, and the room was awash in brightly colored dresses and coats. Suit coats had traditionally been lined with colored silk, but that style had shifted to add a stripe of colored fabric at the hem, collars, and cuffs, or extensive embroidery. Roseli thought it looked garish, but she knew her sense of fashion to be rather lacking.

At the heart of the room, the empress sat upon a gilded throne. Clad in all the symbols of her office, she felt too distant for Roseli to think of as her mother. She wore a royal purple robe over a dress of the same color. On her head rested the golden, jewel-encrusted crown of her office. In her lap lay the royal scepter, a delicately wrought staff set with an emerald the size of a chicken egg. There were a lot of legends about the emerald, but no one knew which were true.

Roseli and Lucia bowed before the throne. Roseli didn't realize until it was too late that no one had taught Lucia the Delphian style of bowing. Lucia pressed one arm flat against her stomach and the other behind her back as she bowed shallowly in the Calliopean style.

Roseli folded her hands in front of her and bowed deeply, staying bent as she waited for permission to stand. She prayed to all the gods that the delicate silver and diamond tiara, her sole mark of office, stayed on top of her head. Normally, Beatrice wouldn't let her out of her quarters unless it was secured in a neat nest of braids and clips. There hadn't been time for that, not after returning from the hospital barely a half hour before the audience.

"Rise," said the empress, choosing not to comment on Lucia's odd bow.

Roseli straightened. "Your Imperial Majesty, Empress Eleanor Almeda of Delphi, I present to you Princess Lucia Caron of Calliope."

"I welcome you to Delphi, Princess Lucia."

"Thank you."

"Come closer, let me get a better look at you."

Roseli knew her vision was perfectly sharp. She was just showing off her power. This did not bode well for the rest of the audience.

Lucia approached the throne showing no sign of being as intimidated as most people in the empress's presence. She was a princess herself, after all.

The empress studied her thoughtfully. "You've your father's look about you, although you seem to have had the good fortune not to inherit his ears."

Lucia didn't seem to know how to respond to that and wisely remained silent.

The empress merely nodded. "I trust you are well? I heard about your misfortune in journeying to Delphi."

"Yes, although many members of my crew were not as fortunate as I. I am grateful for the hospitality you have extended to them."

"It is nothing. I trust they have all they need?"

"Yes, Your Majesty."

"You are better mannered than I expected you to be. I suppose you must have learned it from your mother. She was a Varcian princess, after all. I hope you are not as prone to swearing and yelling over video screens as your father is."

Roseli hated how the empress could say anything she wanted while everyone else had to be unfailingly polite. Would she be so cutting if people could talk back to her? Knowing her, she would, but that didn't excuse the behavior.

Lucia shifted uncomfortably but let the second insult against her father slide. Something about how the edge of her lip twitched suggested there was truth in that particular insult. "I am an admiral of the Calliopean fleet. I never conduct myself in any way unbefitting of my rank."

"I can't say I've ever had much expectation for the conduct of sailors, but perhaps you will be an exception. I think you will make an acceptable daughter-in-law. We must speak more about the details of your marriage contract and the associated treaty, but this is not the place for it. I invite you to dine with my family this evening."

"Thank you," said Lucia.

The empress stood, and everyone other than Lucia fell into a low bow. Lucia glanced at Roseli and then copied her motion. She did not straighten until Roseli did. Her eyebrows drew together in confusion when she saw that the rest of the room was still bowing. Roseli linked an arm with hers and propelled her toward the door, whispering, "They can't stand until we're gone."

In the hall, Roseli let out a breath as they headed down the hall. "That could have been worse."

Lucia gave her an odd look. "She insulted my father's ears and his manners."

"She didn't insult you, though. That's positively gracious by her standards."

"Good to know."

"Can I interest you in lunch? I can tell you all the other ways my mother is terrifying."

The ghost of a smile came to Lucia's lips. "I must regretfully decline. I need to check on my crew in the barracks and see if we have received a response from Calliope yet."

"I will see you at dinner, then."

They bowed and went their separate ways. At least, they attempted to. Lucia made it about three steps before she seemingly realized she did not know where she was going.

"The barracks is one left turn and then two right turns," said Roseli.

The moment Lucia was out of sight, she leaned against the wall and took a deep steadying breath. They'd gotten through the audience; surely, dinner could be half as difficult.

Roseli used her wrist strap to let Alexis, Julia, and Beatrice know they could join her for lunch as she walked back to her quarters. She returned to find her small sitting room largely dominated by flower arrangements. Some were large, some small, but they were all variants of red and orange, traditional for weddings. All the vases and pots had labels with little numbered tags. Beatrice stood at the center of the foliage, frowning at the tablet in her hand.

Julia was lounging on one of the couches, and Alexis had taken a seat in a chair on the other side of the table.

"Beatrice, they all look the same to me," insisted Julia.

"And you?" snapped Beatrice at Alexis.

Judiciously, Alexis said, "You've chosen a fine selection. I'm sure any of them will do."

"Bloody useless, the both of you," grumbled Beatrice. She turned to Roseli as she entered. "Roseli, my darling, for the sake of my sanity, pick a number between one and twenty."

Roseli crossed the room to Beatrice and slipped an arm around her waist. "What will you do if I don't, lovely?"

"I spent the entire morning getting a contract worked out with the florist, and these are the choices they sent. We need to give them an answer within the hour, or the price will go up. I have made so many decisions this week that I just have no more in me. If you don't choose a style of flower arrangement, I'll let Meredith do it."

That was a sobering idea. She'd have gone for the one that was made entirely of carnivorous plants.

"I'll save you, I promise," said Roseli. She kissed Beatrice and made a quick circle of the room, at least pretending to consider each flower arrangement. "Let's go with number twelve. I like tulips."

"Thank you, darling," said Beatrice as she quickly tapped at her tablet and set it down.

They all compared notes over lunch, which they ate informally at the low sitting-room table rather than going to the dining room. Although she had not been much use where flowers were concerned, Julia had been busy. "I've worked it out with the speaker of the Senate. There will be a special session later this week for the Senate to vote to approve the marriage contract."

"I thought that was settled," said Roseli as she reached for a dumpling. The last thing she wanted was one more thing to worry about.

"It is mostly a formality, but it is still symbolically important. After the whole business of your mother marrying Prince Ambrose shortly before Mycenae fell, the Senate passed a bill that gave it the authority to vote on all future royal marriage contracts. They felt they had not been properly consulted on such a significant matter of state. Your mother could have used her veto to overrule the bill, but the Senate at that time was unified enough that they could have managed the two-thirds majority needed to overrule her. She didn't challenge the bill for fear of losing face." For a junior senator, Julia was well-versed in Senate history and procedure. Early in her career, she'd made friends with the Senate librarian and still had tea with the old woman at least once a month.

"There isn't a chance they are going to vote down the marriage contract, are they?" asked Roseli. "The wedding is already set."

"They had best not. We truly need those ships now," said Alexis.

"Don't worry. The vote is just a way for the Senate to publicly assert its power. I know for a fact that both the majority and minority coalition leaders were involved in the contract's drafting. They will approve it now," Julia said.

"Good, that is settled, then. Thank you, Julia." Roseli had just leaned over to kiss her when the door to the sitting room banged open loudly.

"Princess Roseli! Have you seen this contract?" Lucia stormed into the room, two of Roseli's servants at her heels frantically trying to stop her with little success. Lieutenant Laurent also appeared to be trying to dissuade her.

Roseli made a mental note to have a word with her guards about not letting people, even her fiancée, into her quarters unannounced. When she stood, Julia and Alexis moved to stand at her sides protectively, although the couch sat between her and Lucia. Only Beatrice remained seated on the second couch, frowning disapprovingly over her teacup.

"Princess Lucia, I was not expecting you," said Roseli.

"Please call me Admiral Caron," she replied tersely, "I prefer to use my naval title."

"I apologize, I did not know that, Admiral Caron."

She held out a tablet. "Have you read this?"

Roseli leaned over the couch to accept the tablet and saw from a glance that it contained a copy of the marriage contract.

"Yes." Well, she'd had Julia summarize it for her. It was all standard. She was less than thrilled that she was expected to carry their heirs, but that was traditional for the future empress.

She hoped to put off that obligation for another year or two. At least with the egg-splicing technology she and a female partner would need to use, they could choose when she carried her first pregnancy. She wasn't averse to the idea of motherhood, but she didn't feel prepared yet.

"And you're okay with it?" snapped Lucia.

Roseli struggled to figure out what was setting her off. She'd seemed so calm and collected every time they had spoken before. "Are you upset that I'm allowed to take other wives? You have to understand that, as the future empress, it is my duty to secure alliances."

"I'm less than thrilled about that but—"

"The contract still guarantees that my first child will be yours and named my heir."

Lucia's eyes narrowed, and she opened her mouth to say something, but Lieutenant Laurent laid a familiar hand on her arm and whispered something. She seemed to rethink what she was about to say. "That is not what I am upset about."

"What then?"

"How can you possibly ask me to resign my commission and remain on Delphi when my planet is on the verge of war?"

Roseli blinked. "I'm sorry, that is just what is expected. Royal consorts must remain on the planet for their safety." Except for her father, and everyone knew how that had ended.

Lucia slammed a hand on the couch's low back. "I will not. I am an admiral of the Calliopean navy, and I have far more important things to do than play dutiful wife in a gilded palace. Change the clause, or there will be no wedding." She wasn't yelling, but she was close to it.

Alexis moved fully between them. Lucia barely seemed to notice and continued to look past her. Roseli had had enough. Fiancée or not, Lucia had no right to barge into her rooms and speak to her like this. "Then you had best take that up with our respective parents. They are the ones who negotiated the contract, not me. It is not my wish to keep you from the battlefield."

"I will." Lucia turned and headed for the door.

"Wait," called Roseli, "Don't go storming into my mother's study. That will not go well."

Lucia stopped without turning. "Fine, I'll bring it up at dinner, then. You'll back me on this, or I will hold no respect for you."

She strode from the room. Lieutenant Laurent offered them all an apologetic bow before turning to go herself.

"Lieutenant," said Roseli. "You're one of her advisors, are you not?"

She looked nervous. "I am a trusted member of the admiral's staff." The way she'd touched Lucia's arm earlier had left Roseli with the suspicion that she might be more than that. Either way, she was the only person likely to be able to talk to her.

"Then do what you can to calm her down before tonight. Admiral Caron can't speak to the empress like she just did me, do you understand?" Roseli did not know what her mother would do, but it wouldn't be good. She had a talent for flaying people with words as easily as a tanner would a hide. Her mother seemed to sense, almost instinctively, what people truly loved and cared about and how to use it against them.

Lieutenant Laurent bowed again. "I understand, Your Highness, I will do what I can." She turned and followed Lucia out of the room.

CHAPTER EIGHT

As far as Roseli knew, no one had used the smaller royal dining room since the last time an ambassador had been formally received the year before. The room had the distinctive smell of a place that had just been aired.

The royal family seldom, if ever, all ate together. Her mother preferred to take her meals at her desk or alone in her private sitting room. Roseli ate dinner with her little sister at least once or twice a week and usually lunched with her adopted father just as frequently.

It was startling to come into the sitting room beside the dining room and find it crowded. All three of her mother's consorts were present, Prince Leon, Prince Ambrose, and Prince Henry. Most people forgot about Prince Henry when they discussed the royal family.

The bespectacled academic was the only new husband Roseli's mother had taken after the Massacre of the Inner Chambers, and he and Roseli had always gotten along well. The empress had wed the youngest brother of the Harper family in order to keep the loyalty of the old noble family and secure a cheaper price for ship-building metal from the refineries during the past war. Despite the title, Prince Henry was technically only a lord, as was Prince Leon. As royal consorts, they were given the title of prince as a courtesy.

Beyond controlling Prince Henry's mathematical research, her mother never had much use for her youngest husband. He made no secret of the fact that he'd agreed to the marriage in order to get royal funding to build a supercomputer. It was rumored that the marriage had never been consummated due to a mutual lack of interest.

Although not publicly acknowledged, Prince Ambrose and Prince Henry had been quietly having an affair for over a decade. It was not unheard of for an empress's consorts to sometimes be involved with each other, so long as they didn't sleep with anyone outside the Inner Chambers. There was a famous Delphian epic, likely much embellished, involving two of the consorts of a long-ago empress. In the poem, space pirates kidnapped one royal consort, and another one set out on a quest to rescue him. The story involved a lot of daring escapes, swashbuckling, and space battles.

It was hard for Roseli to imagine Prince Henry ever conducting any heroic rescues, unless mathematical equations were involved. As she crossed the room to him, she noticed he had put his tie on inside out again. He wore his wavy black hair long, as was the style of his generation of nobles, but had done a poor job of braiding it.

A pair of wire-framed glasses were perched on his nose, lending him an old Earth, scholarly air. It was rare to see a Delphian wear glasses, as most had their vision surgically corrected. Prince Henry had a corneal abnormality that prevented this, which was unfortunate as he was constantly misplacing his glasses.

It occurred to Roseli that Prince Henry was the uncle of Lord John Harper, the young rock musician Roxane was so smitten with. Although he bore a strong physical resemblance to his nephew, he had considerably more academic interests. It was odd seeing him beside the taller and better-groomed Prince Ambrose. If not for the fondness that came into Prince Ambrose's eyes when he looked at Prince Henry, it would have been hard to believe they were more than merely fellow consorts. Roseli was glad for them. Much of the loneliness had faded from Ambrose's demeanor after Henry had entered his life.

Prince Henry was excitedly showing Roxane a tablet with a three-dimensional image of a rotating spiral and some manner of a mathematical equation. "See, I think I've finally worked out an equation that fully explains the weight and gravitational pull of black holes. All the equations we use now are off. I've been saying it for years."

"I'm sure you have, Uncle Henry," said Roxane indulgently, "uncle" being traditional for a daughter addressing one of her mother's husbands who was not her father.

For her part, Roseli had never called Ambrose by anything but his first name and always called Prince Leon by his formal title of "Royal Highness" when she had to address him, and Prince Leon when she didn't. She had been nine when her mother married Prince Henry, and though she'd liked him from the start, calling a stranger uncle had seemed odd to her, and so she'd always called him by his first name, too, just as Ambrose had.

"If you would just come to my lectures at the university, I could explain it all," said Prince Henry.

"You know I'm not good at theoretical mathematics," said Roxane.

"That's because you don't apply yourself." It was an old argument and a pleasant one. He insisted that both she and Roseli had more of a talent for mathematics than either admitted to. He wasn't necessarily wrong.

Roseli had attended some of his lectures in the past but sadly hadn't been able to make much sense of them. Her mathematical ability extended little beyond basic calculus. She had fared considerably better with economics.

Prince Henry caught sight of her and bowed clumsily. Prince Ambrose bowed somewhat more elegantly. While he did not bother with such formality when they were alone, he was careful to never appear to overstep his place when they were among company.

Prince Leon, who had been leaning against the mantel and largely ignoring the others, also offered a shallow bow. He had only begun to offer Roseli that courtesy since her mother formally crowned her as heir apparent at eighteen.

When Roseli was small, he'd always looked at her coldly, but after the Massacre of the Inner Chambers, that coldness had turned to an active dislike. As her mother's first husband, Prince Leon had wed expecting their first child would one day assume the throne. Roseli's survival after her sisters' deaths had changed all of that. Even after Roxane was born, Roseli remained the eldest surviving princess and the default heir.

Sometimes, Roseli wondered how different her life might have been if her sisters had lived. How much more freedom might she have if she was not the heir. How would Princess Isabella have borne that burden if she'd had the chance to grow to womanhood? She tried not to think about it too often. It hurt too much.

Prince Leon had never liked how close Roxane and Roseli were, although he had little power to keep them apart. They were sisters, after all. Roseli had been eight when Roxane was born, and she had adored the tiny, wrinkle-faced infant. She would slip from her room to sit with the nurse and the baby in the nursery when she could. The sweet-natured young woman, Emily, had talked to her, told her stories, and shown her how to take care of her little sister. Her kindness had reminded Roseli of the nurse she had lost with her first sisters.

She would never forget the night that Prince Leon had come upon her in the nursery when she was holding her infant sister. Much like Roseli, Roxane had never been a good sleeper. She hadn't had jaundice or even cried much, but she'd always just lie there watching the world with huge green eyes, as if she'd feared missing something if she closed them.

After feeding the baby a bottle, Emily had given Roxane to Roseli to hold and had taken a seat in a rocking chair in the corner. Emily had dozed off, a book she was reading forgotten in her lap. Roseli had sat contentedly with the heavy bundle in her arms. She'd liked talking to the baby. She had known Roxane couldn't understand what she was saying, but Emily had said that babies learned a language from listening and that it was important to talk to them.

She'd been telling Roxane about how dull her history lessons were when the door to the nursery had opened. She hadn't looked up, assuming it was a servant.

"What are you doing with her?" snapped an angry male voice.

Roseli had blinked up at Prince Leon, who was storming across the room toward her. His tone had startled her, and she'd pulled her sister closer.

"Give me the baby this instant."

The way he'd grabbed at them both had frightened her. "No!" She'd drawn up her knees and wrapped her arms around Roxane. Roxane had begun to wail.

"Get away from them." Emily had woken with a start and had later said she'd seen only the back of a figure looming over both children. She was on her feet and rushing forward to protect them when Prince Leon had turned, and she'd recognized him. She'd fallen down in a bow. "Forgive me, Your Highness."

Prince Leon had turned from the rocking chair, glowering at her. "What is wrong with you? Why are you allowing a child to tend to my daughter?"

"She is her sister."

"She could drop her."

"Princess Roseli is a good girl. She is careful with her little sister," said Emily with her eyes downturned. "I was taking care of my siblings when I was much younger than her."

Prince Leon had turned away with a dismissive motion. "My daughter is a princess, not some common girl to be cared for by a snotty-nosed waif. Do your damn job, or I will dismiss you."

He'd glared at Roseli as he'd said that, but he'd made no attempt to take the baby again. There had been something ugly in his face, not an immediate sort of violence, not even anger, but nothing good. He'd turned and stormed from the nursery.

Emily had comforted the howling Roxane and wide-eyed Roseli. "It's all right, my darlings, it's all right."

Roseli hadn't wanted to let go of her sister, and Emily had not made her. Emily had knelt and showed Roseli how to pat the baby's back and calm her. "Can I not hold her anymore?" Roseli had asked, looking at the sleeping baby in her arms.

"Of course you can, sweetheart."

"But he said—"

"He almost never comes here. Let me deal with him."

"Are you sure?"

"Men like him are all bluster. He doesn't scare me, and he shouldn't scare you, either." As a child, Roseli had not known that such words were practically treason, even from a foreign-born woman, but she would have never told on her even if she had known. Emily had hugged Roseli and Roxane. "All will be well. Now, let's put your sister in her crib and get you to bed."

In so many ways, Emily had shaped who they'd both grown to be. Roseli still thought of her most days and missed her. She had died when Roxane was twelve, from a cancer that reduced her from alive and vibrant to cold and in the earth in less than six months. Roseli had tried so hard to be the big sister that Emily had believed she could be for Roxane.

The old Earth analog clock on the mantel chimed six. When Roseli turned to look, she caught Prince Leon frowning at her. It seemed that the passage of time had done little to lessen his distaste for her.

The door to the sitting room opened, and Lucia strode in. She was still wearing the same suit as earlier but looked to be in a better humor.

She and Roseli traded bows, and Roseli introduced her to the others. Lucia was polite and gracious, even if her eyes were distant. She offered everyone the same shallow Calliopean bow. It occurred to Roseli that she might be using the foreign bow deliberately, in order to avoid making an even more glaring error. If that was the case, she was mildly impressed.

Calliopean royals bowed to all people from emperors to commoners in the same manner, unlike Delphians, who varied the depth based on rank. Lucia was likely unsure where she fell in the Delphian power structure and had not been briefed.

Prince Leon frowned at her disapprovingly, but he never did much but frown. Prince Ambrose bowed, reminding Prince Henry to do the same by lightly tapping him on the back.

Roxane seemed fascinated by her new sister-in-law. As soon as the formality of the greeting was completed, she said excitedly, "You look just like your character in the comics."

To her credit, Lucia managed to only slightly frown in confusion. "Comics?"

Roxane giggled, "You know, *The Adventures of Captain Scarlet.* You appeared in a whole plot arc last year. You helped her fight off an evil pirate captain who tried to enslave a Calliopean colony on a small moon of Altair."

"Forgive me, I genuinely have no idea what you are talking about."

Roxane rolled her eyes and dug around in the bodice of her dress to draw out a small tablet about the size of her hand. After the first time Roxane had done such a thing in Beatrice's presence, Beatrice had gone to great lengths to explain to Roxane that keeping things in her bra, much less retrieving them in public, was vulgar. Roxane had roundly ignored her and continued with the practice. Roseli had been secretly amused but had the tact not to say so to Beatrice. "You're Calliopean. How can you not know about these comics? They are so popular there. They are based on real events."

She held out the tablet for everyone's inspection. An illustrated version of Lucia stood at the center of the screen. She was wearing her dress uniform and striking a dashing pose with a metal saber in hand. She stood back-to-back with a similarly armed woman who wore a long red coat and a large red hat with an ostrich feather. The title read "The Battle for Altair Colony."

It was all Roseli could do not to laugh. "Tell me, Admiral, you didn't rescue an entire colony with the help of a beautiful pirate captain?"

"Nothing so dramatic. Two years ago, Captain Scarlet of the Thalian privateer ship *Star Chaser* contacted the Calliopean navy to inform us that her ship had found the ruins of a Calliopean colony on the third moon of Altair. They believed slavers had attacked the colony and captured the occupants. My flagship and escort were in the area, so I went to investigate and found evidence to support what the privateers had told us. I sent two smaller ships to pursue the slavers' vessel. They caught up to them just outside of Varcian space, forced a surrender, rescued the surviving colonists, and brought the slavers to Calliope to stand trial. The slavers proved to be Varcian citizens, so the whole incident was a diplomatic mess."

Roxane frowned, pursing her bottom lip. "You never fought a battle side by side with Captain Scarlet?"

"I've never met the woman, if the current Captain Scarlet is a woman."

"There has been more than one?" said Prince Ambrose.

Lucia considered the image. "Yes, from what I understand, the name has been handed down through generations of privateer captains. There has been a ship with the beacon *Star Chaser* and a Captain Scarlet commanding it for well over a hundred years."

"It's inherited, then, just like being an empress?" asked Roxane.

"Yes, although not necessarily along family lines."

Roseli wondered if her mother might have preferred that tradition. Perhaps she would have preferred searching for an ideal heir, rather than being so often disappointed in her?

The door opened, and Roseli's mother entered. She had shed her robe and crown, although she still wore the elegant silk dress. She was dictating something about a fertilizer tariff into a tablet in her hand and didn't even look around the room until she finished talking and stowed the tablet in a pocket. She could afford enough tailors to ensure she owned no dresses without pockets.

She inclined her head ever so slightly in exchange for the bows and greetings she was offered and then kept going toward the door that led to the dining room. "Come on, no point standing around like a bunch of courtiers at an audience. I'm married to three of you, I gave birth to two of you, and one of you will soon be my daughter-in-law."

The long wooden table in the small dining room had been set for seven. Moonlight flooded in through the large skylight. Roseli's mother went to the head of the table, and the royal consorts all took a seat on her left.

At Roseli's side, Lucia hesitated as if unsure where she was supposed to sit. "You'll be on my right," whispered Roseli as she headed to sit on her mother's right. "Between me and Roxane."

Her mother sat first and then gave the others a nod that told them they could all sit as well. Servants brought mushroom soup to start the meal. Lucia reached for her spoon, but a quick shake of Roseli's head warned her to set it down.

When her mother took up her spoon, Roseli did the same, casting Lucia a quick glance and offering a nod. It occurred to Roseli that she must have Meredith arrange for some etiquette lessons for Lucia, as more of their customs varied than she had first realized.

Her mother began the conversation, as was the custom, speaking to her guest. "Do you and your crew have all that you require?"

"Yes, thank you."

"If you wish, I can provide a ship to transport them back to Calliope once the injured have recovered enough to travel."

"Thank you, but that will not be necessary. Another ship of the Calliopean fleet, the *Endeavor*, has been diverted to retrieve the crew of the *Intrepid*. They will be here in a month's time."

"Very good."

"When the ship arrives, I intend to go with them. As an admiral of the Calliopean navy, I must return to my duties as soon as possible after the wedding. I will come back to Delphi once the current interplanetary tensions have eased."

"That will not be possible," said Roseli's mother curtly.

Roseli knew things were about to go downhill, but she didn't know how to intervene without making the situation worse.

Lucia frowned. "How so?"

"You will resign your commission and remain on Delphi."

"I will do no such thing."

"It's part of the marriage contract. I know you have read it. I had a copy sent to you upon your arrival."

"It will need to be revised. I can't possibly resign my commission now, not when both our planets are on the point of war with the Terra Nuevans."

Roseli's mother set down her spoon. "It is precisely because of the looming hostilities that the contract was drafted in the first place. I would not be marrying my daughter off to some arrogant foreign princess who doesn't even know how to bow properly if I did not need a military alliance."

"Mother—" began Roseli, but Lucia cut her off.

"I cannot agree to any contract that requires me to set aside my duty to my planet."

"As a princess, your duty is to serve your planet in whatever way is required. Fulfilling the marriage contract is how you do that."

"I do not see why the contract requires me to remain present on Delphi." Lucia thumped the table.

The empress kept her temper better than that. "I would imagine that would be rather obvious. It is a marriage contract."

Lucia was flushed with anger. "If this is about siring an heir, I don't see why I cannot still depart Delphi and return. I can have some of my eggs harvested before I resume my duties to my planet's navy. Sentiment aside, I don't strictly need to be present for in vitro fertilization."

"And blithely abandon my daughter to solitary pregnancy and motherhood? I had a husband like that, the only damn one I chose to please myself. I was enough of an idiot to allow him to remain in the military despite tradition. He got me pregnant, and then he went and died in battle. You won't do that to my daughter."

Roseli flinched. It was never a good sign when her mother started talking about her father. She always spoke of his death like it had been a deliberate betrayal done to spite her.

"Your Majesty—" began Lucia.

The empress held up a hand, silencing her. "I don't want to hear another word about this. The contract has already been written, and I don't intend to debate its clauses with a young fool."

Lucia glared at her. "I am hardly young."

"You are a child compared to me. As for being a fool, well, you may outgrow that in time, but you have not yet."

"I will not resign my commission. If that makes marriage impossible, so be it." She pushed back her chair and surged to her feet.

She had nearly made it to the door when Roseli's mother called after her, "How do you intend to defeat the Terra Nuevan fleet without the Delphian navy?"

Lucia froze. "What?"

"You know our planets did a shit job of backing each other during the last war, and that's why both lost so many ships. The Varcians are a bunch of selfish bastards who won't send ships until their colonies are in danger. As for the Calypsonians, we both know they will never fight in any war until they have enemy ships in their planetary orbit."

"Calliope has a fine navy."

"But still a smaller one than Terra Nueva. Calliope cannot fight them off alone, nor can you trust the Varcians. If you want my ships to come to your planet's aid, you'll stay on my damn planet and marry my daughter. She's stubborn as hell and only reasonably bright, but at least she's pretty. You could do worse."

Roseli could have done without the comment on her intelligence and temperament, but she was used to it.

Lucia stared a long time before she said, "Your planet is closer to the frontier with Terra Nueva and Thalia than mine."

"They'll still come for your home, Princess, and there are a lot of colonies in between that they will destroy on the way. We stop the Terra Nuevans and their allies together, or we both fall."

"Do you realize you are asking me to give up the sole thing I have trained to be since I was a girl?"

"We all make sacrifices. That is what being royalty means. Now, sit down, shut up, and stop acting like the child you so clearly are."

Lucia clenched her hands, but she bit back whatever she was about to say. Her shoulders stayed stiff with anger, but she silently came back to the table. The rest of the meal was awkward, to say the least. Lucia departed as soon as it was over.

Roseli followed her down the hall, trying not to look like she was running to catch up. "Admiral Caron, please, wait a moment."

Lucia turned to look at her, her face utterly unreadable. "Yes?"

"Come have a drink with me."

She looked at Roseli as if she had suggested they go parachuting. "What?"

"You've just lost your first battle with my mother. Trust me, alcohol helps."

CHAPTER NINE

Is she usually like that?" asked Lucia as she accepted a glass of Septian red whiskey and took a seat on one of the finely carved, silk-cushioned chairs in Roseli's sitting room.

Roseli settled on the settee with her glass. "Pretty much. If it's any consolation, she uses the disapproving elder line a lot. I think she waited with bated breath for her first gray hairs to appear just so she could start calling everyone else young and foolish."

Lucia raised her glass to her lips. She took the time to sip it slowly. Either she knew how to appreciate good whiskey, or she was making sure that the alcohol's strong taste was not disguising poison. Not an unwise precaution, all things considered. "She reminds me of my father, although he does a lot more yelling."

"My mother never needs to raise her voice. She's got the whole condescending stare thing down."

"Have you ever won an argument with her?"

Roseli gave that some thought. "I did, once, when I was about seven. I haven't won one since."

"That must be a story." Lucia leaning back in her chair. It might have been the whiskey or simply exhaustion, but she seemed more relaxed. Perhaps she was glad to find a potential ally in Roseli, at least where the empress was concerned.

Roseli took the cue. "A Varcian diplomat brought a rare white purebred Persian kitten as a gift. Having no use for it, my mother gave it to me. I named it Daisy. My mother said I shouldn't name a male cat after a flower. I said I thought it was a girl cat because it was white and fluffy, just like the girl cat in one of my picture books. She made me rename it Simba. It turned out someone had mistaken the sex of the kitten because later that year, Simba had a litter of kittens. After that, I got to call her Daisy."

While Daisy was no longer among the living, Roseli still had one of her descendants, Dahlia, a fluffy black cat with the blue eyes of her grandmother. Technically, Dahlia was an official palace cat and was expected to fulfill mousing duties. In reality, she spent most of her time sleeping on the couch in Roseli's study or hiding in Beatrice's rooms.

Lucia chuckled. "That's the only argument you ever won?"

"You've met the woman." She took another drink. "Ever since I was a child, she'd tell me what to do, I'd dig my heels in, and she'd figure out a way to push me. Eventually, she'd push hard enough, and I'd give in and do what she wanted. My little sister, Roxane, has a much better approach. She never tells my mother no, just ignores her and does what she wants. When confronted, she'll say she forgot or act like she was never told to do something. My mother hasn't figured out how to respond to that."

"I like her. She reminds me of my younger brother, Thomas. My father can go blue in the face lecturing him, and he'll just shrug. It's my eldest brother, John, who fights with my father. They're both the sort to raise their voices. You can usually hear them halfway across the palace when they're having it out over something."

"What about you?" asked Roseli, although Lucia had already proven herself to be more like her father than her younger brother.

"I ran off to join the navy so I wouldn't have to deal with my family."

"Ran away?"

"Not exactly, but my father didn't want me to go into the naval academy when I turned sixteen. It drove him absolutely crazy that both his sons refused to do any form of armed service, but it was the one thing his daughter wanted. He still had to let me join the navy. He promised my mother he would when she was dying, and he is a man of his word."

There was a lot to unpack there. Roseli wasn't sure if she should be reassured or concerned that Lucia had as complicated a relationship with her family as she did.

"I'm sorry about your mother," she said.

Lucia looked at the glass in her hand. "She died when I was fifteen, and I am who I am because of her. She was a Varcian princess and served as an admiral before my grandmother died, and my aunt assumed the throne. My aunt saw her married off to the Emperor of Calliope to make sure she posed no threat to her authority on Varcia. Even though it was an arranged marriage, my parents still respected and depended on each other. My mother was one of the few people my father ever listened to. It was her naval advice that got Calliope through the last war. She was a brilliant tactician. Calliope didn't start losing the war until she died."

"Your father let your mother direct your planet's armed forces but didn't want you to join the navy?"

Lucia shrugged. "I can't say I've ever understood his talent for doublethink. He's a highly traditional man, even by Calliopean standards. Since my mother wasn't Calliopean, that let him set aside most of his expectations when it came to her. My brothers and I are Calliopean, so he expects us to fall in line."

"I know that feeling. The being expected to fall in line part, anyway," said Roseli.

"At least we have something in common," she said, smiling thinly.

"I'll drink to that." Roseli raised her glass. "To our difficult parents."

They toasted and drank. When Lucia lowered her glass, her expression had gone somber. "There is no way I'll change your mother's mind, is there?"

"No, not unless you can get her into a weaker bargaining position. If your father already agreed to the contract, you have little hope of that." She wondered if she should have found a more delicate way of saying it, but honesty seemed simplest.

Lucia scowled and turned the delicate crystal glass of amber liquid. "That's it, then."

"I'm sorry. I would fight for your sake, except I know how much our planets need this alliance."

"I wish knowing that made it easier. I've spent half my life in the Calliopean navy. I'm not sure who I am if I'm not a sailor."

"A princess of Calliope," said Roseli. "And when I assume the throne, I will make you my advisor for military strategy."

Lucia glanced up. "I thought you already had one. That is General Tate's role, is it not? Unless you have separate advisors for the army and navy."

Roseli chose her next words carefully. She still did not know how much Lucia knew about her, and she didn't want to shatter the uneasy peace between them so soon. "Alexis is not officially my advisor. She is my paramour."

"Ah." Lucia's smile was back. "I was wondering when you were going to mention that."

"Me being allowed to keep my paramours is part of the marriage contract."

"Is it? To be honest, I didn't read much past the part that said I had to resign my commission. I was, however, already aware of your relationship with General Tate."

"Oh, did you read up on me?" It wouldn't have been hard, her having official paramours was a matter of public record.

A hint of color came to Lucia's cheeks. "No, but I've seen the video of you and her."

"Is there anyone on the colonized planets who hasn't seen that wretched thing?"

"I'm afraid it made the rounds of the Calliopean navy. If I'd known you were going to be my future wife, I'd never have watched it."

"And do you only respect women you are engaged to?" asked Roseli. "That accursed video was taken without my or Alexis's knowledge. Some scumbag journalist hacked the code to my dressing room and planted a camera. Now the whole damn universe knows my orgasm face."

It could have been worse; they'd been mostly dressed, and the camera had only caught Alexis kissing Roseli before ducking under her skirts to do considerably more intimate things, but it had still been a shock and a violation when the video had hit the web. Even years later, she still cringed at any reminder.

"Forgive me." Lucia sounded like she meant it.

"It's not like you're the only person who watched it."

"If it is any consolation, it did wonders for your popularity in the Calliopean navy. It inspired a lot of drinking songs."

"Songs?"

"Some aren't even that dirty. There's a rather witty one called 'The Dashing General and the Princess Fair.'"

"Lovely." Roseli drained her glass. "It did the same for my poll numbers here. To read the tabloids, you would have thought that having a quickie with a lover in a dressing room was the first properly imperial thing I ever did."

Lucia blinked. "Truly?"

Roseli reclined farther on her couch, waving a hand for emphasis. "Delphians love a lusty empress. It's all part of the image. An ideal empress is a maiden, mother, warrior, temptress, and wisewoman all in one. She must be beauty and grace personified and also have the fierce spirit of a lioness. She needs to be a scholar of war and economics. She is expected to direct troops but never risk herself in battle. She is a dutiful wife many times over and collects a respectable number of lovers. She must also be a loving mother to a sufficient number of heirs and yet magically keep her figure. Above all, she must speak stoically and forcefully on the video screen. That's the most important bit."

No empress had ever been all those things, but the pressure of expectation was still crushing.

"That's a tall order. Tell me, what is a respectable number of lovers? Are you behind your quota having only one?"

"I've got two others, Lady Swann and Senator Veritas. You met them both in the car on the first night and again when you burst into my quarters earlier today."

Roseli saw a flicker of interest in the admiral's hazel eyes. "I can't fault your taste in women."

That was not the reaction she had expected. "I'll take that as a compliment. You have a reputation of your own, or so I hear."

"It's all earned, I assure you." She had a terribly charming smile, complete with even white teeth.

"Now, that just sounds like bragging."

"I have my moments." She finished her glass and set it down, not reaching to refill it.

It seemed to Roseli that although they had drunk the same amount, Lucia was less affected than she was. If the Calliopean navy was anything like the Delphian one, Lucia could likely drink any civilian under the table.

"This would all be so much easier if I could hate you, curse you for the end of my naval career, but you have offered me nothing but kindness since I got here. I can't help but like you."

Roseli struggled to find the right words. Perhaps things truly could work between them. "Can you like me and still hate what you're losing?"

"Yes, I think I can." Lucia reached across the table to take Roseli's hand, her skin warm through the thin cotton of her glove. "You are to be my wife. For that alone, I owe you my respect."

"And is that what we are to have between us, respect?"

"Hopefully, more than that." Lucia was doing a poor job of hiding a grin. "Your beauty is not lost on me, and hopefully, my charm is not invisible to you."

"I'm hardly blind."

"May I kiss you?" It seemed almost ludicrous for a fiancée to be asking permission, and yet, it made sense. The fate of two empires hung between them, and there was no room for missteps.

"Yes."

Lucia initiated the kiss, gently tilting up Roseli's chin and capturing her lips. It was the most confident first kiss Roseli had ever shared but was all too brief.

Lucia pulled back, her hand lingering in a caress on Roseli's face. "I'll see you in the morning."

Roseli was almost too dazed to speak. "In the morning, yes. Sleep well."

Lucia bowed and then departed, leaving an impressed but mildly disappointed Roseli in her wake.

This was going to be complicated. She hadn't expected to like Lucia, much less desire her.

❖

Lucia had no sooner stepped from the hall out into the courtyard than she found General Tate waiting for her, leaning against the wall.

The general bowed and said, "Admiral Caron, I believe we should talk." Although her tone was polite, she might as well have thrown down a glove.

"If you believe it is necessary."

"Please, come with me to my office."

Had Lucia not had two palace guards trailing her, she might have hesitated to follow her across the palace grounds, but she figured that the general's intentions were likely not murder if she had witnesses. They walked past the barracks to what Lucia guessed was the military wing. A dimly lit hallway led them to a finely appointed room, which they left the guards outside of.

General Tate's office was paneled in dark wood and had heavy mahogany furniture. There were paintings of long-ago space and land battles on the walls that would not have looked out of place in a national gallery. If the serial numbers on the small brass plaques beneath each painting were any indication, they were likely on loan from some important collection.

General Tate poured them each a glass from a bottle of Septian red whiskey. Lucia couldn't help but wonder if both General Tate and Roseli had the same taste in alcohol or if one had given a bottle to the other. She sipped carefully as she took an offered chair. Fine as the whiskey was, she couldn't risk her mind being clouded during this conversation after her earlier drink with Roseli. She already felt off-kilter enough.

She'd seen a picture of Roseli before she'd met her and had known she was beautiful, but she hadn't expected her to be so genuinely charming. It had been a long time since she'd wanted a woman so much after only a kiss.

General Tate took a chair beside the small table that held a lamp and a decanter. "I feel I should warn you that if you ever speak to Princess Roseli like you did this afternoon in her quarters, I will have to challenge you to a duel."

Lucia did not let herself be intimidated. "If you do, I'll choose swords, so I hope you know how to use one."

"I fought my last duel with an épée." Her posture was rigid, but nothing in the way she sat suggested aggression.

"Same."

There was a long beat of silence as they considered each other. Lucia could not read what lay behind her gray eyes. What did it cost General Tate to speak to her so calmly?

Lucia knew she had been in the wrong, but she also needed General Tate to understand she would not be pushed around. She would respect that General Tate was Roseli's lover, if General Tate would respect that she was her fiancée.

She set down her glass. "This afternoon, I was upset and acted beneath myself. I should not have spoken in anger as I did, much less to my fiancée. You have my word it will not happen again."

General Tate nodded. "Then I have no quarrel with you."

"If we are not to duel, would you be interested in fencing sometime?" asked Lucia.

"It would be my honor." General Tate raised her glass.

Lucia clinked hers against it. The whiskey warmed her throat. Curiosity got the better of her. "Was your last duel over Princess Roseli?"

"No, another woman, years before I met Roseli. In the folly of youth, I challenged a romantic rival to a duel. It didn't go well for me. During the duel, the woman I loved begged for the life of my opponent, and I spared her. I won the duel but not the woman I fought it for."

"I'm sorry."

General Tate shrugged. "Perhaps it was for the best. They are happily married now, and I am godmother to their children. What about you? What did you fight for?"

Lucia looked into her mostly full glass. "A childhood friend. She dreamed of a life beyond being a palace servant as her parents had been. She passed the exam to become an apprentice courtesan. A few years later, one of her clients scarred her face and destroyed her career. When I learned of it, I challenged the young nobleman who'd hurt her and marked his face the same as he had hers."

"You fought for a far nobler reason than I did."

"At the time, I thought so, but looking back, I can see I acted more in anger than care for my friend. She never asked me to avenge her. I do not doubt that the man who hurt her deserved what he got, but revenge could not take the scars from my friend's face or the nightmares from her dreams."

"What became of her?"

"She's a dance instructor for apprentice courtesans. It isn't what she wanted, but she says teaching brings her joy." Lucia drained her glass. "I suppose I'll never see her again, at least not in person, if the marriage contract is to keep me on Delphi."

The weight of it all was too much. She would never set foot on a ship again, much less drink coffee with her father, hug her brothers, or scoop up her little niece. Of course, she could still talk to all of them over a video screen, but it would not be the same.

General Tate stood, taking the glasses to the cabinet. "For what it's worth, I'm sorry that you are being forced to resign your commission. You were a fine admiral. I am still alive after the Battle of Brahe because of the orbital support your ships provided."

"Thank you." Lucia stood, stretching. She knew she should go, but she hesitated. "What would you do in my position? Would you marry your lover if it meant never leaving Delphi or returning to the field?"

The general turned from closing the cabinet. "In a heartbeat."

Lucia wished she could feel the same. Lovely as Roseli was, she could not set aside her need to protect Calliope and her father and brothers. Accepting that she could best do so by staying on Delphi and marrying was not going to be easy. She wanted to fight, not leave it to others to do for her.

❖

Roseli was restless after Lucia departed. She wanted to speak to someone and at the same time, keep the evening to herself. She knew Julia had an early vote the next morning and was probably already asleep in her townhouse near the palace.

Alexis was likely asleep, too. She had always been the early to bed and early to rise sort. Roseli found such habits strange but assumed that Alexis had developed them from her service in the military.

Fortunately, Beatrice was a night owl like her. She tapped at her tablet, sending a text coded to only make Beatrice's tablet beep if she hadn't put it into sleep mode. *Hey, Bee, you still up?*

A minute later, Beatrice typed back, *I'll be over in just a minute, darling.*

Roseli tapped quickly as she left her quarters. *No, don't get up. Is it okay if I come over?*

Yes.

When Roseli stepped into the hall, the four guards outside perked up. Two remained outside her quarters at all times to make sure they remained secure, and two accompanied her anywhere she went in the palace. If she wished to leave the grounds, she was required to have at least four, the same as the empress.

"At ease, I'm only going down the hall."

Her head of security, Officer Jessica Smith, bowed formally. "We understand, Your Highness, but we must still see you from door to door."

Roseli returned the bow with a slight dip of her head. "You know, I've never been able to figure out if you lot are incredibly dutiful or just paranoid."

"Would you want to face the empress after letting you come to harm, Your Highness?"

"Fair enough. I invite you to accompany me for a brief stroll down the hall."

"I'm honored to accept, Your Highness." She would never let it be said that her guards had no sense of humor, especially Officer

Smith. She'd been guarding Roseli since she was a child and was not intimidated by her.

She had sons Roseli's age, and when Roseli was small, she had never hesitated to yell at her to stay where she could see her or get down from a wall before she fell. Roseli trusted her with her life precisely because Officer Smith cared more about keeping her safe than upsetting her.

Beatrice's suite of rooms was only a few yards down the hall. It was subject to the same level of security as Roseli's, which was the only reason her guards allowed her to enter without one of them going in first to do a full sweep. Roseli would have liked to connect their rooms, but that would have meant cutting off a major hallway.

Roseli had never seen the inside Alexis's small room in the palace barracks. She had visited Julia's townhouse a few times, but the level of security required for the Crown Princess to spend a night away from the palace had been staggering.

Roseli knocked and entered Beatrice's rooms. The front hall was empty, but she heard Beatrice call, "I'm in the bedroom, darling."

Roseli passed through Beatrice's fashionably decorated parlor. In the dim light, she couldn't make out the ornate blue and white print on the low couch and delicate wooden chairs. She was careful not to trip over the coffee table with its intricately carved swans and gold paint. Beatrice loved that table. It was priceless, according to the palace historian. Beatrice had found it in the basement, a remnant of the legendary salon of one of Roseli's great-great-grandmother's lovers, and had decided such a beautiful thing shouldn't be stored away.

While Roseli had little regard for something she considered a hand-me-down, Beatrice fiercely defended the table against all threats of scratches or stains. She had initially talked of putting it in Roseli's parlor but had thought better of it, citing Roseli's tendency to spill things and Alexis's complete and utter disregard for the use of saucers and coasters.

While Beatrice seldom used her quarters to entertain, she conducted enough formal business there that her sitting room still needed to be worthy of the paramour of a future empress. There was no doubt that any seamstress, event planner, or jeweler she received there would tell their next client all about how she decorated.

When Beatrice had explained this, Roseli had initially been troubled. She'd offered to find Beatrice another space to receive merchants so her rooms could remain truly hers. Beatrice had smiled fondly and told her that while she appreciated the thought, that wasn't how it worked.

Roseli passed down the thickly carpeted hall toward Beatrice's bedroom. The door was half-open, light spilling into the hallway. She stepped into the one room Beatrice had decorated for herself. It was alive with warm mixed colors, from the floor covered in throw rugs to the heavy wooden bed covered in a patchwork quilt that wouldn't have been out of place on old Earth. The walls were given to framed posters from the soap operas Beatrice had grown up watching.

Beatrice herself was sitting on the bed in sweatpants and an old T-shirt, her face clean of makeup. She had her beautiful golden curls carefully tucked beneath a bandana. Dahlia purred in her lap, and she had a tablet in her hand.

As far as Roseli knew, she might have been one of the few people to have ever seen Beatrice in sweatpants. Beatrice would have gladly died before wearing such a thing in front of Alexis or Julia, much less anyone else.

Neither Alexis nor Julia had ever seen Beatrice's bedroom any more than she had theirs. Whatever complex relationship balance made it possible for them to touch while in the neutral space of Roseli's quarters, it didn't work beyond those walls.

"Hey," said Roseli.

"Hey, darling," said Beatrice, "Come lie down, you look exhausted."

Roseli did, pausing to undress. She had to get Beatrice's help to unzip the back of her dress and step out of it. Her instinct was to leave it on the floor, but a slight arch of one of Beatrice's carefully plucked eyebrows was a sufficient reminder to set the expensive garment over a chair. She freed herself of everything but her slip before turning back to the bed where Beatrice had drawn back the covers.

The cat, displeased, leaped off the bed and darted out the door, likely to go shed on the salon furniture in protest. Dahlia would not, however, scratch anything. Beatrice wouldn't have permitted the cat in her quarters if she had shown any inclination toward scratching antique furniture. The one time Dahlia had tried, Beatrice had said her name in such a tone that the little cat had frozen like a guilty child.

Roseli climbed onto the bed with Beatrice, who clapped once to dim the lights. She reached over to tug pins out of Roseli's hair. "How was dinner?"

"About as expected. I'll tell you and the others everything in the morning."

Beatrice's knowing blue eyes searched Roseli's face in the lamplight. "All right, darling."

One thing Roseli loved about Beatrice was that she never pushed for answers, even when she clearly wanted to. Roseli kissed the tip of her nose just to annoy her. "Why don't you tell me about your day instead?"

Beatrice scrunched up her nose. "I had to figure out so many equations for the wedding that I was tempted to go to Prince Henry for help. He's got that giant supercomputer at the university, after all."

"I didn't realize that wedding planning and theoretical astrophysics had much in common."

"Can't be much harder. I had to dig up the old event planning textbook from my apprentice courtesan days. You don't want to know how many variables there are in the equation for how much wine to buy for a wedding."

"I would be doomed without you, Bee."

"I know, that's why I stick around. It's entirely because of patriotic duty."

Roseli tilted her head and tried to look charming. "No other motives?"

"I suppose you are kind of cute."

"Only cute?"

"You're welcome to improve my opinion."

Soon enough, they were both naked, Beatrice beneath her. When she pressed her fingers inside, Beatrice made a wonderful moan. With the others, Beatrice made much quieter and far more dignified sounds, but with just Roseli, she had no such reservations.

"Yes, Roseli, yes, harder, like that, yes, fuck me." The sharp bite of the western slums slipped back into her voice.

Beatrice thumped back against the pillow, catching her breath as the aftershocks of her orgasm faded. Soon, she reached for Roseli, kissing down her body and nudging her legs open to bring her mouth to Roseli's core, eliciting moans and cries.

When they were both sated, Roseli pulled the quilt over them.

"Now I remember why I like you," said Beatrice, resting her head on Roseli's shoulder.

"I'm good in bed?"

"That and an excellent cuddler, even if you snore."

"I don't snore."

"You do, darling, just softly. I don't mind."

Roseli ran a hand lazily up and down the curve of Beatrice's back. "You put up with a lot from me."

"You're worth it."

"Even if you have to plan weddings?"

Despite Beatrice's reassurances, a deep part of Roseli feared that she was asking too much of Beatrice. She could tell when Alexis and Julia were upset, but Beatrice…she only showed her pain if she chose to.

Beatrice paused before replying. "Yes. You know I will do whatever is needed to support you."

"You truly don't mind?" Roseli wasn't sure exactly what she was asking.

"Roseli," said Beatrice, "I've known from the start that you would someday marry and that things would change."

"I don't want anything to change between us."

"Things will, and they won't, darling. Change is the nature of life. We'll find our way through it together. Just know that I will remain at your side as long as you will have me."

"I will always want you with me, Beatrice."

"If you say that enough times, I think I may eventually start to believe you." She sounded almost wistful.

"Then I will keep saying it long after we're both old and gray."

"Speak for yourself, I can't prevent getting old, but I intend to dye my hair when the time comes."

"I'll still keep saying I love you."

"Then I will have to stick around."

CHAPTER TEN

Lucia woke to the sound of someone doing their level best to hack up a lung. Several members of her crew who had been treated for smoke inhalation at the hospital had been released the day before to join the rest of the crew in the barracks.

She was so tired, she briefly considered trying to go back to sleep. Her lungs still burned from the smoke after the shuttle crash. She suspected she'd pulled a muscle in her back while helping others to safety.

She turned her head slightly and regretted it. The stitches in the wound there weren't doing her any favors either. She heard a cot creak as someone got up. With a sigh, she opened her eyes and sat up stiffly. She was still the commanding officer for a few more days, at least. She needed to get to the hospital to check on the crew still there.

At least this time, no one tried to stop her. Her visit was as trying as the day before. Her little cousin's skin graft had gone well, but her first mate Jonas was doing worse. She felt as if one of the pillars of her world was crumbling. He should be up and barking orders and scolding the crew, not lying still as death.

She didn't want to leave him in that strange hospital, her other duties be damned. She sat with him for as long as she could, but she needed to get back to the palace. When she stepped out into the hall, she found one of her crew, Lieutenant Grant, quietly waiting. He had come to sit with Jonas, but he hadn't wanted to disturb her. That was some comfort at least. Even if Jonas was too deeply unconscious to be aware of it, the crew was watching over him.

Upon returning to the barracks, she found a handwritten invitation to have tea with one of the empress's consorts, Prince Ambrose. If she remembered correctly, he was the one Princess Roseli had introduced as her adoptive father.

The paper was thick and cream-colored, the ink a cobalt blue, and the calligraphy impressively ornate. Lucia didn't know what to make of it. Was it a Delphian tradition to send such invitations, and if it was, why hadn't she received any others? Then she remembered that someone had mentioned Prince Ambrose was Mycenaean. That likely explained it.

The two guards who had been shadowing her since her arrival on Delphi showed her the way. It took nearly ten minutes to reach the Inner Chambers in the west wing of the palace. From what she could recall of the day before, Roseli's rooms had been several halls in the opposite direction. That struck Lucia as odd. Why wouldn't the royal family's rooms be together? She supposed it might have been a way to make it harder to assassinate both the empress and heir in one swoop.

They had to pass through several gates. The palace she'd grown up in had had none past the main gate to the royal wing. Her father would have never permitted guards in the inner halls among the family. It was supposed to be a private space. Then again, that particular tradition had once nearly cost Lucia and her mother their lives.

At last, they came to a large courtyard with a small reflecting pool. If the tree that filled half of it ever came down, it would probably take half the roof with it. As she was contemplating the tree, someone smacked into her.

The only thing that stopped Lucia from fighting tooth and nail as she fell was the startled yelp the other person made. They hit the hard cobbles of the courtyard.

"Sorry, sorry," said a male voice. The speaker elbowed her in the ribs as he attempted to disentangle himself.

Lucia was on her feet long before Prince Henry sorted himself out. She offered him a hand up, and he accepted.

He blinked and then felt at his face. "Oh no, I think I've lost my glasses. Do you see them anywhere?"

Lucia surveyed the grounds. "I don't see any."

Prince Ambrose entered the courtyard. "Henry, you left your glasses on the breakfast table again. How do you keep forgetting them? I know you can't see without them."

"I was in a hurry. One of my research assistants called. The supercomputer finally finished running my algorithm. I think we may finally know the correct weight of black holes. If I'm right, this could revolutionize space travel."

Prince Ambrose brought Prince Henry his glasses, cleaning them on his shirt before placing them on Prince Henry's face. "Just don't step into traffic on your way to the university."

"Don't worry, the guards keep me from doing that."

Prince Ambrose watched him go with a half-smile, his eyes crinkling at the edges with worry. He turned back to Lucia. "He's the greatest mathematical mind of his generation, and I live in fear that he is going to break his neck tripping over his feet one of these days."

Lucia didn't dispute that. Prince Henry rather reminded her of her cousin, Edward, who was a renowned composer but so absentminded, she once had to grab him to prevent him from falling into a ditch.

She had the distinctive impression that Princes Ambrose and Henry were a couple. Was that normal for the spouses of a Delphian empress? Or expected?

"Come, the tea should be ready."

A low Mycenaean style table had been laid with tea and small cakes and sweets on a blanket beneath the maple. There were cushions on the ground. Did he expect her to sit on a pillow?

Prince Ambrose sat on a cushion, cross-legged. Lucia copied him. If only her mother could see her now. She'd think the whole thing savage and exotic. Then again, her mother hadn't had a good opinion of Mycenaeans or any cultures other than Varcian.

Prince Ambrose poured milky tea into two large porcelain glasses with no handles and set one before her. She sipped the tea and winced. Who the hell spiced tea?

"Never had chai before?" he asked, sounding slightly amused.

"Afraid not."

"What can I get you instead?"

"Coffee, please."

He spoke into a device on his wrist.

Lucia tried one of the small flaky pastries on the table and nearly gagged.

"I'm guessing you don't like pistachios, either?"

"Never eaten one before," she admitted. Was that the weird green filling?

The wind shifted, stirring the brilliant crimson leaves of the maple above them. "My apologies, I should have thought to order something that would be more familiar to you."

"It's all right. I ate breakfast in the barracks mess hall with my crew."

Prince Ambrose took up an artfully wrapped package from the table and handed it to her. "Here, a welcome gift."

Lucia resolved that even if it was as odd as the food, she would at least pretend to like it. She tore the colorful tissue paper and found a thin, leather-bound book. The cover had a title written in a language she couldn't read, although the letters were in Latin script.

"It's a poem called 'The Wanderer,' from Earth. It is in a language called Old English. There's a translation into Moũsain in the second half, so you will be able to read it. The poem is not long, the book is mostly commentary."

"Thank you." She did not know what the poem was or why he was giving it to her, but she sensed it was significant.

"When I first came to Delphi, the empress's father, Prince Hector, gave this to me. He told me that his father-in-law gave it to him long ago. It is the tradition to pass this book down through the generations of foreign-born consorts of Delphian empresses. Prince Hector was from Calypso, and his father-in-law from Varcia. This poem didn't ease my homesickness, but it gave me words for it."

He wrapped his hands around his cup. "Prince Hector was kind to me. I think he'd have helped me more if his dementia hadn't advanced so quickly. He was lucky, I suppose. By the time of the Massacre of the Inner Chambers, he couldn't remember he had granddaughters, much less that he'd lost two."

Lucia was startled by how casually Prince Ambrose brought up the great tragedy of his family. She had assumed it would be something that the surviving family wouldn't want to talk about. "Thank you for the poem, I'll read it."

"If you ever have questions about the Delphian court or just need someone to talk to, I'm here."

A servant arrived with the coffee. It proved to be strong and dark. After years of drinking terrible navy coffee, she'd almost forgotten what the real stuff tasted like. Once she'd set her cup down, she said, "You know, I'm surprised you're being so kind. I expected you to play the protective father."

Prince Henry frowned. "I don't pretend to have the power to protect anyone."

"I've heard the story of how you saved Princess Roseli as a child."

"I snatched up a child and hid. That makes me no more courageous than a cat dragging a kitten to safety by the scruff."

"I've always thought cats to be rather fierce creatures." Her mother had loved them, even had some white Persian cats brought from Varcia. One had taken a fancy to Lucia when she was little. While she had adored the cat, she'd been horrified when it began to leave dead mice in her bed. Her mother had insisted that the cat was doing it out of love. That had been her first lesson in the complexities of that emotion.

"True, but I'm not the one you need to watch out for."

Finally, something useful. "Who should I?"

"If you can help it, don't cross anyone."

"I'm pretty sure the empress has little fondness for me after last night's dinner." A somewhat mutual feeling. She was not off to a good start with her mother-in-law.

Prince Ambrose chuckled. "Eleanor probably thinks better of you now. She likes people with enough guts to stand up to her, so long as she still wins in the end."

"Good to know."

"Watch out for Prince Leon. He takes offense easily, and when he does, he can be a vindictive bastard."

There was clearly no love lost there. "What of Princess Roseli's paramours?" Was that the right word? Surely, they weren't just openly referred to as lovers, were they?

He studied her carefully. "Had a run-in, have you?"

"General Tate was prepared to challenge me to a duel last night, but we came to an understanding."

"That sounds like her. She is an honorable woman, perhaps to a fault. If she gives her word, she will always keep it."

"And the other two?"

"Don't let Lady Swann's smiles or curls fool you, she is highly observant and intelligent. She's a former courtesan who retired from the guild to become Roseli's paramour and manages most of her public appearances. You'll want to stay on her good side."

"How do I do that?"

"Show her you also have Roseli's best interests at heart. She'll likely accept you if you are a help to Roseli rather than another complication."

"And the senator?"

"Don't trust her smiles, either, she's a sly one. She's the oldest daughter of the Veritases, a wealthy and conniving old noble family. Senator Veritas's mother, Lady Teresa Veritas, is the most powerful woman in the capital after the empress herself."

"I'll keep that in mind."

He sipped his odd-smelling spiced tea. "From what I can tell, Senator Veritas does genuinely love Roseli. She has used her position as a royal paramour to advance her career, but she has always protected Roseli's political interests as well. It's her nature to build alliances, and she'll likely see you as a natural ally. If you want to win her over, ask her to explain the Delphian Senate to you, and she will talk your ear off."

"What of the younger princess?" Lucia had liked her, even if she'd had some unusual ideas from comic books.

"Roxane? She is exactly who she seems. She's a sweet girl, if a bit self-centered. Roseli influences her more than the other way around, although even she can't keep her in line. Be nice to her, and you'll have a friend."

"And the assistant, Ms. Cooper?"

Prince Ambrose considered. "I don't pretend to understand Ms. Cooper. She is an odd one. If you talk to her about cats, she'll probably like you. That's pretty much it, aside from Prince Henry. He'll adore you if you listen to him ramble on about black holes, but unless you've got an advanced astrophysics degree, you'll probably not understand him."

"Is that all?"

He gave that some thought. "Don't let the strangeness of Delphian customs get to you, you'll get used to most of them soon enough. Beyond that, try to make as many friends and allies as you can. The Delphian royal court can be a lonely place if you don't."

"Thank you, you've been beyond helpful."

It seemed she had made an ally without even trying, at least if Prince Ambrose was as trustworthy as he seemed.

❖

Upon returning to the barracks, Lucia was informed by a guard at the door that Lady Swann was waiting for her. When she stepped into the room, she heard laughter.

Lady Swann was sitting on the edge of one bunk, perched elegantly with her legs crossed at the ankles and her curls thrown winsomely over one shoulder. Her green dress was an impressive splash of color in the dull gray room.

Lucia's crew was gathered around, standing or sitting on the bunks and floor as they listened with rapt attention to what she was saying. Lucia hadn't seen any of her crew smile like that since before they were attacked, and the sight lightened her heart.

"And that is the story of how I lost my hat. I'm pretty sure it's still lining that gilded eagle's nest somewhere in the nature preserve. Now, I've got an even better story about—" She saw Lucia in the doorway and stood gracefully, bowing. "Your Highness."

Lucia returned the bow. "Lady Swann, my apologies for your wait. I did not know you wished to see me." A glance and some hand motions from her sent the crew wandering off, giving them a chance to talk without too obvious an audience.

"It was no trouble. I had some highly entertaining company. If you have time now, there are several things related to the wedding that require your attention."

Was one of Roseli's lovers planning the wedding? That was bizarre on a level Lucia didn't have the energy to contemplate. She was tempted to tell Ms. Swann that she had far more important things to worry about than cake and flowers, but she caught herself. The last thing she needed to do was alienate anyone so close to Roseli.

"Very well, what needs to be done?"

"If you would like to have tea with me, I'll talk you through it."

Lady Swann led her to a suite of room's next door to Roseli's. They entered a small sitting room. While the room was not excessively ornate, everything from the rich blue carpets to dark wood furniture and landscape paintings on the walls all probably dated back to the time of the previous empress's reign.

Lady Swann ordered tea with her wrist device and then settled on the low couch beside Lucia. "These are to be your rooms after you are married. I've taken the liberty of seeing them made ready so you can use them as a staging place for wedding preparations."

"Thank you." She had not realized that she and Roseli would not share a bedroom, much less have separate suites. Did married couples on Delphi normally sleep apart or just nobility? Then again, considering that Roseli already had three lovers and would likely marry other wives, it was probably for the best they each had their own space.

"When things settle down, I'll make sure you have a chance to meet with the castle steward so you can make any changes you want. These rooms traditionally belong to the first consort of the heir apparent, but until recently, Princess Roseli's guards were using them to store equipment and as a break room. I had the steward quickly refurnish it with what was available from the vaults."

"I suppose that explains the burned-coffee smell."

Lady Swann scrunched her delicate nose. "My apologies. The engagement was somewhat sudden. I'll get someone in here to air the place out."

The absurdity of Lady Swann apologizing to her for not airing out a room was not lost on Lucia. She couldn't tell if she was being genuinely kind or making a show of power by demonstrating that she ran Roseli's household.

Lucia gave her best roguish grin, the one that charmed most women, even the ones she had no intention of sleeping with. Lady Swann returned an equally charming and just as deliberate smile, showing off her dimples. They appeared to be equally matched.

Lucia let her grin ease to a more natural expression and leaned against the low couch's back. "It's fine. I've spent nearly my entire adult life on starships. Anyplace that doesn't smell of recycled air and dirty socks is a luxury to me."

"I'll still see about getting you some air fresheners."

"What wedding matters can I assist with?" Going with what Prince Ambrose had said, being as helpful as possible to Lady Swann was her best course of action.

"First and foremost, you need something to wear. I can get you a dress or a suit. If I pull a lot of strings, I can see about having a copy of a Calliopean dress uniform made."

"A uniform," said Lucia incredulously. "Wouldn't that be vulgar?"

Lady Swann frowned "Vulgar? I don't think so. I know you have been asked to resign your commission, but it has long been the custom on Delphi for retired members of the armed service to wear their dress uniforms for weddings and other formal events."

"People on Delphi do that?"

"Yes, they don't on Calliope?"

"No, it would be considered incredibly rude to arrive at a civilian event in uniform, much less a formal one."

"I see," said Lady Swann. "I apologize, I was not aware of that cultural difference. Here, it is rare to see most high-ranking members of the military out of uniform. I'm fairly certain that Alexis doesn't own any civilian clothes." She paused. "I'm guessing you won't be wanting a uniform, then."

Lucia was almost tempted to say yes to the idea. It would serve her father right if all the wedding photos sent back to Calliope had her in a dress uniform. She might as well prove herself to be the uncultured warrior he seemed to think her to be.

Only the thought of her grandmother, the dowager empress, being disappointed stopped her. That sweet old woman had loved and supported her in everything she'd ever done. Lucia knew that she owed her grandmother good wedding photos to show off. "Thank you for your consideration, but I think a suit will be fine."

"I'll see to it. I'll also make sure someone briefs you on what is expected for the ceremony."

"Thank you, Lady Swann. I appreciate your help. If it is not too much to ask, may I sometimes come to you with questions about Delphian society? It seems that there are many things I do not yet understand."

Lady Swann's face softened. "Yes, I am happy to help."

There was a knock on the door, and a palace servant, dressed in dull gray clothing, came in carrying a tray containing a teapot, cups, and small sandwiches. As she set it down, a stray bit of milk sloshed out of a small carafe onto the tray.

Beatrice frowned at the spilled milk but said kindly, "Are you new, dear? I don't recognize you."

The young woman started, nearly knocking over the milk again. "I just started today, ma'am. My name is Jenny."

Not particularly interested in the conversation, Lucia reached for one of the little sandwiches that looked like it had cucumber in it. She hadn't found anything edible when she'd had tea with Prince Ambrose.

Lady Swann grabbed her wrist before she could bite into the sandwich. "Wait."

Lucia stared, feeling both aghast and mildly confused. The intensely focused way that Lady Swann was looking at the servant stopped her from yanking her arm free. What was going on?

"Have you met the head cook yet?" asked Lady Swann.

"Yes," said the servant, awkwardly straightening.

"What is her name?"

"What?"

"Tell me her name, dear." Lady Swann didn't sound so kind anymore.

"I don't know. I forgot."

All of Lucia's senses were on alert. Something was wrong.

"When you were trained, how many sugar cubes were you taught to put into a bowl?" asked Lady Swann.

"I don't know!" The servant's voice was a wail and her eyes wide with panic.

"How many times are you supposed to knock on a door before entering?"

The servant didn't answer. She started backing toward the door.

Lucia stood, putting herself between the servant and Lady Swann. She did not see any outlines against the servant's clothing that looked like concealed weapons, but she couldn't be sure.

Lady Swann raised her wrist strap and said into it. "Code nineteen-beta. I repeat, code nineteen-beta."

The servant bolted for the door, and Lucia tackled her. She was a small woman, but she struggled like a trapped animal, screaming and clawing. Lucia managed to get one of her arms twisted behind her back and kept her down.

"Let me go, let me go. I haven't done anything."

The door burst open, and two guards rushed in, guns drawn.

"The woman in palace livery is an assassin," said Lady Swann. "Help Princess Lucia restrain her."

The guards came to help cuff the woman and drag her to her feet. She'd gone silent now, still as a rat held by the scruff.

Lucia brushed herself off, her heart still pounding. A faint pain at her neck told her she'd probably reopened her injury. Hopefully, the bandage was thick enough to keep the blood from seeping through to her white neck cloth. She pushed that thought aside; the neck cloth didn't matter. Had she just survived an assassination attempt?

To her left, Lady Swann was speaking to one of the guards, a middle-aged woman in a gray imperial guard uniform with an eagle patch on her shoulder. "Officer Smith, please have the food and tea tested. I have reason to believe it is poisoned. That woman is not a member of the palace staff. She did not know any of the fail-safe questions. Find out who she is and how she got in here."

The guard bowed. "I'll see it done, Lady Swann. If you and Princess Lucia will accompany me, I need to get you both to a safer location."

"Not until I know that Princess Roseli is accounted for," said Lady Swann.

"She is being secured as we speak."

Lady Swann stood. "Then let us go. Admiral Caron, will you accompany me?"

Not knowing what else to do, Lucia went.

CHAPTER ELEVEN

I look like a slutty cupcake," said Roseli as she considered her
reflection. The fluffy white creation was held up by little more than
the designer's optimism and clung to her modest breasts as best it could
before plunging low. It fit like a second skin until it reached her hips,
then it spread into a truly impressive number of white layers of skirts.

"Is there such a thing as a chaste cupcake?" asked Meredith, "I
mean, they are all baked to be eaten, so you know…"

The designer's assistant, a skinny woman with a beak-like nose,
who had brought the garment for the fitting made an offended sound.
"Begging Your Highness's pardon, but this dress is the height of
fashion. It will be the centerpiece of the spring show."

"Everyone will dress like promiscuous pastries?" said Roseli.
She'd had a long day, and it wasn't even noon yet.

"If you dislike the dress, Your Highness, I can take it back to Lady
Debonair and let her know your objections." It took a brave woman to
threaten royalty, but the assistant worked for a fashion mogul whose
rages were legendary. A mildly sarcastic princess held no terror.

"If you have an ounce of loyalty to the crown, Ms. Swift, you won't
pass on a word of what I have just said to your employer." Beatrice had
moved heaven and earth to get the famously difficult designer to lend
the dress on such short notice.

"You have my word, Your Highness." Damn if she didn't look
smug. "Would you like me to show the modifications we made to the
design for you?"

"Modifications?" If she was about to explain how they'd had to
shorten the dress and take in the bust, Roseli wasn't sure her pride
could take it.

"Yes, Lady Swann sent me to talk to the royal historian to look at your mother and grandmother's first wedding dresses in the palace archives so I could make sure this dress complied with all traditions."

"What are those?" Her mother had never told her about any wedding dress traditions, although that wasn't the sort of thing they talked about.

"The pockets."

"I get pockets?" That sounded good.

"Yes, one for the whiskey flask and one for the poison vial. Try not to get those confused. You'll wear a ceremonial dagger in an ornamental sheath on your hip, but you'll have a hidden slit in the dress so you can get to the concealed gun you'll wear in a thigh holster."

It was all Roseli could do not to laugh. Although her mother had insisted she take lessons as a girl, she was a terrible shot. "I wasn't aware that I was to be armed for the wedding."

"According to the palace historian, no crown princess or empress has ever wed without at least a blade at her side. It was traditionally a saber, but your mother had it scaled down to a dagger so she could move more freely to draw the gun if necessary. The whiskey flask was your grandmother's addition. The vial of poison was first carried by an empress five generations ago."

Roseli had a whole new respect for her grandmother. She might need the whiskey flask to get through the ceremony. She didn't want to think too much about what the poison was for. Legend had it that one of her many times great-grandmothers had rid herself of any husband who proved to be a disappointment on the wedding night. Fortunately, at least as far as she knew, women in her family had grown less murderous since.

She was about to ask how to get out of the white silk construction when the door to her dressing room opened, and Alexis came in. She froze when she saw Roseli in the dress. A sad smile graced her lips. "You will make a beautiful bride, my love."

Roseli could not find words. She felt tears at the edges of her eyes and fought them back. At least she wasn't wearing makeup and need not feared staining the dress. If it had been in her power, she would have given her hand to Alexis half a decade before.

Roseli had just taken a step toward Alexis when the door swung open so fast, it caught her in the back, sending her stumbling half a step. The guards that hurried in barely noticed. "Your Highness, there has been an incident. We must get you to a secure location."

❖

The safe room the guards had taken Lucia and Lady Swann to proved to be a small windowless room that consisted mostly of cabinets and a few chairs. There was also a tiny attached bathroom with a sink and toilet. It was bigger than most quarters Lucia had during her time in the navy, but she still felt trapped. Hiding was not what she did when faced with danger.

They had no sooner sat in two of the folding chairs than the door to the safe room opened, and a guard ushered in General Tate and Princess Roseli. Lucia found herself staring at Roseli in a full wedding dress. The ephemeral creation of silk clung to her slender frame, displaying so much decolletage that it could have been made on Calypso. The rest of the dress was done in what Lucia could only assume was a Delphian style, flowing over Roseli's legs into an entrancing sea of skirts.

She was barefoot, and her hair had come loose from its twist to tumble over her shoulders in dark brown ripples. It wasn't hard to guess she'd come from a fitting.

Lady Swann leaped up from her chair and went to her. "Darling."

Princess Roseli pulled her into her arms. "Bee, what's happened?"

"A poisoning attempt...at least, I think so. That or I've just horrifically traumatized a maid who was clumsy enough to spill some milk."

"What?"

"A woman I didn't recognize brought the tray when I was having tea with Admiral Caron. When I asked her if she was new, she said it was her first day," said Lady Swann.

"That was when you got suspicious, wasn't it?" asked Lucia.

"Yes," said Lady Swann. "No new members of staff are ever allowed within a royal apartment until they've been working in the palace for at least a year. That rule is supposed to lessen the chance of an assassin infiltrating the palace in that way. I still wasn't sure, so I asked the woman several security questions and called the guard when she couldn't answer."

"That was why you asked her about sugar cubes."

"Palace staff are regularly quizzed on a series of boring matters of form. All members of the royal family, dependents, and high-ranking members of staff have a list of questions they can ask to check if a person is a member of the staff. I'll make sure you're briefed on that list."

Her mother had enforced a similar system when she was a child. Today had not been the first poisoning attempt she had survived. She shouldn't have been so careless as to simply eat something set in front of her without checking it with a portable scanner. So many years onboard ships surrounded by trusted crew had left her careless.

There was a beep from a panel on the wall, and Officer Smith came on screen. "Your Highness, I have news. Lady Swann was right. The food and tea were poisoned with a deadly neurotoxin. We are currently questioning the woman we captured. I regret to inform you we have found the garroted body of one of the palace staff, Ms. Sonia Jones, in a broom closet."

Princess Roseli closed her eyes. "The head gardener's niece?"

"Yes."

"She just got married three months ago. Has anyone told her husband yet?"

"I have sent Officer Cane to tell him personally."

"Thank you. Are Julia and my family safe?"

"Yes. All members of the royal family have been secured, and Senator Veritas has been moved to a safe room in the Senate."

"Thank you, Officer Smith, please keep me informed."

"I will, Your Highness. Please remain where you are for now while we finish sweeping the palace."

As soon as the screen went blank, Princess Roseli slumped into a chair. She began to hyperventilate, covering her face. Lucia stood to go to her, but Lady Swann and General Tate got there first, so she sat back down. It was not her place to comfort Roseli. They barely knew each other. She still wanted to.

General Tate leaned over the back of Roseli's chair to hug her from behind. Lady Swann knelt, taking her hands. "Roseli, focus on me, my darling. Breathe in with me, breathe out with me, breathe in with me." She spoke gently and firmly and kept talking until Princess Roseli's breathing grew even.

"I could have lost you, Bee."

"I'm all right, darling. I'm here. I'm safe."

"I love you." Tears leaked from Princess Roseli's eyes. She was clutching Lady Swann's hands as if she was the last solid thing in the world.

"I know, darling, I love you, too." Lady Swann produced a tissue from somewhere on her person and cleaned Roseli's face.

General Tate kissed Princess Roseli's cheek, speaking too softly for Lucia to hear.

Lucia turned away, giving them the closest thing to privacy she could. A deep sense of loneliness and isolation settled over her. If Princess Roseli already had such intimacy and trust with her lovers, what room could be left for a wife? She'd been a fool to hope the night before. It was an arranged marriage. She'd be lucky if they managed mutual respect, much less anything else.

She closed her eyes. Why was she letting herself be so troubled? Perhaps it was just the shock of having nearly died. If Lady Swann hadn't stopped her, she'd have eaten that damn cucumber sandwich. Of all the ways to go, that wouldn't have been a dignified one. She'd faced her mortality a few days before when her ship was attacked, but that at least would have been a death she'd seen coming.

Princess Roseli's voice cut through her mental fog. "Forgive me. You and Lady Swann were the ones who nearly died, and I'm the one crying. How are you doing, Admiral Caron?"

Lucia turned back to find that Princess Roseli was now sitting up, her two lovers on either side of her. "I'm fine." She sought for something else to say. "How long do you think we will need to remain here?"

"Probably a few more hours, at least. My head guard is nearly as paranoid as my mother, although she has good reason to be."

"I'm sure we can find a way to amuse ourselves," said Lady Swann, standing. "First things first. Roseli, we need to get you out of that dress."

You could have heard a pin drop.

Lady Swann quickly clarified. "There are spare clothes in here, and if that dress gets wrinkled before the wedding, a certain designer will have me banned from all polite society, or at least, never sell me another dress for you ever again."

Lucia discreetly turned and faced the door as Lady Swann and General Tate helped Princess Roseli out of her wedding dress. Princess Roseli grumbled about the sheer number of stays, laces, and zippers involved. Eventually, they freed her, and she put on a spare shirt and pants from a cabinet.

Lady Swann carefully hung the dress from a light fixture as

General Tate retrieved a whiskey bottle, a couple of sealed packs of cookies and crackers, and a set of cards from another cabinet.

Princess Roseli sat and opened the pack of cards. "Admiral Caron, may I invite you to join us in our 'stuck in the safe room for a couple of hours' ritual?" Her good humor sounded forced, but Lucia was fine with that.

She did her best to return it. "Let me guess, you get drunk and play poker?"

"The winner gets the good chocolates. You're lucky Julia's not here. She usually wins," said Lady Swann.

"I'm still convinced she cheats somehow," said General Tate, reaching for the bottle of whiskey. She carefully examined the wax seal that covered the top of the bottle before cutting it open with a pocketknife and using the corkscrew from the same knife to pull out the cork.

"She does not. You just hate losing," said Lady Swann, picking up one of the plastic packages of cookies, checking its seal, and opening it. She held it out to Lucia.

Lucia took one. "I get the feeling that you're stuck in here often."

"A few times a year," admitted Princess Roseli. "It's usually a false alarm. The last time we had one, it turned out that the man sneaking into the Inner Chambers was just a member of the paparazzi trying to get photos."

"The time before that, it was Roxane's fault," said Lady Swann. "She gave her guards the slip during a ball and snuck out to go to a bar with some of her university friends. I don't think she realized her guards would think she'd been kidnapped and put the entire palace into lockdown. If that girl hadn't already had to face her mother, I'd have had words with her."

"You get the idea," said Princess Roseli. "On the upside, I'm getting better at my poker face."

Lady Swann patted her arm. "You're not, darling, but it is cute watching you try."

Princess Roseli looked to General Tate for support. General Tate just smiled warmly and dealt the cards.

When she was at last let out of the safe room, Lucia tried to return to the barracks, but her guards prevented her.

All of her good humor from drinking and playing cards in the safe room had rapidly vanished when the older of the guards, a burly woman in her forties, blocked her way, bowing curtly. "The barracks are not secure, Your Highness." There was just a hint of aggravation in her voice.

"I understand, but I still need to check on my crew." After everything they had been through, the sudden lockdown had surely been upsetting for them. She was willing to push past the guard if she had to.

The guard bowed again. "As an imperial guard, I lack the authority to forbid you from doing anything, Your Highness, but it is my duty to advise you on matters concerning your safety. If you wish to go to the barracks, I'll need to summon more guards to accompany you, and that will take time."

Lucia finally understood. The woman wasn't just throwing around her weight for the hell of it. "You'd have to call guards back on shift or from other duties, wouldn't you?"

That earned her a nod. "Yes, Your Highness. However, if you wish to send for any of your crew, they can join you in your rooms without additional security precautions."

"Very well. Please ask Lieutenant Charlotte Laurent to come as soon as possible."

❖

It took everything Charlotte had not to rush to embrace Lucia when a guard showed her into a small sitting room. Lucia was standing by the wall contemplating a bookshelf. Her sleeve was torn, and her dark hair was ruffled, but she was gloriously unharmed. Charlotte had been so afraid for her.

Lucia turned, smiling at her tiredly. "Lieutenant."

Charlotte saluted quickly. "Admiral Caron, are you all right? What happened? The guards wouldn't tell us anything besides that you were safe."

Lucia motioned for her to take a seat on the low couch. "I'm fine, lieutenant. There was an assassination attempt with poisoned food, but Lady Swann thwarted it, and the poisoner is in custody. How is the crew?"

Charlotte wanted to shake her and demand how she could speak so calmly after nearly dying. That was just the way Lucia was, though. She always kept it together, at least outwardly. Only when they were alone had Charlotte ever seen that mask begin to slip.

"Worried by the lockdown but otherwise fine. The quartermaster for the palace garrison came by to see if we needed anything. I asked him to procure several sets of cards, whiskey, and a fiddle. He delivered admirably. When I left, the crew was gambling and listening to Ensign Archer play a reel."

Lucia frowned. "What were they gambling with?"

"The quartermaster brought some candy. I divided it up evenly between the crew." None of the crew currently had any Delphian money or the ability to easily access their accounts on Calliope. Charlotte had spent the morning working with the Calliopean naval liaison office, coordinating temporary credit chips and shore-leave funds for the crew. After all they had been through, they deserved it.

"Well done. You handled the situation admirably," said Lucia.

"Thank you," Charlotte couldn't bear this any longer. She reached for Lucia's hand. "How are you, really?"

Just like that, the tension eased from Lucia's shoulders, and they weren't an admiral and a lieutenant anymore but the friends and sometimes lovers they had been for years. "A bit shaken, nothing more. You needn't worry."

"Let me help you feel better." She drew up their joined hands. With tender slowness, she tugged off Lucia's glove and brought her lips to bare skin.

Lucia shivered, want clear in her eyes but she hesitated. "This isn't...we don't know if we are unobserved."

"To hell with them. You need this. You always do after a brush with death."

"You're right." Lucia pulled her into a hungry kiss.

Charlotte wanted the kiss to last forever, rank, looming war, and Lucia's engagement be damned.

It took them three tries to find the bedroom. The first door they tried led into a bathroom and the second a linen cupboard, but the third yielded a simply furnished room with a decent-sized bed.

Charlotte stepped into the room and began undressing with quick, precise movements. She tugged off her gloves and then shed her jacket and pulled her shirt over her head. As she was reaching behind herself to unclasp her bra, she realized Lucia was watching her with rapt attention from the doorway.

"Like what you see?" she asked.

"Hard not to." Lucia closed the distance between them. She reached out to cup one of her small breasts, caressing a nipple.

Charlotte shivered with need and kissed her. "You're overdressed."

Lucia stepped back to shed her clothing, taking her time to place her shirt and pants over the back of a chair.

Impatient as she was, Charlotte didn't mind the chance to appreciate Lucia's pleasing form, long limbs, and lean muscles. When Lucia was naked, Charlotte motioned her to sit on the edge of the bed and knelt on the carpeted floor in front of her. She kissed the inside of Lucia's thigh before using her fingers to part her labia. She licked and pressed directly with the tip of her tongue, sometimes sucking with her lips, working with a hurried precision leaned from years of hasty liaisons.

Lucia tangled her right hand in Charlotte's hair, pulling lightly and drawing an appreciative gasp out of her. Charlotte loved when she did that, the slight edge of pain and the feeling that she was causing Lucia to lose herself to pleasure. She sped up her ministrations, and soon, Lucia was shuddering with an orgasm.

When Charlotte raised her head, Lucia drew her up onto the bed, working her way down her body, kissing and nipping lightly, pausing to suck on a nipple. She needed Lucia too much to wait. "Please!"

Lucia rubbed at her clit with three fingers until her moans grew desperate and then pressed two fingers into her eager body, fucking her steadily. She always knew how to touch her, what she needed. Charlotte let the pleasure wash over her, covering her mouth to stifle her cry as she came.

Lucia slowed the movements, easing her down from her orgasm and then stretched out beside her. "I think you needed this, too."

"Yes." All the fear and uncertainty of the last few days faded away. She wanted to stay like this, alone with Lucia, happy and sated. She reached to caress her cheek, looking into those hazel eyes. There was warmth there and fondness but not the depth of feeling she sought.

Lucia looked away, and Charlotte let her hand fall, sitting up. "I should get back to the barracks, check on the crew."

Lucia laid a hand on her arm. "No rush. From what you said earlier, I'm sure they're fine."

The temptation was too great. She lay back down, resting her head on Lucia's shoulder. "All right." After a moment, she said, "I was so worried about you when the lockdown started."

"I'm sorry I worried you."

"Don't be sorry, just keep yourself safe."

Even after Lucia's breaths grew even with sleep, she could not find the will to leave the warmth of her arms. She would never have Lucia's heart, but she had this, and it had always been enough. Until it wasn't.

She thought of the letter of resignation she had written but never sent. The file was lost now, along with everything else aboard the *Intrepid*. She had intended to leave the navy at the end of her current term of service and go back to Calliope to manage her mother's import business.

She couldn't walk away now, though, not when Lucia was alone in a foreign court with no one to watch her back. Lucia would never ask, never admit she needed an ally, but Charlotte would find a way to stay and protect her.

CHAPTER TWELVE

Julia woke in a cold sweat to the sound of Roseli snoring in her ear. Roseli had one arm thrown across her and was snuggled up against her. The rest of the bed was empty. Alexis and Beatrice had already departed.

As soon as Julia had been released from the safe room at the Senate, she had rushed to the palace. It had been a relief to find Roseli whole and well, even if the guards had already told her as much.

Beatrice's brush with death had been a cold reminder that being a royal paramour was not without dangers. Two years before, northern separatists had tried to kidnap Roseli's lovers to force the crown to release several of their imprisoned members. They had never gotten close to Alexis. She was too often surrounded by other members of the military.

Julia still had nightmares about the men who'd tried to drag her kicking and screaming into a black car outside her office building. She'd gotten free, although her wrist had been sprained in the struggle. One of her guards had been shot but not fatally.

Beatrice hadn't been as lucky. Roseli hadn't named her as a royal paramour yet, and she'd had no guards to protect her. She had been tricked into getting into a car, thinking it had been sent by the palace. The Imperial Intelligence Service had found and rescued her within hours. As far as Julia knew, Beatrice had been relatively unharmed, at least physically, but it wasn't the sort of thing the two of them ever talked about.

After that day, none of them had ever been allowed to go anywhere without at least one imperial guard. Julia still missed being able to run through the capital's central park without an escort or to just have a cup of coffee alone at a café.

She closed her eyes against the warm morning light, but she dared not drift back into sleep. Shortly before dawn, she had dreamed of the black car again, except this time, it had been Roseli being dragged into it, and she had been helpless to save her.

She slipped from Roseli's arms, careful not to wake her, and went to shower. On her way back to bed, she noticed her coat was buzzing, and against her better judgement; she took out her tablet. She had a high priority message from her mother. It read simply, "Come to breakfast at the house."

No question about if she was safe, not even an invitation, just a summons. That had always been her mother's way. Julia considered ignoring it, except that would only make things harder in the end. She loved her mother, but her mother's level of scheming put her political machinations to shame.

She called for a car and was soon walking up the steps of her family's townhouse. The exterior was the picture of dignified restraint, all white walls and square windows. The only hint of the wealth was the two white columns that held up the front entrance.

A servant opened the heavy wooden door before she could knock and ushered her into the lavish hall beyond. The Veritases had been one of the first families to rebuild after the great fire two centuries before. Julia's great-great-great-grandmother had been a fan of baroque revival architecture. Every single bit of wall and ceiling was painted with mythological scenes or embellished with gold leaf.

Had anyone decorated in such a way now, it would have been considered tacky, but when such architecture was inherited, it was the height of class and refinement. Even the thick red carpet that ran along the hall floor had been restored several times at far greater cost than buying a new carpet.

A servant led her up the stairs, down a hallway, up another set of stairs, and at last to the rooftop greenhouse. It was built in the Calliopean style, with fountains instead of a reflecting pool and a lush jungle of potted trees and plants. The ceiling was a beautiful work of iron and glass. Her grandmother had built the greenhouse for her grandfather when he'd grown homesick for Calliope. As a child, Julia had loved nothing more than playing hide-and-seek with her brothers among the ferns. It had seemed a magical kingdom of verdant greenery. If only life could have stayed that simple.

Julia found her mother at the center of the greenhouse in a straight-backed chair at a high table, sipping a cup of tea while reading a tablet.

She set it down at the sound of Julia's footsteps. They had the same sleek red hair, and although she was well into her sixth decade, the elegant twist of her mother's hair showed only a few streaks of gray. While men on Delphi often dyed their hair to hide the signs of aging, women, especially those in positions of power, seldom did.

Her mother had a lean, vulpine face she painted sparingly. While her dress was a muted ash color, the cut and silk were of the finest quality. At her ears hung two teardrop pearls worth a small fortune each. "Julia, dear, so good to see you."

Julia went to kiss her on the cheek and took a seat. The table was laid with fruit, egg-white omelets, and green tea. None were things she liked.

Her mother didn't waste any time. "How are things at the palace?"

"I imagine you already know," said Julia. She wasn't sure how many sources inside the palace her mother had, but she had to have at least one close to Roseli. The last time Julia and Roseli had argued, Julia had barely left the palace before her mother had called her.

She'd originally suspected Roseli's secretary and had her finances investigated. Aside from buying large numbers of toys for her cats, she had no vices and wasn't spending above her means. Julia had been forced to conclude that, while odd, Ms. Cooper was genuinely loyal to Roseli and not selling her secrets. Julia's current theory was that it was one of the maids or a junior guard.

Her mother sipped her tea. "Yes, but I do like hearing things confirmed. Was there truly an assassination attempt against Princess Lucia?"

"If it were not for Lady Swann's tendency to notice whenever anything is out of place, they'd both be dead."

"She's an astute one." Her mother set down her teacup. "If you were half as sly as her, I wouldn't worry about you so much. Julia, you must be careful."

Julia stiffened. Why did her mother have to always have to unfavorably compare her to others? "Don't you dare tell me to stay away from the palace for my safety."

"I wish I could tell you to do just that, especially as I have good information that the poisoner had help from inside the palace, but I can't. If you distance yourself from the princess now, while everything is changing, you could lose her."

Julia ignored the relationship advice in favor of the other

revelation. "What do you mean the assassin had help from inside the palace?"

"There is no way the poisoner could have gained access to the west wing of the palace, much less the rooms of the heir-apparent's fiancée, without that day's security codes. The empress's security forces have not been able to determine who it was or torture any names out of the luckless assassin yet."

Julia narrowed her eyes. "How do you know all that?"

"Dear, it's my business to know this sort of thing. Information is power. Now, there is a matter I want to discuss with you. To what degree do you believe the empress listens to her daughter's counsel?"

"About as much as you listen to me."

"Regardless, the empress has begun to include her in her military council. Surely, she lets her speak sometimes. I want you to find an opportunity to remind Princess Roseli of our family's mines and foundries."

"Why?"

"Because with the way hostilities are going, the navy will soon need steel to repair and build more spaceships. I've stepped up production, so we'll be ready. We provided half of the steel during the last war, but new mines have opened in the north since then. We must secure a royal contract, and to do that, we need to be on the empress's mind."

"I have said before that I will not use my relationship with Princess Roseli for our family's gain."

"What else are relationships for?"

Julia almost said love but stopped herself. It was an old argument and one she had never won. At a certain point, she'd just stopped trying.

"I'm not asking you to trick her or act against her interests. The crown needs steel. Why shouldn't it come from us? You look after her interests in the Senate, do you not? Shouldn't she do the same for you in the palace?"

Julia did not answer.

"Think on the matter." After a pause, she added, "You will be careful, won't you? You've still got the poison detecting device I gave you?"

"I do." Just not with her.

"And are you using it?"

She wasn't. It was just too awkward to poke her food with a little pen-shaped device during meals. She probably should, especially considering Beatrice had nearly been poisoned.

"Use it."

"Yes, Mother."

Early that morning, Lucia had woken up in an unfamiliar bed with Charlotte curled up against her, breath even and deep in sleep. She knew she should send her back to the barracks before the rest of the palace woke up. But lying there in the dim light that filtered through the curtains, Lucia couldn't bring herself to care. It was just too comforting to have Charlotte's warm body in her arms. She was not in the practice of studying sleeping lovers, but something about the moment lent itself to quiet reflection.

Charlotte was a beautiful woman. In her waking hours, sharp angles defined her face, from high cheekbones to her narrow chin. In sleep, all that relaxed. Her dark hair was loose and tangled, cascading about the white pillow. She must have been having a pleasant dream because her full lips turned up in a smile that softened the rest of her features.

Lucia had seldom seen her smile. There was a healing red line across her nose from the evacuation that was likely to scar. Her face was still clear of wrinkles, but Lucia noticed for the first time that there were a few gray hairs at her temples.

Had those always been there? She ought to have been too young. Were the graying hairs from stress or just genetics? Lucia had once met an aunt of Charlotte's, the captain of a small ship, the *Aquila*. She hadn't been old, but her hair had been nearly white.

That woman was certainly dead. The *Aquila* had fallen in the Battle of White Moon. Charlotte hadn't said a thing about her aunt's death. They never talked about that kind of thing. That had been what she wanted, but had it been what Charlotte wanted?

The light outside the window was growing brighter. She needed to get up. She tried to ease away from Charlotte without waking her, but her eyes snapped open.

"Lucia?" She only called her by her given name when they were alone. Lucia had always done the same. When they were alone, she was Charlotte; on the bridge, she was Lieutenant Laurent.

"I'm going to check on the crew. Who knows what they got up to during an entire night without a superior officer?" Hopefully, not much. The crew had all been on their best behavior so far.

"I'll come with you."

Soon enough, they were dressed and on their way to the barracks. When they reached the parade grounds, they encountered a group of about twelve Delphian soldiers at fencing practice.

Several members of her crew had wandered out to watch. All officers in the Calliopean navy were taught fencing in the academy. Enlisted sailors were never given formal training in it, but it was a popular sport. On the *Intrepid*, a favorite pastime was watching officers spar in the ship's small gymnasium.

As they drew closer, Lucia heard General Tate's clear voice giving instructions from behind a white mask. She was fencing with a man a good bit taller and heavier than herself. "Lieutenant Mathers, keep your arm up. Stop just lunging, wait until you see an opening. No, not like that. You've got reach on me, use it, stop hunching."

A whistle blew, and all the sparing fencers drew apart, tugging off their masks to gasp at the warm morning air.

General Tate was beaming. "Well done. You're improving wonderfully. Keep up your practice."

The young man saluted and went to get a drink of water. General Tate seemed to notice Princess Lucia and bowed deeply. "Admiral Caron, good morning."

"General Tate." She returned the bow with a Calliopean one. She was relatively sure that in the palace pecking order, she technically outranked her, but she remained uncertain of exactly what that meant for the depth of bows.

"Would you care to join us?"

Lucia almost refused, but the chance to do something physical after days of inactivity was far too tempting to turn down. She had asked General Tate to spar with her sometime, after all. She just had to hope this would be a sparring match and not a duel. Even with protective gear, épées could do damage. "Yes, I'd like that."

Someone brought her a fencing jacket, a mask, gloves, and an épée. She was relieved to find that the sword had a smooth French grip rather than a pistol grip, which would have been molded to fit the contours of a hand.

Lieutenant Laurent helped Lucia secure her fencing mask, as she had a thousand times before. Thus outfitted, Lucia weighed the sword in her hand. It was a cheap practice blade, and the balance was poor but would serve well enough.

"You're left-handed," commented General Tate, who had been watching her with interest.

"Yes. In girlhood, it meant I got ink on my hand when my father insisted I learn traditional penmanship, but in fencing, it gives me a slight edge."

"Was your offer to spar genuine? Or do you just want to run drills?" asked General Tate. She sounded hopeful. Lucia couldn't see her face behind her mask, but she got the feeling she was smiling.

Lucia was smiling, too. This was going to be fun. She wanted to see if General Tate was as tough as she acted. "Yes."

"Varcian rules?"

"Why not? Shall we go to three taps?"

"Sounds good. Is it all right if my secretary judges? She has a good eye."

"Yes."

They saluted with their blades and waited for the judge to call for them to begin.

❖

While Roseli was to be married in a matter of days, that did not change the fact that she was still the heir apparent. Ever since she had reached her majority, her mother had included her in all major decisions of state.

Perhaps "including" was too strong a word. The empress had her sit silently at her side during the military, economic, and government meetings. Afterward, when they were alone, her mother would ask her what she thought they should do. Most of the time, her mother would say her answer was wrong and go into great detail about why.

Over the years, Roseli had gotten better at it, understanding her mother's decision-making processes so she could give the desired answer. This usually resulted in little more than a curt nod of acknowledgment. Once, several months ago, her mother had even said that one of her economic suggestions was worth trying.

Roseli was not surprised, therefore, to receive a reminder that she was to attend a meeting later that morning, after she'd awakened. She was, however, surprised to find that her mother had included a note.

Bring your fiancée. Try to keep her in line this time.

She went out into the hall and had just raised her hand to knock on the outer door of Lucia's quarters when a guard informed her that the princess had gone to check on her crew in the barracks. Roseli glanced at her watch, frowning. Walking all the way to the east side of the palace and back would take some time. As far as she knew, Lucia didn't have a wrist device she could call. She'd need to get Meredith to see to that. She considered asking the guards to call their colleagues and pass on the message, but that seemed too impersonal. Lucia deserved a proper warning before facing her mother again.

She set out, walking at a quick clip with Meredith and two guards in tow. While she always had to be presentable, on days where she had no public appearances, she preferred to wear simple black trousers and a nice silk blouse. It was easier to move when not encumbered by countless layers of skirts.

Several hallways brought her out into the warm air of a beautiful morning. She could hear cheering and laughter from across the parade ground. She caught sight of a circle of soldiers from the palace regiment wearing fencing jackets, along with nearly all the surviving members of Lucia's crew currently housed in the barracks.

At the center of the wide circle were two white-jacketed figures. Roseli had never had the hand-eye coordination or the reflexes required for fencing, but she knew enough about it to appreciate a truly impressive match.

As she drew closer, she saw that the fencers were both women. Their identities became clear when Roseli heard a sailor yell, "Get her, Admiral!"

In response, one soldier from the palace garrison called out, "Watch your left side, General Tate!"

Roseli froze. Surely, Alexis hadn't challenged Lucia to a duel. She wouldn't do something that foolish. Would she?

Despite the fencing gear, they looked like they were fighting in earnest, darting and jabbing with impressive speed. How could she stop them? Women in soap operas usually flung themselves dramatically between the fighters, but that seemed like a good way to get stabbed.

Officer Smith stepped to her side and said, "Don't worry, Your Highness, it's only a sparring match."

"I see." That was a relief. Now that she no longer feared she was watching a diplomatic incident unfolding, the sight of them in motion was utterly spellbinding.

Alexis was taller, but Lucia was faster and had more strength to work with. Lucia scored a quick tap on Alexis's side. "Tap," called Alexis.

"Point to Princess Lucia," said Alexis's secretary, Lieutenant Thistle, who appeared to be judging the match. "Next point decides the match."

They saluted and sprung back into motion. The match ended quickly. Seemingly bolstered by her recent success, Lucia became overconfident. She lunged, leaving herself open. Alexis slipped her blade underneath Lucia's and scored a tap on her arm.

"Tap."

"Point to General Tate. Match to General Tate, two to one."

The Delphians cheered, and the Calliopeans looked mildly disappointed. Alexis and Lucia took off their masks and saluted with their blades. Roseli went to join them, offering Alexis a nod and Lucia a bow. She wished she could hug Alexis in greeting or even kiss her, but she knew that would embarrass her. Alexis was not one for public displays of affection at the best of times, much less in front of her soldiers.

"That was a fine match," she told them. "Admiral Caron, I hate to take you away from your exercise, but the empress has asked us to attend a meeting with her military advisors in an hour and a half."

"The empress wants me there?" she asked incredulously.

"I wouldn't expect too much of it. She usually just wants me to sit there and listen. Likely, she'll expect the same of you."

"I'll go make myself presentable." Lucia bowed once more and set off toward her quarters.

Roseli and Alexis were left alone on the practice field as the Calliopean sailors drifted back into the barracks, and the Delphian officers gathered up the fencing equipment. Alexis's hair was ruffled from her fencing mask, and her skin was flushed. Seeing her like that made Roseli want her desperately. "Are you free right now?"

Alexis looked back at her with heated eyes but sighed regretfully. "I should get to the office. There are supply requisition forms due this afternoon."

"You'll need to shower first, won't you?" asked Roseli. She tried not to sound too hopeful.

To her delight, Alexis smiled in understanding. "Do you think there is time?"

"Let's find out."

CHAPTER THIRTEEN

A hasty walk later, they were in Roseli's bathroom, a trail of clothes left behind them. They didn't bother to turn on the water when they stepped into the shower stall. Roseli reached for Alexis, pulling down her mouth to kiss her. When they broke apart breathlessly, Roseli pressed her against the cool tile wall, tasting the salt on her neck and breasts. She smelled like spring grass and exertion, her sweat so newly dried that it was still pleasant. Alexis grabbed her and turned them, pushing Roseli against the wall, her mouth claiming hers.

Roseli loved it when Alexis was like this. She was usually so careful and gentle, but if Roseli could catch her at just the right time, there was a fierce, almost animalistic side to her.

"Did you enjoy the match, Princess?" Alexis nipped her ear lightly, cupping one of her breasts and caressing the nipple.

"You were magnificent." Roseli knew not to say it, but she'd also thought the same of Lucia. The sight of them crossing blades had been one of the most utterly captivating things she'd ever seen, worthy of a scene in one of the lurid romance novels she adored reading.

"Was I now?" asked Alexis, who, for all her dignity, was not immune to flattery.

"Yes."

"Did watching me fight make you want me?" This was probably the closest to dirty talk she would ever get.

"Oh yes."

Alexis gently pinched the nipple between her fingers. "How much?"

"So much."

"Use your words, beautiful."

"Please, don't tease, I need you too much." That was also about as close as Roseli got to dirty talk with her.

Alexis slipped a hand between her thighs. "You're not kidding."

"Please."

Alexis obliged, pressing two fingers into her trembling body.

Roseli moaned. "Yes, yes."

Alexis rocked her hand in quick, forceful motions.

"Yes, harder, yes!" Roseli was glad of the metal railing to her right because if she couldn't have thrown out her hand to grab it, she'd likely have lost the ability to stand.

Alexis kissed down her neck and then about halfway across the top of one of Roseli's breasts before nipping.

"Ah," was all Roseli could manage.

Alexis bit hard, just above the nipple, making Roseli cry out at the intensity of the feeling. She was so close. She couldn't bear it anymore. She reached down to find her clit and press hard as Alexis continued to move her fingers inside her. She came with a cry.

Alexis saw Roseli through her orgasm and then helped ease her down onto the rubber bathroom mat. Roseli was breathless, but she wanted Alexis too much to rest. She pressed a hand against Alexis's shoulder, pushing her back against the other side of the bathroom wall.

"Roseli?"

"I want you." Roseli looked up from her kneeling position to smile at Alexis before she used an elbow to nudge her legs open. She found her clit with her tongue, and when she pressed the flat of it against that sensitive bundle of nerves, Alexis nearly howled.

Roseli repeated the motion.

"Inside, too," Alexis said with a gasp.

Roseli brought up her right hand to press two fingers into Alexis as she steadily sucked and licked at her clit. Alexis didn't last long. She came without much of a sound, but her entire body tensed and then relaxed. She sank to sit beside Roseli on the shower floor.

Roseli crawled into her lap and kissed her. Alexis pulled her as close as she could, their naked bodies flush against each other.

"I love, I love you so damn much," said Alexis.

There were other words Roseli knew she wasn't saying, words she couldn't say. "Mine" wasn't a thing the lover of a princess could ever declare.

"I love you, too," said Roseli. "I always will." She ran a hand down Alexi's side, feeling the roughness of the scar tissue there. Alexis never talked about the last war, but the cost of it was written on her body. Now another war was coming, and Roseli was afraid for her.

Alexis was one of the most senior ranking generals with field experience. She would be called to the front. This time, she might come back with worse than scars or not at all. Why should she have to go? If Lucia could be kept safe on Delphi, why couldn't Alexis? She could ask her mother to have Alexis appointed to a domestic defense position and send some other general into battle.

Roseli's waterproof wrist strap beeped, pulling her back from her thoughts.

Alexis kissed her cheek. "We should shower. You don't want to be late to the defense council."

Roseli rested her forehead against Alexis, not wanting to move, not wanting to say anything. What had she been thinking? She couldn't go behind Alexis's back to keep her on Delphi, and Alexis would never agree to let others fight in her place.

Alexis frowned. "Roseli?"

"I…" She would not cry, not now. "I'm scared. I don't want there to be a war. I don't want you to go fight."

"I don't either, my love, but it is my duty."

"I wish it wasn't." So much for not crying.

Alexis cupped her face with a callused palm. "I swear by all the gods, whatever is to come, so long as I have breath in my body, I will always find my way back to you."

It was the possibility of Alexis not having breath in her body that worried Roseli. She didn't say that, just kissed her.

Her wrist strap beeped again. She wanted to ignore it, but showing up to a security council late and smelling like sex was not a good idea. Alexis helped her to her feet, and they showered together quickly.

❖

Lucia arrived at the meeting before the empress or Roseli. She made the acquaintance of the three members of the empress's military council: the head of the army, General Sharp; the head of the royal space navy, Admiral Heart; and the head of the joint intelligence agency, Director Barker.

Admiral Heart was a white-haired older man with an impressive handlebar mustache that had not been fashionable for at least a generation. Despite his unassuming manner, Lucia knew him to be a brilliant naval tactician. He'd retired from the field before she'd had her first command, but she'd studied his battles as a girl. In contrast, General Sharp was only in her late forties, and her braid was still black. Her face bore none of the shrapnel scars so common to soldiers, but she had a watchful and direct nature that suggested she had seen combat.

Director Barker was of an age with Admiral Heart. She wore a well-cut dark suit and twisted back her white hair in a no-nonsense bun. She was polite, professional, and Lucia had the distinct impression she should never cross her unless she wanted her throat slit in her sleep.

As they waited, Director Barker brought her up to speed on several matters.

Roseli arrived shortly before her mother and sat beside Lucia. She looked rather flushed, almost as if she'd run to the meeting. Her hair was wet from a recent shower and smelled pleasantly of lavender shampoo. Lucia wondered why she had taken the time to shower and almost made herself late when she hadn't been fencing.

The empress arrived, and the meeting began with a summarization of troop and ship locations. It didn't take General Sharp long to account for the troops. They were technically still in peacetime, which meant that most of Delphi's ground troops, aside from those still stationed at military bases in some of their more far-flung outposts and colonies, had come home to Delphi.

That seemed sensible to Lucia. Ground troops only made sense in specific circumstances. Much of the last war had been fought with intense ground combat on the surface of lunar colonies deemed by both sides to be too valuable to destroy from orbit, never mind the human cost.

Admiral Heart used a series of three-dimensional images that appeared above the table to give his report. A younger, and likely far more tech-savvy, ensign advanced and moved the images. Three-fourths of the Delphian navy was still guarding colonies and patrolling the farther-flung borders of Delphian-controlled space. The rest had returned and were now docked in several orbital space stations. A few of the flagships were too large for that and remained in a self-sustaining orbit of the planet. That troubled Lucia. Even during the war, her mother had always kept half her fleet close to Calliope.

None of this information came as a surprise to Lucia.

Apparently, it wasn't for the empress either. She made no attempt to hide her yawn. "So all of our ships are still where we left them."

"Yes, Your Majesty."

"You couldn't have led with that, Admiral?"

"Protocol dictates that..."

A slight raise of one of the empress's eyebrows silenced him. The effect was rather reminiscent of a rattlesnake giving fair warning.

Admiral Heart said quickly, "I will endeavor to be briefer in the future."

"What about the Terra Nuevans? Where are their ships?"

Director Barker stood. Beside her, a woman with an eagle pin on her jacket took over the holographic table. The image shifted, now showing primarily red dots against a new star chart.

"Based on our long-range sensors, border patrols, and intelligence network, we believe half their fleet is still close to their planet, a quarter is guarding their colonies, and another quarter is patrolling their borders and stationed on the hidden lunar bases."

The empress tapped the table. "How recent is your information?"

Director Barker shifted uncomfortably. "Our knowledge of the patrol ships is likely no less than a day out of date. That of the colonies is updated roughly every three days. As for the main fleet..." She frowned. "We've had significant disruptions with our spy networks on Terra Nueva and its outlying colonies. We haven't had a new message for over a week."

Lucia was a sailor and used to taking orders, but she was also an admiral. The Terra Nuevans never just went silent. If their movements went dark, they were planning an attack. She'd seen it often enough in the war.

"You mean our spies were likely found and are being tortured to death as we speak." The empress was not a woman to mince words.

"Not all of them. Radio silence is what they are trained to do when there is a breach in the network. When it is safe, the survivors will begin sending information to us again."

The empress shook her head in disapproval. "Then, for all we know, the Terra Nuevan fleet is heading en masse toward our borders."

"Our sensors would pick them up there," insisted Director Barker.

"Unless they were just outside our sensors and somehow avoiding our long-range patrols."

"That is theoretically possible," admitted Director Barker, "but unlikely. Your Majesty, you commissioned the newer, long-range observation satellites yourself. You know exactly how good they are."

"Which is better than what we used to have but still not good enough." The empress let that hang in the air and then looked to her left, where Roseli and Lucia were sitting.

"What about you, Princess Lucia? What do you think the Terra Nuevans are doing?"

Lucia started and then sat up straighter. "You're genuinely asking for my advice on naval matters after demanding that I resign my commission?" Everything inside her was a complex tangle of rage and hope. Her heart was beating so fast, her pulse echoed in her ears.

"Yes. You were an admiral, were you not?"

Lucia had to fight not to grind her teeth. "I still am, for a few more days, at least."

The empress continued to look at her like an unimpressed teacher. "Commissioned or not, I assume your brain still works. Just because I don't want you to get your fool self killed in battle doesn't mean I think you're useless. You are Admiral Valdez's daughter, are you not?"

"Of that, there can be no doubt."

"Then I hope she taught you a fraction of what she knew. She was the sharpest naval mind of her generation. However, if you're just a yelling fool like your father, let me know now, and I'll spare you these responsibilities."

"My father is no fool," said Lucia, her patience wearing thin.

"He is in military and naval matters."

"Mother," snapped Roseli. "Do you think this is the time?"

The empress spared Roseli a glance. "Is there ever a bad time to be cynical about the capabilities of other monarchs?" With a shrug, she looked back at Lucia. "Are you going to just glare at me, or do you have a theory?"

Lucia took a breath before she spoke. She did, in fact, have a theory. "I think they are on the verge of a major attack against Delphi. Their fleet may be even closer than we think. Why else would they have risked openly attacking my ship and escort if they weren't ready for war?"

"To keep you from marrying my daughter and bringing her a lovely dowry of ships?"

"Well, yes, but I think that attack may have been an act of opportunity to sow discord more than anything else. I believe they have been gearing up for war since they began constructing hidden bases in the neutral zone."

The empress's eyebrow rose again. "Do you know something I don't?"

"Not exactly. As an admiral in the field, and thus at high risk of capture, I have never had access to any classified information that wasn't essential for my mission." She hadn't known about the hidden Terra Nuevan bases until speaking with Director Barker, and that knowledge was a revelation. This was worse than she had imagined.

Lucia lowered her voice. "But I've read all my mother's notes and journals more times than I can count. She was convinced that during the war, the reason the Terra Nuevans kept trying so hard to establish bases on out-of-the-way shithole moons and asteroids was because they wanted a midway resupply point between them and the frontier."

"That is possible," said Admiral Heart. "I always wondered why they were willing to sacrifice so many resources and lives for bases that were of limited military significance, especially when they were stretched so thin near the end of the war."

Lucia continued, "My mother believed that if the Terra Nuevans had ever held Kepler and other small terraformed moons that circle lifeless planets, they'd have used them as a place to refuel and supply their ships so they could stay out in space longer. If they achieved that, they'd gather their navy for one massive attack on either Calliope or Delphi without bothering with the smaller colonies in between."

"That's quite a theory, especially considering that the Terra Nuevans never did that in the last war," said the empress.

"No, but they have hidden bases in the neutral zone now," said Lucia.

"There aren't enough of them to stage a major operation," said Director Barker.

"And you think you've identified them all?"

"Probably not," admitted Director Barker. "Our intelligence does have limits."

The empress turned to Lucia. "What would you advise me to do?"

"Call as many ships as you can back to Delphi and put all that are currently in orbit on high alert."

"You wouldn't advise a counterattack?"

"Not until my father's ships arrive. Your fleet is too small to split without leaving Delphi vulnerable. The Terra Nuevans already have the first-mover advantage, and we must not compound that by rash actions."

The empress smiled thinly. "It seems your mother taught you well. I'll give your advice some consideration." She turned back to the other people at the table. "We will not officially declare war until we have better means to wage it, but from this moment forward, we begin mobilization. General Sharp, Admiral Heart, the time has come to call our reserve soldiers and sailors back to active duty."

❖

After the meeting, Roseli and Lucia returned to Roseli's quarters for lunch. They ate at a low table in the courtyard's collecting pool. The warm spring air was pleasant, and fragrant white flowers bloomed on the vines that wrapped the marble columns. Several pigeons were busy bathing in an ornamental bird bath beside the pool. A little black cat stalked the potted plants, eyeing the pigeons but biding her time.

The meal was simpler than most Lucia had been served on Delphi outside of the barracks. Servants brought ham and cheese sandwiches and a spinach salad. There was a pitcher of iced black tea sweetened with sugar. Lucia thought it odd to put ice in a perfectly good black tea, but at least the Delphians didn't spice their tea as the Mycenaeans did. She asked for water, and a servant brought it. Lucia found she had little appetite, despite the food being some of the most familiar since she'd arrived.

When they were alone, save for the cooing pigeons, Roseli said. "I think that went well. My mother listened to you."

"She did?"

"Trust me, that's not something that happens often."

"I get that impression."

Roseli's face fell. "I thought you'd be happier. You want to be a naval advisor, don't you?"

"Yes," said Lucia quickly.

"But?" For someone who had known her for so little time, Roseli was getting remarkably good at reading her.

"It is nothing."

"Talk to me."

Lucia was not sure how much she should share. They were practically strangers, but Roseli was looking at her with such concern that she had to say something. She supposed intimacy had to begin somewhere. "I'm glad to be helping with military decisions. It's just, I never expected to be doing it on a foreign planet. Throughout my childhood, my mother constantly tutored me on naval and military strategy. She intended me to be my older brother's naval advisor when he ascended the throne. I swore that I would always protect my father and brothers."

"Didn't she tutor your brothers as well?"

"A little but not as intensely as me. She was Varcian to the core and never believed that men could be good military tacticians, even after serving with many. She thought it was a woman's place to lead on the battlefield and for men to follow orders."

Roseli paused in reaching for her glass. "You don't believe that, do you?"

"Considering that my father thought women ill-suited to combat, I learned to be dubious of the prejudices of both my parents early in life. Gender is irrelevant to what makes a fine soldier or commander."

Something brushed against her leg, and she nearly startled out of her chair. She looked down to find a pair of oval-shaped blue eyes looking up at her in a soot-black face of fur. She offered her hand for the cat to sniff, and it bonked her with its forehead.

"I think Dahlia likes you," said Roseli.

"I like her, too. She reminds me of my Sasha, except Sasha's fur was white." She scratched behind those incredibly soft-looking ears. The cat made a low purr.

"Childhood cat?" asked Roseli.

"Sasha was the ship's cat on the *Intrepid*. All Calliopean ships have at least one for luck." In her mind's eye, Lucia could see the fat white cat curled up in her lap and feel her purring. The realization that the animal was dead crashed over her. Had Sasha died along with many of her crew when half the ship had lost life support, or had the cat survived and hidden only to die as the ship broke up in orbit? She had failed so many people, and somehow, the fact that she hadn't even spared a thought for the cat was too much. She kept petting the living animal, hoping that Roseli wouldn't see the dampness that had come to the edge of her eyes.

Roseli's voice brought her back to the present. "One of the palace's other cats, Dahlia's sister, just had kittens. You can have one if you like."

"I get a cat of my own?" It was easier to joke than to say anything else. "I don't have to share yours?"

Roseli laughed. "If you want one. You'll see plenty of Dahlia, regardless. She seems to consider everything in this corner of the palace to be her territory. The guards said she was constantly in and out of their break room, even if none of them could remember letting her in. You have those rooms now, so I'm sure she will come to visit you there, especially when we open the door between our quarters."

"I've been meaning to ask you about that."

"The door? It connects the hallways. I think a bookshelf just needs to be moved."

Lucia looked up. "I meant the question a bit less literally."

"Ah." Roseli's face heated. "I suppose at first, we knock."

"And how often does one of us do that?"

"Um…I don't know. There is probably some awful etiquette guide on the subject in the palace library, but maybe it's better if we just figure it out for ourselves."

Lucia nodded. "That's reasonable."

"Your rooms are your space. You never have to let me into them at all."

"And yours?"

Roseli took a moment before replying. "I'm not sure. I think we need some neutral space. Maybe that should be my sitting room and this courtyard, especially since you don't have a courtyard."

"And your bedroom?"

"That is my space…unless I invite you there."

"Will you be doing that often?" She deployed her best grin, combined with a slight tilt of her head that she knew produced a flattering effect.

"If you want me to." There was no mistaking the warmth of desire in her voice.

Lucia could have pushed her advantage then, maybe stolen another kiss, but she needed answers. "Even when you've got three lovers to keep you busy?"

Roseli got a nervous look, biting at the edge of her lip. "I will do everything I can not to neglect you."

"You seem to have a talent for juggling women. None of the three you have in your bed now seem neglected."

"I try," she said, her face coloring.

Lucia did wonder how Roseli managed it. She'd picked up no hints of hostility or jealousy between Roseli's lovers. If anything, they all seemed comfortable and friendly with each other. Surely, Roseli didn't bed them all together, did she?

She rested an elbow on the table. "I must ask you, so that there is no risk of a misunderstanding or trouble later, are we both permitted to take lovers or only you?"

"Officially or unofficially?"

"Is there a difference?"

"Officially, a royal consort may take no lovers."

"And unofficially?"

Roseli looked at her hands. "Duty and tradition aside, I feel I have no right to ask you to sleep most nights in a cold bed, especially not when you haven't chosen it."

That was a relief to hear. The expectation of sexual fidelity had been one of the least appealing aspects of marriage. "Discretion, then."

"More than you can imagine. You have no idea how cutthroat the paparazzi in the capital city are."

"Considering that video they got of you and General Tate, I can imagine."

"Then you understand how careful you'll need to be. After marriage, if you're caught with another woman, especially if there is proof beyond gossip, it will hurt my reputation. If you take a lover in secret, it must be a woman you can trust absolutely."

"I understand." Although she suspected that this was going to be hard. She'd always been private about who she slept with, but she'd never had to be secretive about it before.

Roseli glanced up at her. "Is there someone? Did you have a lover back on Calliope?"

"Not on Calliope."

A light of recognition dawned in Roseli's eyes. "Ah, you're involved with that pretty lieutenant."

Lucia did not deny it. "Yes, but that's ending. I'll be sending her back with the rest of my crew. I was only inquiring what the rules were for the future."

Roseli frowned. "You need not send her away on my account. If she's already part of your entourage, I trust you can ensure the matter remains discreet."

"I'm sending her away for her own account. I will not see her career in the navy end with my own. She is too fine a sailor." It would be for the best. She knew Charlotte would stay if she asked, but she had no right to.

The cat pounced loudly on something among the potted plants. She emerged victorious with a stuffed catnip toy and lolled about on the sun-warmed tiles with it. Roseli glanced at the cat and smiled. She didn't show her teeth, but there was something pleasing in the turn of her lips.

Without thinking, Lucia laid a gloved hand over hers.

Roseli started in surprise and then grinned. "You're getting bold, Admiral Caron."

"For all I have just said, I don't want you to think that I've no interest in you."

"Oh? You must tell me."

Lucia leaned forward, putting them as close as she could with the table between them. "Right now, the one thing I've got to look forward to in all this mess is getting to know you better, Your Highness."

"Perhaps you can start by calling me by my first name."

"Gladly, if you will do the same." She stood so she could lean over the table and kiss her. It was as good a kiss as the last one they had shared. She ached to pull her close, to explore every part of her.

At the sound of a throat clearing, and they both turned toward the courtyard doorway. Charlotte had stopped abruptly at the entrance to the courtyard, causing Roseli's assistant, Ms. Cooper, to crash into her.

Ms. Cooper was not pleased. "I told you, I have to announce you first. You can't just barge into Princess Roseli's quarters. This isn't some barracks."

"And I told you that Princess Lucia would want to hear this news at once," growled Charlotte.

"Lieutenant, what is the news?" asked Lucia.

"Admiral, it's the first mate, Commander Jonas. He's dead."

Another piece of Lucia's world crumbled.

CHAPTER FOURTEEN

In Lucia's experience, death was seldom dignified or painless, but sometimes, it was kind. Commander Adam Jonas drew his last breath in a morphine-induced sleep as he succumbed to his injuries.

His funeral was held before sunset. While such a hasty burial was not standard practice in the Calliopean navy or even on Calliope, Jonas was a practicing Eleusinian. His religion required burial within twenty-four Earth hours of death. It was never talked about, but most Calliopean ships carried a small number of coffins set within crates of dirt to accommodate this requirement of their planet's religious minority.

Lucia made sure that her first mate was laid into the ground properly, even if it was on a foreign planet. The capital of Delphi, Thetis, had a small Eleusinian community, and the local center of worship's reciter helped her make arrangements. It was the last thing she could do for her old friend.

Roseli's guards had not liked them leaving the palace grounds, much less going to a location as difficult to secure as a cemetery, but Lucia had insisted, and Roseli had backed her. She was beside her now, her delicate silk shoes sinking into the muddy ground of the cemetery as a warm spring rain slowly drizzled upon them.

In front of them, a woman wrapped in a beautifully embroidered red robe stood with a hand upon the shrouded body. She was singing in a language Lucia couldn't understand.

Lucia stood stiffly at parade rest, her arms at her side. All the other crew members of the *Intrepid* were the same, eyes forward. The reciter finished her song. She looked at those gathered and spoke in Moûsaian for the benefit of the non-Eleusinians. "Who speaks for this man? Who will send off his soul on its long journey?"

Lucia stepped forward. "I speak for him. I was his captain."

The reciter motioned her forward to the temporary wooden altar where the body lay. "Will you give the blood of your veins to guide his spirit onward?"

"Yes."

"Give me your hand."

Lucia hesitated, then offered her left hand. She knew enough about Eleusinian funerals to understand what was expected. By rights, it should have been a family member who bled, but Jonas had none present. The sight of the ceremonial dagger sitting on the altar was still unsettling.

The reciter took her hand impersonally, as a doctor would, and rolled down her thin white glove to expose her palm. That act should have been scandalous, but in the face of death, it seemed insignificant. So many things didn't make sense anymore. Lucia barely felt the nick of the blade, but she saw the crimson drops fall to stain the snow-white shroud of her friend and shipmate.

Just as quickly, the reciter was pressing a bandage against her hand. Lucia rolled her glove back into place as the reciter finished her prayers.

The rain increased from a drizzle to heavy droplets as the body was lowered into the earth with the aid of several ropes. She didn't want to move, didn't want to do anything but stand there and watch as several members of the Eleusinian center of worship filled the grave with shovelfuls of dirt. She barely noticed when Roseli laid a hand on her arm.

"Lucia," said Roseli. "Please come away before you get soaked."

She couldn't seem to find her voice.

Roseli leaned close enough to whisper. "I don't think your crew will leave without you, and they shouldn't be in this rain, not the injured ones."

That snapped Lucia back to herself. She saluted the grave and headed back toward what remained of the crew of the good ship *Intrepid*.

❖

Roseli accompanied Lucia and her crew back to the barracks for the wake. Although she had not known Commander Jonas, she could feel the deep grief of all those around her, and her heart was heavy in sympathy.

Before the funeral, Roseli had put Beatrice in charge of planning the wake. Food and liquor were laid out on a side table, along with an odd assortment of instruments. There was a violin, a guitar, a hand drum, and a flute. One of the crew, a curly-haired young woman, was quick to take up the fiddle and begin playing.

The first songs were slow and sad, but as soon as the crew had a few drinks in them, the mood shifted. An older man added his voice to the woman's fiddle playing. Soon enough, people were singing along.

Roseli was officially a Unispiritualist, as was expected as a member of the royal family, although she was in practice an agnostic. She'd been to the gatherings that followed Unispiritualist funerals before but none like this one. No one had sung or gotten drunk at the funeral of Roxane's nurse.

Not knowing what else to do, Roseli sat beside Lucia in a chair against the wall and ate and drank whatever was handed to her. She discreetly scanned each item for poison with a device from her pocket. She recognized the bitter taste of Calliopcan whiskey in her mug and was careful to drink sparingly.

The music shifted, growing faster and wilder, something more suited to the countryside than a barracks. To Roseli's surprise, two of the crew got up to dance, and then others joined them.

"Should we?" asked Roseli.

Lucia set down her barely touched mug. "It would set a good example."

Roseli had read a good deal about Calliope, but she was realizing how little she understood. Was dancing at funerals a sign of virtue or just somehow considered therapeutic?

Lucia linked an arm with hers, guiding her into the cleared part of the room. Lucia laid one hand on Roseli's waist and clasped her right hand as they fell into an easy four-step pattern. The Calliopean prohibition against holding hands in public did not extend to dancing, it seemed.

It felt good to move after the solemnity of the funeral. Lucia danced as easily as she'd fenced earlier that day, gracefully and light on her feet. Roseli was intensely aware of the proximity of her body, of the heat of her hand through the silk of her dress.

They finished one reel and then moved through another and then one more, Lucia guiding her through slightly unfamiliar steps. They were both breathless by the time the fiddler took a break. The room had grown hot from all the movement.

"Let's get some air," said Lucia.

They stepped out into the darkness, discreetly followed by the two guards who perpetually shadowed Roseli and the two who followed Lucia. The rain had stopped, leaving the night smelling flagrantly of petrichor and wet flowers. High above, the twin moons, Castor and Pollux, hung heavy, bright enough to be visible through the city lights.

"Fancy a stroll around the parade grounds?" Roseli offered her arm, and Lucia took it. They set out walking the perimeter of the wide, grassy yard, their guards hanging back just enough to give them some privacy. The parade ground was rounded, with a colonnaded walk, but they chose to walk on the grass for the sake of the sky.

"So that's a Calliopean wake?" asked Roseli.

"Yes. Traditionally, Eleusinians don't hold wakes, but the crew needed this. Jonas would have understood."

"I am sorry for your loss. Did you know the man well?"

"Since I commanded my first destroyer. Jonas was the first mate aboard the *Dauntless* when I was appointed captain. He was not impressed that a twenty-six-year-old had been put in charge of a ship of the line and made no secret that he thought it was because I was a princess."

"Was it?"

"Partially, yes, but I was not the only young captain given such an important command. At that point in the war, there was a shortage of experienced captains to take command of the new warships built to replace earlier losses. I'd already been a captain of a smaller vessel for two years.

"When I was a lieutenant commander aboard the *Courageous*, nearly the entire chain of command was killed after the bridge lost pressure during the Battle of the Galileo Cluster. I only survived because I'd gone to oversee emergency repairs on another part of the ship. After that, as the most experienced junior officer still alive, I took command. I was never relieved as captain after the battle, as none of the other ships could spare officers." Her voice had fallen into the easy cadence of someone telling a story she had told many times before.

Roseli's throat felt tight. How many times had Lucia nearly died? She knew how much resigning her commission was costing Lucia, but she could not help but feel relieved she would not be going into battle again.

"After a while, the brass promoted me to captain because it would look bad for a junior officer to have commanded a frigate for so long. I ended up having my first command at only twenty-four. I saw the *Courageous* through more than a few battles until I was moved to the *Dauntless*. I was less than impressed when my new second-in-command treated me like an ensign who'd just passed her exams."

"What did you do?" asked Roseli.

"Held my tongue, was unfailingly polite, and showed him I knew what the hell I was doing. By that point, I'd been a senior officer long enough to know that the fastest way to lose a crew's respect was to demand it without proving myself."

"Did it work?"

Lucia shrugged. "Not at first. He was painfully formal to my face and kept referring to me as Her Royal Highness in my absence."

Roseli laughed and leaned against Lucia. "You are a princess." She was enjoying every aspect of their walk, from the woman beside her to the warm night air.

"Yes, but I don't use that title in the navy. I had to let it go, though. Jonas was well-loved by the crew, and I'd have looked like a tyrant if I, as captain, had picked a fight with a subordinate."

"Is that what it's like, having a command?" Roseli was the heir to the throne, but she had more experience with subjects than subordinates.

"All naval ships have a delicate balance of power. A captain is worthless without the respect and support of her crew. You must be remote and unassailable while still being human and relatable. Your crew must believe you'll never waver in battle, won't bleed if cut, and yet, they also want you to be someone they'd like to drink with."

"Sounds a lot like being a princess."

"My girlhood was good practice."

They reached the end of the parade ground and turned, following the edge of the columned walk.

"How did you work out things with your first mate?" asked Roseli.

"We fought our first battle together. I got the *Dauntless* through the Battle of the Delta Nebula in one piece, which was more than could be said for most Alliance ships that went into the engagement. When it was all over, we shared a drink. Jonas told me that despite being a princess, I was an adequately capable captain. I told him that despite being a judgy old bastard, he was an adequately capable first mate. We got along after that."

"You called him a judgy old bastard?"

Lucia laughed warmly. "I called him a lot worse over the years, and he did the same of me. We kept each other grounded. I made sure he came with me as I was promoted and served on all my subsequent crews. If I ever did anything he thought was wrong, he'd tell me. That made him invaluable. He talked me down from more than a few bad decisions over the years."

"Truth to power." She had learned early in life that being a princess often meant people would say whatever they believed she wanted to hear. Awkward as Meredith's lack of a filter could be, it meant Roseli could rely on her to speak her mind.

"A hard thing to come by. I don't know what I'll do without him. May the gods rest his soul."

They walked on in silence. They had nearly completed their circuit of the parade grounds. "Roseli," said Lucia in a low tone. "When we reach the next column, I'm going to push you against it and kiss you."

Had Roseli not heard the fear in her voice, it would have been a tempting invitation. Something was wrong.

Lucia continued, "After that, when I say go, we both need to get to the side of the column facing the wall and stay there."

"I…"

There was no time. Lucia pushed her against the column, pressing her lips against hers without truly kissing her. They stayed there for half a breath and then, in one frantic movement, Lucia yanked her to the other side of the heavy marble.

All around them, the world exploded into sound as the outward-facing side of the column exploded from the impact of a bullet.

"Get to cover, sniper on the east roof," screamed Lucia at the guards.

Roseli hit the panic button on her wrist strap, although she could barely reach it, crushed against the column as she was by Lucia. Every instinct her told her to grab Lucia's hand and run, but she couldn't move.

There was another sound of shattering marble and a sudden sharp pain in her arm. She could hear her guards yelling and tried to look, but Lucia kept her grip on her.

"Stay still."

The air boomed with the sound of return fire from the sidearms her guards carried. When Roseli turned her head to the right, she saw that three of the guards had made it to the cover of the columns. She didn't dare look to see where the fourth was.

Officer Smith was to her right. Over the fire, she yelled, "Stay there!"

Roseli heard running footsteps, and the tenor of the gunshots changed. She could only guess that meant that palace guards with rifles had arrived. Eventually, there was silence. Her heart was pounding, and she thought she might be sick.

Officer Smith's wrist strap buzzed, and she grabbed Roseli's wrist. "Move, move, move!"

Surrounded by guards and with Lucia at her side, she was rushed through the nearest doorway and down a series of halls before being shoved unceremoniously into a safe room. Officer Smith followed them in. Roseli didn't realize how badly she was trembling until her legs gave out, and she sank to the floor.

Lucia knelt beside her. "Breathe."

Only after Roseli had taken several breaths did she realize her arm hurt.

"Move, let me check her," snapped Officer Smith. She knelt beside Roseli and cleaned her arm with an alcohol pad from the kit on the wall.

"The cuts are shallow, Your Highness. You just need a bandage."

"I think the marble fragments caught her when bullets hit the column," said Lucia.

Roseli heard liquid dripping and looked up at Lucia. The sleeve and shoulder of Lucia's shirt were damp with blood. Her sense of panic that had just begun to calm flared up again. "Shit, you're bleeding, too."

"I'm fine," insisted Lucia. "The shards cut me. I'm not shot."

Roseli ignored her. "Help her first, Smith, she's bleeding more."

Officer Smith handed Roseli a roll of white gauze. "Wrap this around your arm." She motioned Lucia to sit in one of the two chairs and took a pair of scissors from the kit. She methodically cut away Lucia's shirt and sports bra to get at her arm and side. For all the modesty that Lucia always showed when it came to her hands and neck, she seemed to have little where her naked chest was concerned.

Under better circumstances, a shirtless Lucia would have made a stunning sight. She had broad shoulders and arms toned from fencing practice. Her breasts were modest but well-formed, and she had the sort of toned stomach that could only be achieved by regular crunches.

Roseli's attention, however, was drawn to the series of shallow cuts along her right shoulder, arm, and side that were slowly seeping crimson. Guilt was like a stone in her stomach, Lucia had been wounded protecting her.

Officer Smith considered the cuts, then swabbed them with a substance that fizzed and made Lucia gasp and grit her teeth. As she bandaged them, she said, "You won't need stitches, but you'll likely have some fine scars, Your Highness."

"I'll add them to my collection." She tugged on a shirt that Roseli brought her from one cabinet.

At Officer Smith's urging, they both ate some chocolate and drank water. She laid two mats on the floor from a cabinet and gave them each a blanket, telling them to rest before departing to see what she could find out.

As the panic rooms only had one entrance, the palace guards usually stood vigil outside the door rather than inside once the royalty had been safely settled inside. Roseli sat with her arms drawn around her legs. She hadn't felt this scared and helpless since the night her sisters had died.

Lucia watched her from her mat. "You're worried about your lovers?"

"And my family." The guards still hadn't told them anything, but that wasn't unusual. After such a serious attack, they would keep the status and location of all members of the royal family silent until the all clear was given.

"Would a hug help?"

It seemed an almost ridiculous thing to offer, but Roseli was incredibly glad Lucia had. "Yes, I think it would."

Lucia crawled over and to put her uninjured arm around Roseli and drew her close.

"I'm sorry that being engaged to me has put you in such danger," said Roseli.

"I've spent my adult life leading spaceships into battle. Believe me, I am no stranger to peril."

Roseli settled more comfortably against her. "I doubt you've ever been shot at before."

"I have."

"Really?"

"Yes. When I was a little girl, my mother and I were in an inner courtyard garden when she caught sight of a sniper on the roof. She shoved me into a flower bush and fired at the sniper with a concealed gun. Her first shot missed, and the sniper got her in the left arm. She got him in the heart with her next one."

"That's terrible."

Lucia shrugged and winced as the movement no doubt jostled her cuts. "Her arm pained her for some time after that, but she recovered."

"I'm amazed your mother spotted the sniper and could make the shot."

"She was more than a little paranoid. I guess it came from growing up in the Varcian royal court, where she was under constant threat of assassination. Of five sisters, she and the current Empress of Varcian were the only ones who survived to adulthood."

"Her vigilance saved you both," said Roseli.

"It did that day, and I suppose she passed it on to me. My mother taught me to watch rooftops. That's why I caught the gleam of the sniper's scope."

"Then I am grateful to her."

There was a sudden beeping on the wall, causing Roseli to jerk in fear. Officer Smith appeared on the screen. She looked pale. "Your Highness, all members of the royal family and associated dependents have been secured."

A vise of fear loosened from Roseli's heart. "Thank goodness."

"You'll need to remain in the safe room overnight while we continue to secure the palace."

"Did you catch the sniper?"

"Yes. He was shot dead, so we won't be learning anything from him. I'll provide further details in a briefing tomorrow."

"Thank you, Officer Smith, please keep me informed."

The screen clicked off, and Roseli leaned heavily against Lucia. "They are all safe."

"I'm glad."

Roseli felt drowsy as the adrenaline finally wore off. She wasn't sure exactly when she drifted off, but she woke to find herself curled against Lucia's sleeping form. Roseli closed her eyes and let herself sink back into slumber. She dreamed darkly of gardens and bullets and little girls murdered in their beds.

CHAPTER FIFTEEN

Roseli woke to the sound of the door opening and her mother's worried voice. "Roseli, they said you were hurt."

Still half-asleep, she called back, "Mother."

Beside her, Lucia jerked awake, sending them both tumbling from the sleeping mat onto the icy floor. It took a second to untangle themselves from the blankets.

By the time Roseli sat up, her mother had turned her back. "You two didn't waste any time, did you?" Her tone was an odd mix of aggravation and relief.

Roseli stood awkwardly, brushing at her rumpled clothes. "You can turn around. We are fully dressed."

She turned and froze. "Your arm…"

"Just minor cuts," Roseli promised.

They stared at each other. Roseli noticed she was wearing a rumpled dressing gown. She'd likely come straight from her panic room to Roseli's. Her face was drawn thin with worry, and there were dark circles beneath her eyes. Seeing her like that unsettled Roseli. What had the guards told her mother about her injuries to cause her to rush through the palace in such a state?

"You're all right, then?"

"Yes."

"Good."

The moment stretched.

"Have you checked on Roxane?" asked Roseli.

"Not yet, but she's safe. The guards said they had to lock her in with the youngest Harper boy. She had him in her room last night when the alarm sounded and wouldn't go into the safe room without him. When did those two happen, anyway?"

Roseli had to fight down a laugh, "A while ago."

Her mother rubbed at her temple. "I see." When she looked up, she seemed to finally take note of Lucia. The shirt the Calliopean princess had borrowed from the cabinet was short-sleeved and didn't cover the thick white bandages on her arm.

Her mother's eyes narrowed. "You appear to be hurt worse than my daughter. The guards said you shielded her during the firefight."

"I tried to, Your Majesty."

She gave Lucia a respectful nod. "The guards also said you spotted the sniper before they did."

"I come from a long line of incredibly paranoid women."

"Considering your mother was a Varcian princess, that is not surprising. If you can continue to keep my daughter alive, I will find you to be an acceptable daughter-in-law."

Lucia bowed. "I will do my best, Your Majesty."

Her mother straightened, returning to business as usual. "Princess Lucia, you should go shower and see if you can't make your hair look less like a startled hamster. You're due in the Senate after lunch."

"I thought the marriage contract had already been approved," said Lucia.

"Yes, but you must still appear before the Senate to renounce all other loyalties and obligations, or they won't grant you Delphian citizenship. This must be done before the marriage may proceed, another of their damn rules."

"Is it safe for her to leave the palace?" asked Roseli.

"Obviously not, someone tried to shoot you both last night," said her mother. "However, rumors of the assassination attempt have already leaked. At least one of you needs to appear publicly as soon as possible."

"I'm going with her," said Roseli. She would not let Lucia risk herself again, not without her.

"No, you aren't," said her mother in a tone that brooked no argument. "The two of you together are far too tempting a target. She'll go to the Senate under heavy guard, and you will remain here under the same. The wedding is in two days. There are preparations you need to get to."

"Mother." Roseli crossed her arms, which probably made her look more childish than she realized. "The risk of assassination aside, you can't send Admiral Caron to face the Senate alone. You know what they're like. Don't you remember what happened the first time I went to speak before them after you named me heir apparent?"

Her mother remained impassive. "If you're so worried, send that senator of yours along with her. If Senator Veritas can't get your fiancée through that congressional pit of vipers, no one can."

❖

Charlotte had never been more certain of a decision in her life. She couldn't leave, not now that Lucia had nearly been assassinated twice in less than a week. The moment the guards showed her Lucia's sitting room, she rushed to embrace her.

Lucia made a sharp gasp of pain and tensed.

Charlotte drew back hurriedly, looking her over. Lucia's arm and shoulder were bandaged. What the hell? The guards had said she hadn't been shot. "You're injured."

"It's nothing, just a few cuts."

"I shouldn't have let you go onto the parade ground with only the princess and palace guards. The Delphians are incapable of protecting you. I'm going to work out a roster to make sure you always have two crew members with you." Why hadn't she thought to do it before?

"None of our people are trained as guards, and they won't be here for much longer anyway," said Lucia.

"Then I'll stay with you." She wasn't letting her out of her sight again.

Lucia shook her head. "Listen, there's something I need to tell you."

"No." She was prepared for this. She'd spent half the night in the barracks rehearsing it in her head.

"What?" Lucia sounded genuinely surprised.

"The answer is no. You're about to say that you're sending me home with the rest of the crew, and I'm telling you I'm not going."

"Lieutenant, in case you have forgotten, your posting isn't your decision."

If Lucia wanted to retreat to their formal roles, that was all right. She could do that, too. "I've already filled out the paperwork to transfer to a liaison position with the Delphian navy's central command office here in the capital. I'll help facilitate communication between the Calliopean and Delphian navies. As my commanding officer, you need only sign a document to permit the transfer."

Lucia sat on the couch. "I can't let you throw away your career on a desk position. You're due to be promoted to lieutenant commander soon. You would have already had your first command if you hadn't turned down your last transfer."

"I'd rather serve with you than be captain of my own ship."

"If you stay on Delphi, you won't be serving with me at all. At noon, I have to go to the Delphian Senate and resign my commission. I won't be an admiral or even part of the Calliopean navy anymore."

"I don't care. All I want is to stay with you." She'd never dared say that before.

"I can't let you do that, not for my sake."

"It's my life and my career. Why can't I?" She crossed to stand in front of her, grasping the edge of the couch armrest. She'd never been this angry at Lucia before.

Lucia raised her tired eyes. "Because I don't love you, Charlotte, not the way you love me. If you stay, you'll grow to hate me for it."

Charlotte felt something go cold inside. Hearing the truth did not make it any easier to bear. She stepped back, looking away. "Do you think I'm some girl fresh out of the academy, giddy with her first fling? I've always known you didn't feel the same way."

"Then you'll go?"

She almost did, but the bandage on Lucia's arm, the other on her neck, the sheer look of exhaustion on her face held her. She looked so lost and vulnerable. "No. I know you don't love me, but you still need me. You're about to be all alone in a strange court with no allies. You don't have to keep me in your bed, but you still need someone on Delphi who's loyal to you."

Lucia sat up, an expression of weary determination on her handsome face. "I know you're trying to be noble, but I am still your commanding officer, and I will order you back to Calliope."

"You're only my superior officer for a few more hours. When you resign your commission, I will become the highest-ranking Calliopean naval officer present."

"You still can't sign your own transfer papers."

"No, but I can send them back to HQ in the next data transfer, and there is no reason they would refuse to allow an officer in good standing to transfer to a liaison position, especially as they are going to need more such officers once the treaty is signed."

"You are certain about this?"

"I am. You can sign my transfer papers, or someone back on Calliope will, but I am staying on Delphi."

Lucia sighed. "You don't leave me much choice, do you?"

"I'm sorry. I don't know what else to do. I can't leave you alone, not after someone's tried to kill you twice. You need an ally."

"And you think that person should be you?"

"I don't care if you never share your bed with me again, but I'll never forgive myself if you come to harm when I could have protected you. You know you need someone to watch your back." She felt as if her heart was breaking in whole new ways.

Lucia went silent, her expression unreadable, the way it always was when she was making a decision upon the bridge of a starship. Then her shoulders slumped, as if the weight of all she carried had become too much. "Bring me the tablet, and I'll sign it."

Charlotte took a tablet from a satchel over her shoulder and tapped at it before holding it out to Lucia.

Lucia scanned the document. "Just promise me one thing."

"Anything."

"If you ever start to hate me or grow sick of Delphi, you'll transfer back to Calliope. Don't sacrifice your happiness out of a sense of duty. You deserve better."

"I could never hate you."

"Promise me anyway."

"You have my word."

Lucia tapped her name into the bottom of the document and pressed her thumb against the screen to sign it. Charlotte accepted it with shaking hands and sank onto the couch across from her. She was amazed her plan had worked.

"Do you think you'll miss it?" asked Lucia. "Being on a ship."

"The endless days of tedium broken by occasional hours of sheer terror?" She wasn't sure if she wanted to laugh or cry.

Lucia smiled weakly. "Let's not forget the lovely smell of recirculated air and all the bitter, burned coffee you can drink."

"I won't miss the constant feeling of being boxed in. At least I won't have to worry about my claustrophobia anymore. Looking at the stars through a screen just isn't the same as raising my face to the sky."

Lucia frowned. "You never told me you were claustrophobic."

"It's pretty bad. I have to take anxiety medicine for it while I'm aboard a ship, or I have panic attacks."

"And you stayed in the navy?"

"By the time I realized it wouldn't get better with time, I'd already been promoted to lieutenant junior grade. It was too late to change course, and resigning during wartime wasn't an option. When the armistice came, I was serving aboard the *Intrepid*, and by your side, it was bearable." She shook her head sharply. "I can't do it again. I can't face those narrow halls and tiny rooms alone for a second time. I can't go back and be a captain, not when I feel like I'm suffocating half the time. I can't resign, either, not with a new war coming."

She'd never told anyone other than the ship's doctor who'd treated her first panic attack years ago. She'd not meant to ever tell Lucia, much less right then, but the words had escaped. She did not regret speaking them.

"Forgive me," said Lucia. "I've known you for years, and I never even guessed."

Charlotte crossed her arms, hunching slightly. "We've never talked, not really."

"Yes, but we've..."

"Sleeping with a woman doesn't mean you know her."

"No, it doesn't. Lieutenant...Charlotte, in a few hours, I'll be a civilian and not your commanding officer. Perhaps we can begin again, this time honestly and as friends."

"I would like that." For the first time in all the years they had known each other, she felt that Lucia was truly seeing her. The fragile new understanding between them wasn't what she had dreamed of, but it was real, and that was enough.

❖

A few hours later, Lucia was sitting in the back of a car on her way to the Delphian Senate. It was the first chance she had to get a good look at Senator Veritas. Like all of Roseli's lovers, she was strikingly attractive in her own distinctive way.

Senator Veritas had a narrow face framed by high cheekbones. Her pale skin had a light dusting of freckles, and she had plaited her red hair into a neat braid. A well-tailored black suit showed off her trim figure to full effect without being overly suggestive. She watched Lucia with shrewd green eyes but didn't begin the conversation.

"I suppose you're about to put me on notice, just as Princess Roseli's other two lovers have," said Lucia.

"Oh?" Senator Veritas feigned ignorance. "And how did they go about it?"

"General Tate offered me a drink and then told me if I ever spoke to Princess Roseli disrespectfully again, she'd challenge me to a duel."

She laughed. "Sounds like her. For the record, she only ever fought one duel, and it was some time ago. She's just never shed the reputation."

"I've fenced with her and lost. Whatever reputation she has is well-deserved."

"I heard. There were pictures in the tabloids within the hour. It's been good for your public image. Delphians love a good fencing match. It is a shame no one got a video."

Lucia frowned. "I never saw a camera."

Senator Veritas shrugged. "The tabloids here are serious business. I'm sure some member of the palace regiment sneakily took a photo with their tablet and made a nice sum selling it. Never believe yourself unwatched until you've closed all the curtains and scanned the room."

"Good to know."

"What did Beatrice do? I doubt she threatened you with a duel. She is hardly the violent sort."

"Lady Swann showed me my new rooms and asked if I needed anything. She left me with little doubt who runs Princess Roseli's household."

"She has mastered the art of aggressive courtesy."

"And you?"

Senator Veritas shrugged. "I can't threaten you with a duel. I'm an indifferent fencer at best, nor can I use courtesy as a weapon the way Beatrice does. I've never been the sort to make threats. If the Senate has taught me anything, it's that it is a lot easier to get people to do what you want if you give them something in return."

It seemed Prince Ambrose had been right when he'd told her Senator Veritas was sly. She'd been the last of Roseli's lovers to talk to Lucia alone, after General Tate and Lady Swann had both shown their hands.

"And what do you want of me?"

"For you to treat Roseli well and not come between us."

"You have my word if you will do the same," said Lucia. She knew an offer of alliance when she heard one.

"I will," replied Senator Veritas formally and then in a gentler tone, "Roseli said you saved her life last night."

"And my own. I've done a few heroic things in my life, but yanking a woman behind a column and hiding ranks low among them."

"You still saved the woman I love."

"You can show me your gratitude by telling me what to expect in the Senate," said Lucia, feeling uncomfortable at Senator Veritas's sincerity. Maybe she wasn't as calculating as she'd though.

"Ah, right," said Senator Veritas, straightening in her seat and handing over a tablet. It showed several lines of text. "You'll need to resign your naval commission and renounce your Calliopean citizenship, as well as your claim to the Calliopean throne. You'll swear loyalty to Delphi and receive Delphian citizenship."

"Do I even get to keep my last name?"

The senator's lip quirked. "Until the wedding, then I believe you take Princess Roseli's last name, Almeda. Your last name, Caron, will become your middle one. That is the tradition for imperial consorts."

It was such a small thing, a last name, but it was still another piece of herself being stripped away. What would be left of her in the end? She shook the thought away. If the cost of keeping her planet safe included her name, she would pay it. "Is that all?" she asked.

"After you read the prepared speech on the tablet, you will answer questions from the Senate before a vote to approve your citizenship is held. Don't worry, it will pass. However, about a third of them are going to be hostile, try to trip you up, or even publicly humiliate you."

"If they are hostile, why did they approve the marriage contract?"

"They had no choice, not when a military treaty depended on it, but they aren't happy about it. They resented how the palace, not the Senate, conducted the negotiation process and feel the treaty strengthens the empress's position."

"The Delphian Senate doesn't want a strong empress?"

Senator Veritas frowned. "It's complicated. Some senators do and some don't. Delphian politics are a balance between the monarchy's traditions, the Senate's customs, and our written constitution. The empress is the head of state, but her power is not absolute. The Senate carefully guards its authority, especially the levying of taxes. Trouble began about twenty years ago when a fringe political party, known as the Populist Party, gained seats in the Senate. They want to increase the power of the Senate and exclude the monarchy from government."

"The empress permitted them to form as a party?" asked Lucia.

Senator Veritas shrugged. "Empress Eleanor is no fool. You don't slam the top on a pot when it's boiling over. She never interferes with the formation or operation of political parties unless they call for or incite violence. To their credit, the Populist Party aren't fools, either. They have never publicly advocated for anything more radical than a constitutional amendment to allow for a prime minister."

"My planet has a prime minister," said Lucia. "Calling for one doesn't sound unreasonable. The Calliopean Prime Minister's authority is weaker than my father's. Mostly, she just heads the parliament and makes speeches."

"The Populist Party wants a more powerful prime minister than Calliope has," said Senator Veritas flatly. "Their influence is limited, for now, at least. They have only a fourth of the seats in the Senate and are not part of the majority coalition, but they are highly vocal."

"How do I best deal with them?"

"Stay as formal and collected as you can, never rise to the bait. The senators aren't who matters, the people who will watch clips of this hearing in the nightly news are. This is your chance to impress the Delphian people." The car pulled into an underground parking lot, and they disembarked. Four guards escorted them as they made their way up into the Senate Hall through a series of dull gray halls and service elevators. They stepped into a small, wood-paneled office through a hidden doorway that appeared to be a false bookshelf.

"Through the next door is a side entrance to the Senate Hall. Are you ready?" asked Senator Veritas.

"As I'll ever be." For the first time since arriving on Calliope, Lucia felt a flicker of true trepidation. She had never liked public speaking. It was one thing to give orders on the bridge of a ship and another entirely to charm a roomful of politicians. There was a reason she'd chosen the navy over more princess-like public relations duties.

Senator Veritas motioned to the guards, and one opened the door. They stepped into a cavernous room. It was shaped like a half circle, with row after row of wooden desks reaching backward to the far wall. At the front was a speaker's podium with several desks flanking it. At each desk sat an expectant senator watching Lucia as she followed Senator Veritas to the podium.

Senator Veritas took the microphone and introduced Lucia to the Senate. Far too soon, there was moderate applause, and Senator Veritas motioned to her.

Lucia was glad for the tablet. She read her statement, barely feeling the meaning of the words. "I, Princess Lucia Valdez Caron of Calliope, come before you, honored senators, in accordance with the laws of

Delphi. I resign my commission with the Royal Navy of Calliope and renounce my Calliopean citizenship and my claim to the Calliopean throne. I pledge my loyalty to the planet of Delphi and request to be made a citizen of Delphi in order to wed my fiancée, Crown Princess Roseli Abram Almeda."

In three sentences, she'd renounced the loyalties that had guided her life. She wondered if this was how her mother had felt when she'd done the same to marry the emperor of Calliope. She kept her head up and eyes forward, the way she had been raised.

An older woman at the desk behind the podium had a large wooden gavel and spoke into a microphone. "Princess Lucia Caron will now take questions as required by the Senate bylaws before a vote will be held. Priority for questions goes by the number of seats each party holds. Questions may take only five minutes to ask and answer. Let's get to it."

The first question came from an elderly man from the United Party. He wanted to see if Lucia would be serving in the Delphian navy or if she would still have any control over allied Calliopean ships. Lucia answered in the negative for both.

The next question came from a middle-aged woman from the Centrist Party, who asked if Princess Lucia was renouncing her claim to the Varcian throne as well. Lucia answered that her mother had renounced such a claim in perpetuity when she'd wed. Lucia and her brothers had never been in the Varcian line of succession.

The third question came like a shot across the bow from Senator Rain, a member of the Northern Alliance Party. "Tell me, Your Highness, do you suffer from your grandmother's madness?"

It seemed it wasn't just the Populist Party who wanted to make her look bad. Lucia knew when to play dumb. "I am not aware the dowager empress of Calliope suffers from anything beyond an occasional bit of forgetfulness. She collects ceramic cats somewhat obsessively, but I doubt that can be called madness."

"Your other grandmother."

"I cannot speak to the mental state of Empress Aria during her life as she died years before I was born."

The senator was not impressed. "She was insane. She had her political enemies and anyone else who displeased her tortured to death, often as a form of entertainment at state dinners. Your aunt is not reputed to be much better."

As a girl, Lucia had heard a lot of stories about her maternal grandmother. When she was eight, she'd asked her mother if any of it was true. Her mother had gotten pale and walked out of the room. Lucia had never asked again.

Senator Rain forged onward. "Have you ever had a psychological evaluation?"

Lucia relaxed. She had an answer for this. "Yes, all future officers are required to have such an evaluation before admission to the Royal Calliopean Naval Academy and again before graduation. I have twice been evaluated and found to be of sound mind."

There was a buzzing sound, which meant the questioner's time was up. The next question came from a young man, Senator Baker from the Populist Party. "Your Highness, what do you believe is the proper role of a parliament in a governmental system?"

"I am no political scholar and would not presume to give such an opinion."

"I'll be more specific, then. What do you make of the differences between the parliaments of Calliope and Delphi? For example, Calliope has a prime minister, and Delphi does not. Which approach seems better to you?"

While not subtle, the question still backed Lucia into a corner. To praise one system was to denigrate the other. She charted a careful course, pausing as long as she could before speaking. "I believe both planets have different histories and traditions and are best served by their unique forms of government."

"You don't think Delphi should have a prime minister?"

Lucia opted for humor. "I believe I am too new to this planet to give an informed opinion on much of anything. This morning, I scalded myself in the shower because the hot water faucet was on the left instead of the right, where it has been all my life. Yesterday, I spooned salt into my coffee because I didn't realize salt bowls are blue and sugar bowls are yellow on Delphi. I think it best I refrain from commenting on governmental systems until I've at least figured out this planet's basic plumbing and tableware."

Her words earned her a warm ripple of laughter from much of her audience.

Mercifully, the bell rang, signaling the end of the question. Going forward, the questions got repetitive and sometimes odd. As Lucia would learn later, while Delphi had four large political parties, it had a lot of small ones, some of which held only one or two seats in parliament. Every party got five minutes.

The senators asked if she was fertile, to which she replied she had no reason to believe she was not; if she bore any loyalty to Varcia, to which she replied she did not; and if she thought the palace should hold more balls, to which she had no opinion. The last senator who belonged to the Privateer Party asked if she had ever met Captain Scarlet. Lucia did not know why this was relevant, but maybe he was a fan of comics like Princess Roxane. She said she had never met the woman in person, although their ships had communicated. The buzzer rang before Lucia could tell the Senate the same story she'd told Princess Roxane a few nights before.

The senator with the gavel called a vote. It took less than a minute. There was a large screen at the front of the hall with each senator's name, and one by one, their votes lit up as yes, no, or abstain.

Lucia wasn't sure why her citizenship had to be voted on when the marriage contract had already been approved or why she'd had to undergo an interrogation for the citizenship or even why she needed to be a citizen of Delphi to marry one of its princesses.

The woman with the gavel spoke into her microphone. "Voting is closed. Yeses have it by three-fourths. The Delphian Senate officially grants Princess Lucia Caron Delphian citizenship with all duties and protections. I call an hour recess for lunch."

The room erupted into enthusiastic applause. Lucia was not sure if this was for her or for lunch. At least it was over.

CHAPTER SIXTEEN

That evening, Lucia found herself staring at a bottle and contemplating getting incredibly drunk. There was an entire liquor cabinet in one corner of her sitting room, complete with glasses and unopened bottles. She was not normally prone to drinking heavily. She had too many responsibilities between being a princess and being an admiral to let herself lose control.

But she wasn't an admiral anymore. She had no crew to protect, no fleet to command. She wasn't even in the Calliopean line of succession anymore. All that was expected of her now was to marry, have some of her eggs harvested, and sometimes provide military advice. She was usually not in the practice of feeling sorry for herself, but it seemed like the sort of night to make an exception.

She was just reaching to open the bottle when she heard the front door of her rooms open, and Ms. Cooper poked her head into the sitting room.

"What are you doing sitting around? You're going to be late for your engagement party."

"My what?"

"Princess Roseli's and your engagement party, didn't anyone tell you it was tonight?"

With a jolt, Lucia realized that Charlotte had told her the day before. She'd meant to find Lady Swann and ask her what was customary for a Delphian engagement party. She'd completely forgotten amidst everything else. "Do I need to change?" She was still wearing the suit she'd worn to the Senate.

"You're fine. Come on, you're already late. There is food and booze and music. You're a sailor so you like those things, right?"

"Yes." At the moment, she wanted nothing more than peace and solitude, but she knew she could not escape this obligation.

"Then come with me. I invited your whole crew since you don't have any friends here."

Lucia had been to her fair share of engagement parties, mostly those of fellow sailors. It was common for officers in the navy to marry each other, especially as married couples could serve together. The same was true of enlisted men and women, although they were only entitled to a curtained bunk in the married dorms instead of a tiny cabin.

On one memorable shore leave, while attending the engagement party for two friends Lucia had come through the academy with, she'd woken up the next day in bed with the two hungover brides-to-be. The couple remained two of her dearest friends, and it had not been the last time she'd shared their bed.

The engagement party she and Roseli's assistant entered appeared to be tamer than most she had attended before. There was an abundance of pink and purple streamers and balloons attached to nearly every surface.

The surviving crew of the *Intrepid* were mingling with Delphian nobles of varying ages. The sailors appeared to be behaving. Under other circumstances, especially when faced with as much alcohol as was sitting on the side tables, they'd have all been well on their way to drunk. They might still have been nursing their hangovers from the wake the night before.

Beside her, Ms. Cooper made a delighted sound. "Ooh, tiny cupcakes." She made a beeline for the table with the food.

Lucia was left alone, uncertain about what to do. She saw no sign of Roseli. She decided to see what there was to eat. Nearly everything on the table was some kind of sweet or other, from cookies to cupcakes. The only non-sugary foods were little sandwiches and crackers with cheese.

"Admiral Caron."

Hearing the title that had been stripped from her was a cold shock. She turned to find an elderly man wearing a Delphian naval dress uniform with five stars over his heart. She recognized Admiral Heart and his unmistakable handlebar mustache. He had to know that she was no longer an admiral. Perhaps he had merely addressed her from habit.

He bowed deeply. "I've been hoping to speak with you."

Lucia bowed in return. "I am at your disposal. What did you wish to talk about?"

"The Battle of Galileo."

Lucia could have happily lived the rest of her life without thinking again of those terrible hours.

Admiral Heart must have seen the distress on her face because he said, "I apologize. I know you took heavy losses during the battle. It cannot be an easy subject for you to return to."

"I had twenty ships under my command when the siege began. Five remained at the end." Her small armada had arrived to protect a crucial joint Calliopean and Delphian mining colony on Galileo, the third moon of Copernicus, barely hours before a much larger Terra Nuevan fleet. There hadn't been time to evacuate the civilians.

Her only choice had been to set up a defensive perimeter and pray that more Alliance reinforcements arrived before it was too late. Help had come in time for the colony, but not most of her armada. The weight of all those lives would weigh upon her until her dying day.

The old man reached out and clasped her shoulder. "My son was one of the colonists. He is still among the living because of your sacrifice."

"It was my sailors who died for Galileo, not me. I spent the battle safely on the moon's orbital defense platform."

"That's what I wanted to talk to you about. I've seen the battle reports. What you were able to do with that platform was incredible. It should have been impossible to defend the colony with the size of the force you had, but you did."

"The credit goes to the engineers who designed it. Had I ever used one outside of a simulation, I could have been more effective." There was no way to know. The Battle of Galileo had been the first time a newly developed Beta Gamma Platform had been used in planetary or lunar defense. Most had been completed near the end of the war.

"I was so impressed after I read the battle report that I convinced the empress that we needed one to protect Delphi. She agreed to a technology-sharing treaty with Calliope to get the designs. It was finally completed after the war ended."

"You built one?"

"Yes. We used simulations to train several of our field generals in its operation. Admiral Conor will be the first platform commander.

She goes up to take command from the interim captain later this month. When you have time, after the wedding, could you come speak to her and her crew about your experience on Galileo?"

"Yes, if you believe it will be helpful."

"Thank you. I'll have my secretary get in touch." He bowed and departed. Feeling slightly stunned, Lucia continued to wander through the party.

"Princess Lucia," called out Princess Roxane. "Come join us." She was sitting on a couch at the edge of the room wearing a dress that could only be described as pink and sparkly. It matched her eye makeup. She was leaning against a young man, a skinny noble who wore his blue-streaked black hair long enough to reach his shoulders but didn't have it braided or tied back the way an older Delphian man would have. His attention appeared to be entirely devoted to Princess Roxane.

Not knowing what else to do, Lucia went to sit at the same table, offering a Calliopcan bow before sitting. She was still unclear if, as the future wife of the heir, she outranked the second in line for the throne or if it was the other way around.

Princess Roxane smiled eagerly. "Princess Lucia, let me introduce you to Lord John Harper." She tilted her head toward the young man. "He's Prince Henry's nephew. I wanted his band to play for the party, but Beatrice said rock music would not be traditional. Sometimes, she's no fun."

Lucia had noticed a string quartet playing in one corner of the room.

"It's a shame," said Lord John. "The acoustics in here are great, way better than the crummy bars my band usually plays at."

"Aw, I like those bars, even if it is hard for me to get my security detail to let me go," said Princess Roxane. "Do you like the decorations for the party?" she asked Lucia. "Beatrice let me pick them out. She had to let me help since I'm the maid of honor for the wedding and am supposed to help organize the engagement party. I wanted more glitter, but she said it would be tacky."

"The streamers are nice," said Lucia. She felt a shift of fabric on her neck. Since the shuttle crash, she had been wearing a white silk handkerchief, as it fit better over the bandages on her neck than a ribbon. The bulkiness of the cloth had forced her to use a different knot that she was less familiar with. It was coming loose.

She ducked her head, praying that no one had noticed as she quickly tightened and fixed the knot.

Princess Roxane watched with an expression of fascination, like a child seeing something new.

Lucia was beyond mortified.

"What exactly is the deal with the gloves and ribbon?" asked Princess Roxane.

"They are traditional for women on Calliope," said Lucia, forcing herself to lower her hands now that the cloth was secured.

"I know that," said Princess Roxane. "But why?"

Lucia had not been expecting to have to explain her planet's clothing practices. She tried her best. "It is a matter of modesty."

"Modesty? Do you ever take them off?"

"Not in public."

Princess's Roxane's lip twitched, and then she laughed. "Hands and throats are considered sexual on Calliope, aren't they?" She was loud enough that several nobles standing near the couches turned their attention to the conversation. "I'm right, aren't I?"

This was not the sort of conversation Lucia wanted to be having with Roseli's little sister. "It is more complicated than that. Wearing gloves and a ribbon isn't that different from wearing a shirt."

"Why is it just women?" asked Lord John. "I mean, both men and women have hands and throats, so why does only one gender on Calliope cover them?"

Lucia was well out of her depth and floundering. "I suppose they are viewed differently."

"It's a form of patriarchal oppression, isn't it?" said Lord John.

Lucia glanced at Princess Roxane, who explained. "He's taking a gender studies class at the university."

"It's just a tradition." She knew that wasn't much of an answer, but what else could she say? It was a practice she herself felt conflicted about. Her mother had always said that wearing gloves and ribbons for the sake of modesty was a stupid and sexist practice. She grudgingly wore the garments in public but absolutely refused to within the family's private wing of the palace, the sensibilities of servants be damned. This had deeply embarrassed Lucia's father, but he'd had the good sense to pick his battles.

However, while Lucia's mother might have been dubious of the practice, her childhood governess had not. Lucia had not been permitted to leave her room without gloves and a properly tied ribbon since she was five. As an adult, she felt naked without them. Finding herself surrounded by women who bared their throats and hands without a thought did not change a lifetime of habit.

"You mean, a tradition that forces women but not men to cover part of themselves." Now Lord John sounded smug.

Lucia was losing patience. Why should she have to justify her culture to a man so young, he barely needed to shave? "Do you consider being required to wear pants oppression?" she asked.

Lord John blinked. "I suppose not. I might if women didn't have to, but I still did."

To Lucia's relief, she caught sight of Roseli crossing the room. Roseli offered her a quick bow, which Lucia and Lord John stood to return. Princess Roxane did not rise. Perhaps she was not required to greet her sister formally.

"Princess Lucia has been telling me about Calliopean customs," said Princess Roxane. "Want to join us?"

"Later. She and I need to make a circuit of the room first." Roseli offered Lucia her arm, and she took it. As they walked, Roseli asked, "Calliopean culture?"

"She asked about the gloves and ribbons."

"Oh dear."

They made their way through the crowd, bowing and greeting guests. Roseli handled herself well, introducing Lucia to a seemingly endless stream of Delphian nobles. After an hour, they were both flagging.

When Roseli spotted Princes Ambrose and Henry sitting on an out-of-the-way couch, she led Lucia over to join them. Roseli inclined her head to both, and Lucia bowed.

"Sit, eat some tarts before Henry destroys all of them," said Prince Ambrose, motioning to a second couch on the other side of a small table.

There was an entire silver tray of tarts that Prince Henry must have appropriated from a servant. About half had been picked apart. He was systematically plucking the little strawberry slices and other berries off and eating only those while discarding the rest of the pastry. His face was drawn tight with an expression of utter devastation.

"Is everything all right?" asked Roseli.

"Henry is just pouting," said Prince Ambrose.

"I'm not pouting."

"Yes, you are. It's how you react every time our wife tells you that you can't do something."

Prince Henry glared at him, although without much malice.

"The empress put a security restriction on Henry's current project."

Prince Henry abandoned his tart destruction. "Yes, and now I can only work on it in a government lab with assistants who have been vetted. That means none of my graduate students can be part of the project anymore."

"Aw, Uncle Henry, we all know you just like working with grad students because they are so in awe of you that they will patiently listen to you ramble for hours. Anybody else eventually tells you they have no idea what you're talking about," said Roseli.

"I prefer working with students rather than older scientists because they have open minds. They never tell me what is and isn't possible."

"There are times I wonder if you understand the meaning of impossible," said Roseli.

"Well, this time, dear girl, I'm right, and my algorithm showed it. I've created a formula to calculate the true weight of black holes."

"I thought we already knew that," said Lucia. "The equation for it is part of how the Difference engines on spaceships work." In the academy, her time had been spent mostly learning navigation and combat tactics rather than engine mechanics, but she understood roughly how ships used the gravity of the galaxy's supermassive black hole to essentially slingshot themselves when they traveled long distances.

Travel between solar systems still took hundreds of years. No ships had left the Moũsai system since the generational ship that had brought their shared ancestors. Traveling between planets within the system normally took months. Even if war were to be averted, she would likely never make the long journey between Delphi and Calliope again.

"All long-range navigation programs have a margin of error, and I have suspected for years that it's because the equation used to calculate the weight of black holes was wrong. This discovery has all kinds of applications, not the least of which is potentially creating faster ships." He sighed. "This could change the nature of shipping and travel. My wife, however, can only see military applications."

Lucia could not help but wonder if Prince Henry should be talking about his research if the empress had put a security restriction on it. However, it sounded like the project had been public and largely a matter of theoretical astrophysics until it proved successful, so the cat was likely already out of the bag. It also didn't seem like Prince Henry had any kind of filter.

"Henry," said Prince Ambrose gently. "I think even you can see how the potential to make faster ships may have defense applications."

Prince Henry went back to picking apart a new tart. "I still don't think a military grade classified level is necessary. I suspect the Terra Nuevans may have already cracked the equation and gone further."

Lucia jerked forward on her couch. "What?"

Prince Henry looked up. "I can't be sure, since my dear wife won't let me correspond with any Terra Nuevan mathematicians, what with them still being our enemies, truce or not, but I hardly came up with the entire algorithm on my own. I got the idea from an article I read in a Terra Nuevan scientific journal I had smuggled in a diplomatic pouch. I suspect that poor Dr. Elis must have had a gag order put on her after that because she never published on the subject again."

Lucia's blood chilled. "Did you tell the empress about the Terra Nuevan paper?"

"I didn't think to. She gets annoyed when I complain about my lack of access to Terra Nuevan scientific journals and how far ahead of us they are."

Lucia surged to her feet. "We need to talk to the empress now."

A quarter hour later, the empress, Roseli, Lucia, and Princes Henry and Ambrose all gathered in the empress's private sitting room. The empress paced on the heavy red carpet while the others sat.

"For the love of the gods, Henry, this is the kind of thing you are supposed to tell me."

The normally bumbling royal consort was sitting on one of the low couches and looking offended. "I didn't think it was relevant. You don't care about the details of my work. You never listened to anything I said about black holes until I mentioned ships."

The empress whirled, her normally controlled face showing a hint of anger in the pursing of her lips and narrowing of her eyes. "Damn it, Henry, how stupid can you be? Obviously, I care when it involves the Terra Nuevans potentially having military technology that we don't! The entire reason I ordered you to move your supercomputer to a government lab was because I didn't want to risk the Terra Nuevans getting access to it. Now you're telling me you got the damn equation from them?"

Prince Henry frowned at her through his thick glasses. "You're the one who said to stop wasting your time with minor details. Don't blame me if you don't have enough mathematical knowledge to understand half of what I say."

The empress scowled, deepening the crow's feet at the edge of her eyes. "Which is why I keep trying to give you assistants to translate for me, but you keep rejecting them."

"You keep finding me stupid assistants."

"Or maybe you're just too proud of a son of a bitch to even try. Honestly, Henry, the one reason I married you was for your research. If you're the only one who can understand it, what use are you to me?"

"Enough," snapped Prince Ambrose. "Eleanor, you know that yelling at Henry never gets you anywhere."

The empress snorted. "No, but it makes me feel better."

"It's cruel."

"Believe me, a few sharp words are not cruel," said Empress Eleanor. "And he's got a thicker skin than you seem to think, certainly thicker than yours."

Lucia was deeply mortified to be witnessing a royal domestic spat. The general lack of concern she saw on Roseli's face suggested it was normal. However, while Lucia was engaged to the heir apparent, she was still surprised the empress would argue with her husbands in front of her.

Roseli cleared her throat. "Mother, I think you need to listen to what my fiancée has to say."

The empress came back toward the table, taking a chair between the two parallel couches on opposite sides of the table. "I suppose I had best. Go on."

Lucia said, "If everything Prince Henry has said is correct, it may explain how the Terra Nuevans ambushed my ships. We still don't know how they knew where I would be, but that was likely some internal betrayal. The question is how a battle-level cruiser appeared out of nowhere without showing up on any of my ship's long-range sensors. One moment, there was nothing, and the next, a cruiser was beside us with its weapons charged. That shouldn't be possible."

"And you think it is related to my husband's theories?"

"I do not know, Your Majesty. I thought at first that the surprise nature of the attack meant some failing of my ship's sensors or a more practical trick. Now I am thinking the Terra Nuevans have more advanced technology than we previously believed."

"Shit," said the empress. "Do you realize the broader implications that could all have?"

"Yes, Your Majesty."

The empress turned her attention back to Prince Henry. "Do you truly think it is possible to make faster ships with this equation?"

He threw his hands up in exasperation. "I don't know, Eleanor. It's all theoretical. I'm a mathematician, not an engineer."

"But is it possible?"

"Yes, I think so."

The empress closed her eyes, leaning back in her chair. "Henry, I'm going to get you a team of the best engineers on Delphi. For once in your life, I need you to play nice with others."

Before Prince Henry could open his mouth, Prince Ambrose spoke for him. "He will."

The empress looked back at Roseli and Lucia. "Princess Lucia, first thing in the morning, I need you and all surviving members of your bridge crew to explain to my military advisors and the team I am forming for Prince Henry about what happened when your ship was attacked."

"We will," promised Lucia. After a moment of deliberation, she added. "We have the bridge's black box. We'll share that, too."

The empress's thin eyebrows drew together in vexation. "You did not feel the need to share that before?"

"It was classified," said Lucia.

"That hardly seems in the spirit of a military alliance."

"You weren't exactly offering to share the specs of your battle fleet, either."

"I hope we are past that point now, for the sake of this alliance."

Lucia could think of some choice things to say in that regard, but she bit them back. She was getting good at that. "I hope so as well."

CHAPTER SEVENTEEN

The next morning, Roseli was surprised when she was ushered into her mother's sitting room instead of her study. Her mother usually preferred to speak to her from the other side of a desk.

The sitting room was one of the simplest and yet most exquisitely furnished in all the palace. All the furniture was made of dark hardwood, carved by master craftsmen in the time of Roseli's great-grandmother.

The carpet was ash gray. Even through her shoes, Roseli could tell how incredibly soft it was. The walls were white and unembellished, save for several landscape paintings of the countryside outside the capital. A small artist's signature in the left corner of each painting marked them as the work of John White, a deceased painter who had been famous for his eye for realism. The only time Roseli's mother had seemed pleased with a gift was when Roseli had given her one of those paintings years before.

Her mother was already sitting on the couch and sipping from a delicate porcelain cup of coffee when she entered. She glanced up after Roseli bowed. "Sit."

Roseli sat on the couch across from her, reaching to pour herself a cup. She emptied about half the milk carafe into it. She knew how strong her mother liked her coffee.

"If your fiancée can avoid getting assassinated in the next twenty-four hours, you should be married by this time tomorrow. After last night's revelation, I spoke with Emperor Alexander of Calliope and convinced him to direct part of his fleet toward Delphi sooner than planned. The ones patrolling near the border should arrive in a week. I have called back as many of our forces to Delphi from the border as I can and still leave it defended. I've also spoken with the Varcian empress, and she has said she will send some ships. We shouldn't expect much from her. The Varcians are only interested in risking their ships when it is a matter of conquest, not defending allies."

"I know." Her concerns about her upcoming marriage were starting to seem inconsequential in comparison with the coming war.

"You'll have to put off your honeymoon. I want both you and Lucia to remain in the capital for the time being. Now that Lucia is removed from the Calliopean navy's chain of command, she'll be the ideal person to liaise with them."

"Could she not have done that better as an admiral?" Roseli failed to keep the resentment from her tone. She knew how much losing her commission had hurt Lucia.

Her mother shook her head. "No, were she still a Calliopean naval officer, she would be obligated to act in her planet's best interests before Delphi's. I doubt an oath has truly changed her loyalties, but she seems the honorable sort, and now, at least, she can do what is best for Delphi with a clear conscience."

"Just not fight for it."

"You know, there was a reason I tried to teach you to play chess. Your future wife is more valuable as a queen than a knight. Don't risk losing her in battle if you don't have to."

Roseli's childhood chess lessons had not gone well. She had no talent for tactical strategy, and her mother was not the patient sort. Most games had ended with her mother explaining in cutting words why she had lost after only a few moves and Roseli finding herself nearly at the point of tears. It had been a relief when her mother had finally given up on the idea.

Her mother barely seemed to have noticed that she'd said nothing. "While military decisions take up my time, I will expect you to assume most of my regular imperial duties. You are no great military strategist, but you have a good sense of economics and governance. You've also got far more patience for dealing with the old families and guilds than I ever had. I'll have Roxane take over your social engagements. She's not the brightest in matters of governance, but she has a talent for charming people."

That was her mother's way: she wrapped compliments in subtle insults and made praise sound like a dull statement of fact.

A nagging worry tugged at Roseli. "There is no preventing this war, is there?"

"Not since Terra Nueva attacked Princess Lucia's ship and escorts. Even if war has not been declared yet, that was the first shot fired. If only the truce could have lasted just a little longer." She sighed. "Some of my economic reforms were finally showing results. We've only just paid down the debt from the last war." She rubbed at the bridge of her nose. "There is no point dwelling on what we cannot change. An empress does not choose the era over which she reigns."

"Is that something my grandmother said?"

"No, your great-grandmother wrote that in one of her journals. Your grandmother was the one who said war got in the way of a good time." She took a sip of her coffee. "Speaking of which, there is another matter."

"Yes?"

"My mother spoke with me the day before I first married. I thought I should do the same for you."

Roseli had a brief flash of panic that her mother was about to give her some sort of talk that would go badly for them both. It had been Roseli's childhood nurse who'd explained to her where babies came from. As Roseli had been five at the time and her nurse rather conservative, the old woman had explained babies grew in their mother's tummies without elaborating on how they got there or how they got out.

Roxane's far more liberal nurse, Emily, had furnished further details to Roseli years later with the help of an age-appropriate book, including how babies grew in the uterus, not the stomach, and could be conceived naturally or artificially through egg or gene splices. She had only vaguely hinted that sex was something humans might do for pleasure. When Roseli had reached her teenage years, Emily had quietly given her a few more books that clarified matters.

Roseli's mother had never seen the need to comment on the topic. The closest she had ever come to offering Roseli relationship advice was after things had gone south with Roseli's first lover and lady-in-waiting, Lady Heather. Her mother had told her, "She was a fickle, faithless little tart. Try to pick a better one next time."

Her mother seemed in no rush to speak this time.

At last, Roseli cleared her throat. "What did your mother tell you?"

"To be honest, I hardly remember. I was so angry with her, I didn't listen." Her hands clenched on the table. "My mother caroused with more lovers than any empress in generations, and yet she had the gall to forbid me from marrying the man I loved. She couldn't understand why I wanted your father at my side as my consort, not just in my bed. She said it was my duty as the crown princess of Delphi to wed husbands who could bring me the loyalty of the old noble houses, not some lowborn soldier."

Roseli didn't have the faintest idea what to say, but her mother wasn't waiting for an answer.

"She was right in the end. I needed a first husband who could strengthen my future reign. I was young, though, and I resented her. I barely spoke to her for months. If I had known how little time she had left, I would have made peace with her sooner."

Her mother paused, and something in her expression softened. She looked almost unsure, which was not an expression Roseli had often seen on her before. "You don't resent me for this, do you? You've never asked to marry any of your lovers, but I suspect that is because you already knew what the answer would be. If the Veritas girl ever comes into her inheritance, she may be an option for a later wife, but not the illegitimately born general or the courtesan."

"I…" There were many things Roseli resented her mother for, but the obligations of her birth were not among them. She knew when it was her mother speaking and when it was the crown. "No, I don't. I know my duty."

"Then you are wiser than I was at the same age. Perhaps you can avoid the same mistakes. I was not kind to Lord Leon in the first years of our marriage. I regret that. We had been childhood friends, and I threw that away with my coldness and indifference toward him after we married."

Her mother looked at her cup on the table, turning it between her palms. "Despite that, he always helped me politically without failing. When I assumed the throne, Prince Leon brought me the loyalty of the Stewart family and the other great northern houses. Without him, those damn northern separatists might have finally gotten some real traction during my first year as empress.

"Prince Leon wasn't happy when I married your father, but in his quiet way, he was there for me when your father died only a few months later. He didn't have to be, not after how I'd treated him. He remained patiently at my side, even when I had no use for him or anyone else for a time after…after that horrible night." She fell silent.

"Mother?" Roseli ached to reach for her, to bridge the distance between them. For an instant, she was again the frightened little girl who'd lost her sisters and nurse. The child whose mother couldn't bear the sight of her for nearly a year after her sisters' deaths and had left her to the care of others until she was old enough to begin serious lessons.

Her mother looked away as she had so many times before. When she turned back, her face was a carefully crafted mask of dignity. "Enough of the past. What I mean to say is, try to be kind to your first wife. She seems like a decent enough woman and may be a valuable ally to you."

"I will," said Roseli. Only after she left did it occur to her that her mother had just given her the same advice as Prince Ambrose.

❖

Lucia spent her morning reliving one of the worst days of her life. She sat with Admiral Heart and Director Barker in a small room as they reviewed the data from the *Intrepid*'s black box, including watching footage of the bridge during the attack.

She had faced her fair share of battles, but it was still chilling to listen to the horrible crashing boom that had echoed through the *Intrepid* when it was hit. Her stomach knotted as she watched the grainy footage of the frantic evacuation of the bridge before it depressurized.

She saw herself barking orders. There was her cousin Penelope, stepping up to one of the control panels to replace an unconscious crewmate. In the video, Lucia could only see her tapping frantically, but she knew from speaking with Penelope later that she had been trying to seal the damaged sections of the ship before they'd vented too much oxygen. Then there was the panel explosion that had nearly destroyed the girl's hands.

From the impassable distance of a few days, she watched smoke filling the bridge, saw her first mate Commander Jonas dragging the stunned and injured ensign to safety, the smoke growing thicker. Another explosion caught Jonas in the back, throwing him over the girl.

Lucia watched herself and another crew member fight through the smoke to pull them both to safety. There was a wrenching sound as the bridge depressurized only seconds after the door was sealed. The void of space sucked away the flames.

The video didn't show it, but her ship's two escorts, the *Valiant* and the *Endeavour*, were both destroyed during the surprise attack.

"Turn it off." Although the room was silent, she could still hear the screams and yells. She smelled smoke and burning wires.

Neither Director Barker nor Admiral Heart said anything. Admiral

Heart politely averted his gaze, giving her a moment. Director Barker cast her a thoughtful glance but kept her peace.

Lucia forced herself to focus. She and the bridge crew had retreated to a secondary command center on the other side of the ship and had limped the vessel the rest of the way to Delphi. The black box they had taken with them when they scuttled the ship wasn't the one from the bridge but a backup.

She turned to the tech running the computer, and the screen attached to the black box, which was neither black nor a box but a green disk. "Play back the ship's scanners just before the attack."

Data and video from the ship's external sensors flowed across the screen.

She saw what she'd seen on the day. At first, there was no sign of any kind of ship or satellite anywhere close, and then a Terra Nuevan ship appeared on the sensors. She shuddered. She had to be missing something.

"Play it again."

Still nothing to offer any sort of explanation.

"Again."

"Look, see there, there was a surge of electromagnetic energy," said Director Barker. She was pointing at the reading from one of the ship's long-range sensors.

"Those are just fairy lights. They can happen with faulty equipment or in deep space for no apparent reason," said Admiral Heart dismissively.

In the Calliopean navy, they had called them gremlin's fire. One of Lucia's first lessons as a new captain had been to learn to identify when energy spikes were random or not. Had she missed something on that fateful day?

"How often do you see fairies before an unexpected attack?" asked Director Barker, leaning toward the screen like a hound that had caught a scent. "Bring up all the data on the energy spike."

Lucia watched the screen fill with numbers as the tech at the computer hit a few buttons. Now that she looked at it all broken down into code, she saw that what she had so easily dismissed as just a random fluctuation was unique.

"Fuck." She seldom swore, as it was not befitting for a princess or an admiral, but she made exceptions. She ran her hands over the screen to outline the pattern.

Director Barker smiled in a way that bared her teeth. "More like, fuck the Terra Nuevans. Now we know what to look for. If any of their new ships come within spitting distance of our long-range sensors, we'll be ready for them."

❖

When Roseli entered Beatrice's rooms, she found her sitting in her small office, surrounded by screens, speaking tersely into a phone when Roseli came in. It was the most simply decorated and functional of all the rooms in Beatrice's suite. Beatrice had always said there was no point going to much trouble with the room since as she used it for neither receiving visitors nor relaxing.

"No, daffodils will not do. How can you be out of tulips the day before a royal wedding? You either find more or pay the penalty for defaulting on the contract. Yes, I know that could bankrupt you. Well, maybe you shouldn't have promised flowers you couldn't deliver. I don't want more excuses. You have an hour before I go to your competitor." Beatrice turned off the call.

Roseli leaned over the deck chair to hug her from behind. "You're sexy when you act all mean and business-y."

Beatrice barely seemed to feel the touch. "This is me being nice. If I were being mean, I'd just bankrupt that fool of a flower wholesaler. Now that he knows I'm serious, he'll find me more tulips."

"Have lunch with me."

"There is too much to do."

"Will anything blow up if it's not done?"

She swiveled her chair so that she could see Roseli. "No, I don't think so. For all their faults, at least flowers don't explode."

"Then come eat. I've ordered some food."

They went out to Beatrice's sitting room, and Roseli settled onto one of the low couches with Beatrice beside her. Although Beatrice's makeup was as flawless as ever, Roseli could see faint lines of exhaustion beneath her eyes. The last few days had not been any easier on Beatrice than they had been on her. She did not want to ask more than she already had.

"What is troubling you, darling?" asked Beatrice.

Roseli blinked. "How could you tell?"

"You're chewing on your lip the way you do when you're nervous about something."

There was no arguing with that. Beatrice had known her the

shortest time of her lovers but was the best at reading her. She had never lost the skills of observation she had cultivated for her previous profession. "I need a favor."

"Anything."

"Can you keep an eye on Alexis and Julia tonight? I know we all agreed that it would just make things harder to spend the night before the wedding together, but I still don't think that you or Alexis or Julia should be alone."

"You're mostly worried about Alexis, aren't you?"

"Yes," she admitted. "Although I know it will be hard for Julia and you as well."

"I understand. I'll ask them both to eat dinner with me tonight. I'll see that there is sufficient wine to relax and speak easily but not so much that they are hungover tomorrow."

"Thank you. I know I can always depend on you."

As they settled down to eat, her thoughts were still troubled. With the honeymoon delayed and the new responsibilities her mother had given her, she'd be lucky to spend any real time with Lucia in the coming days, much less Alexis, Julia, and Beatrice. Everything would be so much simpler if a war was not looming over all of them.

She wished she could step back in time a few weeks to when her biggest worry had been dancing with the Terra Nuevan ambassador and telling Alexis, Julia, and Beatrice about her engagement.

CHAPTER EIGHTEEN

It seemed rather ridiculous to Lucia to spend her entire afternoon attending a wedding rehearsal at a temple. She knew that the ceremony would be broadcast live the next day, but did anyone think that she and Roseli needed to practice standing and repeating a few lines?

All the same, it had been a relief to be called away to the rehearsal and spared another round of reviewing the black box data. After initially identifying the energy spike, she'd had little left to contribute. Further analysis lay in the capable hands of Director Barker and her team.

The sun was setting, and she and Roseli were both tired and hungry by the time the rehearsal finished. Roseli invited her back to her rooms for an early dinner. They sat in the courtyard, enjoying the warm spring evening. Lucia updated Roseli on what she had discovered that morning. Roseli listened intently, her attractive face drawn tight with worry.

When the food was gone, Lucia stood. "I should be going."

"You can stay if you'd like," said Roseli. "It's nice out, and the servants just brought the Septian whiskey. We may not have another chance to sit and talk like this for some time, especially with the honeymoon delayed."

Lucia frowned. "You do not intend to spend the evening with your lovers?"

"No, we all agreed that would be too hard. Beatrice promised she would look after them."

"I see." She still wasn't sure how things worked between Roseli, General Tate, Senator Veritas, and Lady Swann. Did Roseli sleep with them separately? Together? Were any of them ever intimate together without Roseli? She could hardly ask unless Roseli offered that information herself, but that didn't stop a few wildly erotic possibilities from skittering across her imagination.

Roseli frowned. "If Lieutenant Laurent is waiting for you or you simply want some time alone, I understand."

"No, she's not." She could never ask Charlotte to her bed again, not now that she understood the unequal depth of affection between them. That evening, she had intended to go back to her room and try to sleep, not that sleep was likely to come easily. She sat back down.

Roseli poured the whiskey into small blue glasses. "How are you holding up? Are you ready for this?"

"The impending conflict?" She shrugged. "I've known more years of war than peace during my adult life. I've sent others into danger while I remained in the relative safety of a flagship or once on an orbital platform, but I've never been completely on the sidelines. I am glad I was able to help today with the black box, but the thought of not going back to the front when the fighting begins again, that is hard."

"I know it's not much, but I think after today and yesterday, I can convince my mother to make you a permanent member of her advisory council."

"Thank you. At the very least, I want to be useful." She took a sip, enjoying the smooth way the whiskey burned down her throat.

"You are already that and more." Roseli leaned back against the couch. "Matters of interplanetary importance aside, how are you feeling about tomorrow?"

"Oh, are we doing something tomorrow?" said Lucia. She was happy to be talking about anything other than her lost commission.

Roseli laughed. "You know, the whole thing with the temple and me wearing a ridiculously puffy white dress."

"I like the dress."

"Do you now?"

Lucia's thoughts flickered to holding Roseli in her arms two nights before. What would it be like when they hadn't just barely escaped death? "I like the woman who wears it even more."

"Flatterer."

"So what about you?" asked Lucia. "Are you ready?"

Roseli shrugged. "As much as I can be. This is my first wedding, too. I barely got through my debutante ball. A wedding is going to be on a whole other level."

"You have official paramours. Was there no ceremony with them?" The entire idea of lovers having official status rather baffled

Lucia. While it was not unheard of for Calliopean nobles to take lovers, or even keep mistresses, they did it quietly.

Several years after Lucia's mother had died, her father had become involved with a widowed duchess. Lucia had seldom been home, but even she had seen the positive effect the sweet-natured and patient woman had had on her still-grieving father. Duchess Dupree had moved into the palace and accompanied her father to royal events, but he was careful to never refer to her as more than a dear friend. It would have destroyed Duchess Dupree's reputation if Lucia's father had ever openly acknowledged her as his mistress.

Roseli grinned. "No, my grandmother collected and dismissed lovers so fast that the official protocol to elevate a lover from unofficial to official status was simplified. All I had to do to acknowledge Alexis and later Julia and Beatrice was tell the royal steward to add royal paramour to their title the next time we were announced entering a ball."

"You don't strike me as the rapidly dismissing sort."

"I'm not," admitted Roseli. "There was only one woman before Alexis, and she left me rather than the other way around."

Lucia sensed there was a story there but suspected it wasn't the time to ask. "I cannot say the same of myself. I have had my share of bedmates but few for long."

"Never?"

"There was a girl during my last year in the academy. Her name was Stephanie. We thought perhaps…" There was no point thinking of what might have been. She took a drink to steady herself. "We were stationed on different ships, and hers was lost during her first battle."

"I'm sorry." There was genuine concern in Roseli's voice.

"It was a long time ago." Sometimes, Lucia still wondered what kind of woman Stephanie would have been if she'd lived long enough to be promoted to the rank of lieutenant. Could the bright spark of desire and young love between them have matured into something lasting and deep? She would never know.

The silence hung heavy between them.

Lucia raised her glass. When all else failed, a toast was often a good idea. "To all the women we have known before."

Roseli raised her glass and lightly tapped Lucia's, "And to new beginnings."

Lucia wasn't sure, but she thought she saw something akin to an invitation in her eyes. "We just have to get through the wedding first."

Roseli set down her glass. "Not necessarily."

"What do you mean?"

Roseli reached to cover her hand with her own. "We don't have to wait until after the wedding unless you want to."

Lucia could feel the heat of her palm through her glove. "Is that so?"

"It is our last chance to lie together as anything other than wives." Roseli looked at Lucia coyly through her dark lashes. There was no mistaking the desire there.

When she was a child, Lucia's nurse had once told her a fable about a man who was chased by a tiger and came to a cliff. He climbed down a vine trying to escape the tiger only to find another tiger waiting for him at the base of the cliff. While the man clung to the vine for dear life, two mice began to chew on the vine up above. As he trembled in fear of death, the man saw a strawberry vine on the cliff with a single ripe strawberry. Faced with impending doom, the man ate the strawberry. It was delicious.

Lucia had never understood the story before. Now she was starting to. She'd lost so much in the last week, and the future was filled with danger. In front of her was a beautiful woman who wanted her. She moved her free hand to press against the back of Roseli's neck and kissed her.

"A picnic?" asked Julia as she stepped into the small bower of rose frames and bushes ringing a stone bench and spring grass at the edge of the palace gardens. She had wanted to go home, but Beatrice had insisted.

The light had already faded, but there were dim outdoor lights set in the ground and several strings of small ones among the roses. A blanket had been laid out with several trays of food and drink.

Beatrice was reclining casually on her side on the picnic, her head resting on her elbow like a girl in a classical painting. Her silk sundress only added to the effect. Alexis sat cross-legged, looking oddly regal and straight-backed for a woman on a bright pink blanket.

"The weather is warm enough, and I thought the palace gardens would be lovely," said Beatrice, flashing a white-toothed smile that looked forced.

The garden was also neutral ground, something which Julia, a woman who spent her days amidst political intrigue, could respect. With a shrug, she joined them on the blanket. She'd likely wrinkle her suit, but that was what dry cleaners were for, not that she picked up or dropped off her dry cleaning herself.

She considered the food. "You even got the kitchen to make those little cherry cupcakes. How did you manage that? Wasn't Roseli just saying the head cook gripes when she asks for those since they are so much work?"

"I can be incredibly charming when I need to," said Beatrice. "Also, I always ask how her granddaughters are doing."

"That's the real trick," said Alexis.

They settled down to eat. It was a beautiful evening. Beatrice had acquired some fine Calliopean red wine. One thing Julia would never fault Beatrice for was her taste. As the food slowly vanished, so did most avenues of casual conversation. They quietly sipped their wine, none wanting to be the first to remind the others of why they were there.

Surprising even herself, Julia broke the silence. "This bit of the garden is where I met Roseli."

Beatrice startled, sloshing her wine. "Seriously?"

"Yes. On that stone bench over there. She was hiding from Duchess Hawthorne during a ball."

"Didn't Duchess Hawthorne marry Lady Monroe? I think I just saw a notice in the paper about their first child's naming ceremony," said Alexis.

"She did, but before that, she was chasing Roseli like a cat in heat while you were away on Calliope liaising with their military, not that Roseli ever took any notice of her," said Julia.

Alexis's expression went stony. "I had no choice in that. The empress ordered me to go."

From what Julia had heard at the time, Alexis had been one of the few surviving Delphian generals who had led multiple joint operations with Calliopean forces. General Harding and General Swift had both died in the last year of the war, and General Potter had taken his own life a few months after the armistice.

"I know," she said carefully. "Roseli missed you terribly while you were gone."

"And you had no scruples in easing that loneliness?" It was impossible to tell if Alexis's tone held acceptance or recrimination.

"For the record, she kissed me first," she told them.

"Oh?" asked Beatrice.

"Yes, although maybe the first kiss didn't count. When Duchess Hawthorne found us, Roseli pulled me into a kiss. It worked. Hawthorne stormed off in a huff."

Alexis smiled thinly. "That sounds like Roseli. I met her for the first time during a ball in a different part of the gardens. She was hiding in a clump of bushes like some kind of forest nymph, trying to avoid awkwardly running into her former lover Lady Heather and her wife."

"That's our girl," said Beatrice. "Very conflict-averse."

"She asked me to get her some snacks. I did, and things went from there," said Alexis.

A thought occurred to Julia. "She kissed you for the first time in the garden, didn't she?"

To her credit, Alexis didn't blush or even look embarrassed. "She did, and she wasn't trying to ward off some unwanted suitor, either."

Beatrice laughed, her face softening with a true smile. "Should I feel disappointed that I first met her at a poetry reading and didn't get a kiss?"

"You wasted no time in becoming part of her life," Julia told her. "I think you knew her about a week before you were helping her choose dresses. Not that I'm complaining. You did wonders for her wardrobe and saved me from having to go to as many balls. There is a limit to how much even I can network."

"For that, I am also grateful, Beatrice," said Alexis. She glanced at Julia. "To your credit, you also spared me from having to attend as many social events as I had to when I first became Roseli's paramour. I fear that navigating high society has never been my strong suit."

Beatrice brushed a loose strand of hair from her forehead. Her normally carefully styled curls were caught in a loose bun that was unraveling. "I find your approach to high society to be rather refreshing. You never say anything you don't mean."

"Which, unfortunately, goes over badly sometimes."

"I don't know. I'm still laughing about how you told Lady Kadish that her dress looked like a pumpkin at the spring ball," added Julia.

"She asked me what I thought of it. The dress was voluminous and orange. I assumed the resemblance to a gourd was deliberate. I intended no offense."

"To be fair, dear," said Beatrice, "I don't think she took any. Your comments have become notorious enough that any woman who asks you what you think of a dress or a hat is deliberately fishing for a funny story to tell her friends." She sat up to refill everyone's wineglasses.

Julia had known Beatrice long enough to recognize when she was controlling a conversation, pulling it in an inconsequential direction to relax those around her. Even with all of them playing along, it wasn't working. She didn't want to pretend everything was all right anymore.

"What now?" she asked.

"Tonight, we drink wine, and in the morning, we watch Roseli get married," said Alexis.

"And after that?" She studied the ruby liquid in her glass.

"We keep supporting her in whatever way she needs," said Alexis. "The same as we always have."

"Just with a wife added to the mix." She didn't know why she was talking so openly; she didn't usually, not with Alexis and Beatrice. There was something about the night, though, the smell of roses and the softness of the electric lights in the trees that made her feel outside of time.

Beatrice pressed her shoulder. "Yes, things are going to change, but we'll figure it out."

"You think so?"

"What other choice do we have? Leaving isn't an option, at least not for me. I love her too much. As long as she wants me, I'm not going anywhere."

"Same," said Alexis.

"Yes," said Julia. She raised her glass. "To love and the strange places it leads us."

They all toasted.

A flash of inspiration struck Lucia when they reached the bedroom door. She placed one hand against the small of Roseli's back and the other behind her knees and lifted her.

Roseli made a startled gasp and clutched at her shoulders and then laughed. "What are you doing?"

"It's traditional on Calliope to carry a new bride across the threshold."

"Not on Delphi," said Roseli. "And we're not brides yet."

"Consider it practice." Lucia carried her the short distance to the bed, setting her down and following her onto the blankets.

What followed was the usual awkward scramble of two new lovers trying to undress while still kissing and touching at the same time. They were both breathless and desperate by the time they were free of their garments, her gloves and ribbon included.

Lucia drew back to look. She had seen her fair share of naked women in her time, but such a sight never ceased to fill her with a sense of awe, especially when faced with a woman as beautiful as Roseli.

She was slim but still pleasingly curved in just the right places. Her skin was smooth and pale, her cheeks and chest flushed pink with desire. Only the bandage and medical tape that still covered her shoulder and part of her arm intruded upon the moment, filling Lucia with a vague sense of guilt. She'd tried so hard to shield her and had failed.

She must have betrayed something in her expression because Roseli brought up a hand to cover herself. "Not what you were hoping?"

Had Lucia not been caught up in her need, it might have amazed her that the heir to an empire, and a woman of no small charms, was still insecure under the gaze of a new lover. She said quickly, "You're lovely. I was worried your arm might be hurting you. It's still bandaged."

"You were hurt worse than me." Roseli ran a hand up Lucia's arm on the unbandaged side. "You know, you're pretty easy on the eyes yourself. You must work out a lot."

"There tends not to be a lot of other options to spend off-duty hours on a ship." She had no intention of joining a folk band, a bridge club, a chess club, a poker night, a prayer group, a video gaming group, a writing group, or a book club.

"Hmm." Roseli's hands wandered across Lucia's collarbone and then lower, circling a breast and brushing against a nipple. The touch was like an electric shock.

Lucia decided that the time for discussion was done. She kissed Roseli again and pushed her back against the covers. Roseli went eagerly. Lucia wanted to take her time to explore and caress every part of her intended. She kissed down Roseli's neck to her collarbone, and her moans grew desperate.

"Impatient," Lucia murmured as she caressed a breast.

"Don't be a tease."

"Who says I'm teasing?" Lucia shifted so she could run a hand up Roseli's thigh. She slipped two fingers through her folds to press her clit lightly.

Roseli gasped.

Lucia pressed harder and made a series of slow circles.

"Fingers inside, please."

That was all the invitation Lucia needed. She pressed two fingers into the warmth of Roseli's eager body. She brought their lips together again as she moved her fingers. She loved the thrill of learning a new lover's desires. When she moved too slowly, Roseli bucked her hips so Lucia moved faster and harder. Her breath grew ragged.

Lucia could already feel the first fluttering of internal muscles that signaled Roseli was on the edge of orgasm. She adjusted her hand so that her thumb brushed Roseli's clit with each motion, and that was it. Roseli did not scream, but her sharp gasp was pleasing. Lucia would have happily seen her to another orgasm, but Roseli was already moving, pushing at her shoulders.

"I want to touch you." Her dark eyes were bright with need. She nudged Lucia onto her back, kissing her collarbone and lower, running appreciative hands over her breasts and toned abs. "Seriously, how many crunches do you do?"

"I don't like to brag."

"You should."

While Lucia was enjoying the admiration, she was getting desperate enough she needed things to progress.

Roseli looked up, a devilish smile on her lips. "What would you like?"

Lucia had never been a woman who hesitated to ask for what she wanted. "Your mouth."

Roseli, rather frustratingly, seemed to be in no rush, thoroughly kissing every bit of skin she could get to. At last, she nudged Lucia's legs open and ducked her head.

Lucia clutched at the bedsheets and wondered if Roseli had won the affections of all three lovers purely through her talent for oral sex or if her skills resulted from having three lovers to practice with. She seemed to know instinctively how hard to press with her tongue and where. Lucia might have made some undignified sounds when her orgasm overwhelmed her. She still felt dazed when Roseli crawled up and kissed her on the cheek.

"Worn out?" Roseli teased warmly.

"Hardly." She was nearly boneless, but she wasn't going to let on. "I don't suppose you have any toys, do you?"

Roseli had a sudden fit of giggles. "Which kind do you want?"

"Strap-on?"

She smirked. "Hang on, I'll fetch the box."

"You have a box?"

"Several." Roseli scrambled from the bed and went to the heavy wooden wardrobe. She returned to the bed with a soft-sided storage box and thumped it down. "Take your pick."

Lucia sat up and began sorting through an impressive and varied collection of dildos and similar toys. "Which is your favorite?"

"The blue dildo and the red harness."

Lucia fished both out of the box. "The blue one is kind of big."

Roseli blushed, which was an impressive feat, as her face and chest were already flushed from their earlier activities. "You did ask which my favorite was. Er, just to make sure we're on the same page, did you want to use a toy on me or the other way around? If...um, you want me to fuck you, you should pick out the toy you want for it."

"Versatile, aren't you?" Lucia pulled her into another kiss. "I would like to fuck you with a strap-on if that is what you want."

"Very much so."

While this model of harness was unfamiliar and involved a few more small buckles than seemed strictly necessary, Lucia had wrangled enough harnesses in her time to figure it out quickly. "How do you want to do this?" she asked Roseli.

"I want to ride you." For such a sweet woman, Roseli could sound wonderfully dirty when she wanted to.

Lucia wasn't eager to be on her back again so soon, but she aimed to please. She reclined against the headboard and beckoned Roseli to her.

Roseli used her fingers to slick herself with a bottle of lube beside the bed and then crawled over Lucia. She kissed her deeply before bracing a hand on the headboard to pull herself up and guide the toy into herself. She made a low moan as she sank down.

The sight of Roseli over her utterly entranced Lucia. Her dark brown hair had come loose from its twist, and it tumbled all over her shoulders. The position showed her breasts to full effect, soft and round with alert, rose-colored nipples. Lucia reached up to cup a breast. Roseli whimpered when Lucia caught the nipple between two fingers and pinched lightly.

"Ah."

"That a good or a bad ah?"

"Good," Roseli managed. "You can keep doing that." She rested one hand on Lucia's shoulder and the other on the headboard as she rode up and down.

Lucia pinched harder. "Still good?"

"Yes, very."

Lucia paid attention to the other breast in the same way and got appreciative sounds. Roseli moved more quickly, falling into steady movements. Positioned as she was, there wasn't much Lucia could do other than touch her. She could feel the pressure of the dildo against her mons and clit, and that was nice but not enough to get her off.

Roseli moved with more determination, moaning as she did. Keeping one hand on Lucia for balance, she reached down to press her clit and came with a cry and then collapsed onto her.

Lucia held her, kissing her cheek. After a moment, Roseli wriggled, and Lucia let go so Roseli could rise enough to get off the toy and then settle back against Lucia's right side.

Roseli undid the clasps of the strap-on that Lucia had yet to disentangle herself from. "Can I get you off again?"

"You have the energy after that?"

"Not much."

Once Lucia was free of the harness, Roseli found her clit with deft fingers. Lucia was so wound up from what they had just done, it did not take her long to tense in release, pulling Roseli even closer as she did. Roseli snuggled against her, head resting on her shoulder. Lucia lazily ran a hand through her hair. She could feel herself already nodding off from the soporific effect of two orgasms so close together.

She did, however, have the presence of mind to reach for a blanket they had kicked out of the way and tug it over them.

She wondered if she should offer to leave. Roseli turned her head just enough to kiss Lucia's collarbone, and Lucia decided she wasn't going anywhere. She drifted off listening to Roseli's soft snores.

CHAPTER NINETEEN

Julia Veritas woke up alone in her bed in her townhouse, only mildly hungover. She almost wished she were genuinely hungover or sick or had some way to get out of attending the wedding. Beatrice had by some wave of her hand put an end to any new bottles of wine after a certain point as they'd all sat talking in the palace garden the evening before. Beatrice had gently suggested they should all get to bed. Alexis had returned to her small room in the palace barracks, Beatrice to her rooms, and Julia to her townhouse.

She slammed a hand into her alarm. She ached to go back to sleep, but she needed to get up and get ready for the wedding. There would be cameras, and as an official royal paramour, she couldn't risk giving the tabloids anything, not even unevenly painted lips. She dragged herself into the bathroom.

Sometime later, she was ready to go. Her hair lay smooth about her shoulders after considerable efforts with a straightening iron to suppress her natural frizz. Her makeup was flawless, and she wore one of her best recently dry-cleaned suits.

She almost made it out the door before her housekeeper, Ms. Hadley, intervened. "Breakfast is laid out in the dining room," the stout matronly woman said loudly.

Julia froze. "I need to get going."

"You have time to eat. If you leave now, you'll arrive unfashionably early," insisted Ms. Hadley.

Julia thanked her and went into the dining room because all else aside, it was nice to have someone in her life who cared if she ate or not. Technically, she was employing Ms. Hadley, but respect went both ways.

She was halfway through an uninspiring breakfast smoothie that was supposed to be healthy when she heard the front door open and Ms. Hadley arguing with someone.

Her mother strode into the room. "Good, I've caught you in time."

"Mother?" asked Julia, setting aside the smoothie that she had never particularly wanted. Something significant had happened if her mother had come across town unannounced instead of summoning her to the family home.

Her mother was not dressed for a royal wedding. Her suit was wrinkled, and her hair and makeup looked as if they had been done the day before and had never been touched up. "You will not be attending the wedding."

"Why?"

"You need to call the palace and tell them you're sick or make some other excuse. Whatever you do, you cannot go."

"I'm pretty sure the gossip columns will have a field day if I don't. It is expected of a royal paramour," said Julia dryly. Why it was expected, she wasn't entirely sure; she thought the opposite might be kinder, but who was she to argue with tradition?

Her mother crossed to the table. "No, you don't understand. It's not safe."

Julia stood. "What do you mean?"

Her mother glanced around the room and sat, leaning close. "Have you been diligent about sweeping for bugs like I taught you?"

"Yes, Mother." Well, Ms. Hadley had, anyway. The seemingly sweet old woman was a retired imperial guard and diligent about seeing to household security. Julia had hired her for her security expertise rather than her dubious smoothie-making talents.

Her mother took out a small clamshell-shaped noise-canceling device and set it on the table. It began making a low-pitched buzzing sound as soon as her mother opened it. While highly effective for preventing electronic surveillance, Julia found them too annoying to even own one.

"I have new intelligence. I don't know who, but I'm certain someone in the palace has been aiding the assassination attempts, and they will not stop. You must not go to the wedding. I can't risk losing my heir and daughter."

It was no surprise that she would put heir before daughter; that was the Veritas way. "If what you say is true, we have to warn Princess Roseli."

Her mother frowned. "I got this information through a leak in the palace security services. The empress already knows. She has tripled security and locked down the palace like a vault while her people try to identify the traitor, but she can't cancel the wedding, not without endangering the treaty or frightening the public. The palace has brought in reserve troops to patrol the area around the Great Temple, but I don't think it will be enough."

"And you're sure the wedding will be the next target?"

"I have no proof, but every instinct in my body tells me so. I don't want you there."

"All you have is a hunch."

"My hunches are seldom wrong." There was no doubt in her voice.

Julia chewed on her lip, torn as to what to do.

Her mother's voice softened, growing cajoling. "I am so sorry, Julia, but there is nothing you can do. We must keep you safe and trust the princess's guards to do the same for her. If you do not feel capable of calling the palace, I can do it for you. I'll say you are ill, and likely, everyone will just assume you are too upset about the wedding to go."

Julia knew that tone from her girlhood. Her mother had used it for everything from getting her to eat broccoli when she was a toddler to convincing her to get a nose job when she was sixteen. She still regretted the nose job. Her natural nose had been a bit long and pointy, but it had been her own.

"If Roseli is going into danger, I can't let her do it alone."

"You can't possibly stop the wedding. If you try, everyone will think you are doing it out of jealousy."

"Then I won't." What chance did she have if the empress was letting the wedding go forward when she knew the risks? "I will warn her guards of your fears, and I will face what comes with Roseli."

Her mother blinked. "What?"

"If you thought Dad or Papa were in danger, would you abandon them?"

"That is different. They are my husbands. I will always protect my family."

"And Roseli is my lover!" Julia had never spoken to her mother like this before, but she'd never been so afraid, either. "She is family to me."

"I don't care who she is to you. I will not let you risk your life for her sake."

Julia stood. "That is not your choice. If you are so concerned, then use your damn spy networks for good for once and figure out who's trying to kill Princess Roseli. That is the only way you can keep me safe."

"Julia, stop being ridiculous. Even if I could, which is beyond my power, there isn't time. The wedding is in a few hours."

"And I will be there." She turned and walked out of her living room. The effect would have been more dramatic if she hadn't had to wait on the porch for her chauffeur to bring the car around.

Her mother caught up with her. "You're being childish."

Julia said nothing.

"And idiotic."

She did not reply, just kept looking straight ahead.

Her mother let out a hissing breath through her teeth and then unexpectedly laid a hand on her shoulder. "I can't talk you out of this, can I?"

"No."

"Then be careful. If I'm wrong about today, then I'm going to call in favors and see if I can't use my resources to figure out where the attacks are coming from. I won't have you in danger again."

Julia turned her head to look at her mother. Her forehead was creased with worry, and her lips pressed so thinly together, they would have been white if not for her lipstick. She was genuinely afraid.

Julia had never seen her like that, and it deeply unsettled her. There was no going back, though. She was many things, but she was no coward. "Thank you."

As soon as she was in the car, she called Roseli's head guard. Officer Smith was polite, but Julia got the impression she wasn't telling her anything she didn't already know. She reassured her that every precaution was being taken, but that proved to be less than reassuring when Julia could hear the worry in her voice.

When she got to the temple, she spoke rapidly in hushed tones with Beatrice and Alexis, who had already been seated. She wanted to talk to them alone, but all three of them stepping away so close to the ceremony would be noticed.

Alexis listened solemnly and then spent all the time until the wedding subtly scanning the temple without obviously turning her head. Beatrice's face was locked into a rigid smile. She clutched a little purse in her lap so tightly, her knuckles went white. Julia wished she hadn't said anything. There was nothing any of them could do, and now she'd frightened Alexis and Beatrice.

❖

On the day of her wedding, Roseli sat in her dressing room swathed in layers of silk as a swarm of makeup artists and hairdressers made last touches. The well-coiffed and painted woman in the mirror was a piece of art. Roseli feared that if she so much as sneezed, she'd mess up all her attendants' careful work.

Her thoughts wandered. She was well-versed in pomp and circumstance. It had defined so much of her life. One lesson that she had learned early was the power of symbolism. A garden party had been planned for her ninth birthday, and that had meant being scrubbed and shoved into a scratchy dress.

She had hated being touched by the cold and impersonal hands of servants after her first nurse's death. She had gotten to the point where she wouldn't even let anyone but Prince Ambrose brush her hair. He had no particular talent for combing a child's hair, much less the angel-fine and easily tangled locks she'd had as a little girl, but she'd trusted he was at least trying not to pull it.

That day, though, he'd been called away, and rather than let a servant de-snarl her hair, Roseli had gone and hidden in the bushes of one of the courtyard gardens. Dragging an upset princess out of a shrub, especially one prone to biting when distressed, was above any of the guards' or servants' level of loyalty to the crown. Someone went to find Prince Ambrose.

He had knelt and peered into the bush. "Found a burrow, have you?"

"I'm not going, and you can't make me."

"I wasn't planning to."

That had filled her with optimism. "Then I don't have to go?"

He had sat on the grass. "No, you still need to go, but I will not make you. I'll talk you into it."

"I hate parties." She had crossed her arms.

"I know, but this is your birthday party. How will it look if you don't go?"

"I don't care. No one asked me if I wanted a party. I won't have any friends there anyway. It will just be a bunch of stupid courtiers and their kids. They don't care about me, just that I'm a princess."

"You're not wrong, Roseli."

"Then why do I have to go?"

"Because people have come to see a princess, and they will be disappointed if they don't."

"That is their problem."

He had seemed to consider what to say before he spoke. "You know that show you like, the one with the little witch who does science experiments?"

"Melody is so brave and awesome. She's friends with dragons and trolls, and she blows stuff up with baking soda and vinegar." Roseli had crawled closer but had still stayed within the protection of the bush.

"Yes, and you understand that while Melody is fictional, there is a real girl who is an actress and plays Melody, right?"

"Yes," Roseli had said carefully.

"And you care about the fictional character, not the actress."

She was feeling lost. "I guess so, I don't know the actress."

"And that's okay. I'm sure she has friends and family who care about her for who she is."

She did not reply.

"Being a member of the royal family is a lot like being an actress. It is your job to play the part of Princess Roseli for the Delphian public."

"Why?"

"Because they need a princess who is brave and kind in the same way you need a little witch who is fearless and smart. Do you understand?"

"Kind of," she had grumbled. "When do I get to be me, though?"

"When you are among people whom you love and trust and away from the eyes of the public."

She had grudgingly crawled out from behind the bush and had gone to her birthday party. Looking back years later, it had struck her as terribly sad that her adopted father had told her it was her duty in life to play a part. Likely, he had been told the same as a boy. All the same, his advice had seen her through countless years in her public role as Princess Roseli.

Just as the servants were finishing with Roseli's appearance, Roxane rustled in wearing a sea of pink taffeta. "My father says I can't go to the wedding!"

"What?"

"He says it's too dangerous, and Mother agrees."

Roseli sent the servants from the room with a wave. "Has something happened? Is there new intelligence from the guards?"

Roxane shook her head, the movement causing her chandelier-like crystal earrings to jangle. "I'm not sure. I think my father just got Mother alone this morning. He convinced her that after all the assassination attempts lately, it was a bad idea for both princesses to risk being outside the palace at the same time. I can just picture Mother saying that she doesn't want to risk both her heir and spare at the same time."

"I'm sorry, Roxane," said Roseli. "I know you were excited to be my maid of honor." Normally, she'd have happily gone to bat and argued with her mother for Roxane's sake, but with her wedding looming, she lacked the energy or time. Considering that she had been shot at two nights before, perhaps it was best if her little sister stayed within the safety of the palace walls.

Roxane huffed. "It's not fair. Everybody else gets to dress up and have fun while I'm stuck in the palace with my father."

"Prince Leon is not going?" She did not care one way or the other, but it was out of character for the royal consort to miss a public event at the empress's side.

"He says he wants to make sure I don't sneak out."

Considering the number of times Roxane had done exactly that, even slipping past her supposedly elite guards, that was not an unreasonable precaution.

Meredith poked her head into the room. "It's time, Princess, we need to get you to the temple."

Roseli turned back to Roxane. "I know it won't make up for missing a royal wedding, but I promise we'll spend some time together next week, okay? Just the two of us."

Roxane perked up. "Can we watch music videos and eat cupcakes?"

"I promise."

Roseli wished her cares could be so easily set aside. It had been years since a new episode of *Science Witch*, and sweets were enough to make her feel better.

❖

As the highest-ranking Calliopean naval officer on Delphi, Lieutenant Charlotte Laurent was invited to the royal wedding. She would not attend. She drew the line at watching the woman she loved, even one-sidedly, marry someone else. She had considered getting drunk that morning, but she had never been the sort to drink before noon.

Instead, as the rest of the city flocked to the temple or prepared to settle in front of their video screens, she went to the naval central command office. It was not in the palace but several blocks away, set in a large block of administrative buildings.

She took her time as she walked over, pausing as she crossed through a small city park to look at the arching blue sky. Her heart ached for what could never be with Lucia, but a new life that lay ahead of her on Delphi filled her with hope.

She breathed in the scents of wet pavement, cooking dough, and trash. There would be no more sterile-smelling recycled air and silence punctuated only by the sound of human voices, mechanic beeps, and vents. At last, she was free of the slowly crushing pressure of windowless metal walls.

At the edge of the park, she stopped to buy a cup of freshly brewed coffee from a small cart with the credit chip she had just been issued. The cost surprised her until the vendor explained it was mostly a deposit for the heavy plastic cup that would be refunded when she returned it to a green kiosk. She thanked the vendor and walked on, sipping her coffee. It was the best she had ever tasted.

She arrived to find the communications department of the central command building deserted. Most of the higher-ranking officers were at the wedding, and the rest of the staff gathered around a video screen in the break room, waiting for the wedding to start. She headed to the small office she had been assigned the day before. Hopefully, she could finally get through the packet of onboarding information she had been given.

She had no substantial work to do yet. While there had been a half dozen Calliopean liaison officers in this office during the last war, things had grown lax during peacetime. The limited amount of coordination required for joint border patrols had proven simple enough to be handled by direct communication between admirals. From what Charlotte understood, that was all about to change, and she could only hope she was equal to the task.

A knock on her door startled her. "Come in."

Lieutenant Lavine entered. The friendly, short Delphian officer was about a decade older than her and had a somewhat obsessive interest with Calliopean culture. When he had shown her around the building the day before, he had talked nearly incessantly about several local restaurants that served good Calliopean style food and a small independent movie theater that played classics from the golden age of Calliopean film every Friday night. He still seemed reasonably competent and had taken the time to help Charlotte complete her onboarding paperwork the day before, which she had appreciated.

He set a tablet on her desk and without preamble asked, "Do you know how to read code?"

Charlotte set her coffee down. "I'm not a communications officer or a decrypter, at least not officially. On my last ship, our decrypter died of a heart attack, and I had to take over his duties until the end of the war."

"Can you look at this transmission?"

She accepted the tablet and flipped through the message. It was from Admiral Robertson of the Fourth Calliopean fleet, who normally patrolled the frontier as part of a joint operation with Delphi. The message gave his projected arrival time as early as next week.

She handed back the tablet. "It looks standard. It's just a second confirmation of the message they sent yesterday."

"This time, there are spelling mistakes that weren't in the original."

"How many?"

"Just a few, but it is weird. Even within the document, some words are spelled right the first time and wrong the second. If someone knows how to spell 'fleet,' why would they also type it as 'flaet,' and then 'fleit'?"

Charlotte snatched back the tablet and scanned the document again. Now that she knew what to look for, there was no missing the mistakes. "I served with Admiral Robertson as a young officer. He once took away my recreation privileges for a week when I misplaced a comma in an internal memo. There is no way he let a message with this many mistakes be sent from his ship unless it was deliberate."

"It's a code, isn't it?"

She hesitated, staring at the tablet. Deliberate spelling mistakes in regular communications was a way to encode emergency messages but was such an overused trick. She didn't know how the Terra Nuevans had never caught on to it. "Yes, I think it is, but without a cipher machine, this could take me at least a day, maybe two, to figure out. There isn't one in the office, is there?"

Lieutenant Lavine shook his head. "No, I've been arguing for years that we should have one, but the Calliopean higher-ups have never wanted Delphi to have access to a cipher machine or a copy of the codes, allies or not."

Charlotte frowned. "If Admiral Robertson knows Delphi does not have a Calliopean naval cipher machine, why would he send something in code?"

"He probably thought Lieutenant Cartwright would see it."

"Wait, not Lieutenant Mary Cartwright?"

"Yes."

"She served with me on the *Intrepid* as a liaison officer, part of an exchange program with the Delphian navy about two years ago. She's the only woman I've ever met who could decode messages without a cypher. Where is she?"

"At the wedding."

"Call her back, we need her."

Roseli watched the city slide past through the bulletproof glass of the armored car carrying her to the temple. She waved at the gathered crowd of strangers, head held high and regal as she had been instructed to do since childhood. Beside her, Lucia did the same.

Roseli reached for her hand.

Lucia startled slightly and then grinned. "Forward, aren't you?"

"We are about to get married."

"I don't suppose I can talk you into eloping instead."

"Not in this dress. I can barely walk, much less run."

The car rolled to a stop outside the steps that led up to the Great Temple, a towering structure of white marble columns and a triangle-shaped roof. Roseli had never understood the Unispiritualist obsession with Greco-Roman architecture, as the religion itself had no relation to the ancient Roman or Greek pantheons of old Earth.

When a guard opened the door, the cheers of the crowd that filled the courtyard before the temple steps bombarded her. Lucia stepped from the car first and turned back to offer Roseli her arm. The crowd grew louder at the sight of them.

A lifetime of lessons flowed through Roseli's mind. Chin up, back straight, smile set. She held her bouquet firmly in front of herself. It had, she noticed, a satisfactory number of white tulips. Beatrice had won her battle with the florist.

She and Lucia climbed the steps to the heavy wooden doors that were open for the occasion. When they walked into the cavernous main room of the temple, the wedding guests, sitting in long rows of chairs, went silent and stood to bow.

Music—probably recorded, as Roseli saw no sign of an orchestra—played as they walked down the aisle past the watching nobles. To Roseli's horror, her low heel caught on an uneven bit of the marble floor. Lucia kept them both upright through their linked arms. Roseli straightened, gave Lucia a grateful smile, and they kept walking.

As they neared the front of the temple, Roseli saw Beatrice, Alexis, and Julia sitting in the second row near the front. It was not the place of paramours, even official ones, to sit with the royal family. Alexis was stone-faced, and Julia was chewing on her lower lip. Beatrice offered a smile that was only a little strained.

Roseli's mother and two of her stepfathers sat in the front rows. Prince Henry, with his usual lack of regard for anything approaching etiquette, waved at her. Prince Ambrose caught her gaze, eyebrows drawn together in concern. Roseli could remember seeing that look countless times as a child when he escorted her to parties or events.

She needed only to nod in response, and he'd make some excuse to help her escape before she became overwhelmed. Roseli smiled back to reassure him. The worry lines eased at the edge of his face.

Her mother gave her an almost imperceptible nod of approval, and Roseli returned it. It occurred to her that her mother had walked down the same aisle four times before, thrice for duty and once for love.

Despite every eye in the room being on her and Lucia, Roseli felt calmer than she had in days. She was glad to have Lucia at her side. They approached the heavy stone altar where the head priestess waited in her starched gray robes. The matriarch of the temple opened a scroll and read. While the recent trend had been to shorten the long and rambling traditional Unispiritualist wedding ceremony, the head priestess showed no inclination toward this. Halfway through the ceremony, Roseli was aware of the sound of people shifting in their chairs and the occasional cough.

Her feet hurt in her impractical shoes, but it helped that her eyes had an appealing face to rest on. Someone with a makeup kit must have tackled Lucia. Her eyelashes were darkened and curled, her eyelids had been dusted with a shade of blue, and her lips were lightly painted. Despite the heat of the crowded room, her face did not shine. She wore a well-tailored linen suit that did her athletic figure every kind of favor. It was a rich blue, and the back and cuffs of the jacket were embroidered with water dragons in the Calliopean style. She had traded her usually white neck ribbon for a blue one. The shirt beneath the coat was white silk, so fine and soft-looking that Roseli wished she could run her hands over it. She promised herself she would later if they weren't exhausted after the wedding and reception.

Roseli and Lucia remembered their cues, exchanged ceremonial golden bracelets at the correct times, and said the proper words. At last, the priestess declared, "I pronounce you consorts for life."

Lucia drew Roseli into her arms, tipping her backward with a hand against the small of her back. Their lips met with every bit as much passion as they had the night before. For one moment, Roseli let herself forget everything but the woman in her arms.

She did not know what the future held but, she was glad she would be sharing it with Lucia. As the crowd applauded, one voice rose above the others.

"Get down!"

CHAPTER TWENTY

The crack of a gunshot boomed through the temple. Lucia grabbed Roseli and dove for the floor as a second shot echoed among the pillars. When Lucia raised her head, she saw the priestess on the ground beside them in a growing pool of blood, her eyes already glassy. The crowd was screaming and pushing toward the exits. Two rows of chairs back, General Tate struggled with someone on the ground. A handgun lay nearby, kicked out of their reach.

The would-be assassin threw General Tate off, but the guards descended upon him, grabbing him roughly and forcing his hands behind his back. He wore an imperial guard uniform.

Alexis tried to rise, then sank back to the floor. She clutched her shoulder, blood seeping through her fingers. Lucia had to get Roseli out of there, but she was afraid to let her up until she was sure there wasn't another shooter.

"Alexis!" Roseli wriggled free, dodged running wedding guests, and ran to Alexis, kneeling beside her. Lucia followed, frantically scanning the crowd for any sign of danger. When Roseli sat back up, the front of her wedding dress was stained scarlet.

"Put pressure on the wound." Lady Swann pushed past to hand Roseli a folded coat. Senator Veritas forced her way through the fleeing crowd to reach them.

"Roseli!" The empress pulled free of the guards trying to hurry her from the temple. She made it three steps toward them before a booming sound shook the entire temple.

One of the great columns and a chunk of the roof came down, separating the altar from the nave in an explosion of debris. Lucia stumbled, falling to her knees. Roseli screamed, the sound barely reaching Lucia through her ringing ears. She cast about wildly, only to find Roseli less than a few steps away, struggling against Officer Smith and another imperial guard to get back to General Tate.

Lady Swann was kneeling beside General Tate's still form, keeping the bloodied coat in place. Senator Veritas picked herself up from the floor. The side of her face was bleeding.

"We must get you to safety," Officer Smith yelled.

Roseli sobbed. "No, I won't leave her."

Lucia's first instinct was to help Roseli out of danger, but she couldn't leave someone bleeding on the floor. She doubted Senator Veritas and Lady Swann had enough strength to carry an unconscious woman on their own.

"Go, we've got her," Lucia promised.

Roseli looked at her with huge frantic eyes and nodded. The guards pulled her into the billowing smoke. The entire temple had to be on fire.

Lucia reached under General Tate's arms and dragged her in that direction. General Tate was heavy, but Jonas had weighed twice as much, and she'd dragged him from a shuttle. A familiar calm descended over her. With a clear course of action, there was no room for hesitation.

General Tate moaned but didn't open her eyes.

"Stop," snapped Lady Swann. "She's bleeding too much."

"We'll suffocate if we stay in a burning temple. One of you, get her feet," said Lucia.

Senator Veritas did, and they were able to lift General Tate. Lady Swann stayed at her side, keeping the coat against her shoulder. They picked their way through the gathering smoke and debris. Lucia almost tripped over something that felt like a body. Horror and guilt tore at her, but there was no time to stop and check. She promised herself she would come back.

The ceiling made a horrible shifting sound. Lucia glanced up to see more debris raining down. "Hurry!" They made it out a side door, stumbling into the brilliant light of the spring morning.

"Get back. Get back! It's coming down," someone yelled. Another crashing noise filled the air with even more choking dust.

Stuck on the steps, Lucia lowered General Tate to the ground, Senator Veritas following suit. They shielded her as best they could. The world became lost to a swirling gray cloud. Lucia's lungs burned, and she tugged her shirt over her face.

When the air cleared, the Great Temple was nothing but a collapsed ruin. Anyone who hadn't gotten out yet wasn't going to now.

❖

Roseli thought that Lucia, Beatrice, and Julia were only a few steps behind her with Alexis. But when she and her guards had emerged from the temple, there was no sign of them. She hadn't seen her mother or Ambrose or Henry outside either, although she remembered she had heard her mother call her name. Oh gods, that meant she'd been near the front of the temple where the column came down. Roseli had tried to go back into the burning temple, but her guards dragged her to the car.

She grabbed at the door as they pulled away. It was locked. "Go back!"

From a thousand miles away, she could hear Officer Smith saying her name. She didn't care. When someone touched her arm, she shrugged her off and kept tugging on the door. "I said, go back."

She straightened in shock as cold water cascaded over her head. She sputtered, brushing her wet hair from her face.

Officer Smith held an empty bottle from the car's mini-fridge. "Your Highness, please get control of yourself."

"As your future empress, I order you to turn this car around."

"I am sorry, Your Highness, my oath to the crown supersedes even my oath to you. I must get you safely to the palace. All members of the royal family and your paramours will be sent there, too."

If they were still alive.

Roseli took a slow, steadying breath the way Prince Ambrose had taught her. Her heart and her mind were in turmoil, but she was still the Crown Princess of Delphi. She didn't have the luxury of letting rising panic consume her.

As soon as they arrived at the palace, Officer Smith hurried her into one of the larger underground safe rooms where Roxane and Prince Leon were waiting.

"Roseli!" Roxane leaped to her feet and rushed to embrace her. She had changed out of her bridesmaid dress and wore a pair of sweatpants and a tank top. She hadn't washed off her makeup, and dark lines ran all over her face from crying. "I was so afraid. They said you were shot, and the temple blew up and…" She dissolved into tears.

Prince Leon sat utterly still against the wall, his eyes wide and mouth agape in shock. When their eyes met, his face snapped closed like a book. He stood with his usual rigid dignity. "Where is the empress?"

"I don't know." She began to shake. Roxane led her to a chair. She was not there long before the door opened again, and Beatrice, Julia, and Lucia entered, all three covered in dust and blood. Roseli met Julia and Beatrice halfway, clutching them both frantically. Some of the tightness in her chest eased.

Lucia hesitated in the doorway. Roseli kissed Beatrice on the cheek and squeezed Julia's hand and then let go. Lucia seemed slightly startled when Roseli hugged her, but after a few seconds, she hugged her back.

"Is…" Roseli tried to say Alexis's name, but her throat tightened.

"We got her out of the temple and into an ambulance," Beatrice said.

Roseli's knees gave, but Lucia supported her. There was a knock on the door frame, and they all turned.

Officer Smith bowed as she entered. "I have just been in touch with my colleagues. The empress is alive but injured. She was struck by falling rubble in the first explosion. Her guards and consorts carried her to safety. She is unconscious, but her condition is stable. She is being treated in the palace infirmary. Prince Henry sustained a broken arm, but Prince Ambrose is unharmed."

Roseli nodded, still feeling dazed.

"Your Highness, I must remind you that, with your mother incapacitated, you are the acting empress."

"I am?" She shouldn't have been surprised. She'd been training her entire life for this moment, and yet she felt like another bottle of cold water had been dumped over her head.

"Yes, Your Highness. When you're ready, please come to the briefing room. Director Barker is already there, and the rest of your mother's council will be soon."

"I can come now." She let go of Lucia and started toward the door.

Officer Smith frowned in concern. "Your Highness, I think you should shower and change first."

Roseli made the mistake of looking down. Alexis's blood had turned the beautiful layers of white silk into a horrifying mess of crimson. It took all of Roseli's self-control not to cry again. The last thing her mother's security council needed to see was their princess in a bloodstained wedding dress. "I will do so and be with you shortly."

As soon as Officer Smith was gone, Beatrice reached for her hand. "Come on, I think there's a bathroom in the next room."

Roseli followed. She had been pulled back from a chasm of unimaginable grief but was still sick with shock and fear for Alexis, her mother, and all of Delphi.

❖

Roseli's hair was still wet when she sat with the security council. She brought Lucia, Beatrice, and Julia with her so she wouldn't have to repeat things to them later. As acting empress, she had the authority to bring anyone she wanted.

Meredith sat to her left. She had materialized with her tablet when Roseli had left the safe room. She had remained in the palace that morning to ensure that everything was ready for the reception and was still dressed in a blue taffeta dress covered in cartoon cats in top hats and wedding veils.

General Sharp, Admiral Heart, and Director Barker sat across from Roseli. Both General Sharp and Admiral Heart had been in the temple. She was covered in dust, and he had his arm in a sling and his head bandaged.

Director Barker wore her usual impeccable black suit. Not a strand of hair was out of place from her tidy bun. In the back of her mind, Roseli couldn't help but wonder why she hadn't been at the wedding. Had she known something?

Her lined face was set with worried determination; Roseli saw nothing furtive there. Dr. Barker couldn't be a traitor. She'd served the crown loyally for decades. Roseli had played with her daughters as a child.

Officer Smith cleared her throat. "We have confirmed that a member of the imperial guard drew his service weapon and fired upon you and your wife during the wedding, Your Highness."

"Who?"

"Officer Michaels, a relatively new member."

"Michaels?" Roseli had only met him a few times, but she'd made an effort to learn the names of her guards. Michaels was a freckle-faced young man who had been too shy to look her in the eyes. At least, she'd thought it had been shyness. She shivered.

"Yes, we are questioning him now," said Officer Smith. "We believe that a series of explosive charges were laid before the wedding and were set off after the shooting. They seemed to be concentrated near the front of the building, likely with the intent of killing as many members of the royal family and high-ranking government officials as possible.

"Fortunately, the seating plan was changed at the last minute to create a better line of sight for the camera crew. Every seat was set farther from the altar, so casualties were less than they might have been."

"How many dead?" asked Roseli.

"We're not sure yet," said Officer Smith. "About a third of the guest list is unaccounted for. Many may simply be injured. Among the confirmed deaths so far are the High Priestess and seven of your senior naval officers."

"Seven?"

"We were seated together on the right side of the altar," said Admiral Heart, his voice ragged from smoke. "The column beside us exploded." He clenched his hands. "I'm alive because my seniority got me a seat on the aisle."

Roseli looked at Officer Smith. "I don't understand how we missed the explosives. You told me the temple would be swept repeatedly."

Officer Smith rubbed her forehead. "In all honesty, Your Highness, I don't know for sure. I oversaw an inspection of the temple early this morning, and I personally checked the area where Admiral Heart's comrades sat. I swear to you, I scanned with multiple kinds of equipment and did a visual inspection. If there was something there, I would have found it."

"You mean you think they were placed later? Who oversaw those inspections? What has Officer Lancet said?" The absence of the head of imperial security was odd.

"Lancet is dead," said Officer Smith. "His body has not yet been retrieved, but we believe he didn't make it out. I am now the acting head of security for the imperial guard until you replace me."

"You don't suspect…"

Officer Smith shook her head. "I knew him for nearly twenty years. He was no traitor. I think there are more traitors in the guard than just Michaels. I cannot yet prove it, but it is entirely possible that a guard or two could have hidden the explosives during or after the final safety inspection."

It made so much sense. How else could the first assassin have gotten into the palace to poison Lucia or the second one onto the roof to shoot at them? Roseli shivered. "I can't trust my security?"

Shame burned in Officer Smith's face. "Yes."

"How far do you think this reaches?"

"I don't know, but you have my word, I will find out."

There was a buzzing sound, and Director Barker took a tablet from her pocket and glanced at it. Her face went pale. "Your Highness, the Terra Nuevan fleet just entered Delphian space."

Roseli hadn't realized there was any ground left beneath her to fall away. Panic and fear welled inside, and she fought them down. She didn't know what to do, so she did what she'd seen her mother do at meetings, gather more information. She just forewent her mother's usual barrage of insults. "Why didn't our long-range sensors pick them up?"

"We don't know. It's as if they just appeared."

"How many?"

Director Barker tapped at her screen, her face going even more ashen. "Impossible to be sure. Our closer sensors only picked up a few ships before they were destroyed, but the Terra Nuevans usually send scouts ahead of larger forces. For all we know, this force could include all ships in the Terra Nuevan fleet that we haven't been able to account for in the past month. Hundreds."

"How long do we have?"

"Based on Prince Henry's estimations, it could be anything from days to hours."

That was not helpful. Roseli looked to Admiral Heart and General Sharp. "Give me options."

General Sharp brushed dark hair out of her eyes. Her braid had half come loose into a tangled and ash-stained mess. But she was as cool and collected as ever. "All my active-duty troops on the planet are currently positioned to guard key assets in the case of a ground invasion. If it comes to it, we will give them hell."

"It won't come to a ground invasion," said Lucia, speaking for the first time. "If the Terra Nuevans get through Delphi's fleet and orbital shields, they'll destroy as many cities from orbit as it takes to force a surrender rather than risk their troops. That's what they did in the last war when they took the Calliopean colony on the third moon of Andromeda."

"She's not wrong," said Admiral Heart.

"Do we evacuate the cities?"

Director Barker leaned forward. "With all due respect, Your Highness, that isn't possible in a matter of hours."

"It could be days before they arrive."

"We don't know that, and if you call for a civilian evacuation, all the major roads across Delphi will become gridlocked right when we need to move personnel and equipment. Civilians could be trapped on the roads and exposed during a bombardment. The capital and the other major cities have extensive subway systems. Those are the civilians' best hope."

Roseli didn't like it, but she saw the sense. "General Sharp, I am giving you emergency authority to keep the roads clear for the rapid movement of emergency personnel and supplies. However, if there is panic, and civilians begin to flee the cities, your orders are not to stop them but to regulate the flow of traffic, is that understood?"

"Yes, Your Highness."

She turned to look at Admiral Heart. "What is the status of our navy?"

"I can have every ship that's sound to fly in a defensive formation around the planet within the hour. Between that and the planetary shields, we should be able to hold our own until our other ships return and reinforcements arrive from Calliope."

"What of the orbital defense platform? It is finished now, isn't it?" asked Roseli. She'd heard her mother complain about the cost more than once.

He shook his head. "The Beta Gamma Platform may not be as effective as we'd hoped. Admiral Conor died in the temple, and Admiral Parker was badly injured. Conor was the most promising of the admirals trained in the use of the orbital defense platform, and Parker was a close second."

"Can you not train someone else?" asked Roseli.

"There is an interim crew currently on the platform commanded by Admiral Winters, but he doesn't have half the mind for tactics that Conor had."

Roseli narrowed her eyes. "Why do I get the feeling you have a better option in mind?"

"She's sitting to your left."

"Me?" said Lucia.

"Yes. Right now, you are the only person on Delphi with combat experience commanding a Beta Gamma Platform."

"Wait," said Roseli. "Are you seriously suggesting I send my wife up to the orbital platform during what will likely be the bloodiest space battle Delphi has ever seen?"

Admiral Heart nervously tugged at the edge of his mustaches but didn't back down. "Yes, Your Highness. I am suggesting it for the good of Delphi."

"That is far too dangerous," she said.

"Princess Roseli," said Lucia evenly. "I am no stranger to going into danger. If I can help, then I must."

"What if the platform is destroyed?" Roseli could still hear the crack of the gunshots that had almost killed them both and had wounded Alexis, smell the smoke of the burning temple. To survive that only for Lucia to again go into danger was unbearable. She had to fight to keep her breath even.

"I have been prepared to die in battle since I took my first oath as an officer at eighteen. I won't be the only person going into danger today. I'll be safer on the platform than the rest of your fleet."

Roseli scrambled for a reason to keep her safe, to keep her near. "It's not just your life I'm thinking about. If you die, your father will surely blame me and refuse to send ships."

"No," said Lucia. "Despite what your mother seems to think, my father is an honorable man. He would never withdraw support from an ally during a war."

Roseli laid a hand on Lucia's arm. "We just got married. I can't lose you."

"We'll both lose everything if Delphi falls. Let me fight for you and my new home." She held Roseli's gaze with steady hazel eyes, fierce and determined.

Roseli wanted to spend the rest of her life looking into those eyes. "All right, but I won't let you go up as a civilian advisor. You deserve more than that. You will be in command with Admiral Winters." She looked at Admiral Heart. "Can you make her a temporary Delphian admiral?"

"That is also within your authority to do, Your Highness."

Roseli turned back to Lucia. "Then, by my authority as acting empress of Delphi, I, Roseli Abram Almeda, name you, Lucia Caron Almeda, an admiral of the Delphian Imperial Navy."

Lucia bowed her head. "I am honored to serve you."

"Then make sure you come back to me."

"Is that an order?" Somehow, despite everything that had happened, Lucia still infused her words with warm implication.

"Yes." Roseli found that, of all things, she was smiling. Why did Lucia have to be so damn brave and noble, and why did that just make Roseli want her more?

"I will not fail you."

A shrill buzzing sound shattered the moment. Director Barker took out her tablet and went white as milk. "A series of small explosions have taken out key force-field transponders across Delphi. The planetary shields are down."

CHAPTER TWENTY-ONE

R oseli had often resented her mother for the cold and detached way she treated everyone, even her family. As the mantle of empress settled about her shoulders and she was forced to send away everyone she loved, she understood.

After she dismissed her security council to carry out her orders, she kissed her wife for what she prayed would not be the last time. They had known each other for such a short time, and yet it tore out a chunk of her heart to let go of her.

Lucia was slow to end the embrace. There was an animation in her eyes that Roseli had never seen before, something fierce and almost joyful, like a hound loosed upon the hunt. "Hold the ground upon the earth, and I will defend you from the heavens. Together, we will see a new dawn."

The lines were achingly familiar to Roseli. Since her girlhood, she had heard them repeated in everything from puppet shows, to operas, to bad television series. The epic poem had originally been written in French by one of the first Delphian colonists, and the rhyme scheme did not carry over into the Moûsaian translation.

"I never took you for a fan of Delphian poets," said Roseli warmly.

"My planet only ever produces good love poets. Yours has the ones that write the best adventure stories."

"Do you think they'll ever write a story about us?" She knew she was delaying, but she couldn't help it.

"With the fate of Delphi on the line, I'm sure there will be several. You'll be imperial and flawlessly beautiful, I'll be commanding and dashing, and history will forget how afraid we both are right now."

"Come back to me, and we'll find a poet who will write the whole story, fear and all."

There was a knock on the door, and Meredith poked her head in. "Admiral Heart says he has arranged a shuttle to the orbital platform, and your wife needs to get to the airfield."

They parted, and Roseli watched Lucia stride from the room, her back straight and step confident. She was left with Beatrice and Julia in the briefing room. She sat between them and collected her thoughts before she spoke. Beatrice took one of her hands and Julia the other. Their touch grounded her.

"We need to get Roxane out of the city. With the planetary shields down, the capital will be the Terra Nuevans' primary target, and there is no guarantee the city's shields will hold."

"You should leave, too," said Beatrice. She had found somewhere to wash her face and brush her hair while Roseli was showering, but her dark blue dress was stained with blood and ash and torn at the hem. Her eyes were red from the smoke she'd stumbled through, and her left hand was bandaged.

"You know I can't. All the communications equipment and infrastructure are here. And..." She could almost hear Prince Ambrose's voice in the back of her head. "The people of Delphi need to see that their acting empress has not abandoned the capital or them. I must be here."

Beatrice smiled sadly. "I will stay with you."

"No, Bee, I need you to go with Roxane."

"Don't you dare try to send me away to safety when you're in danger," snapped Beatrice with far more vehemence than Roseli had ever heard from her.

"You misunderstand. I'm sending you to protect her."

"I am no guard or soldier. In the face of danger, what can I possibly do but grab Roxane's hand and run?"

"That is precisely what I need you to do. Beatrice, you are one of the smartest and most observant women I have ever met. I trust you will see danger in time to get my sister away before it strikes."

She lowered her voice so that just Beatrice could hear. "And you're a survivor. You rose from the slums to become a courtesan. You came through in one piece when you were kidnapped during our first year together and came back to me unbroken. You can make it through anything. If..." She could barely find words. "If the capital falls, if my mother and I die, then Roxane will be Delphi's last hope. It will be up to you to keep her safe and hidden from the Terra Nuevans."

"You realize what you're asking of me. I can face anything with you but alone..."

"She's my baby sister. There's no one else I can trust with her safety."

"Then I will fight for her as I would you."

"Thank you." Roseli hugged her and pressed their foreheads together.

"How will we get out of the city?" said Beatrice. "Officer Smith made it clear we can't trust the imperial guards."

Roseli turned to Julia. The ash of the temple had dimmed the brilliance of her flame-colored hair, giving it an almost rusted hue. Worried green eyes looked out through a pale and bloodied face. There was a cut on her cheek that no one had bandaged yet.

"How much do you trust your mother?" asked Roseli.

Julia startled as if Roseli had poked her in the ribs. "My mother?"

"Yes, how much do you trust her? Is she loyal to the crown?"

Julia frowned. "She is loyal to the Veritas family and not much else, but if she gives her word, she will keep it."

"Can you ask her to use her network to get Roxane out of the city and keep her hidden?"

"Yes. She may try to find some advantage in it, but she'll do it."

"Good. Call her and arrange it. Use your phone. We can't trust the palace phones right now."

"You're not sending me out of the city, too," said Julia firmly.

"I wish I was, but first, I must send you to the Senate to get me emergency powers."

"If you declare a planetary emergency, you can claim those powers without the Senate giving them to you, even if they haven't officially declared war yet."

"Yes, but it will look better if I gain them through a Senate vote. Right now, I need the people of Delphi behind me, and I know the Senate has as much sway with them as the crown does."

Something dimmed in those beautiful eyes. "I'm just a junior senator. I don't know if they will even listen to me."

Roseli let go of Beatrice to hug Julia. "They will because you are brave and inspiring."

"That is assuming I can get a chance to speak."

"You will if you invoke your Right of Oration."

It was an old Senate rule that was seldom used but had long been romanticized and dramatized in movies and books. All senators had the right once in their career to speak for fifteen minutes uninterrupted on the Senate floor. Some used it early in their careers, and others saved it to give their retirement speech.

A laugh bubbled up in Julia's throat. "I'm not going to get a more dramatic moment to use it, am I?"

"I know you will be amazing."

Julia pressed her forehead against Roseli's "If the shields fail, if this is the end, I'll be in the Senate, and you'll be here."

"I know." Roseli should have run out of tears at some point. But not yet.

"We won't be together if…"

Beatrice leaned over Roseli to hug them both. "Stop it. None of us are going to die. Not Roseli, not you, not me, not Alexis, and not Lucia. We are all going to fight for our lives, and we will come through this."

Julia stiffened, then accepted the embrace. "You truly believe that."

"I have to."

❖

When Roseli returned to the safe room with Beatrice and Julia, she found Roxane and Prince Leon arguing. They were both standing. Prince Leon had his arms sternly crossed, and Roxane was stamping her foot. Roseli had a feeling Roxane wasn't going to like her plan.

"I'm not going, not when Mother is hurt, and Roseli might need me," snapped Roxane, glaring at Prince Leon.

"It is for your protection, and I'm coming with you," he said.

Roxane turned to Roseli. "You won't let him send me away, will you?"

Roseli frowned at Prince Leon. "Where are you sending my sister?"

"We are leaving the city to go to one of the emergency bunkers. After the temple this morning, I don't intend to wait for the assassins to come after my daughter."

"I agree," said Roseli.

He frowned, seemingly mistrustful that she agreed with him. "Good. I have spoken with the guards. We will depart in a few minutes."

"That is not a good idea," said Roseli. "Officer Smith thinks there are more traitors among the guards. I've made other arrangements for Roxane. You may go with her."

He huffed. "Your head guard is a highly paranoid woman. I would put no trust in her."

"One of my lovers was just shot by an imperial guard," snapped Roseli. "You will understand if I don't entrust my little sister to anyone else among that service until we have found the traitors."

He straightened to his full height. "You can't possibly send a princess out of the city without guards."

"I'm not. Roxane and you will be under the protection of the Veritas family."

He took a step back. "You must be joking. You would trust a daughter of the House of Stewart to the protection of the House of Veritas?"

"Are you implying my family is not trustworthy?" said Julia.

"Your grandmother crippled my great aunt in a sword duel."

Roseli lost her patience. "This is not the time for history lessons. I trust Julia, and she vouches for her family. They will keep you and Roxane safe."

Prince Leon crossed his arms, puffing up in a way rather reminiscent of a pigeon. He'd been athletic as a younger man, but now, much of that muscle had given way to girth. "No, absolutely not."

"This is not your decision. As acting empress, I am sending Roxane out of the city. You can choose to go with her or not."

His face screwed up into something ugly. "You little…" He stopped himself from saying what he clearly wanted to. "Your mother will wake up soon, and she will not approve of this."

"She seldom approves of anything I do," said Roseli. "How will this be any different?"

Roxane finally seemed to remember that she had a voice. "I don't want to go before Mother wakes up."

"I know, Roxy. I'm sorry, but I wouldn't ask you if there was another choice."

She looked at the floor. "You have to keep the spare safe, right?"

Guilt tugged at Roseli's heart. She reached for her sister, and Roxane rushed into her arms like the frightened teenager she was. "You're not just a spare."

"Don't pretend." Roxane was short enough that she could hide her face in Roseli's shoulder, getting makeup all over her clean shirt.

"You're the night watch, the rear guard, the last hope of Delphi."

Roxane looked up with mascara-smeared eyes. "What do you mean?"

"I have the easy job. I get to stay and fight. You have to go hide. Being still and waiting is harder than acting. I would never have the courage to do what you have to."

Roxane clung tighter. "I can't do this."

"I'm sending Beatrice with you. She'll guide you."

"Bee's coming too?"

Prince Leon snorted. "You're sending the retired whore with us? What's she going to do, seduce any potential assassins?"

Roseli had never been a violent person, but she dearly wanted to slap him. "Insult my paramour again, and I will not permit you to go with my sister."

"You wouldn't dare."

Roseli let go of Roxane. "I am acting empress. I can order all the white roses in the garden painted red if I want to. Don't test me." If she ever ordered such a thing, the Senate would catch wind and promptly have her declared insane, but theoretically, she had the authority.

Prince Leon fell silent.

Roseli had no more time for the matter. She kissed Roxane on the forehead. "I love you. Stay safe."

"You'll take care of Mother?"

"I will."

There was a knock on the door, and Meredith told her the empress was awake.

❖

Roseli's mother lay on a hospital bed in a small infirmary deep beneath the palace. Prince Ambrose had a chair beside her bed, his dark blond hair still dusted with ash. Prince Henry was in a chair beside him, leaning against him, eyes closed. His arm was in a sling.

At the sound of Roseli's steps, Prince Ambrose looked up. He smiled at her wearily. One of his front teeth was cracked. "They said you were safe, but it is good to see you with my own eyes." He did not stand, yet Roseli could see the tension ease from his body. He had never been the hugging sort, even when she was small. For a man who had spent his life painting, he relied almost entirely on words when it came to emotions.

"How is she?"

"Not dead yet," said her mother, her eyes flickering open slowly.

Relief beyond words flooded through her. "Thank the gods." She took her mother's hand, where it lay on the blanket. Her skin was cool and dry, and she did not squeeze back.

"Stop blubbering, loud sounds hurt." She was at least as cranky as usual.

"I'm so glad you're awake."

"Don't get too excited. I've got a concussion, and the doctors say I'm not supposed to think, or I'll make it worse. Which is a fine state for an empress to be in." She tried to sit up and failed, slumping back with a gasp of pain.

"Mother!"

Her mother looked at her with eyes the same dark brown that she saw in the mirror every day, and yet these were infinitely older. "I hoped it would be years before I had to place such responsibility on you, but until the world stops spinning when I raise my head, you are acting empress. Remember everything I taught you, and don't fuck it up. I expect to get the planet back in good working order."

"I swear, I'll keep Delphi safe."

"Don't swear, just do it."

Her eyes drifted closed, her face tight with pain. Her breathing slowed in sleep. Roseli could see how pale she was beneath the bandages that covered most of her head. She looked...vulnerable. Without thinking, Roseli reached out to draw the blanket over her sleeping mother's thin shoulders.

She turned back to Henry and Ambrose. Henry had woken up during all the commotion and sat up. His eyes had the slightly glazed look of someone who had taken painkillers.

"Sensors have picked up a Terra Nuevan fleet on its way," she said, "and the orbital shields are down. We can't trust the guards. More of them may be traitors. I'm evacuating Princess Roxane, Prince Leon, and Lady Swann from the city. I think you should all go with them. Can my mother be moved?"

Now that Roseli knew her mother could not resume command, she needed to get her to safety. The empress and the heir couldn't be in the same place during an invasion.

Prince Ambrose shook his head. "Not easily. The doctors want to keep monitoring her in case she shows any sign of a brain bleed. She needs to be within fifteen minutes of an operating room."

"She needs to be somewhere safer than just a secure room."

"What about the catacombs? They run deep below the palace and are set in solid bedrock," said Prince Ambrose. "If there's one place in the capital that might survive an orbital bombardment, it's there. If there's a ground invasion, we'll also have a way out."

When Roseli was a child, her mother had taken her and Prince Ambrose down to see the tombs beneath the palace several times. There was an escape tunnel in the catacombs that connected them to a cave system that went for miles, all the way to a dry well outside the city. No one knew about it but the royal family. Her mother had forced her to walk it until she could do it with her eyes closed, even as she shivered in fear. She'd only been able to do it because Prince Ambrose had held her hand every time.

Roseli had not sent Roxane through that route because she had such severe claustrophobia that she was incapable of going beyond the outer gates of the catacombs. The one time their mother had taken them both into the catacombs, Roxane had screamed and howled, digging in her heels until Roseli had to carry her. Even then, she'd clung to Roseli in terror and had sobbed inconsolably. They had never tried again.

Roseli hated the thought of sending her mother into that icy darkness, but Prince Ambrose had a point. It was the best option. If her mother's condition worsened, she could be brought back up to be operated on in the palace infirmary. And even if the capital burned, they would still have an escape route.

"Take Dr. Brook with you. She's treated our family since I was a child. I cannot believe she would ever be a traitor." Which left the problem of not being able to trust the palace guards. An idea came to her. "I'll send soldiers from General Tate's office to guard you. Her staff are fiercely loyal. Hopefully, that loyalty extends to the crown."

"That sounds like a plan," said Prince Ambrose.

Prince Henry reached out to press Roseli's arm with his uninjured hand. "Don't look so afraid, dear girl. Ambrose and I will keep your mother safe. He's good at looking after people. Go do what you need to."

"Thank you, both of you."

Having done everything she could to protect her lovers and family, Roseli went to see what she could do for her planet.

CHAPTER TWENTY-TWO

Julia dearly wished she had a clean shirt or at least a hairbrush. She almost called her secretary to bring those from her office and meet her outside the Senate. She quickly dismissed the idea. She had spent enough years in the Senate to know the power of political theater. She needed to walk into the Senate Hall with her clothes still covered in ash and her shirt stained with Alexis's blood.

Her one concession to her appearance was to detangle her hair with her fingers and tug it back into a messy version of her usual braid. Even if the world was ending, she'd rather not look like Medusa.

An odd calm settled over her as she stepped from the car into the underground parking garage. Two of her mother's guards flanked her. She had half expected the car to whisk her away to somewhere her mother deemed safe after the guards had collected her, but it hadn't. A Veritas never broke her word.

As for getting Princess Roxane out of the city, her mother had been more than happy to have the second-in-line to the throne placed in her protection. If all went well, the empress would owe her a favor. If things went badly, Julia could easily imagine her mother leading an underground Delphian resistance with the princess as a figurehead against Terra Nuevan conquerors.

There was no time to think of that. She had to make the speech of her career. She walked through a familiar maze of corridors and past multiple security checks. The Senate guards started at the sight of her, but none stopped her. The idea of a senator stepping onto the speaking floor when it had not been yielded to them was unthinkable.

She pushed open the heavy wooden door that led to the floor and stepped into a room full of voices and light. The speaker of the Senate, Senator Morrison, had called an emergency session. She was angrily banging her gavel to little effect as everyone tried to talk at once. Senator Sonoma was speaking into a microphone on the podium, but the noise completely drowned him out.

Julia walked to the podium. Several senators fell silent at the sight of her disheveled state. Senator Sonoma faltered and then covered the microphone with one hand. "Senator Veritas. You look a fright. Did you just come from the temple? Are you bleeding?"

"The blood isn't mine." At least, most of it wasn't. She had more small cuts than she could count, but none were serious. "With all due respect, Senator Sonoma, I must ask you to yield the floor to me."

The room had fallen nearly silent. The elder senator frowned at her, drawing heavy white eyebrows together. While they were members of different parties and coalitions, Julia respected him. Julia's party, the Liberal Economists, was part of the minority coalition, while Senator Soma's party, the Centralists, was part of the majority.

He took his hand away from the microphone so he could be heard. "Senator Veritas, on what grounds do you ask me to yield the floor?"

"I invoke my Right of Oration."

He turned to look at the Speaker of the Senate. She gave a nod and spoke into her microphone. "It is your right. Please speak, Senator Veritas."

Senator Sonoma bowed and stepped back from the microphone, telling Julia as he passed, "Good luck, kid." He was old enough to get away with saying that.

Julia stepped up to the microphone. The Senate was about three-fourths full. Not everyone had been able to get there amidst the chaos. She took a breath, gathering her thoughts before she spoke. She had only one chance to get what she needed.

"I come to you today not only as a senator but also as a royal paramour, to speak on behalf of Princess Roseli Abram Almeda, the current acting empress of Delphi." It was a risky approach to take and might destroy all her credibility as an independent senator for the rest of her career. However, all that mattered was making sure there was a future. An emotional plea from a lover was likely to work better than just a junior senator's speech.

The room, rather predictably, exploded into a cacophony of voices and questions. The Speaker of the Senate banged her gavel and barked into her microphone, "Hush and let her speak!"

Gradually, the room quieted.

Julia resumed. "At ten this morning, an assassin tried to shoot

Princess Roseli and her new consort at their wedding. My fellow royal paramour, General Tate, thwarted the attempt by tackling the assassin. It is her blood you see on my clothing. Right now, she is in surgery, and her survival is uncertain. After the gunshots, a series of explosions brought down the temple. Every member of the royal family escaped, but others were not as lucky. The empress received a head injury and is in stable condition. Her eldest daughter has assumed all imperial responsibilities until she is fit to rule again."

The level of noise rose. Julia didn't let her chance slip away. "You already know most of this. Princess Roseli has charged me to inform you that our navy detected a Terra Nuevan fleet at our borders. As of this moment, Terra Nueva and Delphi are at war."

Even with the microphone, there was no hope of anyone hearing her for almost a full minute. It was worth it. Julia waited patiently as Senator Morrison banged the Senate back into silence.

When she had control of the room, she told Julia, "I must remind you, Senator Veritas, that our constitution gives the Senate, and the Senate only, the power to declare war."

Technically, even the Speaker shouldn't interrupt a senator who had invoked their Right of Oration, but that didn't matter. She had just given Julia the opening she needed.

"On behalf of Princess Roseli, I respectfully request the Senate to declare war on Terra Nueva and grant her emergency powers."

"As a junior senator, Senator Veritas, you have the right to propose such a vote, but your party head must second you." The speaker looked across the room toward Senator Claiborne, the head of the Liberal Economists. She was also Julia's great-aunt on her father's side.

Senator Claiborne frowned at Julia in a way that suggested she'd like to strangle her for not informing her of her plans. To the room, she said. "I second both votes."

The Speaker thumped her gavel. "Then both votes will be brought to the floor. Senator Veritas, you have five minutes left of your time. Use them wisely."

Julia knew she had to be careful with what she said next. The Senate was televised. She needed to reassure the public even as she fought to get the Senate to her side.

She could say nothing of Terra Nueva's faster ships or the failed orbital shields. It would be impossible to keep it a secret for long, but every minute the news was delayed bought more time to move troops and equipment. If the public learned of the failed shields, there would be panic as people tried to flee the cities, causing a gridlock on the roads.

"I know you will all vote to declare war. The Terra Nuevans already struck the first blow when they attacked Princess Lucia's ship. Now they are launching another attack, and we must be ready. Princess Roseli needs emergency powers to act rapidly and unilaterally. She must be able to move people, goods, and weapons without seeking Senate approval first."

Senator Rain, a member of the Northern Alliance Party seated in the first row, jumped to his feet and yelled, "Like hell. We must not give a royal the powers of a tyrant. The last time the Senate granted an empress that power, she suspended all civil liberties and executed my great-grandfather for sedition."

It seemed that no one was respecting the no-interruptions rule.

"Read a history book. Your great-grandfather was a traitor," yelled another senator. "Empress Titania was a national hero."

"My great-grandfather stood up for the rightful autonomy of the north, you complacent southern coward," yelled Senator Rain.

Had the other senators not stopped them, the two men might have gotten into a fistfight.

Julia sensed she could quickly lose the room. "This is not a time to speak of history and empresses past. Princess Roseli is not her ancestor, and she will not use these powers lightly, nor impinge upon any civil liberties she does not have to. She will relinquish her emergency powers as soon as the crisis is over. She believes in our constitutional monarchy and will act to preserve it. I give you my word that you can trust her in this."

"Just because you're fucking her doesn't mean she won't turn into a tyrant. The word of a lover is useless." Senator Rain's last outburst was one step too far, and the speaker thumped her gavel.

"The next person who speaks out of turn will be held in contempt! Senator Veritas, I grant you an additional two minutes."

Without meaning to, Senator Rain had given her another rhetorical opening. "I know Princess Roseli better than nearly anyone else precisely because I am her paramour. I have seen her in times of strength and weakness that few others have. I can say with authority that she believes you, Senator Rain, to be an aggravating blowhard but a stabilizing force in your party. I also have heard her repeatedly call the Senate a slow and verbose institution that is essential to the Delphian governmental system."

Roseli had never said either of those things exactly, but Julia had no compunction about taking a bit of creative license. "Were Princess Roseli a tyrant, she could have simply declared a crisis and given herself emergency powers. Instead, she has chosen to send me to plead for them."

She allowed a beat of silence for emphasis. "I have known Princess Roseli intimately for over three years, and in that time, I have never found her to be anything but a brave and honest woman. She puts the needs of Delphi before herself and gives everything she has to it. She just sent her new wife, Admiral Lucia Caron Almeda, to command the orbital platform to defend the planet."

A buzzer cut her off, and the accursed gavel banged again. She stepped back from the speaker's podium as the vote began. She had done all she could for Roseli. Now she had to do what she could for Delphi as a senator.

❖

Lucia's heart leaped as the shuttle lifted off the ground. No matter how many times she left a planet's surface, she never lost her sense of wonder. The first time, she had been eighteen and on her way to her first posting on the *Courageous*. She had been excited and afraid, the way any girl heading into the unknown would have been. That fear had faded with the first sight of Calliope falling away, projected on the wall of the shuttle for the passengers, an orb of blue and green. She had never known it would be so beautiful. The sight of the *Courageous* looming before her, all gleaming metal and lights, had quickly become the second most beautiful thing she had ever seen.

The Delphian naval shuttle was much smaller than the sort she was used to. She was strapped in beside the pilot, who had barely said two words to her as he intently flipped switches. The screen before them showed mostly the sky above, at first blue and then darkening into inky blackness speckled with the white dots of stars as they rose. A small image displayed the rear camera.

Delphi was the same colors as her home, but instead of a jigsaw of continents, she could see only one large one, shaped like a boot. At the heart of the landmass was the capital city of Thetis and the woman she had married just a few hours before.

She's spent all the years since graduating from the academy fighting for her planet until the armistice. Most of it had been in the cold void of space, struggling to hold the battle lines back from the colonies. She'd fought for herself, she'd fought for her crew, and when she became an admiral, she fought for her fleet. She'd known distantly that she was fighting for Calliope, but the planet and everyone she loved there had been faraway and safe.

It was not until the Battle of Galileo that she had held civilian lives in her hands, and it had been the most terrifying thing she had ever done. In every battle she had fought before, there had been the option of a strategic retreat, and she had used it when necessary. She had valued her ships and crews over imaginary boundary lines.

At the Battle of Galileo, there had been no time to evacuate the colony, and retreat hadn't been an option. She had learned what it was like to have her back against the wall, to fight for survival and not just victory, what true guilt and terror felt like. She'd sacrificed so many of her sailors' lives for that little colony. Just before the end of the battle, before help arrived, she'd thought she'd done it all in vain, and that fear had been utterly crushing.

The Battle of Galileo had been for several million souls. This time, it was billions. If she let it, the weight of that responsibility would crush her. She forced herself to take slow, painful breaths as she fought for clarity.

An image flickered across her mind. She saw Roseli as she had been that morning, warm and naked beside her in the safety of soft blue blankets. In the light that filtered through the blinds, Lucia had been able to make out a faint scar just beneath Roseli's left ear, likely a remnant of some childhood mishap. When Lucia had tried to pull away to go shower, Roseli had mumbled her name and snuggled against her. Lucia had lain back down until Roseli's assistant had knocked on the door to wake them. It was only a moment frozen in memory, and yet it was something to hold on to.

Charlotte's head hurt, and numbers and letters were swimming before her eyes. Her hands felt cold, the way they usually did after an intense shock. In less than an hour, she had gone from thinking that Lucia was dead because of a miscellaneous early news report to learning from a later report that she was alive.

There wasn't time to process any of her feelings. After being unable to locate Lieutenant Cartwright, she'd had no choice but to decipher the message herself. There was no definitive list of dead and injured yet, but Cartwright had likely perished in the temple. Charlotte had a horrible sinking feeling that the message might be a useless warning about the bombing, but she wouldn't know until she read it.

It was not a quick process. She had determined that the code was hidden in the vowels of the misspelled words, and she was looking at a line of letters. She thought she might be closer to at least guessing which style of cipher had been used.

None of her former crew's communications officers had survived, but she still had help. Lieutenant Lavine had found her a mousy young woman, Petty Officer Mercer, who was the office's best cryptographer. They now sat in a small room with a high-powered computer running combinations and variants as Charlotte guessed at them. Little by little, they were getting closer.

❖

"This is ridiculous," Prince Leon said for what was not the first time. "I have never traveled in such an undignified manner in all of my life."

Beatrice saw nothing particularly undignified in riding in a windowless van. How else were a royal consort, a princess, and a royal paramour supposed to get out of the city unrecognized? Even in the cheap generic clothes the Veritas guards had insisted they put on, there was no mistaking any of them.

The back of the van lacked seats, and they had to sit on the floor. Roxane sat beside Beatrice rather than her father. She had promptly fallen asleep from the emotional exhaustion of the day. Beatrice hadn't had the heart to push her away when she'd leaned against her. She was currently snoring loudly in Beatrice's ear in a way oddly reminiscent of her older sister. Apparently, some things ran in the family. Roxane looked so like Roseli but much younger. Her face was rounder, and her cheeks were scattered with freckles. Beatrice had never had a sister, but she was determined to keep Roseli's safe.

Prince Leon, sitting across from them, and had spent most of the trip glaring at Beatrice and complaining, as if she was responsible for their travel arrangements. "We could have at least taken a hovercraft."

Beatrice did not bother to reply. He would keep complaining no matter what she said.

There was a plainclothes guard in the back with them, sitting with his back against the divider to the front of the van. He was of middle years and held himself as tensely as a hound keeping watch. He told Prince Leon, "That would not be advisable, Your Highness. All hovercraft flights in the capital are logged and tracked. We cannot transfer to a hovercraft until we are outside the capital."

Prince Leon scowled. "I, for one, am not convinced of my step-daughter's paranoid theory of corruption in the guard."

"I understand, Your Highness," said the guard. "I can only reassure you that we have been given orders to protect you, Princess Roxane, and Lady Swann as we would a member of the Veritas family."

"That is less than reassuring." Prince Leon took a tablet from his coat and tapped at it.

The guard straightened. "Your Highness, what is that?"

"What does it look like?"

"You were explicitly told not to bring any technical devices," said the guard.

Prince Leon raised an eyebrow. "A foolish requirement."

"Your Highness, I must insist you give that to me. If that tablet gives out any kind of signal, it can be tracked."

Beatrice felt a cold shiver run down her spine. Was the man such a fool that he had knowingly endangered them all?

"I assure you, it is secure."

"Your Highness, for your protection, you must give it to me."

"No."

The guard spoke into his wrist strap, "Stop the car, we have a problem." Then he said to Prince Leon. "Please, Your Highness, if you will not give me the tablet, we must take it from you. We cannot risk the princess being tracked by assassins."

Prince Leon narrowed his eyes. "You would forcibly take some-thing from a royal consort?"

"We have orders." The car ground to a stop.

Roxane stirred in her sleep but did not wake. For the first time, Beatrice began to wonder if Prince Leon was simply a fool or an actual threat.

"Fine, take it, you impertinent bastard, but know that every action you take will be reviewed in a royal inquest later. You'll never work in the capital again." He held out the tablet, forcing the guard to come get it.

"I understand, Your Highness." The guard took the tablet and talked into his wrist strap. The car moved again. He broke open the back of the tablet, popped out the data card, and snapped it before dropping it to the floor and crushing it beneath his boot.

Beatrice watched in silence. When she snuck a look back at Prince Leon, she caught a brief impression of something that looked like panic before his sharp features settled back into indignant annoyance. He knew something she didn't. The only question was what.

❖

"General Tate is out of surgery," Meredith said without looking up from her tablet. "She's in stable condition and breathing on her own. They saved her left lung, but she lost...wow, that's a lot of blood. How much blood is in the human body?"

Roseli suppressed the urge to wrench the tablet from her hands. "She'll live?"

"I hope so. I like her. The last time I asked her about one of my dresses, she said it suited my personality perfectly." Meredith seldom liked anyone, so this was high praise.

Roseli was numb with relief. She still wished she could be at Alexis's side, waiting for her to wake up. Instead, she was deep beneath the palace in the emergency command center. It mostly consisted of a large room with a lot of screens and little desks where civilian, military, and naval staff tapped at consoles.

Meredith's tablet chirped. "Julia's calling. Do you want me to put her on the screen?"

Roseli hesitated. "Can you put her on just your tablet?"

"Yes." Meredith handed her the tablet, and the screen flickered to an image of Julia.

She still had a smudge of dried blood on her forehead that either she hadn't noticed or hadn't cared about. She was standing in what appeared to be a bathroom stall, if the toilet behind her was any indication, and beamed with triumph. "The Senate has declared war on Terra Nueva and granted you emergency powers and stands ready to assist the crown."

"You did it," said Roseli. "Thank you, my love, I knew you could."

"I did." Julia smiled mischievously. "You owe me fifteen minutes now."

Roseli would have thought that flirting, of all things, would be impossible, and yet it came as a wonderful relief, a brief reprise from the pressure. "Do I?"

"Someday, I'm going to demand fifteen minutes of your undivided attention, and you'll have to give it to me, even if it means walking out of a council meeting."

"You have my word. Now, get to the palace bunker. It's the safest place in the capital."

Julia shook her head, "Roseli, I can't leave the Senate, not now."

"You did what I sent you for."

"I know…but there is a lot the Senate still has to vote on and do."

"They aren't evacuating?"

"We can't. We must reassure the public. If we go, they'll panic, and right now, the capital can't afford that."

"You're just one senator. You can leave. Who will notice?" She had been forced to send away everyone she loved. Couldn't she at least have Julia back?

The image on the screen wobbled. Julia's hands were shaking. "I'm a senator, and I swore an oath when I took office. I have to uphold it." She lowered her voice. "You still need me here, trust me. The Senate can easily turn against you."

Roseli almost said, "But I need you here." Instead, she said, "Are you sure?"

"As I have ever been."

Her entire life, Roseli had been told that being empress meant putting the good of Delphi before herself. She'd just never realized how hard that would be. "I love you, keep safe."

"I love you, too."

Then a lot of things started to beep. "Your Highness," said Commander Sharp. "The Terra Nuevan fleet is here."

❖

Everything was in chaos when Lucia stepped onto the bridge of the Delphian orbital defense platform. She had walked through the entire station without being stopped. While it had been common practice on every ship she had ever served on to not worry about internal security, the lack of anyone checking her credentials at the airlock deeply troubled her.

On the bridge, she found a man in his twenties with an admiral's eagle pin on his chest. He sat frozen in the commander's chair breathing slow, panicked breaths. A woman with a lieutenant commander's star on her chest was giving orders. Lucia trusted her instincts and crossed the bridge to the woman and saluted.

"Admiral Almeda reporting for duty. I have received orders from Acting Empress Roseli to take command of this orbital platform." It was strange to use a different last name than she had all of her life, but it was hers now as part of the marriage contract. Changing her last name mattered a great deal less to her than getting back the title of admiral.

The lieutenant commander jerked her head. "What?"

"I have orders to take command."

The officer stared at her suspiciously. Lucia would have guessed her to be in her late thirties. She wore her blond hair in a neat braid and had the tightly set face of a woman with little patience for foolishness. She looked nothing like her former first mate, Jonas, and yet there was no mistaking a career second-in-command.

"Aren't you the princess's new Calliopean wife?"

"Yes."

"You're not even in our chain of command."

"As of an hour ago, according to the acting empress, I am. I have been sworn in as an admiral of the Delphian navy and appointed as the commander of this platform."

Lucia expected further resistance, but the woman saluted. "Welcome aboard, Admiral Almeda. I am glad to see you. I've read of your battles."

She returned the salute. "I must formally take command from Admiral Winters."

"You'll have to accept it from me. I have assumed temporary command."

Lucia didn't have to ask why. She knew what a panic attack looked like. She had seen it often enough in young officers when they first faced combat, or even later, when they had their first command. Some could work through it, and the incident was quietly kept out of their records. Others couldn't and were sent home with an honorable discharge.

What surprised her was that Admiral Winters had ever risen to his current rank. He shouldn't have made captain, much less admiral; likely, he had been promoted rapidly near the end of the last war when few officers were left.

"Thank you…"

"Lieutenant Commander Sullivan."

"I accept command. Now, tell me what is going on."

"Two hundred hostile ships bearing Terra Nuevan and Thalian signatures just appeared out of nowhere and have ringed the planet."

Her blood chilled. "Thalian?"

"It seems they have reverted to their old alliance with Terra Nueva."

Lucia looked at the primary screen and all the blinking lights. It didn't look good. She could understand why the young admiral had panicked. Bright red dots ringed the planet just outside the range of the Delphian fleet.

"Why haven't they attacked?"

"I don't know."

"Admiral Almeda," said one of the bridge crew said. "We have an incoming transmission from the Terra Nuevans addressed to both the commander of the Delphian fleet and the empress. Should I show it?"

"Yes," said Lucia.

Half the big screen switched to an image of a woman close to Lucia's father's age. She had to grab a nearby console to steady herself. She had fought Admiral Patchett at the Battle of Galileo and knew her to be utterly ruthless and uncompromising. Her face haunted Lucia's nightmares. The last time, Lucia had lost fifteen ships and their crews. Now Patchett had come to take so much more. This time, Lucia had a wife and a new home to defend, and no reinforcements were on their way.

CHAPTER TWENTY-THREE

The woman who appeared on Roseli's screen bore a strong resemblance to an eagle. She was lean, with an aquiline nose and a piercing stare. Her hair was gunmetal gray, and she stood as rigid as a wooden soldier. She wore a crisp gray Terra Nuevan naval uniform without a button or fold out of place.

Roseli would have been intimidated, but she'd spent her entire life dealing with her mother, and this woman's scowl wasn't half as fearsome.

The woman bowed formally. "Greetings. I am Admiral Patchett of Terra Nueva, commander of the joint League of Power's second fleet."

Roseli returned the bow shallowly. "I am Crown Princess Roseli Abram Almeda, acting empress of Delphi. May I ask what the hell you're doing on my doorstep with two hundred warships?"

"I would imagine that to be rather obvious. You look like a smart girl. Surely, you know an invading fleet when you see one."

She ignored the jab. "You acknowledge you are violating the Armistice of Tyco, then?"

"Is now the time to quibble over such matters?" Admiral Patchett had the gall to raise a thin eyebrow.

Roseli kept her face blank. "My allies will care."

"And yet, I see none of them present."

"What are your demands?"

"The surrender of Delphi and all associated colonies to Terra Nueva in exchange for a cessation of hostilities."

"Not much of a negotiator, are you?"

Admiral Patchett frowned. At least, Roseli thought she frowned. Her resting expression was so dour, it was hard to tell. "I was trying to avoid being crude, but if I must, I will. Surrender now, and I will not burn your ships in orbit or reduce your planet's major cities to ash."

"How generous of you."

"I am not unreasonable. If you surrender peacefully, I give my word that you and your family will be unharmed. You are newly married, are you not? Do you not wish to protect your wife?"

"Considering that she and I were nearly assassinated this morning at our wedding, you will understand if I don't trust that promise."

"Even if you don't trust me, are you willing to throw away the lives of your citizens?"

"There is more to life than mere survival. Tell me, if I surrender, what happens to Delphi?"

"It will become a client state of Terra Nueva."

Roseli knew just how weak her position was, but surrender wasn't an option. "And what of my planet's system of government? What of our Senate, constitution, and basic rights? I know all about the perpetual martial law that Terra Nueva keeps its client states under."

"Stop acting deliberately dense to delay the inevitable, girl. You are outnumbered, your planetary shields are down, and help will not come in time."

Roseli hoped that history would not judge her a fool for what she said next. "I will not yield."

Admiral Patchett did not look impressed. "You said one of your names was Abram. Was your father General Joseph Abram? I heard the Delphian empress was pregnant when he died and later bore him a daughter."

The question was so out of place and unexpected that it took Roseli a moment to answer. "Yes. He was my father."

"You're the spitting image of him, right down to the stubborn frown. I faced him during the siege of Ptolemy. He held his ground positions so fiercely, even in the absence of naval support, that in the end, there was no choice left but to destroy half the surface of the planetoid from orbit."

Roseli had to lay a hand on the console for support. She had never known her father as anything but a man in stories, an absence in her life, and a deep source of grief for her mother. Some part of her would always be the little girl she'd been before Prince Ambrose had come into her life, the child who hadn't understood why her sisters had a father and she didn't or why her mother's eyes grew sad when she looked at her even before her sisters' death. She'd never had a face or a name to blame for all that pain before.

"If you think that telling me you killed my father is going to get me to surrender, you're an idiot."

"No, I'm trying to talk some sense into you. Your father was a stubborn bastard, a brave one, a noble one, but in the end, he got himself and his troops killed. I gave him one last chance to surrender, and he didn't take it. Maybe he thought help was coming, or maybe he was trying to keep my fleet at Ptolemy and away from the Battle of Zana that was raging at the same time. It doesn't matter. He died for nothing, and he did not die alone."

"How dare you!"

"Your father took thousands with him into the darkness. You hold the lives of your planet's citizens in your hands. If you repeat his mistakes, you'll take billions with you into death."

Roseli gripped the console and forced her breath to slow. She could not speak in anger or pain. Admiral Patchett was trying to use her emotions against her, and she wouldn't let her.

"You have more ships, but I have a defensive position. If you want my planet, then come and take it, you Terra Nuevan bitch."

❖

Lucia's hands danced across the visual display before her, moving half her ships into formation over the capital and the major cities of Delphi. Similar to Calliopean warships, Delphian ones could project joint force fields with other ships, creating temporary shield walls. It still took a ridiculous amount of power and couldn't be done for long.

She waved the rest of her ships forward to face the Terra Nuevans. She could not use the fully defensive tactics she had used in the Battle of Galileo, not when no reinforcements were coming. The only hope was to strike the Terra Nuevans quick and hard, making the battle cost them too much to continue.

When Lucia was little, her mother used to hold her on her lap and use a projector to play three-dimensional recordings of her past naval battles. Her mother had so seldom held her that Lucia had been delighted, laughing and giggling as she'd snatched at the flickering images.

Her mother had patiently explained what was happening, which ships had been Varcian ships, which had belonged to allies, and which were enemies. Looking back, it was both creepy and sweet, like a mother cat showing her kitten how to hunt with a live mouse. Those memories were still some of the happiest Lucia had of her.

By the time Lucia was seven, she could recite the battle plan of each video by heart. At nine, she was running digital simulations with her mother, moving fictional ships across a screen, and re-waging past battles in new ways. It was the same software she'd trained with in the academy. In later years, when the orbital defense platforms were designed, the user interface was made to emulate the training software since all Calliopean naval officers were familiar with it.

So deeply ingrained were the movements and tactics that she barely needed to think. The screen lit up with explosions as the Terra Nuevans and her ship fired torpedoes.

As the impacts began, she saw her first mistake. A single Terra Nuevan ship broke through the line, heading not toward one of the larger cities but the southern coast of the main continent.

When Roseli had reached her majority and the empress had officially named heir apparent, she had spent nearly a year touring the planet, going everywhere from its major cities to its small towns. Her mother had made a similar journey in her youth. At first, she had been excited to be away from the palace and her mother's supervision. Soon enough, the constant pace of travel had worn her down, and all the places had started looking the same.

There were moments she remembered vividly, though, almost like snapshots. She had loved the waterfalls of Amalthea and the fire festival of Perenna, eaten the sweetest cloudberries she'd ever tasted in a tiny village in the mountains of the Northern Province of Avia, and had swum for the first time in salt water at a resort along the coast in the south.

It was traditional for a child to greet the heir apparent and present her with a bouquet of flowers native to the area to formally welcome her. In Vima, the city's mayor had decided it would be cute to have her daughter do this. Unfortunately, the task was too much for the shy four-year-old. The little girl had made it across the stage to Roseli only to drop the flowers and burst into tears when she couldn't remember what she was supposed to say.

Roseli, who had some experience with upset children from helping raise Roxane, had knelt and told the little girl she was pleased to meet her. The child had hiccupped as Roseli wiped her face with a tissue. She'd smiled when Roseli had taken a small silver flower brooch from her dress and gave it to her. The little girl had hugged her before running back to her mother to show her the brooch.

As Roseli looked at the dots on the screen and the footage that showed the destruction of Vima, the guilt was utterly crushing. How could that little girl, much less an entire city simply be gone? Vima had been a small costal city with no military significance and had no shields. No one had expected it to be a target. She had no choice but to push the guilt down, or she wouldn't be able to function. "Call the orbital platform."

The bridge of the platform appeared on the screen at the front of the room. An unfamiliar officer saluted. "Your Highness."

"Get me Admiral Almeda."

The screen shifted to her wife standing at the center of an image of Delphi with icons of orbiting ships floating past her. She looked like some strange goddess of war in her torn and bloodstained wedding clothes. In all the chaos, no one had found her a uniform.

"They got through. They destroyed a southern city," Roseli said, trying to keep her voice from trembling.

Lucia didn't look at her, just kept moving. She shifted and rotated her hands in a half circle, like a woman dancing. "I know. I believe the Terran Nuevans are targeting the smaller unshielded cities."

Roseli knew this, but hearing it confirmed did not make it any easier. "The murdering bastards."

"Smart murdering bastards. If I move ships to protect the smaller cities, then I must thin the ranks of ships over the major cities." Lucia opened both her palms, and torpedoes launched from half the ships on the screen. Several red enemy ships blinked off.

"They have shields," said Roseli.

"Not ones strong enough to withstand a longer assault. Admiral Heart showed me the specs on the way to the spaceport. The city shields were designed as a backup to cover fluctuations and temporary outages of the planetary shields."

"Can't you take ships from the offensive line? We must protect civilians at all costs." She had already failed the citizen of Vima; she would not fail more Delphians.

Lucia tapped and dragged the images of ships over the planet. Her voice was terse and strained. "If that is our priority, then we should surrender now before more lives are lost. I cannot win without an offensive line, only lose slowly at a terrible cost."

Roseli was torn. Every option before her was unthinkable. To surrender would preserve lives but cost her planet its freedom. To fight meant to either abandon the smaller cities to destruction or to weaken the defenses of the larger and more densely populated cities, endangering more lives overall.

"Do you genuinely believe we can win?"

"Yes, I do. It will cost us, but we can."

"Then keep the vanguard as it is. Leave a bare minimum of ships over the major cities and defend the unshielded ones. Win this battle for me before any of the city shields fall." Roseli had been trained her whole life to play this game, and yet now that her hour had come, she felt unequal to the task. How could she sacrifice the lives of others like pieces upon a chessboard?

Lucia gave her a curt nod, never looking from the battle. "Yes, Your Highness."

When the call ended, Roseli ached to close her eyes, to rest for just a moment.

Someone poked her. "Eat." Meredith offered an open packet of cookies.

Roseli frowned at the cookies without interest.

"You haven't eaten since breakfast, and you get bitchy when you're hungry. Eat." Meredith was one of the few people alive who would have dared say something like that to the crown princess, except possibly Beatrice.

Roseli took a cookie and bit into it mechanically. She realized just how hungry she was.

Meredith set a bottle of juice in front of her on the console. "Drink."

When Roseli raised the bottle to her lips, she found she was terribly thirsty.

"Go use the bathroom."

Roseli gave Meredith an odd look but stood. Meredith had been right about two things so far, and this might be the last chance for a while.

When she got back, Officer Smith was waiting in the command center. "Your Highness, we have a problem. I cannot account for the whereabouts of a fourth of the members of the imperial guard. I believe we may have more traitors than we thought."

Beatrice gently nudged Roxane as the car slowed to a stop. "Wake up, dear, we're transferring to a hovercraft." She was exhausted, but she hadn't dared sleep.

Roxane yawned and stretched awkwardly in the limited space of the van. "We're not there yet?"

"Not yet." Beatrice did now know how much farther they had to go. The Veritas guards had not told them.

The door of the van opened, and they stepped into the cool air of the fall twilight. They were far enough out of the city that when Beatrice looked up, she could see a map of stars. She could just make out the drinking cup, the first constellation she had ever learned.

Julia had taught it to her two years before on a trip to a royal lodge set within a nature preserve. It had been on that trip that Julia's wariness toward her and Alexis's stiff formality had begun to soften, when trust and even friendship had become possible. She hoped Julia was safe, that Alexis had survived surgery. The guards had parked the van on a hilltop. The surrounding area was deeply forested. Even with two of Delphi's moons risen high upon the horizon, the night was far darker than anything Beatrice had known in the city. The distant hooting of an owl made her shiver.

A small hovercraft sat upon the flat top of an otherwise jagged rock formation, its red lights shining against the darkness. Hopefully, there was a path because otherwise, it was going to be a steep scramble. Three guards followed from the van, the middle-aged man who had sat with them, an older woman, and a younger man.

"Brr, it's cold," said Princess Roxane, rubbing at her bare arms. She was wearing the thin mass-produced shirt and trousers she had been given to make her less recognizable. Unfortunately, a sweater had not been included.

"Your Highness, please take this," said the younger guard from the front of the van. He had to unsling his rifle to tug off his jacket. He gallantly held it out as countless movies and books had no doubt taught him to do.

"Thank you, you're so sweet."

A shot rang out. The guard fell, his chest caved in.

Beatrice grabbed Roxane by the shoulder and forced her down. The air exploded with gunfire, and she heard the older guard scream in pain. The occupants of the shuttle returned rifle fire in the dark.

"We must get back to the van." Beatrice crawled, pulling Roxane with her. There was a scream and a thud. To her horror, she looked into the pained face of the guard who had sat with them in the back of the van. Before she could even attempt to staunch the streaming wound in his throat, he went still.

All their guards were down. Even if they could reach the van, Beatrice had never learned to drive, and she doubted Roxane or Prince Leon knew, either. The van would only be a cage.

Above them, shots continued to ring out between the shuttle and the forest. She raised her head enough to search for Prince Leon. He was flat on his stomach on the ground, the same as them. At least he had some sense.

Beatrice called to him, trying to be quiet enough that their attackers could not hear. "We must get to the trees, it's our only chance."

"Stay where you are."

"No, we're sitting ducks."

Roxane was crying, sniffing loudly. Beatrice pressed her hand. "Breathe, dear, breathe. We need to keep crawling."

"I'm scared."

"I know. Stay close." An odd calm settled over Beatrice and with it, a sharp clarity. It would have been easier to crawl with both hands free, but she dared not let go of Roxane. The girl was whimpering in fear even as she kept moving bravely forward. They were so close to the edge of the clearing.

"Stay, you bloody idiots," hissed Prince Leon.

"Come with us. We shouldn't get separated." Beatrice kept moving and Roxane with her.

"Roxane, come back. The people in the woods won't hurt us. They are imperial guards, here to save us," Prince Leon called.

Roxane froze. "Roseli said they shot Alexis. We can't trust them."

"She lied. She's trying to seize power from the empress and get rid of you. The Veritas guards had orders to murder us."

Roxane went still beside Beatrice, listening. Beatrice could not believe her ears; she'd thought Prince Leon a fool but not a traitor.

Prince Leon kept talking. "Roseli is a lowborn general's whelp.

She knows you have more right to be empress than her and wants you gone."

"You're lying. My sister would never hurt me." Roxane clutched Beatrice's hand harder, and they crawled again as a fresh batch of gunfire erupted over their heads toward the shuttle up on the rock formation.

"Roxane!" Prince Leon cried.

When Beatrice looked over her shoulder, she saw he had retreated to the temporary safety of the open van door, the spineless traitor.

"Please, Roxane, come back."

As soon as they reached the tree cover, they stood and bolted into the forest. The sound of Prince Leon calling and gunfire followed them. They had run for about five minutes when the earth shook, and the sky behind them lit up.

"What was that!" Roseli asked as she accepted the hand Director Barker offered to help her to her feet. The head of the Joint Intelligence Agency had just been briefing her on the status of the city's defenses.

"Proof the city shields are holding."

Everything rattled, and Roseli would have fallen if not for Director Barker's hand on her arm.

"Probably not for long," said Meredith. "Oh, my poor cats, they must be so frightened, and I'm not there for them. They'll never forgive me."

Roseli brushed the dust from her pants. "If we felt it down here, then so did every soul in this city. I need to give a speech to calm people."

"Better make it quick," said Meredith. "You can't be spared for long."

One of the civilian techs in the room said, "Your Highness, part of the electrical grid is down. What do you want us to do?"

Roseli pushed down a rising wave of panic and brushed a lock of hair out of her face. Her entire life, she had listened to her mother speak calmly, precisely, and clearly upon the airwaves. As acting empress, she had to be that voice for Delphi now.

"I'll keep it short. Meredith, get Senator Veritas on the phone and brief her. I'll need her to follow my speech with detailed directions of what the citizens should do and repeat it with updates every quarter hour." She just had to hope they would all be alive in a quarter hour.

Three minutes later, Roseli stood in front of a blank wall as she was broadcast on every channel and public video screen. She wasn't dressed particularly imperially. She had on a simple white shirt with the cuffs rolled up because they were too long. Her damp hair was twisted back in a hasty braid. She tried to stand as rigidly as her mother always did.

"Citizens of Delphi, as of an hour ago, a fleet of Terra Nuevan warships arrived and began an unprovoked attack upon our planet. The ships of our imperial navy were ready and are bravely defending us. I will not lie to you or pretend that this will be an easy battle. We have lost our planetary shield because of saboteurs. In violation of every convention of war, the Terra Nuevans are targeting population centers to try to force us to surrender."

There was no point in lying about the planetary shields anymore. People had seen the news about the destruction of Vima. Roseli's emergency powers permitted her to broadcast over all public and private communication networks but not to stop the flow of information.

"We must not give in to their intimidation. If the Terra Nuevans do not flinch from murdering civilians during war, I do not want to know how they will treat a conquered people. We can repel this invasion. The city shields are holding, and our ships are protecting the smaller population centers from orbit. Our fleet is on the verge of turning the tide of battle and sending these bastards packing.

"As your acting empress, I am asking you to remain calm. Do not attempt to leave your city. We need the streets to remain clear for military and emergency operations. Take cover in your closest underground shelter. If you are in the capital, that is the subways. I know you're afraid—so am I. But I know that we, the people of Delphi, are greater than our fear. If we hold fast together, we will get through this dark hour together."

CHAPTER TWENTY-FOUR

The early spring night was cold out in the countryside. Beatrice and Roxane stumbled through the dark forest. Beatrice had always been afraid of the dark, but she was far more afraid of the people chasing them. She knew they were making too much noise as they scrambled through the underbrush, but if their pursuers had night-vision goggles or anything similar, there was no point in stopping to hide. They heard yelling behind them and breaking branches.

She tripped over something, and a burning pain shot up her leg. She had to cover her mouth not to cry out.

"Beatrice?" Roxane turned back for her.

She tried to stand, and the pain was terrible. "I think I broke my ankle."

Roxane tugged her arm over her shoulder. "Lean on me and hop. I saw this in a movie once."

"Roxane, honey, I'll slow you down. Leave me and send back help. I'll hide."

"No."

There was no time to argue, and she knew how stubborn Roxane could be. She had that in common with her sister. Beatrice leaned against Roxane and started hopping. She nearly bit through her lip from the intensity of the pain each time her left foot touched the ground, but she kept going.

Roxane was soon gasping from the effort of supporting her, but she didn't complain. "I see lights ahead."

Beatrice looked up. "It's a road, keep going." Hope gave her the strength to push through the pain.

They tumbled out onto a highway into a wash of headlights.

Screaming brakes shattered the night, and a small truck swerved around them before sliding to a stop.

A sturdy-looking, middle-aged woman popped out of the cab and yelled, "What the hell?"

"Please," called Roxane. "We need help."

The woman walked around her truck. "Wait, are you…"

Roxane straightened up to her full, rather modest height. "I'm Princess Roxane, and we're being chased. We have to get away."

The sound of voices drifted from the forest. Fear tore at Beatrice's heart. "Quickly."

"Put your friend in the cab," said the driver.

Roxane helped Beatrice limp to the cab as the driver hurried around the other side. Beatrice barely dared to breathe until they were pulling away. In the side mirror, she caught a flash of movement as a group of armed people emerged from the forest.

"Go, go, go!" She shoved Roxane's head down as gunfire erupted.

The driver floored it, and the truck careened down the highway.

❖

Prince Ambrose's back hurt. He'd pulled something when he and Henry had carried Eleanor from the burning temple. Dr. Brook had offered him painkillers, but he had not taken them. With Eleanor and Henry injured, he had to stay alert.

They were in a chamber with tombs carved into the limestone and marble sarcophagi holding long-departed empresses. The room was just big enough for Dr. Brook to set up a cot and tend several pieces of beeping medical equipment. Lieutenant Thistle, who normally served as General Tate's secretary, was in command of the soldiers. She was a slight, intense woman with a messy blond braid.

She had settled onto a portable camp chair when they'd arrived in the crypt and had not moved since, her eyes trained on the entrance to the chamber and the dark hall beyond. She'd sent two soldiers out to patrol the dark halls to make sure no one had followed them.

Eleanor stirred in her sleep, and Ambrose adjusted the cool cloth on her forehead. They had never loved each other, nor had they shared a bed since the first year of their marriage, but she was still his wife. After over two decades, they had reached a complex balance of duty and obligation.

She'd kept him safe from Varcian assassins after Mycenae fell.

He'd saved her daughter during the Massacre of the Inner Chambers. He'd taken over care of Roseli when Eleanor had sunk into grief. In gratitude, she'd allowed him to unofficially and then officially become the adopted father of her heir, although it was not politically advantageous to the crown.

She'd never come between them, or had even taken much notice, when he and Henry had become involved. In return, he had kept the peace between them when they'd quarreled over the direction of Henry's research.

He glanced down to where Henry was dozing on a bedroll on the cold crypt floor. He was twitching in his sleep. The doctors had said the break in his arm was severe, and he'd need surgery to mend it. For now, there was only the sling and painkillers.

Henry whimpered in his sleep, and Ambrose left his stool to kneel beside him. Henry's hair had mostly come free from the braid Ambrose had plaited for him that morning. It was a dark, tangled mess, and Ambrose wanted to brush it, but he didn't want to wake Henry, either. He stroked the side of Henry's face, and his breath grew more even.

The sound of footsteps sent the soldiers to their feet, rifles in hand. Henry jerked awake and tried to stand. Ambrose helped him up. "My glasses," Henry mumbled groggily, patting at his face.

"Here, love," said Ambrose, "I've got them." He removed them from his shirt pocket and put them on Henry's face.

Two of the soldiers from General Tate's office slipped back into the room. "We saw six imperial guards in the tombs. They were armed and seemed to be searching," said Lieutenant Hopper. He was a skinny, red-haired man who looked a lot more like a computer technician than a soldier. "I don't think they saw us."

"Shit." Lieutenant Thistle looked at Ambrose. "Is there any reason members of the imperial guard would be in the crypt right now?"

He shook his head. "No, they don't patrol the crypts."

"Then we must assume they're acting on their own."

"You mean traitors?"

"Yes."

"Should we call for help?"

"Not when we can't trust anyone. We must go radio silent and hide. You said there was a secret passage?"

"This way." He went to a tomb set back in a niche and ringed by a heavy metal gate. Within it lay the sarcophagus of Empress Phaedra. The rock behind was carved with complex designs. He tugged a key from a cord around his neck and slid it into what appeared to be a heavily rusted lock. It clicked easily, and he tugged it open. "Bring a light. It doesn't look like it from outside the gate, but there is a gap in the left side of the wall."

Dr. Brook was not pleased. "We can't carry the empress on a stretcher through that." She was even less impressed once she'd looked at the narrow tunnel. It looked more like a cave than anything carved by humans. There was barely even room to stand upright. "It's too narrow to set up any equipment."

"There is a small chamber farther on. It's big enough to set down a pallet."

Lieutenant Thistle nodded. "That will have to do. We'll carry the empress and hide the equipment. Dr. Brooks, you said the empress was stable."

"But I won't be able to keep scanning for brain bleeds," she insisted.

"Better to risk that than her death or capture."

Eleanor sat up weakly. "For fuck's sake, I can walk if someone will help me up."

In the end, Dr. Brook refused to permit Eleanor to stand but allowed one of the burlier soldiers, Warrant Officer Allen to carry her in his arms like some parody of a new bride. For all her insistence that she could walk, Eleanor could barely keep her grip on his shoulders.

They disassembled Dr. Brook's medical equipment and carried it into the narrow passage, out of sight. Lieutenant Thistle dragged a blanket across the floor to obscure the footprints they'd left. Anyone looking in would see that a layer of dust had been disturbed, but nothing more. Ambrose locked the gate behind them.

Lieutenant Thistle said, "Warrant Officer Adair, Chief Warrant Officer Balch, I want you to stay behind, just out of sight of the entrance, and make sure we're not pursued. If you hear any sound in the tunnel, don't engage, run to warn us."

They made a slow procession through the narrow winding tunnel, with Ambrose leading the way, Henry, Dr. Brook, and the guard carrying Eleanor close behind, while the two lieutenants guarded their backs.

After fifteen minutes, they came to the small chamber Ambrose remembered. They truly were in a cave now. The space was barely big enough for Eleanor to lie on a pallet and the others to sit.

Ambrose sat with his back against the wall. Henry sat beside him.

Before he realized it, the exhaustion of the day tugged him into sleep. The sound of gunfire startled him awake.

"Shit, they weren't supposed to engage. Everyone, get up, we have to move," said Lieutenant Thistle.

Lieutenant Hopper unslung his rifle. "I'll cover the retreat. I can hold that bend in the corridor just past this chamber."

"No," said Lieutenant Thistle. "We all go."

Lieutenant Hooper shook his head. "I have to do this. Please, Lucy, think of the baby."

As the commanding lieutenant wavered, more gunfire echoed down the tunnel. She grabbed Lieutenant Hooper and kissed him. "Don't you dare die, or I'll never forgive you."

Ambrose was struck by the impulse to offer to stay in Lieutenant Hooper's place but realized the foolishness of the idea before he could voice it. He hadn't used a gun since he'd hunted with his father as a young man, and he'd been a terrible shot.

He couldn't buy Henry and Eleanor the time they needed to escape. Lieutenant Hopper could. All Ambrose could achieve by staying would be a useless death, or even worse, to become a hostage who could be used against Roseli. Guilt still tore at him as they left Lieutenant Hopper guarding the turn in the tunnel.

They had made it only a few yards before the tunnel shook with renewed gunfire, deafening in its closeness. The sound pursued them as they fled through the darkness.

❖

The entire command center shook as the screen at the front of the room went briefly white. Roseli kept her feet and barked, "Status!"

"The northeast quadrant of the city is gone. The shields are down," said Director Barker grimly. She had just arrived to brief everyone.

"Can we bring the shields back online?"

"Not without the primary shield projector that was just destroyed."

Roseli had to fight not to let fear overcome her. Before she could slow her breath, the image of Admiral Patchett appeared at the front of the room. "Princess Roseli, I believe we have matters to discuss. Your surrender being chief among them."

Roseli thought before she answered. "What terms can you offer?"

Admiral Patchett frowned. "Your continued survival. I assume that matters to you."

"I am acting empress. My duty goes beyond myself."

"And the lives of all those within the capital? Do you not value them?"

Roseli had spent her girlhood studying philosophy with Prince Ambrose. She knew all about the good of the few, the good of the many, and the gray areas in between. "Swear to me you will preserve the civilian government, and I will surrender."

Admiral Patchett shook her head. "That's not how this works. Your surrender must be unconditional, those are the terms."

"At least promise you will not imprison or execute members of my armed forces or government."

"I cannot. You have fifteen minutes to answer."

The screen went blank.

Roseli wanted to scream, to howl, to claw at the wall. None of that was an option. "Get me the orbital platform."

❖

Lucia watched as another little green circle representing a single ship of the line and some three hundred souls flickered out. There was a tangle of red and green lights in orbit over the capital.

Farther out, just beyond the planetary orbits, was a different story. Green dots were slowly swarming over the Terra Nuevan rearguard. Her offensive force was exactly where she wanted it. Admiral Patchett was a worthy opponent, but Lucia had fought her before and knew what tactics she would use.

"The acting empress is calling," said Lieutenant Commander Sullivan.

"Put her through."

❖

With no preamble, Roseli said. "What is the status of the battle?"

"I'm wearing down the forces around the Terra Nuevan flagship. General Patchett is focused on the planet, not guarding herself. If I can take her out, I think the Terra Nuevan forces will crumble. I am so close."

"The capital's shields are down. Can you protect it and continue the offensive?"

Lucia's movements wavered but never stopped. "No, I don't

have enough ships." Even if she drew back every ship she had to orbit over the capital, there was no guarantee an enemy vessel wouldn't get through.

"Then focus on the offensive. Your priority is all of Delphi, not the capital."

Lucia froze and looked over her shoulder. "That will leave you unprotected."

"I know."

The video feed was so poor that she looked more into the memory of Roseli's face than the flickering and grainy image. She forced her hands back in motion. She couldn't afford to waste more than a few seconds in stillness, not when every dot and light before her represented so many lives.

"Please, do not ask this of me."

"I am not asking, I am ordering you, Admiral Almeda."

"You ordered me to come back to you. I can't do that if you're dead."

"I know, and I am so sorry. I am giving you full control of the Delphian navy. You may now act in the absence of any terrestrial guidance until the crisis is resolved. Win this battle for me. If you can't, then and only then, you have authority to surrender on behalf of Delphi."

"Roseli."

"Do not fail me, Admiral Almeda."

She'd have gladly given back her title, given anything to keep Roseli safe, but that wasn't an option. All she could do was what Roseli asked of her. "I swear, I will not, Your Highness."

❖

Roseli accepted a handkerchief from Meredith and wiped her face. Her vision blurred with wetness. There were so many things she had wanted to say, but she could not over a communication channel in the heat of battle. She wasn't sure she'd ever get the chance again in this life. "Send out a message. Tell every citizen to get underground. Have Senator Veritas announce it. Now, get me Governor Harper of the Southern Province."

Governor Harper, a black-haired woman close to her mother's age, appeared on the screen and stood from a desk to bow hurriedly.

Roseli wasted no time. "Governor, are you prepared to take

temporary control of civilian governance if the capital falls, as you are sworn to do?"

"Your Highness?"

"Are you prepared? Military command and the terrestrial side of naval operations will also be transferred to the Southern province if the capital goes silent. You will be the acting head of the Delphian civilian government until the conclusion of the crisis, at which point you will rule in a joint committee with the other provincial governors. You will hold this civil authority until a new Senate can be elected. As soon as either Empress Eleanor or Princess Roxane is located, they will resume duties as the head of state. If they cannot be found, you will be entrusted with crowning another member of the royal family. My cousin Elizabeth lives in your city. She is third in line to the throne. She and her children must be protected. Do you understand and accept these duties?"

It was a rhetorical question. Governor Harper had been briefed on all this when she took office as governor of the largest province on Delphi. The backup plan had been in place for generations.

She bowed solemnly. "Yes, Your Highness. I am ready." Then, something in the woman's face seemed to crack. "Is my son there? If I could talk to him…"

Roseli had forgotten that Governor Harper was Prince Henry's mother. Along with him, a significant number of other members of the Harper family lived in the capital. "He's as safe as he can be. I'm so sorry, but there is no time."

"I understand. May the gods protect you all."

Roseli motioned for the call to end. The room was eerily silent, save for the sound of one soldier praying softly.

Meredith nudged her. "This is it, then?"

"I think so."

"Tactically, it is the right decision," said Director Barker. "I wish it wasn't, but it is." She was staring numbly forward.

Officer Smith took a plastic photo from her coat, her hands trembling. She kissed the picture and pressed it against her heart. "I told them to get out of the city. I hope they're far enough."

"Your family?" asked Roseli. One of the few times Roseli had ever seen the stoic woman smile was when she talked about them.

"I know it was a breach of protocol, but I had to get them to safety."

"I hope they made it."

One of the civilian techs began to cry, resting her head in her hands.

Roseli thought of Alexis alone somewhere in one of the hospitals and Julia in the Senate. If the city of Thetis fell, they went with it. At least they would be at the dark gate to meet her. She thought of her mother and her stepfathers in the crypt. Maybe they would be deep enough to survive.

It gave her hope to think of Beatrice and Roxane safely out of the capital. She doubted Beatrice would ever forgive her for sending her away, but it was a small price to pay to know she lived and was there to protect and guide Roxane when she could not be. Her only regret was she hadn't found a way to send everyone else she loved with them. She could still surrender. It wasn't right, and it wasn't fair for her to bargain with the lives of all who were in the capital, but Delphi was greater than one city.

She thought of all the parts of Delphi that she had seen as a young woman. She thought of towns and cities and far more faces than she could have ever remembered. She did this for them.

"Gods forgive me."

CHAPTER TWENTY-FIVE

Lucia was beyond anger, beyond fear, beyond any kind of emotion other than raw determination. She couldn't let herself think about the city or the woman she was leaving vulnerable as she moved her ships. She had to command and nothing else, or she would falter.

She pulled as many ships as she could away from the planet, and in a series of swipes of her hand, sent them against the heart of the Terra Nuevan fleet. One by one, her little green lights flickered out as they were destroyed in the charge, but more red lights faded. She swirled her hands, rapidly changing the formation, pushing forward. She could almost feel her mother's hands over her own, guiding her through the forms she had taught her.

The Terra Nuevan fleet shifted, moving to protect the flagship. They were too late. It cost Lucia ten ships in the charge, but her forces reached the Terra Nuevan flagship and destroyed it.

There was a brilliant rush of triumph as she turned her palms outward, attacking the Terra Nuevan fleet from within. Red lights flickered out one by one as the Delphian ships tore into them. The battle had turned in Delphi's favor. Lucia's euphoria only lasted until the Terra Nuevans regrouped.

A few minutes later, she realized something crucial. The Terra Nuevan tactics hadn't changed. She had fought enough battles to know when she was still facing the same opponent. She had no proof, but she had a sinking feeling that Admiral Patchett had not been on her flagship.

❖

Charlotte nearly jumped out of her skin when the door to the computer room banged open.

"What are you still doing in here? Didn't you hear the alarms? The city is under bombardment, and we have to get to the building's basement," snapped Lieutenant Lavine.

Petty Officer Mercer saluted. "The computer is not portable, sir."

"Grab a laptop."

"Not powerful enough."

"And we think we've finally gotten it. We're just waiting for it to finish running," added Charlotte.

"How much time?" asked Lieutenant Lavine, his face pale with worry.

"Five minutes, tops."

"I'll stay with you."

After four minutes, the earth shook with a nearby explosion, but at last, the message appeared on the screen.

Charlotte was on her feet in an instant. "We have to call the orbital platform."

❖

Lucia watched as yet another green dot flickered out and tried not to think of how many souls would be weighed against her own when she crossed through the dark gate.

The Terra Nuevans seemed to care nothing for their losses, even as the Delphians destroyed two of their ships for each one they lost. It still would not matter in the end. The Terra Nuevan fleet was bigger, and the Delphians were going to run out of ships first.

She wasn't even sure if she'd live long enough to see that happen. The Terra Nuevan forces had shifted their focus to the orbital platform, forcing her to use far more of her ships to protect it than she could afford. The platform's shields were holding, at least for the time being.

In her place, her mother would have kept fighting until the bitter end, making the enemy's victory as costly as possible. This was her chance to destroy as much of the Terra Nuevan fleet as she could to buy safety and time for Calliope and Varcia. The Terra Nuevans might win the battle today, but they would weaken themselves for the rest of the war to come. It was the logical choice.

The memory of dancing with Roseli on the night of the wake flooded through her mind. She remembered the music, the bright lights of the barracks, and the feel of Roseli in her arms as they turned across the wooden floor.

She'd thought she could pay any price that was asked of her for the sake of duty, for Calliope, for the greater good. She couldn't. Roseli had entrusted her with protecting Delphi, and she had to do that, even if it meant surrendering. She would have to trust that her father's navy could defend the home of her birth. She wouldn't let her wife die, even if the damn woman was hell-bent on sacrificing herself.

She had just opened her mouth to tell Lieutenant Commander Sullivan to call the palace back when she spoke. "A call is coming through from Lieutenant Charlotte Laurent at the liaison office. I think you should listen to her."

"Put her through."

"Admiral, I have decoded a message Admiral Robertson sent. He isn't arriving next week. He's coming tonight."

Lucia kept moving her hands through the holograms, guiding ships. "How can that be?"

"I don't know, but he sent a frequency code and a swatch of coordinates to scan." She never finished her sentence. There was a crashing sound over the computer system and then static.

"Get her back on the line," barked Lucia.

After a frantic half minute, one of the bridge crew said, "There is no response."

"Did she send the frequency code?"

"Yes."

"Then use it to scan with the long-range sensors."

She returned her attention to the battle. A minute later, Lieutenant Commander Sullivan informed her, "Normal scans show nothing in that area of coordinates, but when we searched with the frequency, we picked up fifty signatures. I think Admiral Robertson must be using some kind of cloaking technology we've never seen before."

Lucia did not let herself hope. "How far is he?"

"Maybe thirty minutes."

That changed everything. She did several quick mental calculations before she swept her hands downward, shifting the fleet back toward the planet. She could hold her ground for that long, and with fifty additional ships, she could destroy the Terra Nuevans.

"Call the palace, get me Princess Roseli."

"We lost contact at the same time we did with Lieutenant Laurent."

She stumbled as if the platform had shifted beneath her. She tried to tell herself she didn't know for sure; it didn't help. The grief welled up, vast and overwhelming, ready to drown her.

She slammed a door on her emotions and turned her focus back to the battle. She had to fight for the planet her wife loved.

❖

Ambrose's hands shook as he fitted the key into the lock on the grate that lay over the abandoned well. He finally got the key in, and it turned with a click and swung up with the assistance of hinged springs. He climbed out first, reaching back to help Warrant Officer Allen lift Eleanor over the rim of the well. She put her arms around his neck to help, but her grip was weak.

Ambrose set her on the ground, leaning against the crumbling stone of the well, and turned back to take Henry's hand and help pull him up. With only one good arm, he couldn't climb easily. Dr. Brook was spry for a woman in her late sixties but still accepted a hand. Lieutenant Thistle slid her rifle onto her back and hauled herself up. Warrant Officer Allen followed. Ambrose slid the grate closed behind them, hearing the lock click.

He wondered how long it would delay their pursuers. He hadn't heard them since the earlier gunshots and did not know how close they were. The moon had just risen, and he could see well enough to make out the surrounding forest.

"Where are we?" asked Lieutenant Thistle.

"An imperial nature preserve outside the core of the city. We aren't far from a gamekeeper's cabin where we can seek help. I'll guide us," Ambrose told her.

In the years since the city's founding, urban sprawl had encompassed the nature preserve, so it was a small island of green amidst a sea of buildings.

"I'm staying to hold this position. Warrant Officer Allen, you have command," said Lieutenant Thistle.

"Don't be stupid, girl," snapped Eleanor without bothering to open her eyes. "I don't have enough guards left for any more heroic sacrifices."

That settled the matter. Warrant Officer Allen lifted Eleanor again. They made slow progress through the forest. The path was nearly indiscernible during the day, much less at night. Ambrose had memorized it carefully when Eleanor had shown it to him and Roseli.

They crested a hill. Thetis, the capital city of Delphi, was half in darkness and half in flames.

"No," murmured Ambrose. He couldn't tell where the palace was amidst the smoke, but if the city's shields had fallen, it had to have been the first target.

He had been on Delphi when Mycenae fell to the Varcian invasion, and his father's palace burned. For years after hearing the news, flames and the screams of his mother and sisters had filled his nightmares. In those dreams, he was always helpless to save them.

A year later, on the night of the Massacre of the Inner Chambers, he'd been able to carry a single child to safety. He could still remember the warm weight of Roseli in his arms, how she'd clung to him, too scared to cry. Roseli had been the same age his smallest sister would have been if she had lived.

He'd had no one on Delphi, and then suddenly, a little girl had needed him. Protecting and caring for her had given him a reason to fight his way free of the grief that might have otherwise consumed him.

Now, the capital was burning, and he wasn't there to help her. His eyes stung. Roseli had to be safe, she just had to.

Henry took his hand, saying nothing.

"Don't look back, keep going," Lieutenant Thistle told them. "Move."

They stumbled onward into the darkness. Ambrose almost turned his head for one last look at the city, but a half-remembered fragment of an Earth legend stopped him. Something about a pillar of salt.

❖

Lucia lost her balance and fell gracelessly onto her hands and knees as a direct hit shook the orbital defense platform's shields. "Status," she snapped as she picked herself up.

"Shields holding, no damage," said one of the bridge crew.

Her remaining ships were stretched so thin, she was amazed the platform hadn't taken more hits already. They just had to hang on. Their sensors showed that the Calliopean fleet was only minutes away, although they had still received no direct communication from them.

Lieutenant Commander Sullivan said, "We're getting a hail from Admiral Patchett."

That proved one theory. The old war dog wasn't dead. "Which ship is it coming from?"

"I can't tell. It's scrambled."

"Put her through."

Admiral Patchett appeared on the bridge's screen and bowed. "Admiral Almeda, I am honored to face you again. Please, don't be as stubborn as you were on that moon of Galileo. This is turning into a slaughter. Surrender, and I will spare your remaining ships."

"I decline to do so."

"This is the last time I will make this offer. I know your wife gave you the authority to surrender. You are the only person left on Delphi with the authority to do so."

"Again, I decline." She had never hated anyone more than she did Admiral Patchett in that moment.

"Then the blood is on your hands, Admiral Almeda. I will end this one way or another."

The call went dead.

Barely a breath later, Lieutenant Commander Sullivan said. "We're receiving a hail from Admiral Robertson of Calliope."

An image of Robertson's bald and gray-bearded face appeared on the screen at the front of the bridge. Lucia had known him since she was a child. He had been one of her mother's most trusted admirals. When she was small, he used to bring her plastic models of spaceships to play with and when she was older, books on military strategy.

He'd been the captain of the *Courageous*, the first ship she had served on as an ensign. Despite all his duties, he'd taken several hours a week to teach the ship's younger officers. He would show them recordings of his past battles, and at the end of each, he would say, "Now, tell me everything I did wrong." It was from him she had learned how effective humility was in gaining the respect of one's subordinates.

"I have never been happier to see you, Admiral Robertson."

He bowed. "Admiral Caron? Are you in command? I thought you would be on the planet."

Her old last name sounded strange. In only a few hours, she had become accustomed to Almeda. "I am currently in command of the Delphian navy and this orbital platform. The planetary shields and those of the capital are down. I have thirty ships left under my command. What is your status?"

"Fifty ships, all fighting fit."

"Do you remember the specifics of an Eagle Spear maneuver?"

"I taught it to you."

"Let's do this."

When the Calliopean ships were in position, Lucia waved her ships forward in a close formation as Admiral Robertson brought his ships at the enemy from two curved sides, like an eagle closing its wings.

❖

The one thing that Roseli hated above all else was feeling helpless. She sat in the eerie red glow of the command center's emergency lights, keeping out of the way as everyone else ran about frantically, tugging at wires. The last person she'd sent up to look said that fire raged to the east of the palace, and the rest of the city was in darkness. She had to hope that the military and emergency services were still functioning, even if they had also lost communications.

No one was sure what had happened, but Director Barker suspected that the last bomb might have put out an electromagnetic pulse. The palace staff were rushing to restore the backup systems. Her advisors' current theory was that the Terra Nuevans were trying to take out strategic targets rather than destroy the capital as they had Vima. If they won, it would be far easier to control Delphi from its capital.

Director Barker and a technician were busy doing something with a device that looked like a tangle of wires in a box but was a radio transponder strong enough to reach the orbital platform.

The device crackled, and Director Barker grabbed a little plastic microphone and talked into it. "This is the Imperial Palace calling Beta Orbital Defense Platform. Do you copy?"

A voice crackled back. "This is the Orbital Defense Platform, provide confirmation codes."

Director Barker rattled off a series of numbers from memory.

"Affirmative, code acknowledged." The voice went fuzzier and quieter as the woman speaking to them turned her head away from the microphone, "Admiral Almeda, it's the palace. I've got them on the radio."

After a few seconds of static, Lucia's voice came over the air. "Roseli?"

"Lucia." To hell with titles, even if they were on the radio. They had both just stared death in the face.

"Are you safe?"

"Yes. We just lost communications, that's all."

Director Barker leaned over to speak into the transponder. "What is the status of the battle?"

"Reinforcements arrived with fifty Calliopean ships. We've forced the Terra Nuevans back from the planet. They are retreating."

Roseli's hands shook, and she clasped them together to hide it. She was still acting empress.

"What are your orders, Your Highness?" asked Lucia, her tone formal again.

"What is the status of our fleet? Do you advise pursuing the retreating ships?"

"Greatly diminished, even with the Calliopean reinforcements. Over half of the remaining Delphian fleet has sustained damage, and most ships are not fully supplied. The Calliopean reinforcements took minor damage but were near the end of their patrol run and are all low on supplies. I would advise you to keep all ships here to repair and restock. Sending any ships after the Terra Nuevans before further reinforcements arrive from Calliope would be inadvisable while Delphi is still without planetary shields."

The radio crackled, and for a few seconds, Roseli couldn't hear her. "...and even if we had the ships, Admiral Patchett is a cunning old warrior. I wouldn't put it past her to be setting a deliberate trap. The Terra Nuevan fleet all appear to be moving at normal speed and not currently using the drive that allowed them to arrive at Delphi so quickly. It could be that their damaged ships can't use the drives, and the others are remaining with them to deter pursuit, or Admiral Patchett could be trying to draw us out."

"I agree," said Roseli. "Keep all fully functional Delphian ships in defensive positions around the planet. Begin moving the damaged ships to the orbiting maintenance platforms and start repairs at once. Divide the Calliopean ships between a defensive orbit and close-range patrols. We don't know when the Terra Nuevans will strike again, and we must be ready."

"Yes, Your Highness."

The lights came on as the backup generator finally kicked on. The room buzzed with sound as all the consoles turned back on. There was so much more Roseli wanted to say, but it wasn't the time. She realized with a sudden jolt of euphoria that there would be time later. The battle was won, and they had the rest of their lives.

"Stay in communication and update me on changes."

"I will."

She handed off the radio to one of the technical staff and leaned against the console, numb with relief. She had to move her hand quickly when she realized she'd accidentally activated it. A digital screen flashed, demanding a password.

She heard an almost maniacal giggling to her left. "We're alive," Meredith told her.

"Yes, we are."

"I'm going to see my cats again."

Director Barker came over to them. "We've established communication with some parts of the city and are picking up the sensors and cameras that were outside the area hit by the electromagnetic pulse."

"Get me a report on the damage to the city as quickly as you can. I need to speak with Admiral Heart and General Sharp. After that, I want Senator Veritas on the line. I must tell her how to update her broadcast." And she needed to hear Julia's voice.

"Yes, Your Highness." Director Barker and stepped away to speak to several techs.

Roseli drew the first deep breath she'd had in hours. She was amazed to be alive. She knew something was wrong when Director Barker came back. Her mouth was turned down, and the crow's feet at the edge of her eyes had deepened with worry. "Your Highness, I'll have General Sharp on the line in just a few minutes."

Roseli's stomach dropped. "And the others?"

"We have not been able to reach Admiral Heart or Senator Veritas. I am sorry, Your Highness, but we now have confirmation that the Senate building and the naval command building were both destroyed, along with the weapons depot."

She couldn't breathe, couldn't move. She managed a few words. "What about the bunkers?" All government buildings had them.

"We don't know yet."

"Send someone to find out." Half the room turned to stared at her, and she realized she must have yelled.

"Yes, Your Highness."

Her hands shook. She'd sent Julia to the Senate. She'd told her to keep talking over the airwaves. Even if the Senate bunker had come through, had Julia been in it?

"Your eyes are wet again," said Meredith, pressing a tissue into her hand.

Roseli wiped her face and blew her nose. Was this why her mother had been so impassive? Had there been a moment, or perhaps countless ones, where she'd had to build walls around her heart to keep doing what had to be done?

She forced herself to breathe. When she was again capable of speech, she said. "Meredith, please find out how Alexis is recovering." What she didn't dare ask was if the hospital had come through the bombardment.

"I will," said Meredith.

She noticed Officer Smith standing silently a few steps away, waiting for orders. "Officer Smith, I need you to confirm that my sister, Lady Swann, and Prince Leon have safely arrived at the Veritas estate. Also, send someone to bring my mother and stepfathers up from the crypt. Best they do not stay in the cold and darkness any longer than they have to."

"Yes, Your Highness."

She sunk back against her chair. She was feeling almost calm when Officer Smith said, "Your Highness, there is no sign of your mother and her consorts in the crypt, and the gate to the escape passage is open. We are investigating the tunnel now."

The gamekeeper's cabin looked as if it could have been in a fairy tale. It was small and wooden with a slanted roof. Ambrose knew better. He had just lifted a false slat of wood beside the door to find the hidden panel when the front door opened.

A small elderly woman with hair the color of snow looked out. She was wearing the simple brown and green clothes of an imperial gamekeeper but stood as rigid as a soldier. She had a modern-looking rifle in her hands. "Get inside, hurry."

Something between instinct and exhaustion led Prince Ambrose to trust her. He'd seen genuine surprise in the woman's wrinkled faced when he'd opened the door. She'd not been expecting them. Surely, if she was a traitor, her allies would have warned her to look out for the fleeing empress and her consorts.

"We are being pursued by what we believe to be traitorous imperial guards or imposters," said Lieutenant Thistle.

The old woman shouldered the rifle. "Best we take the hovercraft, then."

Lieutenant Thistle looked around the cabin doubtfully. "Hover-craft?"

"In the shed, this way."

The shed looked even more dilapidated than the cabin. As the old woman unlocked the door, a shot rang out. Warrant Officer Allen's head turned into a bloody mass, and he crumpled, dropping Eleanor.

Ambrose acted without thinking, grabbing Eleanor with the help of Dr. Brook. Lieutenant Thistle returned fire. Eleanor proved capable of scrambling with help, and they got her into the dubious safety of the shed. Lieutenant Thistle kept firing out the door.

The gamekeeper lifted a false panel on the wall and hit a button. Part of the floor fell away, and a sleek black hovercraft rose on a platform. The gamekeeper tapped another button, causing the roof to open, and then ran to open the shuttle's sliding side door and climbed into the pilot's seat. Ambrose and Dr. Brook helped Eleanor into the hovercraft with Henry following close behind. It was a military-style one with seats against the walls and an open middle area.

The hovercraft hummed as it turned on. "Get in," yelled the gamekeeper.

Lieutenant Thistle fired off one final round and ran for the hovercraft. The door of the shed burst open, and gunshots pelted the hovercraft as its sliding door hissed closed.

The gamekeeper showed absolutely no sign of fear and deftly piloted the hovercraft up through the open roof of the shed and into the sky above.

Dawn was breaking as they rose over the city. The fires were now burning out. At first, Ambrose could make out little through the dim haze of smoke that blanketed the city. Then, the wind changed, and with a sob of relief, he glimpsed the golden dome of the palace shining and undamaged.

CHAPTER TWENTY-SIX

"Your Highness."

Roseli jerked awake. In her dream, she'd been in her sitting room playing cards with Lucia, Alexis, Julia, and Beatrice. As she blinked against the harsh light of the command center, she found Meredith standing beside her chair. She wasn't sure what time of day it was.

"Meredith?"

"I have an update. The naval bunker was destroyed. Admiral Heart and his staff are gone."

She knew she should say something about the courage of all those lives lost in defense of Delphi, but she was too numb with her pain.

"And the Senate bunker?"

"It's intact. It's buried under rubble, but rescuers have established communications. Senator Veritas is alive. Everyone there, senators and staff, made it to the bunker in time."

Had she not already been sitting, she'd have needed to. With the intense relief came tears. Meredith had a tissue ready. How many of those things did she have in her large, owl-shaped purse?

"I spoke with the hospital. General Tate is in stable condition. Lady Swann and Princess Roxane just called. They were attacked on their way to the Veritas estate but escaped thanks to the help of a trucker. Prince Ambrose has also established contact. He, your mother, Prince Henry, Dr. Brook, and the others in the crypt had to flee traitorous members of the imperial guard. They got away to a hovercraft and are currently in a secure location."

It was a lot to take in. An odd omission struck her. "What of Prince Leon? He should have been with Beatrice and Roxane."

"Director Barker and Officer Smith are waiting to brief you fully on that in the next room."

She walked there in a daze. The rest of the day passed in a haze of one crisis after another. She was beyond exhausted when Meredith told her that rescuers had finally dug out the Senate bunker, and Julia was on her way to the palace.

Roseli barely looked up from the damage report. "Have her brought here as soon as she arrives."

Officer Smith, who was tapping at the console beside Roseli, shook her head. "Your Highness, perhaps it would be best to see her alone first."

Roseli just looked at her groggily. "Why?"

"I don't know about you, but I'm probably going to sob hysterically for a good hour when I see my husband and sons again. If you will take my advice, go see your lover, and then take a nap. You've been up for over a day and a half."

"I can't leave the command center."

"If something happens, you'll be woken up. Tired brains get stupid. I'm already making the staff take naps, so you can do the same."

That was hard to argue with. Roseli let herself be led to a nondescript room in the palace bunker. It had a cot that had been folded down from the wall. Julia wasn't there yet.

She sat on the cot because there was nowhere else to sit. She didn't mean to drift off, but she heard the door opening and leaped to her feet. "Julia!"

Julia still wore her ruined suit from the temple, and her copper hair was a tangled mess over her shoulders, having come loose from her last attempt at a braid. Her face was smudged with dirt and ash. She barely responded at first when Roseli hugged her. She smelled of dried blood, smoke, and fear sweat. Beneath it all was the warm scent of her sandalwood perfume.

"Roseli." Julia's arms tightened around her, and they were clutching at each other, both crying.

Even as she sobbed, Roseli was deeply grateful to Officer Smith. This wasn't something she could have done in front of others. A Delphian princess wasn't supposed to cry, not publicly, and certainly not when she was still acting empress.

"I thought I'd lost you." Her throat ached so much, she could barely get the words out.

Julia pulled her closer, trembling. "I was so afraid. I never thought of myself as a coward, but I was so afraid when I was trapped underground."

"Or course you were. I was terrified during the bombardment, too."

Julia buried her face in her shoulder, "As I stood in the Senate giving the final broadcast, I was at peace. I knew I could face my death with courage. Then my mother's guards grabbed me and dragged me into the basement with the other senators. When the earth shook and the lights went out, I thought the city was gone, that you were dead, and I couldn't bear it. I almost lost my mind in that horrible dark place."

Roseli ran her hands through Julia's tangled hair, aching to touch as much of her as she could to convince herself that she was real. "Can you ever forgive me for sending you there?"

Julia raised her head. "It was my duty to go. Fearing for myself wasn't the hard part. It was fearing for you and everyone else. I just kept thinking of you. I'd have traded my soul to see you again, alive and whole."

Roseli tilted her chin up to kiss her tenderly. "Your soul is yours to keep. I am here with you now and will be so long as I draw breath."

"I love you so damn much."

"I love you, Julia."

There were more tears, and eventually, they made it to the narrow cot. They lay down, arms wrapped about each other, tumbling into an exhausted sleep.

Officer Smith tried to dissuade Roseli from leaving the palace; so did Director Barker. Roseli ignored them and had Meredith order a car for her.

It took an hour to work through the shattered city to the hospital. Most roads had not yet been cleared of debris. Officer Smith accompanied her, along with two soldiers from General Tate's garrison. Roseli was relying almost entirely on the palace garrison to guard her until the loyalty of the remaining imperial guards could be verified.

St. Sydney Hospital was in a state of controlled chaos. There were cots and pallets set up in the halls. Even the entrance of the acting empress did not slow the flow of doctors, nurses, and orderlies hurrying about. Dressed as simply as she was in dark pants and shirt, Roseli realized that many of the people who passed her didn't even recognize her. That was a relief. She didn't have the energy to be a crown princess just then.

Alexis was in what was normally a small single room but now housed four cots with barely a few inches between them, all with steadily beeping equipment. Roseli saw Alexis on the cot by the window and hurried to her even as her guards were still trying to secure the room.

Alexis looked as pale as death, and her hair was an unwashed and ruffled mess, but there was no mistaking her. Roseli reached for her right hand only to find it covered in tubes. She took her left one instead. "Alexis."

Alexis's eyes slowly flickered open. They had a dull glaze to them, likely from whatever painkillers she'd been given. "Roseli?"

"I'm here, my love."

"Run, you must run, someone's shooting."

Roseli brushed her hair from her face. "It's all over. You stopped the assassin."

"You're safe?"

"I'm safe."

Alexis closed her eyes, seeming to drift off for an instant before rousing herself. "Everything hurts. What happened?"

"The assassin shot you. You saved me."

Alexis's hand tightened on her own. "It was worth it to keep you safe."

"I don't deserve you."

"Yes, you do. I am yours. I have been since you kissed me in the palace garden."

"So was I."

"You were so beautiful in the moonlight. You still are now." Her words were starting to slur, and her eyes drifted shut.

"And you are just as dashing." Roseli kissed her on the forehead. Her skin tasted of sweat but wasn't clammy or hot. Alexis's breath slowed as she fell back into sleep. Roseli sat with her for as long as she could until Officer Smith told her she was needed back at the palace.

One week after the Siege of Delphi

Roseli waited on the roof with Ambrose for the hovercraft that was bringing Beatrice and Roxane back to the palace. Her mother was still not steady on her feet and so could not accompany them, even to see Roxane.

The hovercraft was a sleek silver thing with the Veritas crest on the side. The instant the door slid open, Roxane rushed out. She clung to Roseli as tightly as she ever had when she was a child. "Roseli!"

"I've got you, Roxy."

Beatrice was slower. One of the Veritas guards had to help her down from the shuttle. Roseli's heart sank to see her ankle was in a cast. She hopped over with the assistance of two crutches.

"Bee."

"Darling."

There was so much Roseli ached to say, but it was hard when Roxane was crying in her arms. Beatrice merely smiled and let Roseli hug her with her free arm. With the crutches, she couldn't hug her back.

It took everything Roseli had not to fret over Beatrice as they made their achingly slow way back to her quarters. She wished she had the strength to pick her up and carry her. She had tried asking if she'd accept a wheelchair, but that had earned her a curt, "No darling, I can walk."

When they reached Roseli's rooms, Beatrice allowed Roseli to ease her onto the couch in the sitting room and find an ottoman to prop up her foot. Only a week had passed since they'd seen each other, but her face looked thinner, or perhaps it was simply the exhaustion and pain.

Roxane had something of a wild-eyed look. It was odd seeing her with a ponytail and in a simple gray shirt and trousers instead of her normally colorful clothing. Over tea and sweet cakes and a lot of tears, Roxane recounted her and Beatrice's escape and arrival at the Veritas estate. Beatrice let her tell the entire story, no doubt sensing that she needed to get it out of her system.

Roseli had heard it all already over the phone. Listening to Roxane recount running through the darkness of the forest, pursued by armed men, made her want to hug her and never let go. If she ever saw Prince Leon again, she wasn't sure what she would do. She could forgive many things, but sending armed men after her little sister and Beatrice was not one of them.

When the food was eaten and Roxane had worn herself out, she went to see their mother, who was lucid but still recovering and sleeping a lot since her concussion. Ambrose led her away.

After they left, Roseli settled back beside Beatrice, hugging her tight. She smelled of generic soap instead of her rose-scented perfume. "Can you forgive me? I never meant to send you and Roxane into danger."

Beatrice kissed her cheek. "My darling, you could not have known Prince Leon was a traitor, and you had to get your sister out of the city."

"I owe you everything for keeping my little sister safe and bringing you both back to me."

"I think you may owe Roxane. She would not leave me when I broke my ankle. She's a brave young woman."

"How is she handling all of this?"

"Surprisingly well. I think in some ways, this has all been a strange adventure to her. She's upset about her father's betrayal, but they were never close to begin with."

"And what about you?"

Beatrice settled against her, letting out a breath. "It was all terrifying, and my ankle hurts, but in all honesty, my darling, I've been through worse. This time, I wasn't helpless."

"You are never helpless, Beatrice."

"I was helpless when I was a child, and my father beat my mother and me. I was helpless again when the northern separatists kidnapped me to use against the crown. This time, I wasn't. I had the strength to run and Roxane to protect."

"I still wish you hadn't had to go through it."

"My darling, it cost me far more to leave you before the siege and to not know if you still drew breath than it did to run for my life through that dark forest. Please, no matter what, do not send me away again."

"I won't, I promise. It was too hard the first time."

"Good." Beatrice turned in her arms to kiss her tenderly "Whatever lies ahead, we face it together."

Two weeks after the Siege of Delphi

Roseli did not think her mother should be on her feet, much less resuming her imperial duties. However, the only way to stop her would have been to refuse to step down as acting empress, which would have caused a constitutional crisis. Her mother was at least letting her help with far more of the burden of leadership than she ever had before.

When Prince Leon was finally captured, Roseli was surprised when her mother asked her to go with her to talk to him. She wasn't sure if her mother was including her because she wanted her support or because her mother thought she had a right to face the man who had tried to have her killed.

Two of Director Barker's agents let them into a small cell far beneath the palace. Prince Leon sat with his hands shackled before him on the table. His clothes were wrinkled, and he was unshaven. He sat with his shoulders hunched but straightened at the sight of them, his chains rattling as he stood. "Eleanor!"

"Sit down," Roseli's mother told him coldly as she took a seat. Roseli sat silently beside her.

Prince Leon cast Roseli one disgusted look and then ignored her, turning his full focus to her mother. "There's been a terrible misunderstanding."

Roseli suppressed the urge to curse him to the seven hells. She had a feeling they would get more out of him if she let her mother do the talking.

Her mother spoke as calmly as she had in her last press conference. "Director Barker tells me you secretly plotted with the Terra Nuevan agents to murder Roseli and me. You helped the Terra Nuevan agents get into the imperial guard and bribed and blackmailed existing guards. You did it all to see Roxane crowned, even though she would have been a puppet empress under Terra Nuevan rule."

He scoffed. "You believe Director Barker? She's an evil old bitch."

"So am I. I sat in on the interrogations of the guards you were captured with this morning.

"They lied. They kidnapped me."

"Leon," her mother said wearily. "I've talked to Roxane. She told me what you said."

"The girl is confused."

"Lady Swann confirms her account."

"And you trust the word of a whore?"

Roseli let a flash of anger pass. He didn't have the power to hurt her or Beatrice ever again.

Her mother's eyes narrowed, her hands clenching the table. "I do, especially after Lady Swann helped Roxane escape the same traitors you are claiming kidnapped you."

He fell silent.

Her mother rubbed at her temple, as if a headache were starting. "Stop lying to me, Leon. It will not work. There is too much evidence against you."

He slumped, as if a string had been cut. At last, he said, "For the record, I didn't know about the invasion."

"Just the assassination attempts and the explosives in the temple?"

He did not dispute her.

"Just tell me one thing, Leon. Why?"

"Because Roxane is the rightful heir."

Her mother's lips thinned. "Don't even try to pretend you did this for Roxane. We both know the weight of the crown would crush her spirit. She's a sweet girl, but she'd make a mediocre empress at best."

Prince Leon lifted his head. "You're right. I did this because I couldn't bear the thought of that common-born military grunt's whelp on the throne. That bastard had your heart in life. He shouldn't have your dynasty, too."

Roseli clenched her hands but remained silent.

Her mother straightened her back. "You did this because you still resent Joseph? He has been dead for a quarter century."

Prince Leon leaned forward, tugging at the manacles that held him to the table. "I never expected you to love me back, but did you have to rub it in my face that you still loved him every single day of our marriage?"

"I seldom speak his name anymore."

"You murmur it in your sleep." The pain in his voice was as raw as an open wound.

Her mother went still, her thin face unreadable. "And for that you turned traitor to Delphi, to the crown, to me?"

"Yes, and I don't regret it." He slumped back. "If I may have one last request, I want to see Roxane again before I am executed."

"No."

"She is my daughter."

Her mother shook her head. "And mine. You'll never see her again, Leon, and you will not die, not by my order. I'm sending you to one of the imperial estates in the west. You'll live out the rest of your days under house arrest on a windswept little island with no one but you and the guards." She stood. "Good-bye, Leon, I will not see you again."

"Eleanor, please."

She left without another word.

Roseli followed and waited until they were several hallways away to ask, "That's it? You're just locking him away in an estate?"

Her mother paused in her step, turning to look at her with tired eyes. "We both know he can never stand trial."

"Why not? Why can't the bastard be held accountable and shamed before all of Delphi?" Let everyone know him for the traitor he was.

"A public trial would also shame his family and cost me their support. The Leons and their allies are one of the only things keeping the northern separatists in check. I can't risk a rebellion right now, not when all our resources need to go to the war and rebuilding."

"I still don't like it."

Her mother shook her head. "What would you have me to do, Roseli? Have him shot? He's Roxane's father."

That chilled her blood. She'd read enough of her family history to know her great-grandmother would not have hesitated. "You're sparing his life for her sake?"

Her mother turned and began to walk again. "Right now, she hates him, and I intend to keep it that way. A dead father is too easy to forgive."

Roseli fell in beside her. She wasn't happy with her mother's decision, but she didn't have a better solution. When they came to a staircase, her mother stopped, glaring at the ascending gray stone. The palace elevators were still not fully functional.

Roseli held out an arm. Her mother sighed but took it. They began a slow progress upward.

"If it is any consolation, I am sending him to Cordata Island."

"The one where all the flightless cormorants nest?"

"Impressively smelly and noisy birds. I'm sure he'll hate it."

CHAPTER TWENTY-SEVEN

One month after the Siege of Delphi

Lucia sneezed as she stepped from the dim shuttle into the almost blinding summer sunlight. With so much of the capital's communication equipment damaged, remaining on the orbital platform had been the only way to maintain communication with the remaining Delphian ships and allies.

Admiral Robertson had cleared up the mystery of his unexpectedly early arrival and why his ships had not shown up on ordinary sensors. The week before, he and his fleet had been performing the first major trial run of a new cloaking technology, testing to see if they could complete an entire maneuver without appearing on Delphian or Calliopean sensors. The technology was too top secret for him to discuss how it worked over the ship-to-ship intercoms, but Lucia's best guess was that it was some sort of electrical signal distortion.

When the Terra Nuevans had attacked Lucia's ship and escorts, Admiral Robertson and his fleet had not been on the frontier, as their official flight path had stated, but far closer to Delphi. He'd received orders to change course and provide reinforcements to the Delphian fleet. His orders had also included a coded message that there was a suspected information leak in the Delphian navy and that he was to continue to broadcast false coordinates.

As far as Lucia knew, the information leak that had led to her ship's destruction had not been found. She knew there had been traitors in the imperial guard, though, so it was possible that there had been one in the Delphian navy as well. She suspected that the Terra Nuevans had cracked the Calliopean broadcast codes and had intercepted messages between her ship and Delphi.

For the moment, she couldn't ask if there was any news on that matter. The problem with being on the platform was that there was no guarantee that any communications with the ground were truly secure, not with the primitive equipment they were using. Things had reached a point where she needed to speak securely with the remnants of the Delphian naval command and the empress. There were also things she could not say to Roseli from a crowded bridge.

She looked around the spaceport, recognizing the imperial gilded eagle on the side of a waiting black car. The woman standing beside it was not who she had hoped to see. She hid her disappointment and bowed politely. "Ms. Cooper."

"Admiral Almeda." Ms. Cooper returned the bow. "Princess Roseli sends her regrets that she could not be here to meet you personally. The Empress of Varcia called to discuss a defense treaty right before it was time to meet you."

Few people genuinely frightened Lucia, but her aunt was chief among them. She'd never met the woman in person, but she'd spoken to her a few times over a video screen. It had been unsettling how much she looked like Lucia's mother or, at least, what her mother would have looked like if she'd lived to grow old. Her aunt had the same green eyes and high cheekbones as her mother, but there had been a cold intensity in her careful words that left no doubt that she expected to be obeyed.

Lucia had heard her mother's stories about her aunt and knew exactly what she was capable of. Varcia had sent a small fleet to Delphi's aid that was soon to arrive, but Lucia knew better than to trust her aunt's intentions. She'd spent a good deal of time on the orbital platform arguing with her father, convincing him that Delphi had to be protected by an equal number of Calliopean ships as Varcian until Delphi could rebuild its navy. Varcia had turned on injured allies before.

They settled into the back of the car. Lucia was struck by the memory of the last time she had been driven from the airfield, her lungs burning and neck bleeding. She could now draw a deep breath without pain, and her stiches had healed cleanly. The cuts on her arm and shoulder from when she and Roseli had been shot at in the palace grounds were now scabbed and itched terribly.

Ms. Cooper glanced at her tablet and then folded it up and put it in her purse. She had an odd bag shaped like a strawberry. It matched her dress, which was covered in cartoon images of smiling red fruit. She looked at Lucia with intelligent eyes behind her cat-eye glasses. "Princess Roseli asked me to brief you."

"Thank you."

"Officer Smith and Director Barker think they have identified and captured all the traitors in the imperial guard, but the full investigation is going to take some time. The palace could not keep knowledge of this from the public, unfortunately."

"Will the trials be public?" They would have been on Calliope. While the emperor appointed all high court judges, they served for life and could not be removed. For generations, the courts had insisted on complete transparency in all trials.

"No, the empress will hold an imperial tribunal. Only the sentences will be made public."

"Executions, I assume." On Calliope, treason was the only crime that rated capital punishment. During her father's reign, the few times a case of treason had arisen and the defendant had been convicted, the Calliopean emperor had used his imperial authority to commute the sentences to life in prison. Her mother had said it made him look soft, but her father had insisted it was important for an emperor to show mercy. Lucia wasn't sure what the law was on Delphi, but she knew they had capital punishment for some offenses.

Ms. Cooper shook her head. "Probably not. The empress has the right to hold and sentence suspected traitors to anything short of death without Senate oversight, but if she orders any executions, the Senate will be allowed to see the transcripts and commute the death sentences into life imprisonment if they can get a two-thirds majority vote."

"That's rather specific."

"A couple of generations ago, a previous empress got a little overzealous with the executions after an attempted northern coup, to the point of taking out political enemies who were never involved. This prevents that from happening again."

"You have a keen understanding of Delphian politics, Ms. Cooper."

"I have been Princess Roseli's assistant for some time, and I listen when people talk."

"Do you think the Senate would not permit Empress Eleanor to execute the guards who tried to murder her family?" She had never before wished the death of anyone outside of battle, but in this case, she was willing to make an exception.

Ms. Cooper took a small clamshell-shaped device out of her purse and scanned the car before putting it away. "I believe she's more concerned with keeping certain matters from public knowledge. You see, it turns out that Price Leon was part of the conspiracy. He colluded with the Terra Nuevans, corrupted many of the guards, and helped them in their assassination attempts and the bombing of the temple. He is now in custody and under house arrest on a royal estate. In order to keep this matter quiet, the palace has officially stated that he suffered a stroke when he learned of the bombing at the temple and is alive but incapable of speech or public appearances."

She was glad that the source of treachery had been found but was deeply troubled that it had been a member of Roseli's own family, even if Prince Leon was only related by marriage. "Does the public believe it?"

"They have other worries at present." Ms. Cooper looked out the window.

Lucia did as well. They had reached the boundaries of the city and were passing through a transformed landscape. At first, most buildings only showed a mild coating of ash, but soon, they passed several that had fully burned. The effect was eerie: fully burned-out hulks standing between smudged or singed buildings.

"During the bombardment, the fire spread through the city by burning embers on the wind," said Ms. Cooper. "Those that landed on more modern buildings built during Empress Eleanor's reign never caught fire because of the new building codes and fire-suppression systems. She ordered all the buildings in the city upgraded a few years ago, but the process wasn't complete yet, especially for privately owned structures. A lot of those burned to the ground. Casualties were only as low as they were because Senator Veritas was on the airwaves telling all civilians to shelter in basements or the subway system. Most listened to her." Ms. Cooper wrapped her skinny arms around herself. "I'm so glad I chose a modern apartment building. I could have lost my cats. The older building next to mine burned."

The car made a turn. Before them lay an expanse of rubble. For all the battles she had fought, Lucia had never seen the cost of war wrought upon a city before. Before Delphi, the colony of Galileo had been the only civilian population she had directly defended. The sight of the broken buildings came as a cold and brutal shock. If she had fought harder, sacrificed more, could she have spared Thetis this?

"This was the Senate square. You can still make out a few of the building's columns. It wasn't directly hit. The bunker in the Senate basement held up, but the survivors had to be dug out. It took a day because of all the heavy marble. Senator Veritas is still not so good with darkness or small spaces."

Lucia shivered. She had spent her naval career fearing death by loss of life support or sudden decompression. Dying trapped in the dark beneath thousands of pounds or ruble sounded even worse.

They drove on over the cleared but pockmarked road. Through a screen of damaged buildings, Lucia saw what could only be described as a crater. She knew what had happened, but it didn't make it any easier to see. Even a bunker couldn't survive a direct hit. "The naval command building, I assume."

"Yes."

"Have..." How could she even say it? "Have any remains been recovered?"

"Only bone fragments so far, but they have all been too badly burned to extract DNA. They'll be interred in the naval cemetery beneath a memorial."

She thought of Charlotte. She remembered a soft-spoken young woman who'd come aboard her ship years before and had stolen glances at her, hungry but hesitant, until one day, their hands had brushed while looking at a star chart alone in the boardroom. Lucia had asked her if she had any interest in coming to her quarters later for a drink, and Charlotte had accepted.

She remembered a capable lieutenant who'd stood with her on the bridge through so many battles. She thought of the new side of Charlotte that she had only just begun to see, the woman who chose to leave all she had known to begin a new life on a foreign planet for the sake of living beneath an open sky and not among the stars. And for her sake as well. Lucia tried to fight through the emotions choking her. How could such a woman now be nothing but bone fragments and ash?

Ms. Cooper kept rattling on, oblivious to her distress. "The empress posthumously awarded everyone who died in the battle the Medal of Valor, those on the ground included. She heard what your officer, Lieutenant Laurent, did for Delphi. She was able to extend the medal because she was a liaison officer. Do you know who it should be given to?"

"It should go to her parents. Can you see to it that the medal is sent back to Calliope with the surviving crew of the *Intrepid*?" At least her crew had come through. They had all sheltered in the palace's basement during the bombardment, and the building had never been hit.

"I will take care of it."

❖

Lucia's suite of rooms felt both familiar and strange. After a month of disuse, the air smelled stale and dusty. She had nothing to unpack, only a tablet and the borrowed uniform she was wearing. Fortunately, Lieutenant Commander Sullivan had been close to her size. All the insignia was wrong for her rank, and she'd had to cover Sullivan's name with a pinned bit of cloth. Having an admiral's insignia sent up to the platform had been low on the priority list.

She showered and put on black slacks and a gray shirt that had presumably been bought for her. They were slightly too big. In a drawer, she found the box of clean gloves and ribbons that Roseli's assistant had brought her when she'd first arrived.

It was good to put on clean ones. She'd been wearing the same gloves since the temple, and despite washing them several times in the sink of her tiny room on the platform, she'd never gotten the bloodstains to fade to more than a dingy brown.

Then there was nothing else to do. She had to resist the urge to pace. Someone would tell her when Roseli finished her call. On impulse, she went to the door between her rooms and those of her wife. When she tried it, it was unlocked. The hallway smelled of lemon-scented wood polish.

She thought she heard voices and followed the sound to the sitting room. As she drew closer, she caught fragments of conversation that included the words *military*, *aid*, and *food distribution*.

The sitting room was illuminated by golden afternoon sunlight. Several windows were open to let in jasmine-scented air from the courtyard. All three women present fell silent when she entered.

Lady Swann was lying on one of the low couches with her foot in a bright pink brace that was elevated on a pillow. A fluffy black cat was curled on her stomach, oblivious to the tablet propped against it. A set of crutches leaned against the table beside her.

Across from her, Senator Veritas had several tablets scattered on the low table in front of her, along with discarded coffee cups. Her hair was in a ponytail rather than her usual neat braid, and she'd taken off her suit coat.

General Tate sat in a chair perpendicular to the two couches. She looked like she had fought her way back from the dark gate itself. She was terribly thin, and her eyes were deeply shadowed. Her normally olive-toned complexion was ashen, and her right arm was in a sling. "Admiral Almeda, welcome back." General Tate moved to stand, an act that required bracing her left hand against the chair.

"Please, I didn't mean to disturb you," said Lucia, bowing quickly.

General Tate abandoned the attempt, opting for a nod, which the others also gave.

"Please, join us," said Lady Swann. "We just ordered tea."

Lucia hesitated. "Thank you, but there are things I should see to."

"I would advise you to take her up on the offer," said General Tate. "Lady Swann has charmed Roseli's cook, and she'll make her anything she asks. When was the last time you ate something that was not previously frozen or dehydrated?"

As there was no other chair near the table, Lucia went to sit on the same couch as Senator Veritas. A minute later, several servants came with trays. Senator Veritas dutifully cleared the clutter off the table so that cups and little sandwiches and cakes could be set out.

Lucia accepted a cup of tea. The delicate porcelain was absurdly light in her hand after the heavy metal ones on the orbital platform. She recognized Darjeeling, fragrant and divine. Once she had set down the cup, she noticed the others had a few bits of food on their plates. The sheer number of options on the tray was overwhelming. She hadn't had to think about what to eat in a month.

The little cakes and sandwiches looked more like jewels than food, and after all the terrible life and death choices she had been forced to make, she found that this small and inconsequential one was too much for her.

She must have stared for too long because Lady Swann, who had nudged off the cat and sat up when the food arrived, took up a silver set of tongs and started putting things on a plate. "I'm sorry, I'm being a terrible hostess. Most of these must be unfamiliar to you. Here, this is a cucumber sandwich, and this is a honey cake, you must try it."

Her tone was as reassuring as her words.

Lucia picked up a little silver fork and took a bite of cake. It tasted of butter and honey and sunlight. Sometimes, coming back from spending too long onboard a ship was like coming in from the cold, with the sharp pain of skin aching and burning as sensation slowly returned.

Lucia heard a soft *murph* and felt the press of paws and the slight weight of the cat climbing onto her lap. When she looked, the little black creature was leaning forward, sniffing at her plate with interest.

"Don't let her eat your food. She's on a special diet." Lady Swann's tone reminded her of her sister-in-law when she reprimanded her for giving her niece sweets.

Lucia lifted her plate safely away from the inquisitive feline. She tried to think of something to say. "When I came in, you were discussing dispersing aid to civilians, were you not?"

"Yes, the military is helping with distribution," said General Tate.

"We are not discussing work during tea," admonished Beatrice. "Let's try to be civilized."

Senator Veritas laughed. "Oh, come on, even on old Earth, people talked business at meals."

Beatrice sipped her teacup. "Then they were fools for not seeking a proper respite. You give me a half hour of peace with each meal, or you order from the kitchen yourself."

Senator Veritas grinned. "Then I must yield to you because I don't think the cook likes me."

Lady Swann returned a weary smile. "You confused her grand-daughters' names."

"They are identical twins."

"Yes, why do you think I call them both honey? I can't tell those two toddlers apart. Your mistake was acting like you could."

Lucia had lived long enough to know when people were making small talk just to ease an awkward situation. The women around her were working their way through a script because they weren't sure where she fit in yet. She wasn't either. Oddly enough, she was all right with that. There would be time.

She ate the food, and when it was gone, sipped the tea and petted the purring cat, letting the conversation flow around her. A tension deep inside herself eased. She hadn't realized how exhausted she was until her eyes grew heavy.

"Lucia!" Roseli's voice snapped her back to attention.

Roseli stood in the doorway. She was dressed as formally as she could be short of a ballgown, in a dark blue dress with a silk jacket, and her coronet set upon a careful updo. Her face was artfully made up, but nothing could fully hide the signs of exhaustion.

"Roseli." Lucia stood, earning an offended meow from the cat she had displaced. She took a step toward her, then stopped as she remembered where she was. Was she still expected to give a formal greeting when in the presence of others if they were with the princess's lovers and in her rooms?

Roseli answered that question by rushing to hug her.

Lucia hugged her back as tightly as she could, breathing in the lavender scent of her hair. She tried to speak, but her throat was too tight.

Roseli took her hand. "Let's go talk in the courtyard."

The sudden intimacy in front of others was startling, but Lucia found she didn't care. Roseli guided her to the door before pausing. "Please, give me a moment."

"Take all the time you need," said Lucia.

Roseli stepped back into the room. She spoke in hushed tones with Beatrice, trading a brief kiss. She spent longer murmuring with Alexis, resting a hand on her uninjured shoulder. She kissed Julia without speaking.

Everything Lucia had been raised to believe told her that she ought to feel some kind of jealousy. Instead, she just ached to hold Roseli again. She still didn't know how she felt about the matter of her wife having lovers, but she couldn't resent them for caring for the same woman she did or being there for her when she could not.

Roseli came back to her, and they walked through another hall and out into the open air of the courtyard. The sun turned the reflecting pool into a shifting sea of light. All around them, tiny insects, some with gossamer wings and others with tiny yellow and black bodies, buzzed about the flowering vines that ran up the column. Several small birds fluttered in and out of an ornamental birdbath, chirping loudly.

Unable to wait any longer, Lucia pulled Roseli into a kiss. Roseli was gloriously alive in her arms, her skin warm beneath the fabric of her jacket, her lips soft. When they broke the kiss, Roseli's cheeks were flushed, and she was beaming.

"I am so glad you're home."

Such a strange word, home. As a girl, she'd thought it was her father's palace. The first time she'd come back from the naval academy to rooms that were so strange and empty without her mother, she'd known it wasn't home anymore. For many years, she'd found it in the navy. While the ship she served upon changed, the routine and purpose were always the same. She'd never thought to find a home in a woman's arms.

"I'm glad to be back." She was not expecting the sudden sob that rose at the end of her words.

"Lucia?" asked Roseli, her lovely smile fading with concern.

She rubbed at her face, wiping away the tears before they could fall. If she started, she didn't think she could stop. "I was so afraid you were dead when the platform lost communications with the palace."

"I'm sorry, I never should have asked of you what I did."

"You asked nothing more than was my duty."

"Just because something is a duty doesn't make it easier."

"No, it doesn't," said Lucia. "I will gladly fight for you to my last breath, but please never ask me to leave you undefended like that again. To do it a second time would be more than I can bear."

"You have my word."

The second kiss was gentler and sweeter than the first. "How long do I have you?" asked Roseli.

"Three days, then I have to get back up to the platform."

"So little time."

"When communications are back up, I won't need to be there as much."

"You won't be commanding the fleet in the field?"

Lucia's heart leaped. "Your mother would let me? She seemed rather adamant about clipping my wings."

"To be honest, right now, you're one of the few surviving admirals or even captains who are not new to their rank or on the edge of retirement. Any position you want is yours. My mother didn't like the idea, but she said you can leave the planet if you have some of your eggs harvested first. You must also get your father to swear he won't cancel the treaty if you get killed."

To be among the stars again, to be on a ship was beyond her wildest hopes, and yet other worries weighed upon her. She would train others to command the platform, but it would take years to do so properly. She wasn't sure how to instill in an adult the childhood of lessons she'd had from her mother. Even then, could she trust someone else to protect Delphi while she was in some far-flung corner of the galaxy? The late Admiral Heart had been right. She was the best woman on Delphi to command the platform.

"Roseli, I can't be your field commander. I need to be on Delphi to operate the platform if there is another attack and to help you shape Delphi's strategy for the war."

"Is that what you want?"

"It is what I have to do."

"Then I'll have you appointed as naval advisor to the crown and head of planetary naval defense."

Lucia's heart warmed. "Thank you."

They waited for the formality to fade between them, and then Roseli laid a warm hand against her cheek. "I've only got you for three days? We shouldn't waste any of it, then."

Lucia kissed her palm. "We have a marriage to consummate, don't we?"

"Best we get started."

Lucia scooped Roseli into a bridal carry, causing her to giggle in surprise and clutch at her shoulders for support.

Roseli kissed her, and in that instant, despite the battle that lay behind them and the war ahead, everything was perfect.

About the Author

Catherine Young (https://catherineyoungbooks.com/) always dreamed of growing up to be a writer. Somewhat to her surprise, she did. She resides in Austin, Texas, with a large collection of books.

Books Available From Bold Strokes Books

A Good Chance by Ali Vali. Harry, Desi, and Desi's sister Rachel are so close to getting everything they've ever wanted, but Desi's ex-husband is coming back to get his revenge and rip apart their chance at happiness. (978-1-63679-023-7)

A Perfect Fifth by Jaycie Morrison. Streetwise pianist Zara Keller and Lady Jillian Stansfield couldn't be more different, yet their connection brings a new awareness of who they are and what they truly want in their lives—including each other. (978-1-63679-132-6)

Catching Feelings by Ana Hartnett Reichardt. Andrea Foster expected to catch a lot of pitches from the Alder Lions' star pitcher, Maya, but she didn't expect to catch feelings. (978-1-63679-227-9)

Defiant Hearts by Lee Lynch. In these stories, you'll find your lovers, friends, and lesbians you wish you knew—maybe even yourself. (978-1-63679-237-8)

Love and Duty by Catherine Young. All Princess Roseli wants is to marry her three lovers, but with war looming, she must instead marry Princess Lucia to establish a military alliance between their planets. (978-1-63679-256-9)

Serendipity by Kris Bryant. Serendipity brings jingle writer Annie Foster and celebrity pop star Bristol Baines together, and their undeniable attraction keeps them close, but will their different paths drive them apart? (978-1-63679-224-8)

The Haunted Heart by Jane Kolven. A ghost, a ring, and a quest to find a missing psychic—it's a spell for love. (978-1-63679-245-3)

The Rules of Forever by Nan Campbell. After reconnecting at their high school reunion, Cara and Lauren agree to embark on a textbook definition friends-with-benefits relationship, but trying to keep it uncomplicated is harder than it seems. (978-1-63679-248-4)

Vision of Virtue by Brey Willows. When virtue and desire come together, be prepared for sparks in this next installment of the Memory's Muses series. (978-1-63679-118-0)

The Artist by Sheri Lewis Wohl. Detective Casey Wilson and reclusive artist Tula Crane are drawn together in a web of passion, intrigue, and art that might just hold the key to stopping a killer. (978-1-63679-150-0)

Cherry on Top by Georgia Beers. A chance meeting leaves Cherry and Ellis longing for a different life, but when Ellis's search for truth crashes into Cherry's insta-filter world, do they have any hope at all of a happily ever after? (978-1-63679-158-6)

Love and Other Rare Birds by Angie Williams. Ornithologist Dr. Jamie Martin and park ranger Rowan Fleming are searching the Alaskan wilderness for a bird thought to be extinct, and they're about to discover opposites really do attract. (978-1-63679-108-1)

Parallel Paradise by Mayapee Chowdhury. When their love affair is put to the test by the homophobia of their family, community, and culture, Bindi and Rimli will need to fight for a chance at love. (978-1-63679-203-3)

Perfectly Matched by Toni Logan. A beautiful Cupid named Hannah, a runaway arrow, and just seventy-two hours to fix a mishap that could be the best mistake she has ever made. (978-1-63679-120-3)

Slow Burn by Missouri Vaun. A wounded wildland firefighter from California and a struggling artist find solace and love in a small southern town. (978-1-63679-098-5)

The Inconvenient Heiress by Jane Walsh. An unlikely heiress and a spinster evade the Marriage Mart only to discover true love together. (978-1-63679-173-9)

The Value of Sylver and Gold by Michelle Larkin. When word gets out that former Boston Homicide Detective Reid Sylver can talk to the dead, the FBI solicits her help on a serial murder case, prompting Reid to assemble forces once again with Detective London Gold. (978-1-63679-093-0)

Wildflower by Cathleen Collins. When a plane crash leaves seven-year-old Lily Andrews stranded in the vast wilderness of Arkansas, will she be able to overcome the odds and make it back to civilization and the one person who holds the key to her future? (978-1-63679-244-6)